All of an Instant

TOR BOOKS by Richard Garfinkle

Celestial Matters
All of an Instant

A TOM DOHERTY ASSOCIATES BOOK

NEW YORK

All of an Instant

Richard Garfinkle

ALL OF AN INSTANT

This book is printed on acid-free paper.

Edited by David G. Hartwell

Book design by Victoria Kuskowski

A Tor Book
Published by Tom Doherty Associates, LLC
175 Fifth Avenue
New York, NY 10010

www.tor.com

Tor® is a registered trademark of Tom Doherty Associates, LLC.

Library of Congress Cataloging-in-Publication Data

Garfinkle, Richard
All of an instant / Richard Garfinkle. — 1st ed.
p.   cm
"A Tom Doherty Associates book."
ISBN 0-312-86617-8 (acid-free paper)
I.   Title.
PS3557.A71536A79   1999
813'.54–dc21   99–32902
                                                                              CIP

First Edition: November 1999

Printed in the United States of America

0   9   8   7   6   5   4   3   2   1

Dedicated to the teachers and students of
clarion west 1992

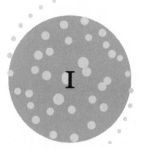

I

T ime is earth and water.

The lower half of time where most people live is solid stone, a hard mass of cause and effect confining human life in walls of inevitability; the stone of time has many strata with gems and metals and a thousand varied riches buried in the multitude of layers that comprise the hard crust of prisoning/treasured temporality.

The upper half of time is an ocean of clear water, rippling with tides of action and change, created wave upon wave by those few people who live in that eternal sea. The waters of atemporality follow the tides from past to future, rippling and crashing with the surf of man-made change. The ocean is varied in calm and storm with neap tide and riptide, with safe swimming currents of alteration and killing whirlpools of transformation, but everywhere from the shallows of time to the deeps the ocean is one and the same water.

No one is born into the waters of time; each ocean dweller lived first in the earth of time, before either pulling himself or being pulled out of the hard strata, yanked away from the prison of causality into the freedom of change.

The first man to so free himself acted in ignorance. He was a seeker after knowledge, a solidifier of the unknown, a laborer in the sciences of matter. Before he saw the Instant he bore the name Dhiritirashta, the name of a mythic ruler of his people. Dhiritirashta in seeking the invulnerable solidity in the untouchable fluidity of the smallest constituents of matter caught a glimpse of the gap in causality that is the Instant, and he saw (the only true thing he ever saw) that between the causal and the acausal, the temporal and the atemporal, was a unity.

But in his blindness he conceived of the unity of time as an earthly unity, a solid place from which he could reach out and grasp all the wealth of past and future. Seeking that prize, he labored for a dozen years to build a machine, a sheath to cover his body, to separate the matter of his form from the solid world around him, a second skin that was causal on the inside, but acausal on the outside, a portable break in the unity between the halves of time, a line drawn down the edge of connection, a barrier against all earthly harm.

He knew that none of the phenomena by which the beings of earth perceive and interact with the world existed in this other side, but he could not conceive of leaving those phenomena behind, so into this second skin he built devices to translate atemporal perception into temporal, atemporal action into temporal analogy. He would see and hear, move and act.

In pursuit of motion and action he discovered that the other side of time laid bare the four-dimensionality of the world. To move in it he needed to take not just his present body but a considerable portion of his past with him. He needed to cut loose not just his life now but the preceding year. This he calculated would give his machine enough strength to move him through the other side of time.

The day came when his machine was ready. He stepped into the half-visible, half-mirrored cocoon and felt it seal around his skin, and then he felt (though he had been certain he would not feel) the strands of the device reach backward through the gaps in causality—back (though he did not understand it yet) through the waters of the Instant to cover his previous year of life.

Sheathed in the dualistic webbing, Dhiritirashta turned on the machine, breaking the bonds of time. The silver shell severed his connection to the solid mass of temporality and cast him, like an untrained swimmer, floundering into the ocean of time.

Shocked by the sudden intrusion, the placid waters were churned into waves by the terrified man who had thrown himself into the deep. Inside his second skin where cause and effect reigned, Dhiritirashta flailed in fear of drowning, though no water entered his lungs, no pressure beat upon him. He was fearful, though without cause of fear. On the outside of the skin, where the acausal solidity he had created touched the acausal liquid of time, there was connection and a jumping across the bridge of probability; large-scale events occurred in a realm that had only known happenings within scales so small that no one could say whether they had happened or not.

Across the gaps the splashing of the swimmer created large waves and deep currents. These waves wrought great changes in the world. The waters that had only determined where an electron might find itself became determiners of events of much greater sweep and compass.

In the solid world left behind, the climactic year of his work was undone and remade by Dhiritirashta's sudden disappearance. His laboratory was deserted, his work abandoned, and the machine he had been building was gone, leaving no trace within the world. Change came to the earth, remarked upon as a peculiar and inexplicable event, and the fate of Dhiritirashta lay at the feet of accident.

In the Instant, Dhiritirashta surfaced in a panic, treading water in an eddy of rippling change, a swirling tidal pool created by his own flailing. He gasped for air that did not exist and that he did not need to sustain his new life. A glimmering of awareness came to him, a feeling of deathlessness, of safety from the ills of the solid world. The first man freed from the bounds of earthly constraint regained his composure and looked out on the gentle calmness of an almost unstirred ocean. He watched the waves of change that rippled out from his new-made aquatic body, a thing of four dimensions: the three of his old temporal body and a tail of the life he had taken from earth. The waves that came from him passed over the earth and altered it, making new chains of cause and effect in the solid world below, the acausal flow penetrating and touching the causal universe, moving an atom here, changing a reaction there, altering the path of a stone in flight to strike the head of a soldier, injuring him so that he missed a battle that would have killed him so that he lived to lead an army and a nation to victory instead of defeat. Such were the changes Dhiritirashta's casual motions created.

In his ignorance of the ocean, he called the place to which he had come the Instant, and conceived of it as a place unchanging, and called the solid world he had left the Flux. In his thoughts he declared that in the Flux all things change, and that in the changeless Instant all change is caused, for it seemed to him that the only real change was alteration of the solid world and that the ripples and waves he created in the Instant were not changes in the ocean, only effectors of change in the earth.

Dhiritirashta, amazed at the ease with which his merest motion could change the world from which he came, was fired by a sudden greed, a desire to control the Flux which he believed to be the real world and to mold it to his conception, to unmake all that he had disliked in the world and make it all that he had desired. He set about to use the waters of the Instant to carve the earthly side of time into the perfect world for men to live in. Or rather into what he in his earthbound mind conceived the perfect world to be.

Dhiritirashta's was a simple notion of perfection. The people he regarded as most valuable in society (scientists in his case) would rule all others. The arts he preferred (computer abstractions) would be pursued. The architecture he liked (tall spires and vast parklands) would pervade. And the supreme being he approved of (himself) would be worshipped, under the title Universal Monarch.

His means of creating utopia was as simple as the utopia itself. He swam a few centuries pastward from the era in which he lived and rippled out waves of change to alter the things in the earthen world that dissatisfied him. Gradually, one wave after another, he made the time in which he was born into the time in which he would have liked to be born.

In the course of remaking society, history, science, religion, and all the other things that had distressed him while he lived in earth, he radically changed every human who lived futureward of the point from which he executed change. In the course of this alteration, he undid the lives of his grandparents and made himself never-born. In reshaping itself to accommodate the changes Dhiritirashta had wrought, the Flux became a place in which Dhiritirashta had never been. And yet he did not vanish from the Instant, he was not unmade by his own unmaking.

The Universal Monarch pondered this paradox, floating above the place and time in which his great-grandparents failed to meet, and wondered at the strangeness of it. Had he thought harder and pursued this clue to the atemporal reality around him he might have gained insight and from it spared the Flux and the Instant the pain that was to come; but he did not. All he saw was that the acausal world around him made him invulnerable to all the effects of all the causes in the world, even aging and death could not touch him in his sheath.

Secure in his illusions, the Universal Monarch completed his remaking of the world, and then lay back upon the waters of time to reign in pleasure, studying the society he had sculpted out of solid time, joying in the results of his labor, dipping down to touch the world and see the progress man made under his benevolent guidance, to watch the advances of knowledge, the spread of art and architecture, the songs of praise sung to him all across the world.

But he had looked with too narrow a focus and neglected that things created in the solid earth have consequences long after their inception. A thousand years futureward a flaw developed in the flawless gem of a society he had carved: another man found the means of entry into the Instant. This man, who abandoned the name of his birth and called himself simply Asura, after those who made war upon the gods, fancied himself a liberator. He dreamed of freeing the world from the legendary atemporal dictator who, it was said, reigned in glory outside of time from the eternal sameness of perfection.

This self-conceived redeemer entered the Instant with two likeminded comrades who also took the title of Asura. Together they learned the ways of the ocean, and discovered that the great powers of the Universal Monarch derived from the simplest of actions in the Instant. The three Asuras who had believed that they would be attacking a terrible and invincible enemy and that they had little hope of success realized that Dhiritirashta ruled all with very little.

The Asuras learned to move through the waters, to push their year-long bodies like fish through the ocean, and they discovered that the rippling of their bodies made waves. They learned in manner quick and painful that sharp motions could make waves that could break the two-sided mesh that had been woven around them. Once the skin was broken, their vulnerable causal bodies would be bitten into and carved up by the waters. Against this attack the webs sought to reform themselves, but often a piece of the person would be lost to the ocean amidst this healing.

Pain and loss from these accidents taught them that they were capable of causing great injury to others in the Instant by the simplest motions of their atemporal forms. Armed with this understanding they swam the thousand years pastward to confront their enemy.

The battle that ensued was fierce but crude, as both sides discovered the fragility of their atemporal bodies. Lasting out their year-long tails, the former master of the Instant and his assailants, raised savage cutting waves that tore each other's bodies into fragments. Each piece of their lives was quickly resealed in the webbing that permitted them to survive in the first place, but of the many pieces of each life only one was alive and could act. In each of the atemporal beings, consciousness was temporally contained, existing in a single moment that carried the illusion of progress and passage from the Flux into the Instant.

Dhiritirashta and the three Asuras had each a taken a solid year of life into the Instant, but this battle whittled away that timeless time, carving out a month here, a week there, until the Universal Monarch, Dhiritirashta the blind king, was carved into a flotsam of unthinking seconds and a tiny scrap of consciousness that subsisted in a piece of his life barely a tenth of a second long, not even time enough to flee the pain of undying death.

Dhiritirashta was effectively gone, leaving the three liberators, the three Asuras, to rule the atemporal ocean.

These emancipators now set to work undoing the tyranny of the man whose life they had shattered into helpless moments. They swam several centuries further pastward and proceeded to remake the world into a place of universal freedom, a grand utopia of time-bound liberation. But to accomplish this great dream for the world, they had to become the rulers, the gods of the solid world. And as they had come together to fight the enemy god who sculpted their earth, so they engendered opposition, seekers and warriors who sought to fight their shapings of time. Another force of warriors, seven proud crusaders, entered the Instant, seeking to oppose the atemporal triumvirate who had remade history according to their whims.

Another battle ensued; destructive waves unleashed by tails lashing in anger fragmented both clans of warriors. But this battle was inconclusive. Both sides retreated from the disputed region of the Instant. Both sides nurtured their visions of a reshaped world, but neither could approach the time they wished to change without risking attack from the other.

Bobbing on the surface of the waters of time, beneath the nothingness that took the place of sky, the men of the two camps whispered to each other in questioning waves, querying and speculating, seeking to find advantage. How do we gain an advantage over our opponents? How can we attack without being destroyed ourselves?

Their words rippled little changes as they deliberated, the discussion itself slightly altering solid time below them. Questions and speculations passed back and forth in minute changes until one of the attackers, new come to the Instant, hit upon the idea. He led his people, swimming three thousand years futureward, and there he dove down and gripped the solid rock of the Flux. This man of the atemporal waters of time reappeared in the temporal earth, temporarily trading his ocean-native tailed form for the bipedal existence he had known before. Those time-bound men who saw him appear thought he was one of them, suddenly, impossibly coming into existence; they could not see his tail of years bobbing in the waters above, for they could not see the waters.

That man, clutching the solid earth like an anchor, looked about him at the world that their change-waves had sculpted. He paid no attention to the society or the people or their lives. All he wanted to find was some object, some device that had been created using the theories that had permitted them entry into the Instant three thousand years before.

He found what he was looking for, a simple metal implement that could be held in the palm of a hand. They were used by the time-bound to strengthen their four-mile-high buildings and keep them from falling over in the winds. The theory on which they were based was long since forgotten. But the man who came back from the Instant knew how they worked, knew that they drew upon strong causal connections, the solidity engendered in things by the narrowing of probability into apparent certainty. He understood that these devices used the earthly side of time itself to make matter resistant to change. He snatched four of them out from the main supports of a tower and tore them from the earth of time as he released his anchor and, passing through the solid sky into the ocean, floated to the surface of the Instant.

The small objects he had taken in his momentarily temporal hands blossomed in the Instant into long strands of thread that covered his tail and the tails of his comrades. When the sharp-edged change-waves of battle struck those silken bands, the crested cutting waves became blunt, smooth flows that washed peaceably over them. Armored against their foes these atemporal warriors returned to the aborted fray and assaulted the three liberators.

The battle that ensued was a slaughter. The protected warriors carved their naked enemies into helpless fragments with sharp waves lashed out from their tails while their newly stolen defensive sheaths kept them safe from the crests of their foes' watery attacks.

Again the Instant was ruled by a single force. Again the Flux was molded according to one unified vision. And again new forces arose to free time from its oppressors. But not just one group entered the Instant; four different factions from four different times carrying four different conceptions of perfection came out of the earth and into the waters to make reality of their desires.

Battle was quickly joined. The same lessons of atemporal warfare were learned by the newcomers. Soon all five factions were diving down into various treasure regions of time to steal from the earth those gems of technology that would be useful in the Instant.

But every raid into the Flux created awareness in the people of earth that the people of water existed. Each raid created new stories, engendered more research, and created new groups of seekers who cut themselves off from the civilized life of earth to join the vikings of time's waters.

The number of sides in that war grew until over a thousand tribes contended for dominance in the Instant, dissolving the placidity of the ocean into a roil of battle. A thousand schools swam the waters of time seeking to impose their views on the earth below them.

In search of weapons the tribes ranged far across the waters of time. At first they only searched futureward from their times of origin, seeking the highest technology available. But the waves of change they themselves created made the deep future seas choppy and dangerous, and the world below them changed so swiftly to their atemporal perceptions that even as their raiders would anchor down to steal a prize it would be snatched away from them in the sudden onset of a new-made world.

Then one tribe, fleeing pastward from a savage battle in which their numbers had been gravely depleted, anchored into a time a dozen millennia before any man had heard of the Instant. This desperate tribe found a city of people living in relative peace, suffering only the mundane time-bound concerns of death, disease, and poverty.

With their superior technology and command of the powers of time the Instant dwellers enslaved the time-bound men and forced them to make weapons for the war outside of time. The atemporal masters even took a few of these people into the Instant to serve as shock troops, expendable warriors to be thrown at their enemies.

This tactic of enslavement soon spread among the tribes so that instead of only ranging futureward in search of weapons, they also swam pastward in search of thralls to labor for them. But in doing so the tribes of time brought the knowledge of the Instant with them to times and peoples who would never have conceived of it. And from these no-longer ignorant peoples new tribes of time were spawned, new factions who entered the Instant to join the eternal war.

Searching for treasure and slaves, the tribes continued to range pastward, unmaking the fixed histories from which their own peoples and their own visions of how things should be had sprung. And the numbers of tribes swelled. Ten thousand bands of warriors swam through the waters of time, each band composed of ten to fifty fanatic soldiers. All told a quarter of a million combatants contended in the Instant, each soldier committed to his tribe's vision of history, and each man's stirrings and strivings roiling the waters of time and muddying the solid earth below.

Back and back the warriors of the Instant ranged, seeking advantage in battle, caring nothing about the wild changes their passage made in the histories of the earth, for each tribe vowed that when it had triumphed in the war that all these sad expedients, all the suffering they had brought upon the earthly world, would be unmade and paradise/true history would be carved from the gems of solid time.

But even this vow-strengthened callousness had its limits. As they ranged pastward, pillaging the world for their needs and unmaking all the endeavors of the time-bound, the marauders of time reached a single place, a single people, a single event, and a single being who they did not dare unmake, for even in their overweening confidence they feared that there was one thing that if changed they could not change back.

In the small community in Africa where the first Homo sapiens lived, they found a single woman from whom all modern humanity had descended. Even the warring tribes of the Instant feared the consequences to their visions of perfect history if they removed the first Homo sapiens from the world.

A ripple of fear washed over the tribes of the Instant as one and all they momentarily saw how their actions placed the solid earth at risk and how the war itself endangered the histories they wished to create. For one moment, the Instant was united by a single terror. But fear-born awareness does not last. Greed conquered their fearful thoughts. The cautious tribes who fled back futureward, fearing to touch this woman and her immediate descendants, were replaced by bold tribes who saw in her and her children the chance to remake all of humanity according to their desires.

The single ocean wave of peace that followed the moment of awareness was replaced by a new war. This one was fought more carefully but no less savagely than the battles occurring further in the future. The tribes that fought over the beginning of humanity did not dare to recklessly slash the ocean with waves of change. Instead they fought seemingly mortal battles anchored into the world as one after another they shed blood and shattered earth seeking to capture and enslave the village of Homo sapiens and their Great Mother.

In the solid world, the first humans knew the terror of endless sudden unpredictable invasion. In the heat of the day they would be laboring at the bewildering tasks their masters had set them, when without warning a squad of strange people, clad in robes of shimmering metal or bands of coruscating rainbows would appear among them. Then their masters would appear to fight off the invaders. There would be flashes of light, and crashes like thunder. Huts would burst into flame; trees would fall; the sky would darken with smoke. And in a few seconds of conflict, the first humans would have new masters whose actions would be as inexplicable as those of their predecessors.

Each new enslavement would bring new changes to their lives. Many of the conquering tribes sought to genetically modify the Great Mother so that all of humanity would be better suited to whatever vision of life they had brought back to the beginning of things. Others sought to lock up the first humans, keep them in boxes like precious gems, only letting them out to breed. Still others sought to indoctrinate them, give them ideas that would become the foundation stones for all humans.

But all the various different slaveries of the People (for that of course is what the first humans called themselves) shared one thing in common: perpetual incomprehension. Where the masters came from and what they wanted were a mystery to the People, a bewilderment that lasted until one tribe of conquerors chose to do to these first humans what was commonly done with peoples further in the future. These new rulers chose to make shock troops out of the men of the People. That tribe of masters conceived the notion that only the genetic heritage of the People needed to be preserved; the individual lives of the People could be used as they saw fit.

By their own lights they were careful and deliberate in their manner of choosing which of the People to bring into the Instant. In order to make sure that what they did would not endanger humanity's existence, only men who had already fathered children and women past the age of childbearing were brought into the Instant. And to make sure that they could always undo their mistakes, they refrained from taking the Great Mother (for such they and all the other tribes of time called the first woman) into the Instant.

The masters of the People created their cadre of slave-warriors to be brute soldiers, so they gave them the minimum capabilities to fight in the Instant and let them have neither armor nor weapons. They declared to the People that these Ghosts would be their defenders, and set them in the shallows of the Instant to take the brunt of any new assault. The Ghosts suffered greatly in the battles that came, but those that survived learned the ways of the Instant and came to understand the nature of the war outside of time.

Eventually, the Ghosts and their masters were conquered by a tribe who styled themselves the Tamers of Evolution and the People were enslaved again. These new rulers saw the value in the Ghosts and gave them greater capabilities. The Tamers spent much effort in pillaging technologies that could be used to augment humans both in the Flux and the Instant. From a time that no longer existed seventy thousand years futureward from the time of the Ghosts they had stolen devices that would weave themselves into a person's nervous system and borrow the speech center of their brain, giving advice to the mind.

The Tamers used this technology to place Voices in the brains of the Ghosts, voices tied to sensors and to memories that would guide them in battle without teaching them too much about the Instant (though it was already far too late to keep that knowledge from them). The new masters also strengthened the atemporal bodies of the Ghosts so they could more easily withstand the rigors of battle, and they gave the warriors an extended sense of touch that greatly enhanced their perception in the Instant. To refill the decimated cadre of warriors, they instituted a series of tests of the living members of the People and chose the fittest among them to become Ghosts.

The Tamers too were eventually displaced by others who saw the value of the Ghosts. These new conquerors, who called themselves the Dragons of the Celestial River actually led some of the Ghosts futureward with them when they went to battle, so the slave-warriors saw firsthand the depths of change and the wildness that was the Flux. They returned to the People and vowed in secret that their native time, the two-hundred-year stretch of earth and water that they called the Now, would not be made to suffer the indignity of arbitrary change.

Away from the senses of their masters they spoke these words:

> *"We are the People.*
> *The People will not be changed.*
> *This is the Now.*
> *The Now will not be Flux."*

And with this vow came rebellion against the Dragons. Knowledge of battle gleaned in secret from their many rulers, weapons pillaged from the fragmented bodies of defeated enemies and hidden in places untraveled by their conquerors, and a drive and determination unseen before in the slaves, all these were revealed in a sudden rage of piercing waves and rippling tides.

This single violent crest of change freed the People of the Now and their guardian Ghosts. In the moment of their freedom the Ghosts made a choice to be unlike all of the other tribes of the Instant. The Ghosts assembled and vowed together, speaking in mortal words and atemporal ripples, that they would not seek to change the future, that their only concern would be the protection of the People, the Now, and the Great Mother. They left the war to the mad tribes of the future and sought only to keep the Now from suffering the horror of change. Thus the vow taken in slavery was renewed and expanded in freedom.

The Ghosts began their eternal vigil by establishing stern protections and strict standards of action. They chose two leaders: an Elder and a War Chief. For Elder they chose an old woman who was one of the first of the People dragged into the Instant. To her was entrusted the duty of making sure that the Ghosts remembered their vow and never strayed. Through the struggles that came the same person kept the position of Elder, always present, always a solid reminder to the Ghosts. The War Chief's duties were less subtle; he it was who commanded the Ghosts in battle and oversaw the protection of the Now.

Unlike the Elder, the position of War Chief changed hands several times. The first man to hold that position was the leader of the rebellion that freed the Ghosts. His name in life had been Fal and he had been the firstborn of the Great Mother. He laid down the basic military structure, giving some of his warriors the tasks of guarding the futuremost border of the Now, others the task of seeing to the Great Mother's welfare, and the rest he kept in reserve to fend off invaders. Fal was destroyed thwarting the next attempt to enslave the People.

The second War Chief, Ein, reinstituted the testing of the People in order to refill the ranks of the Ghosts after they suffered grievously in several assaults. He gave his life preventing the Great Mother from being kidnapped as a newborn.

The third, Hes, struggled mightily to prevent the re-enslavement of the People. During his reign as War Chief, more than two dozen tribes came pastward one after another to attack the People. Each assault caused great changes in the Now, as many lives were unmade and many others created. At the end of his reign only four of the original rebelling Ghosts survived; all the other Ghosts in his command were later additions culled from the People by the testing. So desperate did the third War Chief become that he conceived the notion of bringing the Great Mother into the Instant in order to protect her. One of his own warriors stopped him and the Elder stripped him of his title and exiled him from the Now. Hes was killed several millennia futureward by an enemy tribe seeking vengeance for a defeat they had suffered at his hands.

The fourth War Chief was a great-grandchild of the Great Mother named Nir. The Now that Nir was born into had suffered many alterations from the Now of the rebellion. None of the time-bound People whom Nir grew up with had known the lash of slavery. Instead they lived under the guidance of the Ghosts, proud of their heritage and their defenders. Nir excelled at the Ghost tests and eagerly entered the Instant to join the cadre.

He learned the ways of combat in the Instant: how to attack foes with his ten-year-long tail, how to defend himself with shields and blunting waves, how to keep out of the cutting streams of his comrades while they also battled. He learned how to stretch out his touch and feel the currents of change years and tens of years from his location. He learned to interact with and use his Second and Third Voice, respectively the extra memory and tactical advisors implanted in each Ghost's brain. In short, he swiftly mastered the tactics of time.

Nir was the warrior who alone had prevented the previous War Chief from tearing the Great Mother from the earth of time by tricking him into believing that an enemy tribe was attacking. For the loyalty and ingenuity he showed, the Elder made Nir War Chief and gave him the gift of Fourth Voice, the atemporal analysis tool that was the secret aid of each War Chief in turn.

Once appointed to the position, Nir contemplated the state of the Ghosts and the People. They had been battered and their numbers reduced in the last few onslaughts. His predecessor had been driven to desperation out of fear that the vow of the Ghosts could not be kept. In a moment of changing thought Nir realized that the reason the Ghosts had suffered the reverses they had was their isolation from the war of time. Futureward, the mad tribes raided the Flux for weapons, but no such raiding was possible in the Now. Nir created a new task for his warriors, making some of them scouts who would travel in ones and twos futureward into the wilder parts of time's ocean. Their orders were to keep away from the battling tribes and concentrate instead on snatching weapons from the treasured earth of shifting time.

The Elder expressed concern about this novelty, but when the bounty of Nir's scouts helped the Ghosts fight off the next few assaults without any loss of life, she relented. Under Nir's leadership, the Ghosts and the People began to enjoy a measure of security unknown under previous leadership.

And from security, curiosity arises.

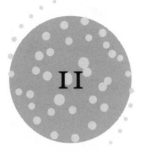

II

From deep in the war-stormed middle of time's ocean, pastward across fifty millennia, Col, one of the Ghost scouts,
came swimming back to Now, clutching to his tail a ragged piece
of flotsam. He had found it floating in a gentle current and picked
it up, hoping that it was some prize he could return to his War
Chief. He had reached out to it with his extended touch and waited
for his Second Voice to tell him its nature, and his Third Voice to
explain its battle uses. But both Voices were silent with incomprehension.

The scout considered leaving the jagged-edged thing of half a
second's extent, and searching further futureward for battle-useful
material. But the muteness of his Voices and his native curiosity,
which had made him an ideal choice for the duty of prospecting
futureward, prevented him from leaving the thing to bob upon the
currents of time. Instead he took the object with him, back through
the danger-laden currents of the middle Instant, back to the Now
so he could present his peculiar prize to Nir.

Floating in his accustomed place one hundred and fifty years
futureward from the Great Mother's birth, the War Chief stretched
out his touch to sense the contours of the object. He pondered

briefly, then called the Ghosts together in a council. Nir's message was sent up and down the two centuries of the Now, tapped out in ripples across the shallow waters of time, "Come to council, come to the seventh day of summer in the Year of Ghosts' Conferring."

The Ghosts swam through the shallow waters of the Now. The Elder and the warriors and the scouts, all save the Great Mother's guards came from their posts and their duties. Navigating with the aid of their Third Voices, they made their way to the correct day and hour. "Twenty years to the Year of Ghosts' Conferring. Four kilometers to the Great Mother's mound. Ten years, two kilometers. One month, fifty meters."

So they swam, guided by Voice and their own sense of touch, feeling the contours of the solid world beneath for the telltale markers that had been carved into that year and that place.

The Ghosts swam to the center of the Now, to the Year of Ghosts' Conferring. The custom of the Ghosts was rigid. All meetings for great matters took place in that year and in one single spot, for it was in that year that the original rebellion had been plotted in subtle talk anchored into the earthly side of time. To the Ghosts it marked the midpoint of their territory, one hundred years after the birth of the Great Mother and one hundred years before the People left their village and ventured out to populate the world.

All twenty of the assembled Ghosts swam together to that spot. They spoke no words in the Instant, keeping to the custom of silence that the rebels had employed to hide their thoughts from their enslavers.

Nir stretched out his touch and felt each warrior in turn. All were present. The War Chief dove down and, touching the floor of the ocean, grasping the solid side of time, vanished from the Instant.

Nir came into being fifteen meters in front of the mound of dirt that held the Great Mother's bones. His sense of touch drew inward until it reached no farther than the border of his skin. Nerves that had recently taken in the press of liquid time tingled at the airy lightness of a summer breeze wafting over the War

Chief's naked form. Nir opened his eyes, useless in the Instant, to gaze up at the sun through the broad leaves of the trees. He sniffed the air and his long-ignored nostrils savored the smell of fruit and nuts, and he listened to the distant singing of the People in their village two kilometers to the west as they celebrated the Year of Ghosts' Conferring.

"You are facing the burial mound of the Great Mother," Nir's Second Voice told him. Second Voice was a useful recorder of facts, but it had no discernment about when to speak and when to keep still.

"Twenty atemporal incursions, ranging from two meters to thirty meters away," Nir's Third Voice alerted him. The tactical warning system also did not know when to keep quiet.

His score of warriors appeared in sudden solidity, forming a ring around the mound, fourteen men whose apparent ages varied from fifteen to thirty, and six women seemingly clustered around their middle forties. Their naked forms were lean and well muscled; a lifetime spent preparing physically for their eternal existences showed in their stern health. In unison the twenty warriors covered their eyes with their hands and bowed first to the mound of earth and then to the War Chief.

Nir looked at each in turn, rejoining in his memory their earthly appearances with the feel of their watery bodies. They were his uncles, aunts, cousins, nieces, and nephews, but none of them had ever been born, just as he had never been born. The Now each of them had known in life was different from the Now each of the others knew. Each of them in their minds held on to the Now they had known and had told it to the others, so that every Ghost knew every permutation, every change that had happened since the liberation—knew every change and cursed every tribe that brought about those changes.

The Ghosts uncovered their eyes, and each in turn studied their War Chief's dark and serious face, saw the frown of concentration that he habitually wore when anchored into the solid world, and watched him shifting his weight back and forth from leg to leg as his muscles reminded themselves of walking and fighting in the earth.

The Ghosts rarely discussed their opinions of the War Chief. He was their leader appointed by the Elder and they followed him. If they had spoken to each other about Nir they would have been surprised at the lack of uniform opinion about him. In truth no two Ghosts thought the same thing about Nir.

One veteran who had served under all but the first War Chief thought Nir a brilliant tactician, but lacking in respect for things already done. Another who had also been under those three felt Nir too hidebound, too stiff in his attitudes. One scout believed the War Chief lacked broad enough vision to see all the opportunities that lay open to them in the deeper waters of time. Whereas Col, who had made the discovery that had brought this meeting about, felt Nir's mind was far-reaching and his grasp of the nature of the Instant unmatched by any Ghost, excepting, of course, the Elder.

"Atemporal incursion, fifteen meters directly ahead," Third Voice said to Nir.

Nir lowered his eyes to the ground for a few moments, then looked up.

A naked woman whose skin had paled to light brown over the sixty years she had lived in solid time had come into being seated on top of the mound; her face was lined with sadness but her eyes gleamed with dark fire like kindled coals. She stood up carefully as if her age had come again upon her, stretched weathered arms out to feel the air, and then turned in a slow circle to survey those around her. Each Ghost covered his eyes with his hands as her fierce glare fell upon him. When she was done gazing upon the gathered warriors, the woman seated herself atop the grave and covered her own eyes for a moment.

"Recite the litany," she commanded.

"We are the People!" the voices of the Ghosts boomed into the afternoon wind. And with those words each remembered his life in the world of stone.

"The People will not be changed!" And each remembered his vow to defend, and the moment of his severing from solid time and entry into the watery existence of a Ghost.

"This is the Now!" The limits of their duty reasserted themselves. To guard this one village for two hundred years, that was what they had vowed.

"The Now will not be Flux!" They would keep their charges safe from the madmen of the future.

"Again!" the Elder said. And the response echoed like the second rumble of thunder.

> "We are the People!
> The People will not be changed!
> This is the Now!
> The Now will not be Flux!"

"War Chief," the Elder said, turning to face Nir.

"Yes, Elder," he replied.

"Speak forth the purpose of this conferring."

"Yes, Elder," Nir said, once more covering his eyes briefly.

Two young boys of the People had slipped away from the village during a break between dances, and, after running along the jungle trail that led to the Great Mother's grave, now crept quietly through the thick growth of trees as they neared the edge of the clearing. They kept low to the ground and cocked their ears, hoping to hear the speech of the Ghosts. They knew they were not supposed to be there, that only the priest of the People and those who were chosen to join the Ghosts were permitted to see them. But the curiosity of youth was not to be denied even by the oft-repeated prohibitions of parents and priests.

"The story is true; they look just like us, only naked," whispered one of the boys as they peeked through a break in the circle of trees. "But I don't see the tails they're supposed to have."

"That one on the left looks like my uncle Col," said the other, "but Uncle Col's alive."

"The old woman in the middle," the first boy whispered, shivering despite the warmth. "She must be the Elder. She is sitting on the Great Mother's bones."

"I wonder which one is the War Chief."

"Two unarmed subadults, crouching in ambush position, ten meters directly behind," Nir's Third Voice said. "Danger presented: minimal."

The War Chief turned his head around and saw the boys duck down, trying to hide their faces from the terrible wrath of the Ghosts. Nir abandoned his grip on the solid world and returned to the cool waters of the Instant. He curled his ten-year-long tail and with a single short stroke swam two hours into the past and two kilometers south to the waters above the village of the People.

The War Chief reached down into solid time and appeared in the carved limestone dwelling that housed the priest of the People, an elderly man named Yal who would have been Nir's father, had Nir's mother ever existed. The priest was dressed in the hide of a lion and carried a long staff of something that appeared to be wood, but which was actually an atemporal intrusion detector. When Nir appeared Yal was already kneeling on the grass floor of the hut with his withered hands covering his eyes.

"Two boys will try to slip away from the village during the dance. They desire to see the Ghosts in conclave. You will stop them, Yal," Nir said.

"I will stop them, O War Chief of the People."

Nir returned to the Instant, swam two hours into the future and two kilometers north, and reanchored himself in front of the mound into a conference that had never been disturbed.

"Col," Nir ordered, "show us what you found in the deeper waters fifty thousand years futureward."

"Yes, War Chief," the scout said. The young-looking man with open wondering eyes vanished into the Instant and the ten-year-long oceanic body of the scout reached out with a coil of his tail to grasp the jagged object he had left bobbing above this moment in the Year of Ghosts' Conferring. The thing he had brought back was only a few seconds long and less than a half a meter in diameter. It felt sharp and cold to his extended touch, like a cracked ball of ice.

Col slid the object down the coils of his tail until it reached that moment in his years of atemporal life where his consciousness resided. He pulled the frozen flotsam to himself and dove back down into solid time.

Col reappeared in the same spot he had left five seconds before. The earthly world accepted his sudden coming into being with a grace born of familiarity, but it did not do so for the thing he brought with him. The icy, ragged bubble tried to bob up away from the world to escape back into the Instant, but with the weight of his tail and the strength of his anchoring Col forced it to come into earthly existence.

It came into being two meters in front of Col. Floating in midair was what appeared to the assembled Ghosts to be a lump of dirt torn from the ground. Blades of grass stuck out from the top of the clod of earth, still gleaming with the dew of dawn in springtime. The lighting in the air above the dirt had an early-morning redness that contrasted sharply with the afternoon's harsh summer sunlight that surrounded the Great Mother's mound.

A bee flew sleepily through the separate light and air and alighted upon the stalk of a flower, sticking up from the blades of grass. But the flower had no top, only a ragged stalk with a few pieces of drooping petals that hung as if suspended in the air. The partial flower wavered in a wind that did not exist in the time and place that the Ghosts were standing.

The bee spiraled up the stalk, seeking for the nectar from a flower that was not there. It touched one of the hanging petals and froze in space. The wind ceased to blow, the grass held still; nothing moved on that lump of earth.

"War Chief," Col said. "I can barely keep the object anchored."

What is that object? Nir asked the Voices implanted in his mind.

"No new thing has appeared needing description," Second Voice said.

"No new threat has appeared," Third Voice said.

Fourth Voice hesitated, which greatly surprised Nir.

What is that object? the War Chief repeated, directing his question to Fourth Voice

"Atemporal conglomeration of unknown characteristics," Fourth Voice finally said. "Collection of objects bound together in a manner similar to the binding of solid time. Observation indicated that objects cannot leave the boundary of the region."

What could create such a thing? Nir asked.

"No known atemporal theory accounts for this phenomenon, hence no source can be deduced."

"War Chief," Col said. "I must let it go. It is dragging me back into the Instant."

"Let it go, Col," Nir said. "Follow it back to the Instant and return with it again."

"Yes, War Chief," the scout said. He, the floating lump of dirt, the demiflower, the grass, the bee, and the early sunlight disappeared. They reappeared a few seconds later. The clod, the grass, the bee, and the flower repeated their actions exactly as they had before.

"Object does not act like a free atemporal entity," Fourth Voice said to Nir. "It displays all the characteristics of time-bound existence, except that it floats of its own accord in the Instant. This object is impossible by all known atemporal theories."

"Fourth Voice says there is something new in the Instant," Nir declared.

The Ghosts covered their ears for a moment at the mention of the War Chief's private voice.

"Let any who wishes to speak on this matter do so," the Elder said, taking back control of the conclave with a stern tone in her voice and then magnanimously permitting the others to converse.

Opinions were bandied back and forth as to the importance or unimportance of this new strangeness, but neither the Elder nor the

War Chief paid much attention to what was said. Both of them knew that any newness in the Instant would eventually create great trouble for the People. An inexplicable newness could not be left alone to become a danger, for new things always arose from the battle schemes of tribes. Some enemy of the People (for all the other tribes were their enemies) must have created a weapon whose effects the Ghosts were witnessing. The enemy had to be found and the weapon taken for the good of the People. With practiced glances the Elder and the War Chief communicated their understanding to each other. When the conclave had finished they returned to the Instant to speak of matters not to be discussed within the realm of the living.

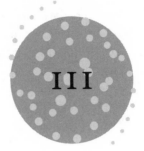

III

The Ghosts were not the only people of solid time captured and enslaved by the marauding tribes of the Instant who had rebelled successfully against their masters. There were many tribes who strove for freedom and then became marauders of time once they were liberated. But only one tribe snatched freedom from slavery the moment they entered the Instant, and they did not become warriors of time.

This unique band was a small clan of Australians that had lived a peaceful though marginal existence in the interior of that continent. The time period in which they had lived in the solid world was some sixty thousand years futureward from the Now.

To the tribes of time, the Now served as a marker for distinguishing the era in which events occurred, since all other time-bound ways of naming eras—religious events, reigns, olympiads, time of the great snows, and so on—were continually changed or unmade under the tides of the watery world. Only the Now was sacrosanct and so could be used to give some meaning to the question "When did that occur?"

This group of Australians had been found and studied by the

Time Warriors of the Eastern Gaian Church. When the Church had existed it had dominated Asia and the Pacific Ocean, but it had been unmade by an attack upon its founder by the Atemporal Cavalry of the West Brythanic Khanate. All that remained of the Church that had conquered two-thirds of the earth was a band of twenty-six people floating angrily in the waters of the Instant.

But the Time Warriors remembered the glory of the Church and kept it alive in songs sung in ripples of ocean waves. They sang to recall the vanished past and the lusted-for future, as every tribe of the Instant did. They sang so that they would not forget the history they fought to recreate. Memory was vital in the Instant, for there was no means of writing in the waters of time.

Each dweller in the Instant had only a limited amount of life in which to store his knowledge; a warrior with a ten-year tail had only ten years of consciousness, which was recycled over and over again. In this allotment of time he had to formulate his thoughts, learn from experience, and set aside what would be worth keeping when his consciousness reached the end of his atemporal life and returned to its beginning. Only the most important or the most ingrained of memories could be retained during the shattering moment in which consciousness bred in earthly time confronted the true atemporality of the Instant

And there was so much to know just in order to survive that many Time Warriors forgot the purpose for which they had entered the Instant, until their comrades would sing them the songs of their people and they would know once more why they were there, what they sought to do, and who their enemies were.

In the songs of the Eastern Gaian Church were verses of history, morality, geography, enmity, and dominance. In the last category was the Song of the Conquered, which listed all the time-bound peoples that the Church ruled. Near the end of the Song of the Conquered was the line, "The Knowers of Dreamtime, bound in body, free in mind."

With this line went the knowledge that a people imprisoned in earthly time had conceived of a place like the Instant and had learned in their minds the skills to comprehend and act in the time out of time.

To the arrogant minds of the Time Warriors of the Eastern Gaian Church these people would be ideal slaves, needing less training than any others. The warriors dove down from the Instant into the Flux of Australia and snatched away a score of this isolated group of humanity, and then with a swift barrage of change-waves unmade all the time-bound natives of Australia so that the knowledge and skills of Dreamtime would be wiped away from the Earth and so no other tribe would be able to make use of that knowledge.

The Time Warriors did not want to make these new dwellers in the Instant into shock troops; they wanted them as thieves to go among the other tribes and steal the latest advances in atemporal warfare. So they gave their slaves five analogue senses. The new slaves could "see" the folds and twists and curves of the waters of the Instant and distinguish the "colors" of soft and angry tides. They could "hear" the splash of oncoming change and the rippling speech of distant warriors. They could "feel" the texture of atemporal objects clutched against their tails. They could "smell" oncoming sea changes, the sweat of approaching warriors and the blood of shattered enemies. And they could "taste" the water around them for the character of the Flux below, distinguishing empty land from occupied cities, rich gem-laden earth from barren wastes, and human habitation from human desolation.

But the Gaians did not want their new slaves to have much memory or much capability in battle. They did not want them to recall their earthly life except to remember their Dreamtime skills, nor did they want the slaves to be able to muster killing waves long or choppy enough to injure any dweller in the Instant. One means existed to fulfill both of these ends; when the Gaians tore the Australians out of the Flux they did not bring much of their lives with them. Instead of tails years long, they gave their slaves only one minute of life each.

One fragile minute could not generate enough of a wave to

injure anything in the Instant, one brief minute could not keep much in memory, one swift minute could not formulate a plan for rebellion, or so the Gaians thought.

For something unexpected arose in those tiny minutes of life lived over and over: pulsing beats of consciousness and emptiness. A new manner of human thought arose in the minds of these Drums, as their enslavers called them.

Most of the dwellers in the Instant were capable of pretending that the life in the ocean of time had a progress, a direction, even a passage like that of solid time. They created this pretense in their own minds by relying on their memory; they recalled things as having happened, therefore they had happened, therefore there was a past in which they happened.

This delusion was only broken when consciousness reached its end and memory recycled. Then the truth would be seen. The Instant had no past or future, only a present that refused to stay the same. The Time Warriors created their conceptions of a past in the Instant by joining together their memories of these states and creating an illusion of a solid past in the watery side of time.

But the memory of a Drum was not like the memory of the longer-tailed Time Warriors. Where a man with a five-year-long tail would pass through that moment of truth only once in five years of apparent accumulated experience, a Drum would have it happen to him once a seeming minute. And while a long-tailed man would seek to forget that event as disruptive to his thinking, the Drum would cling to it as the most coherent thing that happened to him in a life of forgetfulness.

This rhythmic pulsing of memory wrought two effects upon the minds of the Drums. One was upon their memories, those seemingly shallow, confused, bewildered memories that caused their masters to regard them as ignorant, unlistening children. Their masters' view of them was true as far as it went, for when a Drum talked he seemed to be incapable of holding on to a thought for long. And so he would be, for the short-term memories of Drums were much afflicted. But their long-term memory was another matter entirely. Every cycle of consciousness gave a Drum a single bright moment of understanding. At the end of each cycle that moment would sink like a stone into the depths of the Drum's mind, and down below the level of conscious thought those stones would cluster into deep awareness, waiting to be called up by the right stimulus. Beneath the ignorant surface of a Drum was a depth of personalities and skills waiting to be called forth.

The second change that marked their minds was not so deep. It was just below the surface of consciousness that the Drums learned to see the Instant as it is: an infinite moment in which all things happen, not a part of a sequence of events. With this way of seeing came advantages in action that these twenty original Drums used to gain swift freedom from their masters.

The Drum's advantage was most clear in battle, and in battle with the Gaians it was first demonstrated. A long-tail would thrash out a cutting wave and see it as progressing toward its target. But a Drum would see the lashing as a change in the state of the Instant from safe to destructive, and the Drum would change himself, in attitude, in position, in direction and speed of motion in order that he would not suffer from this new state. To the long-tailed attacker the Drum appeared to be anticipating his attack and moving to defend himself before the wave would strike him.

From this came the belief among the long-tailed that Drums could know what was going to happen just before it happened. But it was not so. The truth was that the Drums knew that in the Instant, there is no before, there is no after, there is no happening, there is only the Instant.

This understanding came swiftly to the original twenty Drums. Or rather, it was apparently swift to the Gaian Time Warriors who had anticipated the need to educate their slaves in the ways of the Instant. The teaching began with warfare and the warning that the Drum's tiny bodies were fragile compared to their longer-tailed masters. The slaves seemed to absorb this concept meekly and to cower before their masters.

So the Gaians moved on to the practicalities of battle. In the midst of a lesson on the dangers of riptides in which the Gaians had created a cutting whirlpool that no Time Warrior would dare enter, all twenty Drums dove into and through the savage swirl of change-waves, seeming to the Gaians to be dodging in between the breakers. All of the Drums escaped through this man-made hazard, leaving their bewildered masters behind them, unable to give chase.

The Drums used their smallness to hide in the currents of the ocean and plotted together what they were to do, now that they had been brought into Dreamtime. They floated and talked, but the shortness of their memory made the debate futile.

Gradually, one by one the Drums abandoned the argument, and each swam away alone to find his way in the waters of time. As they traveled about and encountered the various tribes of the Instant, the myth of the Drums with their useless memories and their impossible ability to anticipate action in the Instant spread until it became common wisdom.

Some of the more adventurous tribes sought to create their own Drums by truncating the lives of volunteers among them since it was clear that they could not make slave Drums. Eventually a sizable minority of the tribes in the Instant had Drums to act as spies and thieves.

But none of the later Drums could match the original twenty in skill, for they did not possess the stories and the ways of Dreamtime and so they could not so closely connect their minutes of mortal life with their immortal existences.

Yet those twenty did not survive unscathed in the Instant. Eight of them were destroyed in conflations of circumstance from which even they could not escape, battles so savage that the sharp edges of the waves could not be dodged even by one as small as a minute, colliding typhoons of vast changes that covered and altered the entire world and swept up the Drums only to smash them against countervailing change-waves. Two of those eight were even caught and killed by their greed to steal something. Though they knew their enemies would be upon them, still the desire for treasure kept them rooted to one spot as they tried to make away with baubles stolen from solid time.

Five others were taken more subtly. The stories of those five are all the same: capture by a tribe and slow indoctrination. Weak memory played upon, songs sung, stories told, loyalties insinuated, until the Drum had quite forgotten where he had come from and believed himself to be a member of his captor's tribe.

Six more gradually lost interest in the events of the Instant. They became absorbed in their own perception of the waters and the understanding of the timeless time around them. Eventually each of these six ceased their moving through the Instant and settled down to bob in contemplation on the waters of time.

And so of the twenty Drums taken from the vanished peoples of Australia only one continued as he had begun. His name was Kookatchi, and by practice long and deep he had made himself the greatest thief in the Instant.

The impetus that led Kookatchi to thievery arose as soon as he was brought into the Instant. One moment he was sitting under the hot summer sun in the desert of the Australian outback, and the next he was splashing in the waters of time. His new senses filled him with images of beauty, the iridescent colors of the tidal flows: dark blues for the deep currents, bright reds for breaking waves, a delicate hint of purple for the rippling speech of his captors.

And the feel of the waters washing over his new tail. The sting of sharp crests, the caress of broad change-waves, the tickle of the bobbing waves from his captors. The smell of their long tails redolent of years, aged in the waters of the Instant. The clean newborn scent of his fellow Drums.

"Beautiful," he rippled out, his first word spoken in the Instant.

It was beauty that held him and beauty that made him conceive of freedom from the Gaians. Kookatchi could not bear to be kept from the beauty of the Instant. He wanted to see the ocean of time in all its possible states, to drink in with his Drum's awareness of wholeness the permutations of the waters.

When the Drums escaped Kookatchi struck out on his own, swimming through the Instant, drinking in all the beauties of water, change, tide, and counterflow and sometimes dipping down into the solid world and tasting the myriad variations of the Fluxing earth.

At first he was content only to look, to have the visions of beauty pass through his fleeting consciousness and vanish like bubbles in the wash of retreating memory. But gradually Kookatchi found himself unsatisfied. He wanted to do more than see and forget. He wanted things he could savor through cycle after cycle of his mind.

In spying on the tribes he watched them taking useful devices from the solid earth and hoarding them for their own use. Kookatchi came to see these objects as bright treasures to steal. He began to practice creating distractions, making tiny ripples near the tribe he had chosen to steal from; the ripples were careful imitations of the first waves that marked the approach of an enemy tribe. But to create distractions, one must be able to think like the one being distracted. To do this, Kookatchi learned to move away from a Drum's awareness, to conceal the simultaneous nature of the Instant in the illusion of sequence that the tribes clung to. Kookatchi learned to think and act as if he were once more living one minute over and over again.

Suspended between the two awarenesses, that of the Drum and that of the long-tailed, Kookatchi would work his deceptions. He would watch as the tribe he was deceiving would form itself into a defensive arrangement. With his Drum's awareness Kookatchi would dart through the holes in the tribe's arrangement and snatch away his prize.

The Drum would swim away and bob up and down on the waters, cradling his stolen beauty. While holding such an object, Kookatchi would be continually reminded of his theft, the prize itself serving as memorial of his cleverness. The Drum would keep hold of the spoils and the memory of the theft until he had milked all the enjoyment he could from them. Then he would abandon the object and swim away, forgetting all that had happened.

All save the clear moment of the theft. Those moments formed deep currents in his mind, teaching him the art of thievery and sinking down a knowledge of each tribe from which he stole. Kookatchi's thefts became more and more sophisticated and his study of his victims became quite detailed. He learned their languages and their songs. He learned the way they swam and the weapons they favored. But all this knowledge was buried deep in his memory, to be forgotten once he had left the scene, and remembered if he returned to plague the same tribe again.

The thief's reputation spread all through the Instant. Rare was the tribe that had never been raided by Kookatchi. His origin and motives were unknown and legends grew that somewhere, perhaps anchored down in earthly time, perhaps in some remote corner of the ocean, was a vast horde of treasure that he had secreted away by some means unknown to the other tribes.

Many tribes had sought to chase the Drum after a theft in the hopes that he would lead them to this great store of weapons. But none had succeeded, since the Drum had no such treasury, only his memory of the beauties he had taken.

It was during one such chase that Kookatchi encountered the thing he had never seen before and could not forget once he had seen it.

The Drum was fleeing from the Eternal Warriors of the Vatican Hegemony from whom he had stolen a very pretty bauble that in the Flux looked like a two-foot-wide curlicued mass of silver and gold wires, but in the Instant showed itself to be a graceful spider-web of shimmering blue and red that smelled faintly of blood. The object could be used to involuntarily anchor a Time Warrior. The Vatican's Eternal Warriors had planned to use it to capture and then kill the leader of their primary enemies, the Messengers of Holy Avignon.

But Kookatchi had stolen the weapon before the Eternal Warriors could use it to exact their revenge. And now the Vatican Hegemony's soldiers had a new target for their wrath.

They pursued the Drum across the waters of time that lay above North America fifty-six thousand years futureward from the Now. In that region of the Instant, the tides were very uneven. Regions of choppy eddies resulting from the intermix of battles only a few centuries in the past alternated with areas of slow, deep tides that resulted from changes laid down tens of millennia before.

Kookatchi steered away from the safety of the rich blue waters, choosing instead to surf through the angry red waters where his longer-tailed pursuers could not follow without risking their existences. He darted straight into a clashing riptide fifty miles in radius, propagating futureward, red wave against red wave with the anger of a battle being fought a hundred years before.

One of his pursuers followed him into the clashing waves and was shattered into hour-long pieces. The tang of blood and the scream of the warrior assaulted the Drum's senses. He swam on, dodging each cutting crest.

The fourteen remaining Hegemony warriors circled eastward around the crashing surf and lashed their tails in unison, sending new violence into the century-old conflict. Their lashing sent a deep crimson line washing over the eddies, a huge crested wave that sucked up all the lesser waves and added them to its force.

Kookatchi saw the state of the Instant and knew that there was no place he could move that would be safe from the crash of this wave. Without even bothering to think about it, the Drum reached down and anchored into the solid world.

Kookatchi appeared on a glacier in northern Maine, one short, dark-skinned man dressed in gleaming gold body armor in the midst of a howling blizzard. The snowstorm that battered him covered four hundred miles and had turned sky and ground pure white with ice and clouds. In a crevice half a mile away the starving natives huddled in igloos while the relentless nuclear winter poured down snow and sleet. The Drum studied the whiteness appreciatively and held up his stolen treasure to see how it looked glistening gold and silver against the white.

The wave of change that had been meant to bisect Kookatchi

in the Instant washed over the area. The nuclear war had never happened; there was no glacier. Kookatchi, unaffected by the change-wave, sniffed the air of the old maple forest, watched the red-brown leaves fall onto his treasure, and briefly savored the delicious nip of autumn air.

Two trees a few yards from Kookatchi vanished. A bird's course of flight abruptly changed direction ninety-seven degrees. A rock that had been whole was now broken. Tiny change-waves. Kookatchi knew what they meant, sensed the state of the Instant above him, and released his anchoring just as the Vatican warriors anchored down and leveled their weapons at the spot he had recently occupied.

Kookatchi flicked out a few ripples that indicated he had fled pastward, then swam swiftly away and hid in the rolling surf of a deep-tided region. His pursuers returned to the Instant and turned pastward to follow his false trail, hoping he would lead them to his fabled horde.

The Drum watched them go then until they reached the limit of his vision some fifty years in the past, then he forget about them and floated in the lapping tide contemplating the beauty of his prize.

The web of atemporal solidity that radiated out of the two-second-long instance of the worldly device lay around Kookatchi, pulsing red and green as the gentle change-tides floated over them. Its fixedness amidst the changing waters was the beauty that had first attracted him. No matter how the state of the Instant changed, this spider's trap remained solid, a reminder of the earthly origin of all things that floated in the waters of time.

But its changelessness began to bore the Drum. As the Instant altered around it, it remained the same, and the attraction began to fade. The gem he had stolen lost its luster and eventually became a thing of complete indifference to him. With nothing to keep his attention Kookatchi wandered off seeking new beauties, the trap left behind him to be snatched up by the first tribe that wandered into that area.

Kookatchi swam aimlessly east and futureward. Over Mozambique, sixty-three thousand years futureward from the Now, he
came upon a battle in progress and stayed to watch, hoping that
some item of interest might be shown.

The Roman Republic Time Corps were fighting a pitched battle
with the Tibetan Instant Berserkers. The fight had initially broken
out when the Tibetans had sought to genetically engineer and enslave a particular group of Mozambique natives whose ancestors the
Romans had enslaved. The Romans regarded these people as their
property and took exception to the actions of the Tibetans. The
change-waves from the battle had, of course, unmade the very people they were fighting over, but the fight itself continued.

Kookatchi found the interchange of cutting waves and broken
crests, the slicing up of warriors and the stench of blood, all too
familiar. He ducked down into the Flux to see if the collateral
changes from the war would produce anything worth his attention.

Kookatchi appeared on a paved asphalt road and began to walk
down it. One step, he was in a vast city made of artificially grown
crystals, glittering prismatic towers rising two miles into the sky.
The next step, a clear glass plain, covered with steel ruins, long ago
melted by nuclear attack. A third step, and the blond, blue-eyed
natives of Mozambique were holding a ceremony offering flowers
and computer chips to green marble statues of the Buddha Maitreya
who had only recently lived among them.

Step after step the solid world melted and reformed under the
force of the watery conflict above. Kookatchi continued his stroll
through the chaos until the battle died down and the changes became less frequent.

Realizing that the battle had ended and the troops had gone,
Kookatchi unanchored. The Australian looked around him at the
flotsam of fractured bodies floating peacefully on the green-blue
tides of time. The smell of broken tails, redolent of spilled blood,
stung his senses.

Kookatchi noticed one particularly long fragment; one of the

Romans had lost seven years from his tail. Kookatchi swam over to search the discarded remnant of a man's life.

Kookatchi sidled up to the base of the tail, the earliest moment of the Roman's existence that had been taken into the Instant. The Drum slid slowly alongside the bent and coiled tail, feeling the injuries that atemporal battle had inflicted on the temporal form.

The base of the tail was a boy some fourteen years old.

"They cut their warriors quite young," Kookatchi said to himself, not remembering that he had said the same thing on every occasion in which he had studied the Roman Republic Time Corps.

Kookatchi felt his way along, feeling the body change and grow, until at an age of twenty-one, he encountered the ragged edge of the severing. The smell of blood was heavy there.

"Must have been a riptide," he said as he studied the jagged line of the broken tail. The cut had not been a clean one. The last few minutes of the tail were harsh and serrated, with slices of the soldier's body seemingly stuck together haphazardly. Here the man still had a head, a few seconds later, a torso was added. Arms and legs appeared and disappeared for the next few minutes, until Kookatchi reached the end of the tail fragment where there was nothing left of the man.

Kookatchi had seen enough injured Time Warriors to be able to visualize the back end of the tail that remained to the Roman soldier. A headless corpse, then arms and legs without a torso, then arms or legs missing, until a few minutes farther up the tail there would be a whole Roman ready for battle.

No doubt the soldier would have the remnants of those ragged minutes amputated so he wouldn't have to live through the pain every time his consciousness returned to the new end of his tail. There was nothing on the body worth looting; any atemporal gear had been stripped by whoever had won the battle.

Kookatchi swam away, quickly forgetting about the Roman. He swam across the Instant seeking beauty, but nothing new presented itself. He passed several battles, none of them memorable, and searched a dozen encampments for things worth stealing, but nothing caught his attention until he came to Mongolia fifty-five thousand years futureward from the Now.

A sound came to him. Repetitive and faint, it reminded him vaguely of the tapping language used by the Ghosts of the Now, a tribe he had rarely seen and never found to be of much interest. But it was not a language. Kookatchi waited while his consciousness recycled over and over and his mind focused on the sound, waiting for knowledge to float up from the deeps of his memory.

After only a few passes through the shortness of his life, the knowledge came to him, the knowledge surprised him, and the surprise delighted him. The sound was one he had heard many times while he was time-bound, but never in the Instant. It was the sound of droplets of water striking something solid. But in the ocean of time, water was never found in drops.

Intrigued, Kookatchi followed the sound, swimming eastward. He lost track of everything else, the strangeness drowning all his concerns. Only that impossible sound held his attention. Where could it be coming from? He barely noticed the faint scent of old, stale blood in the water, barely realized that the deep blue tides were becoming redder and darker. That steady drip-dripping pulled him onward.

He swam on until his small tail felt something smooth and hard under it. The hardness snapped him from his reverie. He drank in his full awareness of the Instant, but what he perceived his mind rejected as impossible. There could be no solid place in the waters of time.

Kookatchi coiled his tail to swim on, but he slipped on slick hardness, cold like frost. He slid uncontrollably eastward, flopping like a fish on a sheet of ice, slipping and skidding, and then he fell into the solid world. He did not anchor, did not want to go from Instant to Flux, did not know that he could be taken back down against his will. But fall he did and taken he was.

He was standing on tundra. The noonday sun shone through wispy clouds, illuminating the dry gray grasses. A herd of tall brown horses galloped past him, paying him no attention. The noise of their passage filled his ears with the thudding of unshod hooves on dry ground. The booming of their gallop was everywhere. Then, like the second after a clash of cymbals, there was a deafening silence. A silence that did not go away.

The horses stood frozen in midgallop. Froth spewed in frozen streams from their mouths, their hooves planted on the ground or floating in midair as if where they stood did not matter. The air had become still, almost solid. Kookatchi tried to walk over to the nearest horse, but found himself unable to move. It was as if the moment of time he occupied was the last moment there was ever to be, as if there were no second after the one he and the horses were occupying, no time into which they could advance or through which he could maneuver his atemporal form.

Kookatchi pushed against the solid world, scrabbling back up into the Instant. He could feel his tail straining against this impossible prison of time. He felt the strain, felt the world fighting against his leaving. He heard something crack, and he was free, back in the Instant, sliding again across the icy area. But now he was sliding away from the trap that had held him, sliding back into the welcoming tides of time's ocean.

Once back in the waters, Kookatchi swam away, swam for hundreds of kilometers until he felt safe. Then he turned to survey the peculiar region he had just left. To the east and south of him, and as far futureward as he could see, the ocean of time was still and cold like ice, and like ice there was a thin tracery of cracks covering the unchanging anomaly.

"Beautiful," he said reveling in the uniqueness of the place. "But dangerous. I wonder if I've ever seen anything like this before. I hope I would remember it if I had."

Kookatchi wandered away from the strange cracked area, seeking safer regions and more pleasant things to think about. But each time his consciousness recycled he was startled by a perfectly detailed vivid memory of the fall, the horses, and the cracked glacier in the ocean of change. And each time the same thoughts filled the mind of Kookatchi the Thief: "What kind of weapon created that beautiful place, and who has it? Whoever it is, whatever it is, I'll find it and steal it."

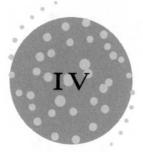

IV

The inhabited region of the Instant extends from the birth of the Great Mother to one hundred thousand years futureward from the Now. There the tides of time have homogenized into deep currents that ebb and flow in great changes, great swaths of flowing possibility that separate the surface of the waters from the solid world below. Futureward of the hundred-millennia mark it is impossible for any being to free itself from the solid world, for as one tries to leave the Flux, the deepest currents rip the would-be Time Warrior into milliseconds.

But one tribe does inhabit the deeps of time's ocean, the largest tribe in the Instant—or perhaps army is a better word than tribe. They are held together not by a desire for a fixed history, but by a single person, their strategist. Her name while she lived in the world was Quillithé. And so she shall be referred to, for the atemporal language of her army uses pictures not sounds, and it is easier to call her Quillithé than to mark her with the picture meaning center of all plans.

The tribe that brought Quillithé into the Instant and made her their leader was a small heterogeneous group of sixteen fearful nomads. These men had not come from one culture. They had not entered the Instant with a desire to see a single history created. They had fled the solid world in terror at the thought of their own destruction.

In the Flux below that deep ocean of time human life was rare. The wars that raged pastward had more often than not wiped out that species from the earth. But if the conflicting waves of previous battles brought about circumstances in which humans still lived, then those time-bound people who existed in that spark of life would have inherited one hundred millennia of Instant warfare. Those dwellers in the earth would know that they were slaves, prisoners to the whims of atemporal conflict, and they would seek escape.

But escape was rare. Most such men died in the crosscurrents. Of the thousands who tried, only those sixteen succeeded. Most came into the Instant battered and scarred; they tried to take long tails with them, but succeeded only in snatching a few months of their lives. They feared the tribes that battled in pastward parts of time's ocean and they huddled together and in crude pictures whispered a question. How could they survive?

They argued and debated until one of them hit upon the notion that what they needed to keep them safe was a champion, a warrior to defend them from the dangers of the other tribes. He proposed that they find one long-lived person and take her whole life into the Instant, a century-long fighter, one who would be so much larger than any opponent that no one would dare attack them.

They anchored down into the swiftly changing solid earth of time and waited. Patience was all they had so patience they used. The world flickered past their eyes, changing from desolation to paradise, from empty space to lush growth. Twice they spotted a likely prospect, twice the world changed before they could grab the hoped-for person. But the endless press of possibility finally gave them the one whom they sought.

A woman named Quillithé, born in a society locked in an interminable war that had been going on for centuries, born on an exhausted earth teetering on the edge of collapse. She managed to live one hundred years amid war, starvation, and disease, hardened by life until she died, almost miraculously, of old age. The sixteen nomads blinked in wonder at her life and grabbed her before the tides of time unmade the world in which she lived.

Nine of the tribesmen threw their bodies between Quillithé and the oncoming tides that sought to shatter her. Forsaking their own safety, they died in millisecond splinters so that she could be brought through into the safer waters above. Their sacrifice was not in vain. Quillithé lost not one second of her century of life. She emerged whole and perfect into the Instant, all of her from the moment she emerged from her mother's womb to the moment when she shut her eyes and died.

But the surviving seven tribesmen did not obtain the warrior they had sought. The shock of entering the Instant and the wild careening of her consciousness from the moment of death back to the moment of birth took away all of Quillithé's memory, and the world in which she was born, lived, and died vanished from her mind just as it vanished from the solid earth. Quillithé opened her rudimentary vision and looked out into the Instant, a newborn native of the ocean of time, newborn with a hundred years of empty life waiting to become a hundred years filled with craft and wisdom.

Her seven fathers still had hopes of making her into the soldier they desired. And they believed that they had the tools to do it. All the flotsam of the pastward arms race had come to them and they could draw upon the best tools ever created for battle in the Instant. The sheath they wove around Quillithé was vastly more advanced than the simple causal/acausal mesh that Dhiritirashta had manufactured for his entry into the Instant.

The seven scorned such primitive tools, confident that their armament would create their warrior. First they broadened Quillithé's sight, the only sense they themselves had in the Instant, stringing the farthest-reaching receptors up and down her century of life. Her analog sight became capable of seeing fifty thousand years across the ocean of time. Her vision cleared, Quillithé began to watch the battles going on pastward from the deep ocean that was her home. She saw the coming together of waves and the forming of tides and the changing of the ocean and the killing of the warriors.

The seven continued their work, joining her hundred years of nervous systems into one atemporal consciousness. Quillithé's mind became a huge echoing cavern, capable of being filled with vast areas of knowledge and of contemplating all the possible uses of all things that came before her. Quillithé's mind began to work, absorbing all she could see and turning the possibilities over in her mind. She began to chart the courses of change and the manners of battle in the Instant.

To protect her body, the seven nomads interleaved wave-dampening shields into her tail. Thus protected against the cutting ripples of time, Quillithé settled down comfortably in the deeps.

Then her seven fathers sought to give her the gift of movement. They joined her nervous system to her tail and attached atemporal motivators by which she could coil and uncoil. Quillithé stretched and unkinked her century and discovered the first limitation of her vastness, for though she could move each part of her tail, she could not bend and ripple enough to make the waters carry her through the Instant. Quillithé could not move herself through the ocean of time, let alone create the sharp killing waves she would need to fight their enemies.

The seven fathers flicked out sad pictures of despair. The plan that had cost them more than half their number had failed. But Quillithé answered them, rippling out from different parts of her body a subtle picture, more complex than any they had ever created. In this image written momentarily on the waters of time she showed her fathers how she would lead them and create an army, the only army in the Instant.

And her fathers rejoiced. Instead of a transitory warrior who might be killed in battle, they had created a strategist who would be able to see and protect them from all dangers, real or potential.

No force of warriors larger than thirty had ever been assembled in the Instant. If more men than that were on one side in a battle then their combat waves would begin to interfere with each other and attacks would backlash; one wave would cut across another, creating a riptide that would flow back and carve up the attacker. Tribes had sought for means to keep track of the currents of time so that such accidents would be prevented. But no one had been capable of following the apparently chaotic courses of intersecting change-waves, until Quillithé was created.

She could see and pick out the progresses of crosscurrents, and her mind could analyze all the possibilities. She could trace and predict and know how each wave front would travel and could order her troops accordingly. She created strategies, organizations, marching orders, battle plans, arrangements of up to three hundred warriors who could fight in the same battle without endangering each other so long as they followed her schemes.

But first she had to have such an army. Her seven fathers were too few and too small to serve well in battle, and had she not been created to protect them? She, their servant, could not put them at risk in battle. She needed to bring up new warriors from the deeps of time's ocean. And here she discovered the second limitation of her size. Quillithé could not anchor; the earthly side of time would not receive her. Too much of her bobbed on the surface, buoyed up by the currents of the ocean of time, and she could not muster the force to pull herself down through the waters to the earth.

So it fell to her fathers to begin the recruiting of Quillithé's army. She devised a means by which they could protect each other from the deep crosscurrents that had cost them nine of their number when she was liberated. She had four of her fathers form a square in the ocean and ripple out counterwaves to the lower tides while the other three anchored down and waited for the world to change appropriately and a likely prospect for recruitment to come into being.

Quillithé wished there had been some way other than risking her fearful fathers, and it had taken much cajoling to get them to do this one thing. Eventually, they agreed, seeing that if they wanted the army that would keep them safe, they would have to risk themselves once more.

Her fathers rejoiced when they freed first one, then another, then another fifteen-year-long soldier for the new army. These recruits, grateful for their release, swore eternal loyalty to Quillithé. The strategist now employed these new officers in her army to obtain still more recruits, and her fathers rejoiced that they no longer needed to risk their own lives. The army swelled until three hundred long-tailed warriors rippled out pictures of loyalty to Quillithé.

At that point she ceased to add recruits. Three hundred soldiers she could deploy in battle and know the interleavings of their chaotic cutting waves. More than that and the intersecting processes of change would become infinitely unpredictable. Quillithé studied this infinite undecidability. She found it beautiful in the way it flowed and filled the caverns and recesses of her mind, but it would be far too dangerous to create it.

Her army bobbed around her, floating in the deep tides, and the strategist looked at them waiting patiently for her orders and considered what she was to do with this force unmatched in the Instant.

Her initial plan was the simplest use for the only true army in the ocean of time. She contemplated the conquest of the Instant and the subjugation of all the warring tribes. With her vision she could see half the inhabited area of the Instant and watch the battles that took place pastward of her. She learned the ways of each tribe and determined how best to defeat them. Some could be conquered by sending expeditionary forces against them, but the larger and better armed tribes would take the whole of her army to defeat safely. And her whole army could only act in concert if she was present to direct them. And Quillithé could not move.

But she could be moved by others. Quillithé stretched out her tail, opening out into her full one hundred years' length. She ordered her troops to roll her pastward by making gentle coordinated waves that would push her vast weight of years along through the tides of time.

The plan worked and by the careful effort of seventy-five of her soldiers, the great strategist rolled pastward twenty-five thousand years to the most futureward region where the tribes of time normally battled.

The arrival of this army struck terror into the tribes. Some fled immediately. Some attacked and were instantly destroyed in coordinated assaults more devastating than any they had ever conceived. Some tried to scout the limits of the force and were swiftly spotted by Quillithé's matchless vision and then wiped out by her army.

The story of the century-monster and her army spread swiftly as the surviving tribes fled pastward. Some disbelievers came futureward to see if there was truth to this impossible rumor, for all the soldiers of time knew that no tribe could have three hundred members and no dweller in the Instant was longer than twenty years in tail length. Those that survived their investigations returned to spread the fear. Despair grew among the tribes of time and the word "surrender" was whispered in the camps of the Instant. Though no tribe could bring itself to give up its vision of a perfect world, still, what could they do against this army and its terrible commander?

Quillithé's plan seemed to be working until she noticed that something unpredicted was happening to her body. In the deep waters where she was born the tides of time were homogeneous and she could float safely, unconcerned about the waves flowing over her. But in the shallower pastward waters, little knifelike wave crests crashed against her repeatedly, taking little nicks and cuts out of her existence. The waves were not strong enough to carve her up or shatter her century, but they could take away a finger here, a toe there, little shreds of her left floating in the waters.

These waves, harmless to shorter-tailed time warriors who could easily move to avoid them, would eventually whittle the giantess into nothing. Quillithé considered dispassionately whether the conquest of the Instant was worth the loss of her existence. She swiftly concluded that it was not, for without her, the army would not be able to function as a whole and eventually some conquered tribe would rise up to destroy them.

The strategist abandoned her plan of conquest and ordered her troops to roll her back to the deep waters of the future. The tribes who had witnessed her prowess in battle rippled out a gentle sigh of relief. But those whose hearts were fixed on conquest could not understand why Quillithé had retreated. Fear spread among them, carried by confusion. And the legend of the incomprehensible monster from the deeps grew greater. That legend took many forms but a common factor among them was that doomsday would come to the tribe if ever again they faced Quillithé in battle, and if ever again she left the waters of the deep surely she would come for them, bearing doom in her vision and in her coils.

Back in the safe deep waters, Quillithé returned to her contemplations. What was she to do with her army if conquest was impractical? She turned her vision once again pastward and regarded the tides of time. All the changes that flowed together to create the environment in which she existed arose from one hundred millennia of battles. All change in the Instant arose from war and she needed the tides of change.

The conclusion was inescapable. Quillithé needed the war, so she would perpetuate it. She kept her vision focused on the battles and the tribes and when it seemed that one tribe was growing too mighty she would send an expedition from her army to weaken them, either by pillaging from them any new technological advances or killing some number of the tribesmen in order to reduce the rising tribe to parity with its enemies.

Why they were subject to such onslaughts was not clear to the attacked tribes. They could not see with Quillithé's eyes or judge with her strategist's mind. They could not know that she predicted their rise. Thus her legend spread further. The monster of the deep's minions attacked without warning, without reason, without purpose. She who was in truth the most cold-bloodedly rational of beings was depicted as a creature of madness, incomprehensible to any rational tribesman, the mad goddess of death who could slay even the immortal beings of the Instant.

Quillithé and her army became the great unknowable horror that lurked at the edge of inhabited time. The tribes began to whisper and wonder what power had created her. They began to believe that she held the great secret to conquest of the Instant. Some dared to sally futureward in an endeavor to take this great secret, but none succeeded and her legend of terror grew.

But Quillithé knew that the perpetuation of the war was only a temporary expedient, she knew that Flux and Instant changed with infinite possibility. Eventually, in the course of those changes, something would arise to give her more purpose than the mere perpetuation of bloodshed.

That new possibility eventually arose, but for the first time since she was brought into the Instant, Quillithé's vast vision was blind to the sight of what she needed to behold.

It began with a matter that hardly took a fraction of the strategist's attention. She had noticed the Greater Antarctic Temporal Battle Corps camped thirty-five thousand years pastward over the Indian subcontinent. From where she sat floating in the deeps of time she observed their actions first with detachment, then with interest. The Antarctics had brought up from the Flux some whip-like objects several years in length and were experimenting with them. Quillithé watched as the Antarctic warriors tied the lashes to the ends of their tails and used them to extend the reach and breadth of their own attacks. A ten-year-long warrior with one of those stingers tied to his tail could make cutting waves twenty years in length.

Quillithé judged the strategic value of the whips, taking into account the strategies of the Antarctics and their longstanding feuds with the Pali Atemporal Insurgency and the Tahitian Soldiers of Mithra, and concluded that the Antarctics would swiftly defeat these foes and take from them some weapons that would operate synergistically with these whips and give the Greater Antarctic Temporal Battle Corps too large an advantage in the war.

In consequence she devised a strategy for her troops to use against the whips, and dispatched twenty-five of her warriors to relieve the Antarctics of their prizes and reduce their numbers from eighteen to ten. At that level she judged that they would no longer be a concern.

Quillithé's soldiers swam pastward and engaged the enemy. The Antarctics, as Quillithé predicted, endeavored to use their whips as a surprise, but her troops had been briefed and directed their cutting waves at the ends of the Antarctic soldier's tails, slicing the stingers from them before they could be used.

Quillithé noted with some pleasure the efficiency with which the leader of her detachment, Adjutant Vanchen, turned her strategy into reality. She turned to contemplating Vanchen's possible promotion.

The battle ended with Vanchen's troops capturing all the whips and killing six of the Antarctics. The remaining twelve fled pastward, swimming swiftly through the breakers. Vanchen was left with a dilemma. His orders were to whittle down their numbers to ten and to bring back the whips. He weighed his options and sent two of his soldiers back to Quillithé's camp carrying the prizes while he led the remaining twenty-three in pursuit.

Quillithé watched this development with interest. The results of Vanchen's decision to pursue would determine whether or not she would promote him. She had some mild distress as the two groups, hunters and hunted, swam pastward to forty thousand years from where she sat. Only ten thousand more years and they would reach the limits of her vision. Vanchen knew as all the officers of the only army knew that they were not permitted to swim pastward of the fifty-thousand-year mark. Quillithé could not judge what she could not see, and what she could not judge she could not use in creating strategy, and without her strategies the officers were helpless.

The fleeing tribe swam pastward and east toward the ocean over China. Quillithé's troops pursued at a steady swim, closing the gap of centuries into one of decades. Soon they would be in striking range of their targets. Quillithé curled a few months of her tail in satisfaction.

The Antarctics reached the ocean of time over the western end of the south coast of China and, to Quillithé's astonishment (a feeling she rarely experienced and relished only slightly), the twelve fugitives became blurry and indistinct. Quillithé focused her vision on the region, ignoring huge swaths of the Instant in order to see more clearly. But all that did was make the dark fog into which they were disappearing become more sharply black against the blue and white waters of time.

Quillithé broadened her vision, taking in more of the area, but all she saw was more darkness, a night black stretch of time that covered most of China, Mongolia, and Siberia at forty thousand years pastward from her. She looked further back into the past and saw that near the limits of her vision, the region of blackness covered almost all of the waters above Asia.

She turned her attention back to the pursued, but she could no longer find them; they had disappeared into the blackness. Vanchen's troops were still following them. Already the twenty-five soldiers she had dispatched were fading from her sight. Quillithé was astonished. Vanchen should have known better than to enter a region with unknown characteristics. Could it be that his limited vision was unaware of the blackness? Was the blackness real or some effect meant to block her specific sight? That was a disturbing prospect; it meant that one of the tribes had devised a weapon to be used specifically against her, a weapon she had not seen developed.

Vanchen's soldiers vanished into the blackness. Quillithé waited, spinning possible explanations for the darkness in the corridors of her mind. An hour of her life seemed to pass, then a day, but neither hunters nor hunted emerged from the void.

Her contemplations had led to no satisfactory conclusion. She did not have enough information to determine the nature of this strange region. There was no choice; she would have to risk some more of her troops in order to learn the answer.

Floating near to Quillithé's body, huddling in fear were her seven fathers, their months-long tails dwarfed by her century. They quaked out ripples of terror as her confusion manifested in idle rollings of her body.

An image rippled out from the four-month-long body of one her fathers: Quillithé coiled up, her tail in many knots, implying disturbance. There was a blue haze over the picture implying a question.

Her father wanted to know what was wrong.

Quillithé rippled out a blank image as smooth as glass against the waters of the deep. An admission that she did not know.

The small being shuddered and cowered closer to the protective century-long life he had fathered, fearful of whatever force could keep knowledge from his omniscient daughter.

Elsewhere along her body Quillithé rippled out another picture. This one floated along the tides to the pastward western edge of the camp until it reached its intended recipient.

Adjutant Irithrué, one of Quillithé's trusted scout leaders and a veteran of many battles against the lesser tribes, floated on guard on the perimeter of the army. The picture order reached her. It showed her swimming swiftly into the center of the three-centuries-in-radius camp where Quillithé waited to brief her.

Irithrué turned her fifteen-year tail and swam inward past the rings of floating warriors practicing their battle tactics, past the armorers with their tightly herded reefs of weapons, past the inner guard whose duty it was to protect Quillithé herself, until she reached the century-long leader and the seven she protected.

The strategist sent a series of swift pictures depicting what had happened to Vanchen. Irithrué shivered slightly, rippling out incoherent nervousness. Her whole existence in the Instant had consisted of fighting under Quillithé's command, and that command relied on the strategist being able to see what was happening. This darkness frightened the Adjutant even more than it did Quillithé.

More pictures rippled from the strategist's body.

Image: Irithrué gathering up six scouts and swimming pastward out of the camp.

Image: Irithrué and the scouts arriving at the dark area and searching.

Image: A tribe with a device creating the darkness. The blue of inquiry limning the tribe and device (seek out whoever created the darkness, identify them and the source).

Image: Irithrué and the scouts in battle with a tribe. Bright green coloring over the battle, bright green signifying negation (do not fight).

Irithrué absorbed the orders and committed every detail of the pictorial instructions to memory. The Adjutant repeated the pictures back to Quillithé, signifying her understanding. Quillithé rippled out acknowledgment and dismissal. Irithrué swished her tail in brief salute and swam out to the place where the scouts were camped, some fifty years pastward from camp center.

Quillithé watched Irithrué gather up her scouts and swim pastward out of the camp. The strategist sent comforting pictures to her fearful fathers. But there was no comfort in her mind. The prospect of darkness covering the Instant, cutting her mind off from the information she needed with which to plan, gave the normally calm strategist the rare sensation of being as afraid as the seven fathers who had created her.

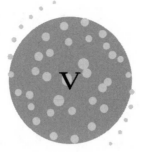

In the Year of Ghosts' Conferring, the Elder and the War Chief sat together in the clearing of the Great Mother's mound speaking together of decisions and dangers. Night had fallen and the two Ghosts savored the feel of cool wind across their naked skins. Above them, above the world, above the sky in the ocean of time, the remaining Ghosts floated, waiting for their leaders to emerge from the earth and command them.

The Elder still sat on the Great Mother's grave; the War Chief squatted on the ground next to the mound, looking up at the old woman with polite determination while she in turn stared back at him with a cold, unshaking resolve.

"You will send four scouts," the Elder said for the tenth time. "Col, who found the object, and three veteran far-travelers."

And for the tenth time Nir tapped his left eyelid with his right hand, signifying disagreement with her commands. "Only Fourth Voice can discern the nature of this threat. I must go with Col to find it."

At the mention of the Voice that only the War Chief could hear, the Elder momentarily covered her ears with her hands.

"The War Chief must remain in the Now," she said, ending the cycle of debate for the tenth time and returning them to the silence of the summer evening. All argument had been exhausted in the ten rounds of repetition. Dispute had given way to a conflict of wills embodied in this interchange: command, rejection, counter-command, rejection.

Each of them sat implacable in attitude, patient as only the timeless can be patient, disregarding their environment as only Ghosts can disregard. The Elder had permitted Nir to innovate before, but she would not allow him to abandon his post. The War Chief for his part would not permit his men to risk themselves to no advantage. He had to go and find out for himself what was happening.

Nir himself had never ventured forth from the Now, never actually experienced the waters of the middle Instant. His only knowledge of the places beyond the shallows came from his scouts. Nir's Second Voice had copied the recorded experiences of each scout from that Ghost's Second Voice. In consequence the War Chief knew the feel of the middle waters, the lapping tides and the savage war pools secondhand; but now he needed to touch them himself and give the experiences to his Fourth Voice, which could not interpret mere recordings.

The moon rose into the clear night sky. Off in the distance, the two Ghosts could hear the drums and dancing of the People as their celebration grew louder in exuberance.

"Your duty is to protect the People," the Elder said.

"That is what I wish to do," Nir said. "My warriors are well trained and well armed; they can stave off an attack from a known tribe. But this unknown is beyond them. Only Fourth Voice can confront it, and only I carry Fourth Voice."

"That can be changed," the Elder whispered, letting the threat waft on the breeze.

Nir's initial impulse was to ignore the insinuation, knowing that the Elder did not wish to replace him as War Chief. But then Nir's agile mind changed and he realized that the idle warning of the Elder contained the means of breaking their deadlock. He covered

both his eyes and bent his back forward, so that his head faced the
ground like a man waiting to be decapitated. "If the Elder mistrusts
my judgment so much, perhaps she should make another Ghost
War Chief."

The old woman gasped in astonishment and the breath of living
air entered her lungs, filling her with a sudden nostalgia for time-
bound life. She remembered the taste of food, the springy step of
walking on jungle grass, the feel of a human form held next to her,
beginning the long task of creating life anew.

She shook such thoughts from her mind and returned to her
vow-born duty. The Elder's vow was to be the one who decided
the course of the Ghosts, what they would undertake for the good
of the People and what they would reject. She and she alone chose
the War Chief. She looked down at Nir's body, studied the short,
tightly bound hair on the back of his neck, the bull-like muscles of
his back, and considered. She did not like the easy way in which
Nir adapted his thinking. She did not like his taste for innovation.
But he had saved the People more times than any of his predecessors and he had lost fewer warriors than any of his predecessors.
There was no one who she could find to replace him. For that
reason she could not let him go.

But she realized that if Nir were not permitted to follow the
course of action he had proposed, then his mind would turn solely
to the problem of finding a way to do what he felt needed to be
done. His value as War Chief would be impaired, and soon he
would become no better than any of the other veteran Ghosts.
Therefore, what benefit was there to keeping him?

"You may go, War Chief," she said. "But if during your absence
I feel it necessary to give your position to another, I will do so, and
on your return you will be relegated to the ranks of the warriors."

"I accept your terms, Elder," Nir said as he raised his head to
face her.

As one they released their hold on solid time, vanishing from
the clearing. For an hour, nothing stirred around the mound of the
Great Mother. Then the sounds of drums and pipes and the rhyth-

mic beat of dancers grew loud in the jungle as the People came to the clearing to give their midnight obeisance to the bones of their ancestress.

In this particular formulation of solid time, the People numbered one hundred twenty-seven. All of them, from the eldest woman to the youngest child, all the People came out on Midsummer Day in the Year of Ghosts' Conferring. They formed concentric rings around the Great Mother's bones and danced her praises in ecstatic circles. At the center of the dance, Yal the priest, who might have been but was not the War Chief's father, cried out the blessings the Great Mother had bestowed upon them.

"For our lives, we thank you."

"For those who have gone beyond to protect us, we thank you."

"And for the sacrifice you made of your own life, we thank you."

"Great Mother, we thank you," all the People cried as they leaped into the air, their stitched-hide garments floating momentarily in the breeze, showing the nakedness of the People that made them one with the Ghosts.

The two young boys who had not succeeded in spying on the conference danced less exuberantly than the others; the harshness of their chastisement for planning to leave though they had not done so still ached on the backs of their legs. The elder boy's uncle, Col, watched them carefully as he led them in the dancing.

Six months later, Col would abruptly vanish, never to be seen again by a living member of the People. Seven years in the future he had chosen to become a Ghost and had had to tear away those years of his life out of the solid earth in order to make his tail. The two boys would never see Col again though he floated above them, protecting and scouting.

In the Instant, Nir dismissed the Ghosts and sent them back to their duties. Only he and Col remained in the waters over the Year of Ghosts' Conferring. The scout paid no attention to the fact that he was swimming above himself. The Ghosts were sternly taught to have no concern for their discarded living bodies.

Nir tapped the tip of his tail gently against the shallow waters of the Now, sending out short burst waves in Col's direction. By means of this tapping, clearly discernible to their extended touch, the blind-deaf Ghosts communicated in the Instant.

"The Elder and I have decided," Nir said to Col. "You will take me with you to the place where you found the object."

"War Chief?" the scout tapped, sure he had misfelt the words Nir had tapped. "Did I understand you correctly? You are leaving the Now?"

"There is no choice, Col," Nir said. "Fourth Voice must be shown the source of this object."

"Yes, War Chief," Col said, tapping his perplexed submission. The Ghosts did not question their leaders' decisions.

"We will go to the Armory," Nir said, turning around in the water so the front end of his tail faced pastward, "and then depart."

"Yes, War Chief," Col tapped as he aligned his seven-year length in the same direction as Nir's ten years. The two of them swam pastward through the shallows. A few strokes of their tails and they had crossed fifty years of water.

In the waters above the village of the People, the Armory of the Ghosts bobbed peacefully. Gathered in a pool of water two miles across by two months long were the coiled-up tails of weapons taken from all the tribes that had assailed the Now since the Ghosts had liberated themselves, as well as the bounty brought back by the scouts.

Two Ghosts floated on the edges of the pool, their sense of touch extended, waiting for anyone who would dare attempt to steal the weapons of the People. "Who comes?" one of the guards tapped.

"The War Chief," Nir tapped back.

The guards extended their touch and felt the contours of Nir's tail, from one end of his life to another. "Advance, War Chief," the guard tapped.

Col swam forward and the procedure was repeated. Then the guards swam aside and Nir and Col poked two months of their lives into the Armory and felt around among the tightly coiled bundles for the weapons they needed.

"How armed will we travel?" Col asked Nir.

"Shields, one atemporal weapon each, and one temporal weapon each."

"Yes, War Chief," Col said. Nir could hear nervousness in the taps of the scout.

"You wonder why we take so little," Nir tapped as he felt through the corner of the pool where the shields floated, tightly wound spirals of antetemporal force.

"If the War Chief wishes to explain . . ." Col said.

"I am temporarily depriving the Ghosts of their leader," Nir said. "I do not wish to deplete their ability to defend themselves any more than that."

"Yes, War Chief," Col said.

Nir felt the bundled forms of the Wavebreaker shields. The Ghosts had over two hundred of these, the most common objects in the Instant. The Ghosts had salvaged many from the bodies of their slain enemies. Some had been part of the Armory since the liberation of the Ghosts, others had been taken in attacks. Only a few had been brought back by scouts; these were the prizes of the Armory, the most advanced defensive devices to be found in the Instant, and the Ghosts had only four of them. Nir slid his sense of touch over these tightly coiled helices of muting force and pondered whether he should take one or avail himself of a more primitive Wavebreaker.

In battle he would naturally have been given the best defense available. The Ghosts could not afford to lose their War Chief. But he was already depriving them of his presence and tactical ability. Still, if he did not take one his chances of survival were much lower, and the risk he took would be in vain.

Grudgingly Nir reached out the end of his tail and touched one of the four new Wavebreakers. At the touch, the compactly bundled spring uncoiled into a line of force twenty years long and half a micrometer in radius. The gentle waves of the shallows that struck that line dulled into nothingness. Nir slithered up to the line and rolled it around his tail, coiling it loosely around his ten years. His sense of touch felt momentarily muffled as if he were wrapped in cotton wool, but the sensors impregnated in his atemporal body swiftly compensated.

Col had also donned a Wavebreaker, but the more primitive kind worn by the scouts, who knew themselves to be expendable for the good of the People. It did not even occur to Col to question the better protection of his commander.

The two Ghosts then swam across the pool of arms to where the atemporal weapons floated and found two Macedonian Tail Spikes. These short vibrating talons added wavelets to the waves they emitted in combat, layering a fractal sharpness onto the crests of their attacks. These month-long scythes were strapped to their bodies, bound by the same force that the Wavebreakers used to mute attacks.

Thus outfitted for atemporal combat they darted swiftly over to the temporal weapons. This flotilla consisted of armaments taken from the Flux and meant to be brought back down for combat in solid time. The War Chief strapped a bandolier of Aztec Solid Helium Grenades to the middle of this tail, while the scout armed himself with a Bantu Positron Gun.

"We are finished," Nir said to the Armory guards as he and Col swam out of the pool of flotsam.

"Yes, War Chief," the two armorers said, and resumed their duties.

Nir gathered his warriors together at the futuremost border of the Now to give final instructions.

"Triple the border guard," Nir said. "And double the Great Mother's protectors. All scouting missions are canceled. All Ghosts are to be on constant alert."

"Yes, War Chief," they tapped in unison, raising a brief flurry of bubbles in the shallows.

"No Ghost is to move more than one century futureward from the Now. Even in pursuit of fleeing enemies. Understood?"

"Yes, War Chief."

Nir extended his touch and felt the contours of each warrior in turn, remembering their capabilities and weaknesses, their strengths and their tendencies to err. A great temptation filled him to load his warriors down with orders, but a great discomfort came with the temptation. The War Chief preferred the improvisation of tactics to the solidity of strategy and he much preferred to exercise his genius for the thick of battle rather than his competence in planning. The temptation changed to a desire to stay back in the Now. It would have been easy for him to believe that staying was the best means of fulfilling the vow of the Ghosts, but he knew better; only his Fourth Voice and his agile mind could find and interpret the source of the seemingly static piece of time Col had brought back to the Now.

In the face of the vow, and Nir's understanding of the vow, temptations vanished. He had given the proper orders; he had prepared as best he could for his absence. The moment had come to let go of the Ghosts and venture out of the Now.

The War Chief turned his tail futureward and tapped out a brief order for Col to attend him, and the two swam off. The mustered warrior Ghosts felt out with their extended touch until the last ripple of their leader's tail strokes faded from their feeling. A ripple of fear flowed among them; they wondered if they would ever feel Nir again, and if not, which of them would be named to replace him.

In the solid time below the futuremost border of the Now, the last priest of the People, a century-old man called Daz, spoke to an assembled multitude of five hundred People. Daz, who had once been a young boy who failed to sneak away to see the Ghosts, and whose uncle Col had one day vanished, stood at the gates of the village and proclaimed that the People were no more, for the Ghosts would no longer protect them.

"It is time for the People to leave the village of the Great Mother and be the People no longer. The Ghosts have proclaimed that we must go out into the world and take it from Not-the-People.

The Ghosts have said that this will happen; this and only this event must occur. All others are subject to the choices of the Ghosts and the attacks of the enemy."

The People groaned and wept, for they had lived all their lives under the protection of the Ghosts and now they would no longer be safe from the marauders of time.

"We must go forth and disperse," Daz said. "Each family of us will go out and settle in another part of the world. From this moment forth we cease to be the People."

And Daz took from around his neck a torque of shells carved with the names of every Ghost who had served the people and took from his face the mask carved from baobab wood, a mask that showed the face of the first War Chief, and laid them on the ground. Daz walked out of the village followed by the five hundred No-Longer-the-People. And so the Diaspora began.

In the ocean above, Nir and Col swam into the Diaspora, the ten-thousand-year stretch of time when Homo sapiens took over the earth. Few tribes of time vied over the Diaspora, and those that did regarded it mostly as a place to experiment with changes rather than as a source of technology or slaves. Thus the waters of that region of the Instant were deeper, full of more changes than the Now, but still relatively shallow.

Nir rocked his tail back and forth, feeling the unfamiliar sensation of many small waves striking him, haphazardly and arrhythmically. Also strange to him was the experience of open swimming space. He had spent the whole of his atemporal existence in the two-century span of the Now, a region only twenty times his own length. But passing through the Diaspora he swam through centuries. Like a fish released from a bowl into a lake he had freedom to move and feel what he had never felt before, the release and joy of open water, open space in which to swim.

Nir began to swim faster by curving his tail side to side like an eel. He generated long change-waves on which he could speed through the centuries. In the Now he would never have dared create such a motion for fear of changing the world the People lived in even a little. Such was the Ghostly hatred of change, that they were cautious in motion and even in the small waves of speech where the only risks were to the quantum states of subatomic particles. Only in battle had he ever swum swiftly and even then his motion consisted of swift turns and rolls, not the long steady strokes he was now achieving.

Col kept silent as he watched his War Chief swim. He, like all the other scouts, had felt this secret joy of swift swimming, though none of them spoke about it. It was taboo among the Ghosts to express pleasure at anything that brought about change in the solid world below.

Nir and Col swiftly crossed the ten millennia of the Diaspora, feeling the deepening of the waters. In the Now, solid and liquid time were close together; only a thin layer of the waters of change lay above the earth. But further futureward, as the waves of alteration accumulated and mixed together, deeper currents of change came into being, small waves gathered and joined larger ones to create the tides and depths of the middle Instant.

Nir's extended touch soon could no longer sense the solid time below; his tail no longer scraped the bottom of time's ocean.

"Col, stop," the War Chief tapped. "I wish to enter the Flux and regain my bearings."

"Yes, War Chief," Col said, and coiled his tail into a floating posture.

Nir swam down through the currents of change until he touched solid time. Touching he gripped, gripping he entered. Nir appeared at the base of a mountain in southern Africa, fifteen thousand years futureward from the Now. A tribe of nomads clad in ragged skins huddled together under patched tents to gain some shelter from a raging storm.

"Ghost," one of the nomads cried. Fifteen thousand years of carefully preserved legends had come to life. Here was their hope of salvation. Here among them was their protector. Here was the man who could restore the herds of wildlife to the continent of Africa so that they need no longer starve.

But Nir did not understand the shout; the language of these nomads was far different from that spoken by the People. Second Voice diligently recorded the word and prepared to assemble enough examples to do a linguistic analysis.

But before another word was spoken a wave washed over the place. Nir was alone amidst the five-hundred-year-old desiccated remains of a necropolis, a broken city of timber and basalt in which a civilization had preserved its dead in the hopes of life beyond.

Another wave, alone on an untouched mountain.

And another wave. A mining camp seeking diamonds to appease the spirits out of time, who two thousand years before had enslaved this people and set them to digging in the ground, then left without warning.

Nir released his grip on solid time and bobbed back up into the ocean.

"We are the People," he tapped, renewing his vow after witnessing firsthand the effects of the war in the Instant. Col echoed the War Chief's words with his own tapping.

"The People will not be changed."

"This is the Now."

"The Now will not be Flux."

The two Ghosts uncoiled themselves and swam futureward into the more heavily populated regions of the Instant.

Most of the battles in the Instant were fought in the sixty-thousand-year stretch of ocean between twenty thousand years futureward from the Now and eighty thousand years futureward from the Now. That region was the most promising for creating the histories desired by the tribes as well as the most bountiful in terms of treasure and slaves. Here the hundred thousand tribes of time swarmed thick, clashing in battle, raiding the solid world and each other, creating the deeps of time with the disputations of their changes.

Into this region Nir and Col swam cautiously. Two isolated warriors could not risk engaging in battle, so they probed the waters around them, feeling for the telltale eddies of nearby conflict and swimming away at the slightest touch of war.

Their course was circuitous. They would swim centuries and thousands of kilometers out of their way to avoid coming near conflict. Once they even had to double back and travel two thousand years pastward to escape a running battle. But with patience and determination they finally reached their goal, fifty-six thousand years futureward from the Now, over the southernmost island of Japan, the place where Col had found the impossible object.

The waters of that region seemed strangely calm, and Nir reached down to touch the solid world below.

"It is shallow here," he tapped.

"Shallow?" Col replied. It had never occurred to him to check for such a thing. He had presumed the waters to be quite deep this far from the Now.

"But War Chief," Col said, "the tribes are fighting all around us. I can feel their change-waves coming toward us. How can it be shallow?"

"Let us find out," Nir said. He began swimming slowly with gentle strokes, as he felt his way through the currents trying to find the source of the shallowness. The two moved slowly west and futureward, crossing above the part of the Pacific Ocean that lay between Japan and China while they traversed the centuries.

As they reached the eastern coast of China, sixty thousand years futureward from the Now, Nir's Third Voice cried a warning into his mind. "Dangerous change-wave approaching from southwest and pastward."

Col had also been warned by his Third Voice. The two Ghosts stretched out their senses of touch and felt through the waters. There in little pinpricks they perceived what their Third Voices had already noticed, sharp-edged waves not yet blunted by the crosscurrents of the middle ocean. A battle was being fought no more than three centuries and a thousand kilometers away. The destructive overflow of the conflict was progressing toward them.

Both Nir and Col were shielded but they both knew better than to rely only on their defenses. The Ghosts straightened out their tails and turned to face the oncoming wave, presenting the narrowest sides to the cutting edge.

They waited, bobbing in the impossible shallows, prepared to ride out the sharp-cutting waves like two pieces of driftwood floating peacefully through a monsoon.

But the anticipated savage wave never came. For no reason that their sense of touch could discern, the huge oncoming torrent broke apart fifty years pastward and two hundred kilometers to the southwest. The wave fragmented from one huge onslaught into a million tiny wavelets that washed forward and struck the Ghosts with no force at all. The tsunami they had feared was no more than a spring shower of tiny change-ripples that danced across their tails with nary a hint of injury resulting.

"Wave fractured by solid interference," Fourth Voice told Nir.

Solid? Nir queried. What could be solid here?

"Unknown," Fourth Voice said.

Two unknowns in the same region. Nir's mind shifted and he knew that they had to be the effects of the same cause.

"I think we are near what we are looking for," Nir tapped to Col. "Follow me, slowly."

"Yes, War Chief."

Nir swam toward the place where the wave had broken. With slow, cautious strokes he approached it kilometer by kilometer and month by month. As he felt his way through the misplaced shallows, his sense of touch experienced a grating in the ocean, a scratchy grittiness unlike the smooth waters and gentle ocean floor of the Now.

Thirty years, seventy kilometers, and Nir's touch found something it had never felt before. Where the waters of time should have been flowing in waves and crests there was a sharpness unlike the changing, twisting saw of a cutting wave. This was a solid sharpness, like a knife lying in the waters, a thin blade of something earthly in the ocean.

What is that? Nir asked Fourth Voice.

The Voice hesitated as if unsure. "A crack in time."

A crack? Nir said. In the ocean?

"The region surrounding the crack has the character of solid time," Fourth Voice said. "But it is not being changed by the water around it."

How can that be? Nir said.

"Unknown," Fourth Voice replied.

"Crack shows defensive value," Third Voice butted in. "It blocks change waves."

Nir relayed Fourth Voice's analysis to Col, who accepted the pronouncement with blind faith. The scout's Third Voice gave him the same suggestion concerning the military usage of such a crack.

Nir stretched out his sense of touch and found that the crack was not isolated. Westward and far into the future and past there seemed to be a network of cracks, most of them no larger than a few seconds long. But Nir's sense of touch dimmed as he stretched out to feel the region, and he could feel no further than half an hour and ten kilometers into the shattered area.

"What do we do, War Chief?" Col asked.

"We see how large this cracked region is," Nir said, "and find out where it came from. We need to know which tribe created this and what use they are making of it."

Nir and Col began to feel their way along the contours of this broken area. Being careful to maintain a distance of a hundred kilometers from the cracking itself, they slowly tracked the fault line futureward. The region was irregular, jagged and coastlike, a zigzag border with jutting promontories and inlets, an impossible island of solidity in the ocean of time.

Their Second Voices traced mental maps as they swam, drawing the outlines of the island in their minds. Their Third Voices gave them constant commentary on the strategic and tactical value of the twists and turns and corners of the broken island. Nir queried his Fourth Voice repeatedly as they went but it seemed to be learning nothing from their travels. The War Chief kept swimming onward, hoping that either Fourth Voice would discern the nature of the breaking or that his own mind would change and he would know what this new thing he confronted was.

While Nir focused his attention on the origin of the breakage, Col's mind wandered into an almost euphoric excitement as his map of the island grew. The scout had come to believe that this region of solidity was a place of safety from change—did it not break the waves of alteration, stopping the ocean's destructive might? Col rejoiced in the possibility that here was the fulfillment of the Ghosts' vow, if he could find the source of this cracked area and return with it to the Now, and use it to make the time of the People a protected island, safe from invasion, safe from change.

Assuming it was safe. Doubt grew in Col. He did not know what was inside the borders they were tracing.

"War Chief?" Col tapped hesitantly. "I ask permission to enter the region."

"No," Nir said. "We continue the mapping."

All the things that had occurred to Col had also occurred to Nir, but the War Chief did not share the scout's overeager joy in this discovery. He could not put into words what troubled him about this mysterious place. Perhaps it was the scratchiness of the shallows. Perhaps the haphazardness of the island's placement. Perhaps it was the fact that no one had challenged them as they scouted the area. But no, there was something deeper in his thoughts, some basic feeling of repugnance at the broken island that he could not yet account for. Somewhere in his fluid mind he came to know that far from being the fulfillment of the Ghosts' vow, this shattered land was the very antithesis of that oath.

VI

As they followed the edge of this impossibility, Nir and Col were themselves being followed, but their pursuer was too far away and too small for them to feel him pursuing them.

Kookatchi had seen the Ghosts when they first approached the region he had escaped from. Their presence was a great surprise to the Drum. He had only been to the Now once, and had not actually entered it. He had come following a tribe that had wished to conquer that region and subjugate the People. Kookatchi had watched the Ghosts in action and listened to their language. He had found beauty in their devotion to protecting a small parcel of time, and beauty in the simplicity of their song. Four lines of vow to summarize all they were doing in the Instant. No tribe could match that singleness and clarity.

But those were the only beauties he had found watching the Ghosts, and those were the only treasures he had taken away from the shallows of the Instant. He had since then occasionally spotted Ghost scouts bringing things back from the middle of time's ocean, but he had never seen a pair of them outside of the Now.

Intrigued, he followed and listened to their tapping speech. He was astonished to hear the shorter-tailed Ghost call the longer one

War Chief. He wondered what prize would lure the leader of the Ghosts into the deeper parts of the ocean. Whatever it was, it would have to be a great prize. And Kookatchi the Thief could not resist following to find out what it was and snatch it away from them when the moment was right.

Kookatchi's astonishment grew as the two Ghosts began to track their way along the cracked area. The Drum conceived the notion that perhaps the Ghosts were involved in the creation of the cracking. As his consciousness recycled, the idea mutated into a certainty. Kookatchi would follow and find out how they had made this region, and then he would steal the secret.

Nir and Col continued their mapping, tracing the outer edge of the broken island futureward through the centuries, then eastward across the Pacific rim, then farther east to encompass all the Pacific archipelagoes for a decade before cutting sharply back west into inland China.

Kookatchi followed them, keeping a distance of two decades and fifty kilometers from the Ghosts. The Drum had to swim swiftly to keep up with the longer-tailed strokes of the Ghosts. Fortunately for him they were not swimming at their fastest, being more concerned with methodical mapping than speedy passage.

"War Chief," Col said when they had covered a distance of more than five thousand years since they had first encountered the cracking. "This island is miraculous. If we could only find out how it was made we could protect the Now completely."

Nir lashed his tail in irritation and tapped out a harsh rebuke. "Do not be a fool, Col. This cracking is a greater danger to the People than an enslaving tribe or even the Flux itself."

Col was stunned. It was an article of faith among the Ghosts that the Flux was the ultimate threat to the People's existence. He tapped out a tentative question. "Why?"

Kookatchi slipped closer, drawing to within a few months and kilometers of the two Ghosts, a dangerous closeness; if they felt his presence he would be within range of their tail lashes. But he had heard Nir's pronouncement, and without a moment's consideration agreed with it. The Drum, who had never been a creature of explanation and contemplation, wanted to hear the reasons Nir would produce to bolster his own intuitive opinion.

"Why?" Nir said. "Because every change made in the Flux can be undone by another change, but this cracking disperses the waves of change by which all things are accomplished in the Instant. We do not know if the process that made it can be reversed."

"War Chief," Col tapped demurely, "that feels like an argument in favor of such a place. If we made the Now such a place, then the People would be safe inside an unchangeable barrier."

Nir tapped an aggravated beat on the shallow waters of the Instant. "Do you know why the Now is safe from change?" he asked.

Col swished his tail pridefully. "Because we Ghosts protect it."

"There are tribes that have tried to protect other parts of earthly time. They have not succeeded. Have they?"

"No, War Chief," Col said.

"And why not?"

"Because other tribes can alter those places from earlier times. They do not dare do that to the Now for fear of killing the Great Mother."

Nir coiled himself into a tense spiral. "But if a line of cracking were laid across the futuremost border of the Now, other tribes could attack us from further in the past without the effects of their change-waves propagating beyond our borders. They could attack us, enslave us, even kill the Great Mother and it would have no effect on events further in the future. The People and the Now would be as vulnerable as any other part of time."

Col was not convinced. The words of the War Chief could not dispel the joy he had felt at the prospect of truly protecting the People. But his next question was cut off by a warning from his Third Voice.

"Worldwide change-wave impinging on this region."

The tidal wave of change that bore down upon them had originated in the late Diaspora, fifty thousand years pastward from where Nir and Col talked and Kookatchi listened.

The Time Warriors of the Aesthetic Eugenicist Conclave had made the change that had created the wave. They were a tribe late come to the battles of the Instant, not concerned with making a specific history but with making humans a perfect species—perfect, that is, in terms of appreciating the world around them. The Aesthetic Eugenicist Conclave was one of those eccentric tribes that haunted the Diaspora, capturing and genetically altering time-bound humans in experiments that had grown more and more absurd as the Conclave's frustration with the wars of the Instant had increased.

This particular change had been wrought on a small settlement of Homo sapiens. The Conclave had altered the genes for color reception in the eyes so that the descendants of these Homo sapiens would be able to see two octaves into the ultraviolet and three into the infrared.

This tribe interbred with others, spreading these genes throughout the burgeoning human population until all of the earth's inhabitants could see these new bands of beautiful light. The resultant change in concepts of beauty and art spread through all aspects of human existence. All of human history was altered by this one act, and that alteration was reflected in the Instant by a tidal wave that grew in force until it covered all the waters above the earth with a savage torrent propagating futureward.

All the tribes of time knew what to do when such a wave was passing. Just before it struck them, each tribe in turn anchored down into the earthly side of time to wait out the savage squall. Once the wave had passed them by they reemerged to continue their battles.

From the Diaspora to just pastward of the deeps all the tribes of time took this expedient measure to protect themselves. Only Nir and Col had cause to consider another course of action. The broken island had shown itself capable of taming violent waves, but they did not know if it could calm the oncoming typhoon.

Nir had never personally been through such a change-wave, but the recorded experiences of his scouts had given him considerable caution. Still, this might give Fourth Voice enough information to formulate a hypothesis about the island.

"We will wait out the storm here in these shallows," Nir said.

"Yes, War Chief," Col replied, tapping carefully to keep the fear out of his voice.

Nir stretched out his sense of touch, reaching down through the years. The first advance waves of the change lapped against his senses, shallow and calm. They had definitely been tamped down by the bulk of the island. But what was that? It was coming from the east and the north. The wave had curved around somehow; instead of propagating straight from past to future, the island had bent it. The change-storm was coming toward them perpendicular to the direction of past and future, coming to them through the spatial directions.

"Down," Nir tapped, slamming his tail against the shallow waters so as to be heard over the oncoming tidal wave.

The two Ghosts dove down and gripped the solid side of time. They came into being in the middle of a crowded street in a sprawling, smog-filled city in Indonesia. Squat gray plastic buildings filled the landscape for kilometers around them. Dozens of men armed with bulbous spiral-barreled rifles were firing acid-filled pellets from open windows down onto a crowd of unarmed youths, chanting something that neither of the Ghosts could understand.

The wave struck, crashing in from all sides. The solid earth twisted around the two Ghosts. There was a moment of a myriad conflicting images dancing before their eyes: cities, jungles, roadways, musical performances, dances. Then the waves passed, resolving into their previous futureward direction. The images settled down into a single place. The gray city was gone. In its place was an open plain dotted with kilometer-high towers of silver-and-green plastic. Stretched between these towers were spiderwebs of solid rainbows that curved gracefully up from the base of one tower to the top of the next, then down again, forming a lattice of multicolored streets that meandered through the air like the smoke trails of drunken fireworks.

People were lying on those many-hued highways in the sky, watching the sunrise and commenting on the aesthetic qualities of the light as it came down through carefully engineered cloud formations.

Col prepared to unanchor, but Nir stopped him and pointed to a short man in a purple-and-gold body suit woven from some metal. Nir had noted the man standing in the crowd of beleaguered youths before the change. He now stood alone on the grassy ground, directly under one of the rainbow bridges.

"Capture him," Nir said.

He and Col vanished into the Instant and anchored back down where the little man had been standing, but he was no longer there.

Kookatchi had momentarily forgotten why he had anchored down in that particular place and time, but when his Drum's awareness realized Nir and Col were about to reanchor, he remembered. He vanished into the Instant just as they were appearing.

"He knew we were coming," Nir said. "He must be a Drum. We have to catch him and find out what he knows about the fractures."

Nir vanished into the Instant before Col could speak the conventional belief that because of their poor memories Drums never knew anything. Col followed his War Chief and they set off in pursuit of Kookatchi, who was swimming away futureward, trying to remember who was chasing him and what he might have stolen from them.

The Time Warriors were gone from the spired and bridged city. A series of small waves flickered over the Flux and reached the spiderweb metropolis. The place became a battlefield for robot tanks, then a ten-mile-square automated idol factory, then a forest that had never been touched by human hands, and so on, and so on.

Kookatchi fled, ducking between the waves of change, trusting his small size and his Drum's innate sense of oncoming alteration to help him escape. He was not overly worried about the pursuit. No one had ever captured him, not once since he took up his life of thievery. At least, he could not remember ever having been caught.

"How do we catch him?" Col asked as the Ghosts swam in pursuit. "I can barely feel him amidst the waves."

Nir had captured a Drum once before, a relatively inexperienced one who had been part of an attacking army. To do it he had ordered a dozen Ghosts to form a circle with their tails, surrounding the Drum while six other Ghosts waited in the Flux to catch him if he tried to escape into the solid world.

There was no way he and Col could duplicate that maneuver on their own.

"We will follow him from several years' distance until he forgets about us," Nir said.

"He will evade us in the waves."

"I do not think so," the War Chief said. "He was near the island. It must be important to him. He will come back to it."

"What good will that do us?" Col asked.

"In the shallows near the island we will be able to sense him. He is a creature of the deeper waters and may not know how easy it is to feel things in shallow waters."

"Yes, War Chief," Col said, feeling a surge of confidence in his leader.

Nir slid to within five years of the cracked region and felt through the barely moving ocean of the Instant. His sense of touch was irritated by that same scraping quality he had felt before in the bottom of the ocean near the island; he forced that feeling out of his mind and concentrated on the moving water. The ripples of change from the past were so damped that he could hardly feel them, but from southeast and futureward he felt a little rhythmic swishing that tickled his sense of touch as if someone were repeatedly brushing a feather against his fingertips.

"That way," Nir tapped, and the two Ghosts set off at a slow, measured swim.

Kookatchi darted through the waters, surfing over the small waves, swimming between large ones, holding still like a piece of flotsam, ducking down a few times into the Flux, using all the tricks he had mastered to evade pursuit. As evasion became the sole occupation of his thoughts, he forgot who he was fleeing from or even why he was fleeing.

Nir and Col stayed decades away, and seemed not to be following him, so Kookatchi quickly lost track of them. Eventually he could no longer see any possible candidates for those who were hunting him, and he gradually forgot that he was being chased at all.

The Drum floated peacefully in the waters over northern Mongolia, sixty thousand years futureward from the Now. Nothing was happening, no one was after him, he had no objects of beauty to contemplate. Kookatchi considered searching for someone to rob, but then he remembered the horses and the fractured time and decided to return and investigate.

Nir and Col had great difficulty following Kookatchi; indeed, they lost his trail repeatedly. Whenever this happened they would return to the edge of the broken lands and slither along it until Nir felt the telltale soft, swift rhythm of Kookatchi's tail swishes. Then they would set out again. Each time they tracked him, Kookatchi would realize the pursuit and flee, then forget about it and return to the waters near the island. The two Ghosts found themselves looping out and back over and over again, slowly closing in on the Drum's haphazard wanderings.

VII

Forty thousand years futureward, Quillithé watched the activities around the region of darkness with great interest. She had focused her vision on the progress of Adjutant Irithrué's unit as it swam pastward, and noted with dispassionate approval how well Irithrué had avoided contact with several hostile tribes.

But the strategist's attention was drawn away when she noticed the tidal wave approaching from the past. She broadened her sight to watch the change-wave pass over the entire world, and noted each tribe as it anchored down to avoid the cutting fury of the tempest.

Surprise rose up in the caverns of her mind as she noticed the wave passing on either side of the black region and saw it impossibly curving around the darkness, so that the changes propagated from east, west, north, and south. That unprecedented bending of the course of change fascinated Quillithé and gave her a valuable piece of information. The region of darkness was not just a blockage of her sight. Something was there, something new to the Instant.

The wave continued its progress, flowing futureward into her native deep waters, where its cutting force was muted by interaction with all the other change-waves that melded into the tides of the deeps. The wave that washed over Quillithé herself was only a gentle ripple making her century of life bob lightly up and down on the waters.

But Quillithé's attention was still focused on the area around the darkness. The wave having passed over, she noticed two Time Warriors unanchor into the Instant. No, not two. There was a third, tiny in size, but intense in brightness, a flickering, glowing being darting through the waters so deftly that it almost looked to her as if he were vanishing from one place in the Instant and then appearing in another. She had seen such sights before; clearly the small shifty being was a Drum.

The two longer-tailed warriors she did not recognize. They were not members of any tribe that frequented the futureward half of the inhabited Instant. Indeed, given the relative clumsiness of their swimming she suspected they might be of that tribe she had only heard about, the legendary warriors of man's beginning.

The Drum and the two unknown warriors seemed to be playing a complex game, darting in and out of the region of blackness, swimming away and then returning. All three showed such a familiarity with the region of darkness that had swallowed her own troops that she began to wonder if they might be the warriors responsible for its existence.

The strategist let the notion echo through her mind; bouncing off possible interpretations, giving birth to considerations, but ultimately leading nowhere. She needed more information before her contemplations could blossom forth into awareness and action.

The strategist shifted her attention to Irithrué's patrol. They were still ten thousand years futureward from the dark region. If the Drum and two far-past-timers continued their peculiar game then Irithrué would catch up with them. Quillithé had confidence in the Adjutant; she would realize that her orders not to fight did not encompass the rare opportunity to capture a small group of Time Warriors.

Quillithé rolled a few months of her tail thoughtfully in the water and returned her attention to the darting and dancing around the dark region. Whatever knowledge the Drum and the early warriors had of the blackness, Irithrué would wring it from them and bring it back to the strategist for absorption into the vast spaces of her mind.

Kookatchi was so used to being futilely pursued that he barely gave it any thought. He presumed as he surfed the shallows near the broken island that his pursuers were probably after his mythical horde of treasure. They could hardly have been seeking to recover something he had stolen since he was not carrying any loot. The Drum, his memory and ideation confined by presumption, could not think of any other possible reason for them to be hunting him.

The closest his thoughts came to the truth occurred once when he swam close to the border of the breakage itself. The thought bubbled up in his mind that perhaps those chasing him might have been the tribe who created the island, anxious to prevent him from escaping with their secrets. Not that he possessed those secrets, but perhaps his reputation had made them believe he knew more than he actually did.

But even if that was so, it did not matter to him; he would escape as he always had. No one had ever captured Kookatchi the Thief.

Quillithé, who had once captured Kookatchi when he tried to raid one of her weapon caches, watched his activities with fascination. Capturing the Drum had been a difficult operation and had given her a certain insight into the nature of the smallest inhabitants of the Instant. She had been fascinated by Kookatchi's apparent ability to foresee her strategic choices and take advantage of any possibilities she left open to him. It seemed impossible to her that such a small being could see options better than she could.

She had created a few tests, laying traps with more than one escape route. One of these would always be an immediate escape with no long-term advantage. The others would be subtler, involving the laying of multiple distractions that would cut off her pursuit of the Drum. In each trap, Kookatchi escaped by the immediate means. She concluded that his "foresight" was only an awareness she did not have.

Then she laid her final trap, one in which there were no avenues of escape. Rings of soldiers in the Flux and Instant lay in wait for the Drum as he surfed the waters of time. They sprang upon him, darting in from all directions, creating a vortex he could not surf out of. Surrender was his only option, and the Drum took it.

Quillithé had interrogated Kookatchi for an apparent passage of days, in order to add his awareness to her own, but she could not absorb into the caverns of her mind that instantaneous flash of pure knowing that the Drum relied upon. She accepted in theory that his understanding of the Instant was true, that the ocean of time had no passage, no progress, that it is and transforms. But she could not add that understanding to her webs of plans and schemes, she could not make it a factor in the creation of strategy. So she reluctantly let it go, to sit and wait in a rarely visited room in the manifold chambers of her vast mind.

The interrogation over, Quillithé had contemplated destroying Kookatchi, but decided against it. Eventually, she might want to try again to take his awareness for her own, and until that point he served as a distraction and a nuisance for the other tribes. She had let him go after convincing his failing memory that he had not been captured; indeed, she implanted in his thinking a belief that he had never ventured into the deeps of time.

Now Kookatchi himself occupied only a small region of her consideration. The Ghosts were of more interest: two Time Warriors engaged in the apparently fruitless effort of catching the Drum. Only two of them. She let the possibilities dance through many of the halls of her mind. Yes, it was barely possible for two Time Warriors to catch a Drum, but it would require a deftness and swift reaction that she doubted existed in the Instant. Certainly none of the leaders of any tribe she had fought had shown the necessary tactical brilliance.

But the great majority of her mind dwelled upon a more complex question. What Quillithé wanted to know was how the two Ghosts were using the dark region to chase the Drum. They were clearly doing so; whenever they lost his trail they reentered the darkness and emerged again on a direct course. What was in there that was so useful? The greater part of her cavernous consciousness sought to spin out possible explanations, but no satisfactory answer came to her.

Quillithé resolved to find out. If the Ghosts found Kookatchi worth their pursuit, all she needed to do was capture the Drum again and use him as bait to lure them into the deep waters and catch them as well.

Image-orders flashed through her camp, bringing fifty of her soldiers to attend upon her.

Image from Quillithé to the soldiers: The detachment of fifty swimming thirty thousand years pastward, then breaking up into twenty-five pairs, the pairs spreading out to a region of five thousand years and ten thousand square kilometers.

Image: If Kookatchi swam anywhere into the region they covered, they were to converge into a tight net and catch the Drum as she had captured him before, half of them to deploy in the Flux and half in the Instant to cut off all possibility of escape.

Image: With Kookatchi captured, they would lure in the two Ghosts and capture them as well, then bring all three futureward to Quillithé.

The fifty warriors left the army and swam pastward to carry out their strategist's orders.

Nir and Col, believing themselves the hunters, knew nothing of the trap being laid for them. The scout had become excited about the chase, foolish though he thought it. He had rarely experienced the odd thrill of following Nir's direct battle commands, of receiving a bundle of detailed instructions from the War Chief.

"Follow at fifty years' distance, close slowly to forty years, follow for a while making few new waves if you can. If he does not seem to have noticed you decrease the distance another decade, and so on."

Col had carried out this command until he had closed to thirty years; then Nir had abruptly countermanded the order.

"Retreat to a century away. Stay still, do not move."

That had startled the scout, but he did as he was told, obeying without comment. Nir had swum away then, taking up the pursuit on his own. The scout had waited and then to his surprise received a broad order with no details, only a reliance upon his own ingenuity.

"Chase the Drum to the futuremost edge of the broken island. Make sure he goes there; do not let him flee outward into the ocean."

Col worked hard trying to carry out this command. He swam far out into the ocean, four hundred years from the breakage, and then sharklike prowled the coast until he felt the tickle of the Drum, and then herded him toward the futuremost border.

Kookatchi accepted the herding for a while, letting himself be pushed back to the island, before darting through Col's blockade, surfing on Drum awareness.

The scout rejoined his War Chief. "I failed. He escaped."

"You did not fail," Nir said. "I used you to push the Drum in order that I might feel how he moved. There is a suddenness in him that I have never felt before. Your obedience gave me the knowledge I needed. Now I am sure the Drum can be caught."

Col was stunned to admiration by the realization that his apparent failure had caused events to work themselves out according to the War Chief's desire.

Nir himself knew that his manner of leading confused his subordinates and disturbed the Elder, but in the Now, survival and success were what mattered. He could not predict when a complex plan would occur to him that would need to be carried out step by step or when only a single perfect action would appear, clear in his mind, or when a goal such as capture would change into a new goal like the gleaning of knowledge. But the War Chief knew and relied upon the fact that his tactical senses had never deserted him. From his first entry into the Instant through half a hundred battles defending the Now from invaders, from dissension, and from the previous War Chief, Nir had never been at a loss in warfare.

Even during this chase, in this doubly unfamiliar region of the Instant, half deep water, half impossibly shallow island; even seeking to do the impossible, to capture a Drum; even here he knew he could rely on his mind to change in the proper manner and give him the understanding and he needed to accomplish what needed to be accomplished.

Nir's mind had turned itself over to concern with the broken island; so had Kookatchi's awareness, and Quillithé's strategizing. Upon the strangeness of the broken island three unique but separate and distinct minds hurtled toward each other, seemingly propelled by their individual seekings for answers. Nir relied upon the feel of his thoughts to show him the way, Kookatchi upon his sudden insight and swift change, Quillithé upon the vastness of sight and thinking. They did not know they were coming together. Each mind believed itself to be working on its own, in command of all things around it. Each was in error. Though Kookatchi sought to escape, and Nir sought to capture him, and Quillithé sought to net them both, in truth there was no hunter and no quarry, in truth the tides of time were drawing the three of them together.

VIII

Kookatchi, carried along by his own confidence, permitted himself to be distracted from the chase. On one of his longer loops away from the broken island, he found himself sixty-seven thousand years futureward from the Now, over Sri Lanka. There the Drum saw an encampment; the Fifteenth Legion of the Byzantine Temporal Fusiliers was floating above that island. One of their number, a soldier named Theodora with great experience pillaging the Flux, was diving down and dragging up any useful bits of technology she could find.

The Byzantine Fusiliers were arming themselves for their planned assault on the Son of the Sun's Featherless Falcons, camped only five centuries futureward of them. This attack was punitive, against the Falcons' recent raid on the Fusiliers and the disruption of their attempt to create a new New Rome in southern Asia.

Kookatchi had no interest in the reason the Fusiliers were so intently pulling treasure out of earthly time. It was the treasure itself that distracted him, a pile of brightly shining objects floating freely next to the spot where Theodora was diving. The Drum's attention was particularly caught by two twinned lines, only a few seconds long, but throbbing with an earthly heaviness that weighed them down so they barely bobbed in the water. Even the waves that passed over them hardly disturbed their languorous floating.

The theft itself was simplicity. The Drum swam slowly into the camp under the cover of the washing tides, then slithered to within a few minutes of Theodora and waited for the splash of her dive into solid time. In that transformation of the Instant when water splashed in all directions, the Drum slipped over, grabbed the heavy baubles, and surfed out of the camp, clutching the few-second lines to his tail.

Escape was swift and simple. The Drum swam east and slightly pastward, skimming over the waves of change, laying false trails and eventually anchoring down in the Philippine Islands.

The Drum ignored the world changing around him and focused on the objects he had stolen. In solid earth they manifested as two half-meter-long rods of steel and quartz. They were remarkably heavy for their size, and some force bound them together so that they could not be held apart farther than two meters. At the top of each rod was a button, and after a certain amount of experimentation the Drum discerned what they were for.

To make sure he was right, Kookatchi stuck the quartz-tipped ends of the rods into the sides of a mountain and pressed the buttons. The rods began to vibrate and the Drum sensed a decided atemporal component to the shaking; the rods were drawing the waters of change down into the earth and using them to force the motion of the mountain.

"Beautiful," he said as the island shook under the force of his man-made earthquake. Wooden . . . stone . . . brick . . . iron houses tumbled . . . remained firm . . . were built . . . shattered . . . killing . . . hundreds . . . no one . . . thousands . . . millions . . . setting off tidal waves . . . tsunamis . . . nothing.

The Drum retrieved the rods and returned to the Instant, rapturous with the beauty of his prizes.

Nir and Col swam relentlessly toward him only two decades pastward from where the Drum emerged, two strokes of his long tail for Nir, three for Col. The War Chief felt the Drum rise up from the earth to the waters in a tiny splash; that splash was like a thunderbolt in Nir's mind, showing him clearly and suddenly how to catch the Drum. All that was necessary was to forget his normal way of thinking and take up a new one for a short burst, then return to normal thought. Nir was not displeased; that willingness to briefly suspend accepted practice was the heart of his manner of command.

"Chase him toward me," Nir tapped to Col.

The Drum heard the words and rippled out a few seconds of laughter. He would most assuredly let the seven-year chase him toward the ten-year. Near the long-tailed warrior he would be nothing but a little bit of flotsam, too innocuous for their extended touch to find. Kookatchi feigned fear, darting this way and that as the scout pursued him, herding the Drum toward Nir.

The War Chief waited. Gathering his control of his tail, he stretched out his sense of touch, feeling up and down his own length, suspending the normal ignorance of his own body that permitted a Time Warrior to believe that his former time-bound self and his new free self were one and the same. The War Chief took this focusing on his body, this exact knowledge of his own contours, and gave it to his own Second Voice, imprinting it in memory. He formed in his mind a shape, coiling and twisting, a maze made of his own ten years' extent. His Third Voice constructed the commands to be given to the atemporal "muscles" that moved his tail.

Kookatchi surfed closer to the War Chief, surprised that the ten-year-long warrior was not moving. He sensed no changes coming in the Instant; the configuration of water and dwellers in the water was going to be the same. The same—no, changed. The Drum leaped back suddenly as the whole shape of the Instant altered. The War Chief was no longer a straight line lying athwart the direction of past to future. The Ghost had without warning bent himself into a four-dimensional coil, a labyrinth made of one body, kinked and curved with twists and bends and cul-de-sacs, each arc of his being no more than five minutes long.

As Nir reshaped himself, Col anchored down into the Flux and waited should the Drum seek to escape that way.

Kookatchi was amazed. To him it seemed as if the Ghost had done something that could only be accomplished with a Drum's awareness. He had changed without passage, moved without going through motion; in perfect suddenness the War Chief had become the maze.

Yet though Kookatchi did not know this, Nir had accomplished this Drum-sudden change without Drum's awareness. The War Chief as yet did not see the way the Drum did, though he knew that only the completely sudden had a chance of catching the apparently prophetic Kookatchi. He had bypassed his own way of thinking, the easy acceptance of passage that the long-tailed all had; he had given up control of his body and let it change according to his will.

The labyrinth shrank, tightening around the Drum into harsh coils, heavy with the War Chief's years, sharp with the force of his body. One cutting ripple from Nir and the minute-long Drum would shatter into consciousnessless milliseconds. In the Instant, that mindless shattering was death.

Nir rippled the end of his tail, and Col, responding to the signal, emerged into the Instant, now that the Drum could not escape by anchoring.

Kookatchi felt a brief burst of ecstasy at the beautiful way in which he had been captured, but that feeling vanished in the recycling of his consciousness. Then fear filled him. One chance remained for his escape.

Kookatchi let loose the earthquake makers to float in the few seconds of space around him. "You want these things?" he asked in the tapping language of the Ghosts.

"No," Nir tapped, sending painful shudders through Kookatchi's body. "We want to know about the cracking."

"Why?" Kookatchi asked cautiously, wondering how these Ghosts could know about the strange island that existed in the middle Instant. Why did they care about something that occurred so far from their home?

Nir rippled his tail; Kookatchi convulsed, feeling the fragility of his minute-long self.

"We want to know who made it," the War Chief tapped through the body of the Drum.

"I do not know that."

"Then what do you know about it?"

Kookatchi's consciousness reached the end of his tail and flickered back to the beginning. He was surprised and briefly joyous to find himself trapped in somebody's coils, but as before the joy turned swiftly to fear. The Drum tapped the earthquake makers. "You want these?"

Col's patience was wearing thin. He had dutifully followed his War Chief through the complex maneuverings, the backtracking, the loss of trails, and the risk of exposure to enemy tribes, and now they had found their goal; they had captured the Drum. The scout was amazed at this impossible feat and wished to speak to Nir about how it had been accomplished, but—all that effort for someone who could not possibly know anything, someone who had clearly shown the uselessness of his memory.

"War Chief," Col tapped, interrupting the interrogation. "Is this not wasteful?"

"Feel and learn, Col," Nir tapped in patient response. "A Drum's knowledge is buried and must be dug up from the treasury of his memory."

"How do you know that, War Chief?" Col asked.

"Fourth Voice told me when first we captured a Drum."

Col fell silent, unable to challenge the authority of Fourth Voice.

Nir returned his attention to Kookatchi, who had been momentarily fascinated by the interchange between the Ghosts. The Drum wondered what Fourth Voice was and how he might go about stealing it.

The War Chief knew that he was only going to get one question answered for each cycle of Kookatchi's thoughts, and he would have to use the Drum's forgetfulness to his advantage to gain the element of surprise with each new question.

"What is it like to be in the cracked area?" Nir asked.

Kookatchi paused, unsure of what to say. A squeeze from Nir made it clear he had to speak. "There is no water; it is like crawling along the bottom of the sea. But the bottom is fragile."

The Drum's consciousness reached the end of his tail and flickered back to the beginning. He remembered being captured, knew that his captors were Ghosts, but could not remember what they wanted. Ah, he was carrying loot; that must be it. Kookatchi tapped the earthquake makers, no longer aware of what they were or how he had come by them. "You want these?"

"No. Tell me about the fragility of the broken island."

The Drum was startled by the Ghost's knowledge. But he could feel the threat of the coils around him and chose to answer. "There was no need to anchor. I fell through the bottom into the Flux. But the Flux was not being changed, and it was unconnected, many solids, not one solid."

Kookatchi's consciousness recycled. He was being held prisoner by Ghosts. They knew about the broken island. They had no interest in his loot.

"Did you break the ocean? Did you make the island?" the Drum asked.

"No," Nir replied. "What does it mean that the Flux is unconnected?"

"Events just stop. All motion ceases. One second does not lead to the next."

Kookatchi's consciousness recycled. Captive of Ghosts. Possibly they had made the broken island. Who had a better motive than the haters of change from humanity's dawn? "Why did you create the cracking?"

"We did not do so," Nir said. "How does it feel when one second does not lead to the next?"

"Helpless, powerless," Kookatchi said, and his tapping took on the rhythmic qualities of an earthly drum as the beginnings of a song were forming his mind. "The time-bound are trapped, prisoners of solidity. But they have past and future to comfort them and give them hope. In the broken island, there is neither past nor future comfort. . . ."

The Drum's consciousness recycled and he finished the words, though he wondered what they meant. "Nor hope."

"Twenty enemies approaching, fifty years pastward, two hundred miles to the west," Nir's Third Voice warned him.

The Fifteenth Byzantine Fusiliers had realized the theft almost immediately after Kookatchi departed from their camp. They had gathered up the remaining bounty of Theodora's raid and set out to find the thief. There was no wake to follow, no tides created by the tail of their quarry. By the lack of such signs, they concluded that Kookatchi the Drum was the robber they hunted. They did not come to this out of any brilliant leaps of intuition nor out of any clever reasoning; the Fusiliers like all the tribes of the Instant were liable to blame Kookatchi for any inexplicable disappearance. Thus they had set out to find him in the hopes of winning his hidden treasure for themselves and for the history they wanted to impose on the world.

Their strategy of pursuit was not a bad one considering they had nothing to help them. Their leader, the Basileus Michael Thalleus, once emperor of half the world before he gave it up to enter the Instant to seek revenge, had hit upon the plan of searching the nearby tribes and seeing if any of them were chasing a thief. Michael Thalleus's scouts had spotted Nir and Col giving chase to something they could not see, and knew it had to be Kookatchi. When the two Ghosts stopped and settled in one place, Thalleus, his mind clouded by greed, concluded that they had found the hoard and were about to pillage it. The emperor whose throne, empire, and people had never existed, and who in consequence was just another barbarian chieftain in the Instant, led his warriors to the attack.

Nir did not even consider battle with twenty well-armed Time

Warriors. He flicked a signal to Col and the two of them swam off eastward, leaving Kookatchi in sudden isolation.

Kookatchi's consciousness reached the end of his tail and flickered back to the beginning. He wondered why he was standing still when an angry tribe was bearing down on him. He also wondered who the two other Time Warriors running away to the east were.

The Drum surfed away on the forward wake created by the approaching Byzantines. It was a temporary expedient; they would soon catch up with him. But all he needed was one recycling of his mind to remember all the means of escape, and a second recycling to recall the Byzantine Fusiliers and their long-standing enmities with other tribes. It was simplicity born of long practice for Kookatchi to lay a false trail leading off toward a camp only eight hundred forty years and seven hundred kilometers away where the Radical Turkic Liberation Front sat brooding on their recent defeats and wanting revenge on one enemy or another.

The Drum watched briefly as the two armies clashed into a wild whirlpool of battle. Satisfied, Kookatchi swam futureward, hoping to see something new and beautiful unlike the ugliness of the broken island.

Quillithé had watched the meeting between Nir and Kookatchi, and the sudden intervention that broke it up, with interest. The longer-tailed of the Ghosts had actually conceived of and implemented the one means of capturing a Drum she had envisioned, and he had done so without the advantages of her labyrinthine mind.

It seemed to her contemplations more and more likely that the Ghost was responsible for the creation of the darkness, and more and more likely that he had done so for the specific purpose of thwarting her. But still, in the deep corridors of Quillithé's thoughts there remained other possibilities, and she was not one to fix on a single idea until it was definitely established. Even then she would continue to look for holes and weak spots in the solid surety.

Meanwhile in bits and sparks she watched the tiny wake of the Drum surfing casually toward her trap. If all went well she would soon have some answers.

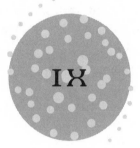

IX

Nir and Col swam eastward from the Fusiliers, then ducked down into the Flux in the area of the Hawaiian Islands and waited until they were sure their pursuers had passed them by.

"War Chief," Col said, "What did you learn from interrogating that Drum?"

Nir watched silently as the five-thousand-meter spiral castle of King Mahonahona vanished and was replaced by a spaceport that covered the Hawaiian Islands and the water between them. Gray-and-white arrow-shaped spaceships flew off toward the stars on pillars of fire, then disappeared as the decades of work that went into them were undone by a war that had been started a dozen centuries pastward by the One-Planet-Is-Enough tribe. The ripples of this change spread through the Flux, out beyond earth, unmaking the lives of millions who would have terraformed and colonized half a dozen moons around the solar system before stretching out their hands to touch a hundred star systems beyond.

Col waited, but Nir said nothing. The young Ghost deliberated, then covered his own eyes and asked in formal tones, "What did you learn, War Chief? I seek to know for the good of the People."

"Uncover and I will answer," the War Chief said.

Col removed his hands and looked up into Nir's face. Nir studied his subordinate, presently appearing to be twenty years old, his dark skin unmarked by any mortal battles. During the life Col had led, the People had not been attacked; the Ghost had grown up with the dictates of vigilance but no firsthand understanding of the dangers he faced.

Since he had entered the Instant, Col had learned better, but his face still bore the placidness of one raised without true fear.

"I learned what the Flux in the cracked region is like. I learned that the Instant is fragile, perhaps too fragile to support us. And I learned that the cracking was important enough to be remembered by a Drum."

"Thank you, War Chief," Col said, and lapsed into respectful silence, waiting while his commander decided what to do next.

Futureward, Kookatchi had been trapped again, was terrified again, and was being interrogated again. This time his captor was Quillithé, the monster of the deep; this new captivity brought back to the surface of his memory his previous prisoning in her coils. The Drum recalled that she had interrogated him long and hard about his means of perceiving the Instant, and that she had clearly been dissatisfied with his answers, but that she had let him go for some unfathomable reason of her own.

Kookatchi also recalled that his only hope was that she be willing to let him go again. She held him captive, floating in the center of her nine-ringed army camp. Each ring was composed of long-tailed soldiers, arrayed in perfect uniformity, willing to obey without question. Along their tails lay shields and weapons that gleamed and sparked and rippled with atemporal power, a rainbow of savage sharpness that tugged at his senses, inciting his lust for their beauty and terribleness.

But though some of his thoughts were turned to the hopeless task of contemplating theft here in the camp of the deeps, most of his consciousness was focused on the grace and power and fearfulness of the monster herself. All around him she floated, coil upon coil, no broader, taller, or deeper than any normal human, but oh the atemporal length of her. A century united into one mind, one action, one contemplation. Such beauty, and the only way he could possess any part of it would be in the memory of this interaction.

And when the Drum realized that, he ceased to have any reticence. He would surrender to her and speak and listen and take the joy of the interaction away, if she let him live. And if she did not release him, if instead she shattered him into milliseconds, then frozen in each of those millisecond bodies would be a memory of her.

Kookatchi rippled out a pictograph, a shorthand version of Quillithé's full image speech, his body being too small to create the grand sweeps of picturing that the strategist and her army created.

Image from Kookatchi: The Drum submitting himself before her, she rippling out blue-tinted question pictures and he giving answers.

Quillithé responded with vast multicolored canvases showing huge stretches of time's ocean and the events occurring on them.

Kookatchi stared with joy at the rippled-out images flowing across the waters, glistening liquid images kilometers and months on a side. Such beauty, and he would never possess it save in memory. His short brush of a tail could not answer it in kind, he could not produce that beauty, but he could make a beauty of his own in his calligraphy.

Quillithé sent an image showing Kookatchi's capture by Nir. The maze-trap of the War Chief's tail was subtly depicted; each twist, each turn, each knife-sharp angle was brightly shown. Nir's form was limned with the subtle blue glow that meant a question in the picture speech. Quillithé wanted to know who had captured the Drum.

Pictograph image from Kookatchi: The Instant, shallows to deeps, shallows limned in a bright white of answering.

Quillithé's suspicions were confirmed; they were the legendary Ghosts of man's origins. She sent another question, this time limning the interchange between Ghost and Drum. "What did they want to know?"

The Drum's recollection was fuzzy. The beauty of the monster he was speaking to had driven all other beauties from his mind. But there was something—oh, yes, that was it.

Image from Kookatchi: Island in the ocean, cracks in the island. The island limned in white. That was what they had asked him about.

Quillithé had never seen the island, but she quickly realized that it must be what was concealed in the darkness.

Image from Quillithé: The ocean of time, the dark region marked. Then an image of the island, questioning blue to ask if they were the same thing.

Kookatchi replied with a series of ideographs, showing the island about two centuries inward from the area of darkness. Kookatchi assumed that the blackness was only a form of questioning he did not yet know. He did not realize that Quillithé could not see what was so clear to his much narrower vision.

Image from Quillithé: The island, limned in gold and blue, a request for general information.

Kookatchi tried to answer her question, but it was very difficult to explain what had happened to him in the Flux using a language created to discuss the Instant. The worst part came when he tried to make a picture of the immobile horses. The Drum's capacity for speech failed him as he tried to show immobility in the native language of change.

It took a while for Quillithé to understand the changelessness of the cracked region, but she immediately understood how fragile it was. If it could barely support Kookatchi's one-minute tail, it would never hold her century-long bulk. There was a strange reversal in this island, for the waters of time buoyed up her body, yet this solid place would collapse under her. The more she thought about it, the more likely it became that the region was created specifically to bar her presence. The darkness and fragility almost guaranteed this. But still, there were other possibilities.

Image from Quillithé: Nir and Col, limned in gold and blue. A request for general knowledge.

In the elm-covered courtyards of the Hawaiian University of Linguistics, Nir had finished contemplating what Kookatchi had told him and decided that he did not yet know enough about the broken island to decide how the Ghosts should respond to it. Indeed, though it was clear that the fragment Col had brought back to the Now was related to the cracked region, Nir did not yet know how it was related.

"We resume scouting," Nir said. He and Col abandoned their grip on the Flux and swam back to the shallows around the island to resume their mapping. Taking care not to permit any part of their tails to get closer than ten years to the cracked border itself, they resumed tracing the contours of the fragile area. They carefully mapped the barely flowing waters just futureward of the broken island.

They had finished mapping the futuremost border, which covered India and southern China at a period sixty-three thousand years futureward from the Now. The border now turned pastward, and they had begun to make their way along it when Col managed to pluck up his courage and ask his leader a question that had been troubling him since they first found the area.

"War Chief, do you have any idea why none of the nearby tribes are camped near this area when it affords excellent protection against the ravages of change?"

"I wish I knew," Nir said. "I also have been troubled by that question. Perhaps the madmen are too busy raiding each other to investigate this area."

Nir doubted his own words even as he tapped them out. He had always believed, as did the rest of the Ghosts, that every other tribe in the Instant consisted of self-deluded lunatics who never rested from trying to kill each other and enslave the solid world.

The Ghosts held it as an article of faith that all the tribes of time had the same motto: Attack, attack, and attack again. But Nir the tactician could not accept that any tribe, no matter how insane, would ignore the combat usefulness of the broken islands and the shallows around them. Surely some had tried to use it.

The two Ghosts continued their scouting, eventually completing the map. The cracking formed an irregular island, some ten thousand years long and six thousand miles wide, a hard lump of broken solidity amidst the churning sea of time. Their Second Voices dutifully recorded the existence and extent of this new landmark in the ocean of time, creating perfect maps that could be called upon at need. Their Third Voices chimed in with comments about its defensive value. Nir's Fourth Voice was still unsatisfied. It neither knew how the cracking was created, nor could it give advice should the War Chief encounter the cause of the cracking. Fourth Voice was insistent. It needed to have more information. Nir agreed with it, though for his own reasons.

"Do we return home now?" Col asked.

"You do," Nir said. "Give the map to the Elder, and, with her permission, dispense it to the rest of the Ghosts."

"What about you?" Col asked.

"I have to find the answer to your question."

"What do you mean?"

"I intend to find out why no tribe goes near the cracking."

"But War Chief, you should not be out here alone. You are too valuable to the People. I must stay with you."

"No, Col. You must bring back what we already know. The map and the Drum's words must be given. The Elder will be angry at my absence and she may replace me as War Chief. If so I will bring back to the new War Chief such knowledge as his Fourth Voice will need, before mine is silenced."

Col wanted to protest further, but in matters of warfare Nir's decision was not to be gainsaid.

"Go," said the War Chief, and Col went.

Nir waited until Col had vanished from the range of his touch, then turned back to begin an in-depth examination of this ten-millennia anomaly.

Col swam pastward through the regions of warfare to the relative calmness of the Diaspora and then on to the placidity of the Now, where he reported to the Elder and let his Second Voice transmit to her Second Voice the map of the broken lands.

The Ghosts met in early spring in the Year of Ghosts' Conferring. A storm was raging, pouring lightning and rain down on the clearing of the Great Mother, but the Ghosts cared nothing about that. What mattered to them was that they met without their War Chief to hear about the great strangeness far in the future.

With the Elder's permission, Col transmitted the map to his comrades and narrated the events of their journey.

"Why did Nir stay behind?" the Elder asked Col from her perch atop the Great Mother's bones.

"The War Chief needed to learn more. He said that Fourth Voice was unsatisfied."

The assembled Ghosts dutifully covered their ears with their hands, then uncovered them.

The Elder tapped her bony right knuckles against her left shoulder. Nir had disobeyed her implicit requirement that he keep Col with him and that he return swiftly. But Fourth Voice belonged only to the War Chief. She was empowered to give the Voice and to take it away if necessary, but only he could hear it and decide how best to fill its needs. The Elder surveyed the assembled Ghosts and considered whether or not any of them could take Nir's place. Not yet. Two of the veterans among them had the potential to be good, if uninspired, leaders. She would deputize them and give them temporary command of the Ghosts. If one proved worthy she would make him War Chief, unless Nir returned before that eventuality.

That would suffice. But still she wondered what had prompted

Nir to stay behind. Was it Fourth Voice as he claimed or was it something native to his strange one-moment-orthodox-the-next-unorthodox mind?

The Elder stroked her wrinkled chin. "Why did he stay behind?" she whispered into the afternoon air.

Far futureward, Nir contemplated the true answer to that question. It was not the promptings of Fourth Voice that kept him away from his duties in the Now, though those could not easily be ignored. It was a deep foreboding, a fear in his mind and an anger as well. His mind nurtured a feeling of suspicion that had first arisen when he heard Kookatchi's description of the broken lands. If the Drum was telling the truth then beyond the border Nir and Col had mapped lay an area of real changelessness. To the War Chief of the Ghosts, the idea of that true stasis stared at the pretense of stability his warriors maintained in the Now and mocked it.

Before they were cut loose from the real world, all Ghosts-to-be swore to protect the Now from alteration. But unlike most of his warriors, Nir knew that oath to be a sham. When their consciousnesses recycled, most Ghosts forgot the horror of alteration that had been visited upon the People by the attacks of other tribes. The War Chief alone, aided by Fourth Voice, remembered the many different Peoples there had been.

Nir recalled with perfect clarity the unmaking of his descendants, then the destruction of his maternal ancestors up to and including his grandmother, who had been the first daughter of the Great Mother. She had been killed at the age of three during a raid by the Vatican Combine, and so had never borne Nir's grandmother, who had not birthed his mother, and so down to his own nonexistence.

The true stasis of the broken island tempted and disturbed the War Chief. He knew that the more reactionary elements among the other Ghosts would want to use this cracking in order to protect the People, regardless of the effect on the region surrounding the

Now, and that the Elder herself would lead that reactionary element.

Once Nir returned, the Ghosts would confer and a debate would begin on what to do about the cracking. Nir knew that the Elder would side with the fanatic Ghosts, that she would order him to find out how to create such a region, and then she would command the cordoning off of the Now. As he had told Col, such a barrier would not truly protect the People, but the Elder would command it anyway.

So for the good of the People and the true fulfillment of the vow, Nir stayed away until he could find arguments against that view.

Searching for clues, Nir swam futureward to the border of the broken island and searched diligently, looking for signs that any tribe came near to the broken island. He needed to know the answer to Col's question. Why was no one nearby? The War Chief extended his sense of touch, feeling for the ripples of nearby tribes. There, one was approaching swiftly and another behind it.

The Imperial Sudanese Atemporal Raiders were on the run, fleeing from a skirmish with Charlemagne's Paladins of the Ages. The Sudanese had been trying to reshape the destiny of West Africa in order to recreate one of the satrapies of their long-destroyed empire, but they had been thwarted by their hereditary Carolingean enemies who had attacked them over the forest preserve in central Sudan.

Only half a dozen Sudanese had escaped the battle. The other fifteen, including their centurion, had been torn to fragments, the jagged pieces of their shattered tails strewn across the Instant by a unified wave-front attack from the Paladins.

The Imperial Sudanese out of stubborn adherence to their time-bound origins only altered the history of that part of the earth from which they had sprung. Hence they knew nothing about the broken island that floated above Asia. Now fleeing to that strange region they were about to discover why no one else was camped nearby.

Nir was about to find out as well.

The Sudanese had a thousand-kilometer and twenty-year lead over their Carolingean pursuers as they swam toward the island. Nir shadowed them, keeping a distance of ten years and fifty kilometers, hiding in the wake of their passage.

En masse, the Sudanese swam blindly into the cracked region and fell through the shallows into the static Flux below. Their long tails thrashed out angry ripples as they vanished into solid time. The multiyear-wide waves of their panicked descent vibrated along the edge of the region. Nir felt the waves shaking the broken fragments, shivering through the cracks, widening them, making them longer, consuming more of liquid time, breaking the bottom of the ocean.

Refracted and reflected by the fractures, a sharp riptide erupted out from the broken lands. To Nir's astonishment, the interfering wave fronts cracked a dozen more years and a hundred more kilometers in every direction out from the border. The fall of the Sudanese had broken more of the Instant, stolen more of the ocean to create dry land.

The War Chief turned to flee before the fissure lines reached him, but as he uncoiled his tail to swim away the gently washing Instant under Nir froze, the ocean seeming to turn to ice, ice that shattered under his weight. The War Chief fell through the fragile solidity of the ocean floor into a newly broken piece of earthly time.

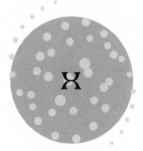

Buried alive; that was the first coherent thought Nir had. Then a memory from his earthbound childhood, a choking feeling that had come upon him at the age of five when Yal, who then had been his father, had told him that the Great Mother was under her mound. He had wondered if she could come out, or if the dirt and stone were holding her in, keeping her down under the earth.

Down in the earth of time. The shard of time he had fallen into, five kilometers by two kilometers by half a kilometer by forty-seven seconds, held him trapped, prisoned as if he were one of the time-bound.

But the War Chief was not one of the truly time-bound, who did not know that their lives were captured in stone, who had the illusion of progression of past and future. Nir knew about his imprisonment; he could feel the coffin of earth holding him down. His whole ten years of existence was held in this claustrophobic less-than-a-minute stone. It was not like anchoring, not that temporary resumption of illusory life, where one seemed to exist in a three-dimensional body experiencing one second after another. This falling into fractured time was different. His ten-year tail had been forcibly coiled up, bent back upon itself manifold times so that he could be squeezed into this forty-seven-second stone.

His life lay all around him, from twenty years old to thirty, scattered in multiple images, multiple Nirs across the area of the shard, a decade of War Chiefs littering that defile of time.

A flash of memory. Falling in, the sharp edges had tried to cut him into pieces, but his Wavebreaker shield had protected him, kept him whole, so instead of being carved up and falling into a multitude of fragments, he had slipped, then bent. Twisted and knotted on himself, he had been coiled up into this one piece of stony time.

To the four people, three rabbits, and two cows that lived in that temporally isolated meadow, caught in the process of meandering through their earthbound lives, it seemed as if an army of identical naked men had appeared all around them. Most of the multitude of same-persons were standing on the ground; a few were floating in midair caught in the midst of a fall. Some were sticking up out of the ground, displacing the grass that the humans had brought the cows to nibble on, disputing the rights of the rabbits to their home territory.

To the time-bound perspective of these creatures, it appeared as if the thousands of invaders were flashing in and out of existence, incapable of keeping still. As each moment passed a horde of Nirs would vanish and another horde would appear in different places.

Nir, whose awareness of the situation was much closer to the reality than the time-bound observers, could feel his consciousness flicker moment by moment up his tail, changing his place and time in the stone. He spent a split second at the futuremost border of the fragment, watching a line of his younger selves that stretched across the fragment from the east end to the west. An apparent moment later he was in the center of the region staring into the confused brown eyes of one of the cows.

He grasped a second of coherence and tried to unanchor. It had always been easy before this, just a matter of letting go, but here the Instant would not support the bulk of his tail. He would fall up, then slip back into the narrow confines of the fractured moment. He wondered for one split second how many other Time Warriors were trapped in shards in the broken lands, watching themselves flicker in and out in endless variation, unable to extricate themselves. Then the sequence of his life fell again into fragments.

His mind tried to cope with this confusion of changes. It thrashed around, seeking a new way of taking in the bewildering existence that trapped him. For one fractured moment it grasped a Drum's simultaneity, and the War Chief felt the whole of his being, conceived of his atemporality in the midst of the temporal. Nir's fluid mind tried to hold on to that pure awareness, but habit and memory intruded, the need to think of a next moment destroyed that moment of understanding. Conventional thought reasserted itself and Nir fell once more into the madness of irrational passage.

Nir's Third Voice, overwhelmed by the multitudes, failed to recognize that the myriads of people around Nir were all Nir himself. Reacting to the apparent invasion of Time Warriors it screamed warnings about armies of atemporal attackers, appearing and vanishing all around him. Whenever Third Voice paused in its rantings to reevaluate the situation Fourth Voice took over: "Temporal fracture, temporal fracture, impossible circumstances. Environment cannot exist. Temporal fracture."

Nir entered a stretch of his life that lasted a full five seconds before teleporting him off again. In those seconds he shouted a single command to his subsidiary Voices: Silence.

It was a command all Ghosts knew about, but none had ever given. The Voices were crucial to Ghostly armament and the safety of the Now. Yet to save his sanity Nir, War Chief of the People, had turned off the advisors that were among the greatest treasures won in the rebellion of the Ghosts.

Silence for one brief second, and in that second Nir's fractured thoughts cohered and his mind changed. He felt the means of escape through the emptiness, through the fractures. But then he lost it as his life again fell apart into millisecond-length pieces. His eyes blurred with overloads of images from being first on one end of the shard, then another. Underground, smell of dirt. Sky, stink of ozone, lightning forming. Upside down in a pool of water, drops just entering his mouth. Remembered thirst, unfelt since he had entered the Instant.

There, eight seconds of connected existence, enough to begin the escape. Nir pushed a few minutes at the rear of his tail out of the solid time, slipping it up and over the edge of the shard into the Instant. The sharp edge of the fragment bit into him, but the Wavebreaker blunted the assault, leaving him whole. Slippery, ice-like, the shard tried to push the few minutes back down, but Nir laid that part of himself across the gap between this fragment and the next one. Was that a tingle he felt, water, drops of fluid change flowing under those few minutes of himself?

Nir pushed farther, dangling bits of himself onto shards, bending and twisting his tail so that no piece of time held more than a few seconds of his life.

Nir learned quickly how much of his weight each nearby shard could hold as he bent and kinked his tail into an awkward curve lying across the broken Instant. By cautious pulling, tugging, and distributing of his massive decade, the War Chief slowly extricated his ten years from the forty-seven-second trap. In ones and twos and then tens and thousands, the images of Nir vanished from the shard that had prisoned him, until with one last push against the solid world, he was gone. The four people, three rabbits, and two cows no longer remembered that he had ever been there.

Finally freed, Nir lay on top of the fragile shell; most of him lay on the gaps between fragments. The gritty, serrated edges of broken moments tried to grate him into a milliard pieces, but the Wavebreaker kept his ten years of life intact. Yet he was not safe. Beneath him the cracked fragments cracked even more; shards a minute long broke into smaller shards of a few seconds each. He could feel parts of his tail starting to sink back into the real world.

Shifting to keep his balance, Nir cracked more of the impossibly solid Instant. He was losing his support. He tried to feel around him, but his extended touch felt only sharpness alternating with mushiness. It was as if he were surrounded by a foam with tiny pieces of glass in it. His only sense could find no clue as to how far he was from the edge of the broken island.

Speak, the War Chief commanded, reactivating his voices.

"Second Voice recording," Second Voice said.

"Third Voice awaiting danger," Third Voice said.

"Fourth Voice analyzing," Fourth Voice said.

Show me the map of the island, Nir said to Second Voice.

An image appeared in his mind, displaying the entire region as a block of ice floating in the ocean.

Focus in on the place where I fell in, Nir commanded.

A region of the map expanded in his thoughts. He saw a coastline, ragged with inlets and harbors.

Nir tried to orient himself to the image, but his sense of direction had been badly disrupted by his tumble into the broken Flux and further hindered by the intricate maneuvers he had undergone in order to extricate himself. Worse, the new cracking had rendered the map inaccurate.

Where am I? he asked Second Voice.

"Unknown. Please supply a source of orientation."

A thought, swift, quick. The War Chief again stretched out his sense of touch, feeling along the cracks instead of through the shards. He could just feel a subtle vibration in the foam; it had to be the damped pulse of change-waves flowing in their natural course from past to future. Nir marked that direction as pastward, Second Voice took in the information and oriented the map accordingly, rotating the picture in Nir's mind.

A marker appeared in his thoughts showing Nir where he was. More ground cracked beneath him; an hour of his life slipped into the Flux. The War Chief yanked it up and slithered off in the direction he hoped was east, toward the edge of the island. He kept his tail on the cracks and moved in gentle pulses, slipping a month here, a week there, sometimes as little as a day of his life eastward.

The vibration in the cracks grew stronger, and the fuzziness that muffled his touch faded. Water, he could feel it not too far away, the tides of time moving in wash and backwash like the beating of a mortal heart. He was close, only a few kilometers, only a few weeks.

Little by little, the War Chief dragged his way back into the ocean of time.

The shallows near the island held no comfort for Nir; the grating feel of the ocean bottom felt too much like the digging sensation of laying his tail across the cracks in time. The War Chief swam eastward swiftly to get away from the island and the shallows. He swam for over a thousand kilometers, swam until the tides of time had deepened the waters so his tail no longer scraped across the bottom.

Floating on the waters over Australia, Nir coiled his tail and searched his length for any injuries had suffered. The War Chief felt up and down the length of his tail. There was some minor damage to his body: a finger was missing for five minutes, two years back. Both ears and one hand had been severed from an hour-long part of him near the upward end of his tail. Somewhere in the middle both legs were gone for nearly a week. Nir was relieved; nothing vital was missing. Once he returned to the Now, the Elder would be able to heal him without amputating any of his tail.

But that would require his return. Did he have enough to dissuade the Ghosts from making the Now into an island? Did he know enough about the cracking to be satisfied? That depended on Fourth Voice.

Explain what happened in the cracked region, Nir commanded Fourth Voice.

"Unable to do so."

Why?

"Recent events are not consistent with established understanding of the Instant."

Elaborate, Nir said.

"The ocean of time cannot be solid, therefore the island cannot exist. But it does. New understanding is necessary."

Nir tapped his tail arrhythmically against the waters, sending out gentle change-ripples. He had no choice. He had to remain. None of his subordinate Ghosts were capable of garnering a new understanding of the Instant, nor were they capable of seeing that such a new awareness was necessary for true fulfillment of the vow. The Ghosts conceived of their vow as a simple matter of battle to protect the People. Only he could accept that gaining a new aware- ness might be necessary to fulfill the duties of the Ghosts. It was because of this accepting that the Elder had made him War Chief, though she herself did not know it.

It was also (though Nir did not know this) why the Elder was not yet seriously considering a replacement for him. Nir's absence troubled her greatly, but she knew how unlikely it was that any of the possible replacements could match his abilities. And she had seen what a War Chief pushed beyond his limits would attempt. She remembered the desperation that had driven Nir's predecessor to his act of folly, an act of folly she had not suspected he was capable of. Only Nir had realized what his War Chief was contem- plating and only he had acted in defiance of orders to save the Great Mother.

Memory and worry about his status in the Now washed away as Nir floated in the waters of change, his mind turning in all di- rections seeking the way he had to travel in order to find the in- formation Fourth Voice needed.

Three hundred years futureward, Adjutant Irithrué and her detach- ment of Quillithé's soldiers swam slowly toward Nir, seeking to take that choice away from him.

Irithrué and her scouts had covered the forty millennia between Quillithé's camp and the broken island without any mishap. Follow- ing orders, Irithrué had avoided all contact with enemy tribes and had focused single-mindedly on her mission of discerning the nature of the black region.

Irithrué and her scouts possessed, as Quillithé did, only the single sense of sight. Though their range of vision was much more limited than the strategist's grand vision, it was adequate for the tasks assigned them. Irithrué could discern events up to a thousand years and two thousand kilometers in any direction, and she could focus her perception down to objects one second long. But despite this sharp vision, she could not see the broken island.

Her vision relied on the tides of change, and there was no change on the island. Thus, as she and her scouts came within a thousand years of their goal and swam pastward toward the darkness, Irithrué, expecting to see into the blackness as she approached, was horrified to find that all she saw was deeper and deeper darkness.

Despair washed over the Adjutant. She had come forty thousand years to see inside the blackness, and she could not do so. If no means came to hand, she would have to return and report her failure to Quillithé. The strategist would not punish her or berate her, but Irithrué knew that Quillithé's opinion of her usefulness would decrease and she would be given less demanding and important work. For Quillithé's soldiers there could be no greater humiliation than to be reduced in the strategist's vision.

But then something happened that gave Irithrué hope—an opportunity to rise in Quillithé's awareness. She saw a warrior emerge from the blackness. He swam slowly out at first, then hastened his strokes as he fled. There could be no other word for it; the warrior was escaping from the land of darkness. But no one was chasing him, nothing else emerged from the ebon shallows in pursuit. Irithrué rejoiced; here was a source of information. Quillithé's orders not to engage in battle would not extend to her pitting her five soldiers against one lone Time Warrior.

"Five Time Warriors, average tail length twelve years, eighty years futureward," Nir's Third Voice warned him.

The War Chief anchored down into the Flux, presuming that the five were simply swimming from one place to another and that they would pass him by. He appeared on a small Pacific island, uninhabited—covered by a two-mile-high green glass arcology—set aside as a playground for the family of earth's emperor—set aside as a prison camp for the natives of the Bantu nation who were blamed for all the world's problems—set aside as a retreat for those who wished to give up the physical immortality mankind had attained and accept the traditional practice of dying.

A series of small rhythmic waves passed over the island, changing the positions of seven palm trees on the beach. "Long tails passing in the Instant above," Third Voice said. Nir waited until it was reasonable to believe that the five were long gone, then he released his hold on solid time.

Quillithé's soldiers had been instructed by the master strategist; they had been carefully taught how to deal with the tactic Nir had employed. They had indeed passed over the place where Nir had hidden, but they had stopped not far from it, forming a ring ten miles and two months across around the place Nir was likely to emerge, and had continued to swish their tails in a rhythm that grew quieter and quieter as if they were still moving, retreating farther away.

The War Chief rose out of the solid world into the waters of the Instant. His pursuers struck just as Third Voice shouted a warning. The three warriors pastward of him lashed sharp-peaked waves in his direction. Nir rolled west and futureward. He coiled his tail and lashed back, blunting the oncoming ripples with his own countercurrent.

But the assault had been a distraction. The remaining pair of Irithrué's warriors swam forward and knotted their tails together into two twisted helices coiled parallel to Nir's body. If he moved in any direction, they would catch him.

"Coiled tails, four meters and six seconds in all directions," Nir's Third Voice said.

"Unable to identify origin of attackers," Second Voice chimed in uselessly.

One of the soldiers sent a rippling picture toward the War Chief, requesting his surrender. But Nir did not know the language of Quillithé's people and in his blindness could not see the shape implicit in the wave that flowed toward him across the Instant. All Nir's extended sense of touch could feel was an erratic, tickling sensation that washed over his tail, doing no damage.

Nir took advantage of the momentary lull in battle to grab the bottom of the ocean and anchor down into the Flux. He was met by the three soldiers who had made the initial assault; they had anchored down while their comrades encircled the Ghost.

Nir's real-world senses returned, and he opened his eyes to see his attackers. What confronted his vision was a motley group of three completely different-looking people; the uniformity and coherence of their Instant appearance was belied by their Flux bodies. One of the three was a gray-skinned woman dressed in metallic yellow armor that rippled across her two-and-a-half-meter height like a snakeskin shining in the sun. The second was a one-meter-tall man, completely hairless with dark blue skin, covered with some sort of synthetic plastic patches where parts of his natural derma had been burned away. The third was a woman, naked as Nir himself; her body was covered with short tufts of red fur sticking out from every joint, and there was a golden glow about her body from which emerged a sharp smell of ozone forming.

Their appearances were all different, but the cobalt blue rods they pointed at Nir had a disturbing uniformity. Nir had seen too many weapons in too many shapes held in too many confident hands to be able to doubt that the blue batons were lethal.

"Attackers fit description of no known tribe," Second Voice said. "Weapons fit no known temporal or atemporal classification."

The red-furred woman opened her mouth and spoke. She said a single word in a language Nir did not know and Second Voice had never heard. Then she said another word, again unknown. She repeated this procedure eight more times before she hit upon the language of the Mayan Stalkers of the Seventh World, a tribe the Ghosts had once defeated. The word was simply this: "Surrender."

The War Chief was startled at the request. Traditionally, the tribes of the Instant neither asked for nor gave an opportunity to surrender. Battle was carried through until death, capture, or escape. Whoever these strange warriors were, they belonged to no group that Nir was familiar with. He weighed the odds of battle against the value to the People of his life and knowledge.

Nir covered his eyes and bowed his head in surrender.

Irithrué did not know how to interpret the War Chief's gesture. But she concluded that, as he was making no hostile moves, he had assented. "Your surrender is accepted," Irithrué said in the same language she had used before.

Nir uncovered his eyes and looked with calm boldness into the face of his captor.

Irithrué gestured upward with the palm of her hand toward the one-meter-tall soldier, who vanished into the Instant. Then she did the same to Nir, who interpreted the gesture correctly and released his grip on solid time to return to the ocean. Irithrué and the other soldier swiftly followed. Her troops were arrayed in a pentagon around Nir, two futureward of him and three pastward; their tails were interlaced and coiled together, forming a five-sided net around the War Chief. It was not a perfect prison since he had several directions in which he could move out of the pentagon, but its purpose was clear, and Nir understood that if he tried to leave they would reshape their pattern and attack him. With a tap of his tail Nir acquiesced and let himself be herded futureward.

As they swam away from the middle Instant toward the deeps, Nir felt his captors and endeavored to discern what they were doing. But their behavior only confused him, and of all mental states Nir most disliked confusion; it implied that things were going on that his agile mind could not swiftly adapt to. The first source of his bewilderment was the lack of an obvious language on the part of his captors. No taps or pulsed ripples passed between them. But after a few millennia of travel he noticed that occasionally one of them would coil up one or two months of his life and emit a complex wave front, too slow moving and blunt to be combat useful, and the others would react to it. Nir could not imagine how such a premeditated, slow-to-generate process could be useful for speech in the Instant where combat demanded swift orders, but he had to conclude that it was just that; this cumbersome form was somehow a language.

But how was it perceived? His extended touch could not make sense of the wash of waves, here deep, there shallow, here intricate, there plain.

"Remember these wave patterns," Nir ordered his Second Voice.

He was also perplexed at their behavior toward him. They had not sought to disarm him; he still wore his Wavebreaker and his tail spike. Nor had they cut off pieces of his tail to reduce his danger to them—many tribes who took prisoners carved them up into month-long segments, the unconscious pieces were discarded, flotsam of war. The single month that happened to hold the prisoner's mind was then made captive. A one-month Time Warrior was too small to do injury to the longer-tailed foes, but had enough life span remaining to retain all their useful memories. Indeed, having accepted his surrender, Nir's captors showed little apparent concern for any danger he might pose to them.

Nor did they seek to question him. This troubled Nir, it forced him to conclude that he was being taken to someone who would interrogate him. This puzzled him. Had his Ghosts captured someone he would have expected them to gain at least some cursory information about the captive before bringing one back to him for more formal inquiries. The War Chief's mind changed and he realized that whoever he was being taken to must inspire such great confidence in his or her subordinates as to make such preliminary work unnecessary. He wondered what kind of chieftain could create such a sense of reliance in these soldiers. And whether that reliance could be used against that chieftain.

Adjutant Irithrué's confidence came from the knowledge that as they swam futureward, they were under the broad, clear gaze of Quillithé. Though still thirty-five thousand years pastward of the army, Irithrué knew that they were being watched and that the strategist would formulate a plan and implement countermeasures should anything untoward happen, such as the prisoner escaping. Irithrué was confident that as long as she followed Quillithé's orders, everything would work out as the strategist desired.

Irithrué's confidence extended so far that she had no curiosity about Nir. Any questions about the warrior's origin and his ability to survive in the darklands would be answered once he was brought into the strategist's presence.

After captive and captors had swum ten thousand years futureward from the broken island, Nir began to wonder how far the camp of this tribe was. Most of the tribes did not send out scouting parties for long distances; few let any of their members venture more than a single millennium from the main body of warriors. His tribe was an exception, but they had a place to defend, which no other tribe had.

Nir began to wonder if somewhere far futureward there was a place, a definable locale like the Now. But no, that seemed quite impossible.

Indeed, as he swam further futureward and felt the deepening tides of time, felt the interacting change-waves creating deep currents, Nir became surer that there could be no place out there, nothing like the Now. His extended touch could barely feel the ocean bottom below him, and he knew that soon all he would be able to feel would be water and change in every direction.

Nir's confidence solidified as he lost contact with solid time. No, there could not be a place to defend, not if the solid side of time were subject to this much change. No, nothing to keep a tribe here, nothing to protect. There had to be another explanation of the distance these warriors had traveled from their tribe.

Nir turned to his Voices for suggestions. Second Voice had no useful information on the remembered wave patterns, nor could it identify anything about the tribe. Third Voice was displeased at their tactical position, and its unhappiness was compounded by the observation, "Warriors show best-known adaption to Instant."

Elaborate, Nir said. Third Voice switched to its verbose non-combatant mode.

"They swim with greater facility and hesitate less when dangerous change-waves are coming. Their Instant reflexes are also swifter. They adapt quickly to any changes in our posture. And . . ."

Nir was startled. Third Voice rarely hesitated.

And, Nir prompted.

"There is evidence that their sensing range is much greater than ours."

What evidence?

"No tribe has impinged on our sense of touch since we were captured. Therefore, hypothesis offered: They are avoiding any contact with other tribes, and doing so with greater range of perception than ours."

That is likely, Nir said. Presume that they have greater sensory range when making tactical analysis. Cease elaboration.

Fourth Voice? Nir queried, faintly disturbed at the silence of his primary guide.

"Estimate twenty-five to thirty-five thousand years until we reach their native waters."

Native waters? Nir said.

"Adaptation requires greater depth to the sea of time."

A long journey, Nir thought. One hundred thousand years from the Now. A pang of loneliness struck the War Chief, of separation from the calm, placid shallows of his native time. He had swum so far, and had so much further to go. It came to him quite suddenly that he had no real conception of that distance. He had traveled in easy strokes, his sense of touch giving him an awareness of decades around him, and he had accepted that awareness and believed that it showed him the truth of the Instant. But what were his decades of perception to the great stretch of time he was crossing?

A shiver of panic ran up and down Nir's ten years of life. Rare, the feeling of fear, to one who had faced and contemplated death so often. But it was not death he feared, it was helplessness in the vast ocean of time. Too much space, too great a distance from any help. He had come into the deeps from an awareness of his duty, but that duty did not encompass being captured. Nir's thinking changed, a sudden flash from old thought to new; no remnant remained of his passive acceptance. No longer would he accept the superiority of his captors, in their numbers or in their perceptive or combative capacities. He was War Chief of the Ghosts; it was his duty to escape and he would do his duty.

His mind transformed, Nir stretched out his sense of touch, focusing his attention on everything around him, in order to find any useful matter from which he might create the moment of his release.

Opportunity came when he and his warders reached the true deeps of time, eighty thousand years futureward from the Now, a mere twenty millennia pastward from Quillithé's camp, well within the strategist's close-in vision.

The five warders relaxed their grip, spreading out, giving the War Chief a little more room in which to swim. Nir could not understand why this was happening; his best guess was that some enemy tribe was nearby. His limited touch could not sense what they could see, that scattered around them for a thousand years were troops of Quillithé's army. The scout force had met up with the net the strategist had laid across the upper reaches of time.

Across a gulf of a hundred years, Irithrué exchanged pictures with the commander of the force of fifty scattered warriors.

Image from Irithrué: Blue limning of the fifty. A request to know the reason they were there.

Image from the commander: Net around two long-tailed warriors and a Drum. Answer: They had been sent to capture these three.

Image from Irithrué: Blue limning around the warriors and the Drum and the net. What success had they had in securing the proposed captives?

Image from the commander: Bright gold limning around the Drum, silver limning around the warrior contained in a pentagon, tinge of green to indicate irony. Black limning around the other fleeing. We captured the Drum, you captured one of the long-tailed, the other has escaped.

The pentagon stretched itself out. Room to maneuver, just a little, Nir thought, that is all I need. The War Chief began to rhythmically dip parts of his tail deep into the water, as if adopting a longer swimming stroke to deal with the complex currents washing below him.

The strokes grew longer, a week of his life dipping down, angry cross currents pushing him east and west, trying to tear apart his body; a month, riptides below him, harsh as the cutting waves of battle, his Wavebreaker the only source of safety; six months, deep heaving tides like world-changing waves, trying to pull him to pieces, there: the bottom. Nir grabbed hold of the earth and anchored into solid time, his body kept whole by the blunting defense of his shield.

Irithrué was stunned by the loss. Did not the man know how dangerous these waters were? No one of Quillithé's people would anchor into the Flux without special protective gear. He must have been destroyed. No, there was no sign of fragments. He had survived. The prisoner was hiding in the Flux and Irithrué could not chase him.

Image from Irithrué to one of the scouts: Swimming into the

camp to receive orders. Irithrué knew that Quillithé would have already seen what had happened to the captive.

The scout darted off, coiling and uncoiling his tail as he skimmed across the surface of the deeps, making his way toward the camp twenty millennia futureward.

Quillithé herself was fascinated by what had happened. Two simple possibilities lay before her: either the man had been fortunate enough to be wearing the correct protection, and so had survived the dive, or he knew the nature of the deeps and was prepared. Or, a third possibility tingled up, he had taken advantage of the deeps, not knowing their nature but improvising on the spot. That fit with what she had already seen the War Chief do.

Quillithé decided to dispatch one of her soldiers carrying a protective Shimmering Dive Helix. The soldier would meet Irithrué's scout halfway and give over the device so that Irithrué would be able to retrieve the prisoner. No, wait—a subtly better variation, yes, that was most likely to appeal to the Ghost who had shown such a talent for improvisation.

Quillithé rippled out a picture to the soldier and made sure he understood its subtleties before sending him off.

Too fast, the world was altering too fast for Nir to take it in. Apparent deci-second by apparent deci-second everything changed completely. Before his new-opened eyes could focus on a thing it would be gone, replaced by something else. Ground vanished . . . centuries-old trees appeared . . . the scent of the air was perfumed with lilacs . . . toxic with cyanide . . . stinging from methane . . . drunken with new-crushed grapes. Nir reeled under the rapidity of the change.

It was like being imprisoned in the stone, things changing so fast. But here, he was the fixed thing and the world was twisting around him.

Second Voice screamed, "Overload, incapable of processing. Sensory overload, incapable of processing."

Cease recording! Nir shouted to the noise in his mind.

"Senses cannot compensate," Third Voice said. "Cannot warn against oncoming danger."

"Perception of transformation too swift," Fourth Voice said. "Perceived passage cannot accord with actual change."

Nir's mind altered again and again, seeking for a thing to concentrate on, a seed from which it could grow an understanding of the swiftly flying world around it. The only unchanged thing—that was it. Words formed in Nir's mind and he spoke them aloud in the language of the Ghosts. One hundred thousand years after the Great Mother's birth, Nir spoke these words in the first tongue: "I am standing."

He felt his own body, remembered his limbs, recalled his form, concentrated on the truth of his words.

"I am standing."

"I am standing."

The blur of change became just that: a blur around him, a fog of twinkling colors and confused impressions. The War Chief no longer tried to make sense of it all; he simply refused to let it affect him.

In the waters above Nir's immovable stance. Quillithé's messenger slipped the protective Helix around Irithrué's tail, dimming the Adjutant's sight. No longer could she see for a thousand years; now a mere fifty years of time were open to her vision. But that was a small price to pay for the ability to survive passing down through the tides of the deep.

Image from Irithrué: Two people, one threatening the other with a weapon. The threatening gesture was limned in blue. Was she to capture the Ghost?

Image from the messenger: Two time-bound people standing, mouths open, hands stretched out. Gold limning around their open mouths. Quillithé's order, repeated several times, was that Irithrué was to parlay with the Ghost.

Image from Irithrué: Two time-bound people mouths open, hands stretched out. Scene limned in questioning blue. Irithrué needed clarification in the concept of a parlay. Such a thing had never been done in the Instant.

Image from the messenger: Two Adjutants discussing, pictures passing back and forth. To parlay is to discuss as equals.

Image from Irithrué: Adjutants limned with black and gold with drops of red indicating confusion and a slight hint of horror. How could Quillithé demand that she treat any out of the army as an equal?

Image from the messenger: Quillithé commanding. The order had been given.

Image from Irithrué: Irithrué coiling up before Quillithé. The order was accepted.

Another image from Irithrué: Two time-bound people mouths open, hands outstretched. Mouths limned in blue. What was she to parlay for?

Image: Quillithé and Ghost, rippling pictures and forth. To have the Ghost come to the camp and speak with the strategist.

Image: Irithrué coiling up before Quillithé.

The Adjutant dove down through the savage tides, watching as the Helix deflected the waves so that they bounced off her body. Down through the currents until she reached the bottom, grasped it, and appeared.

"Atemporal incursion, fifty meters south," Nir's Third Voice warned him.

"I am standing," Nir said, focusing on his feet as he stood on the side of a mountain. Irithrué stepped toward him, ignoring the wild changes around her.

Step: The mountain became a forest preserve, the last home of a thousand types of deciduous trees; all the rest had been frozen two ice ages ago.

Step: A warren of underground caves in which there lived the remaining two hundred survivors of a weapon that had set off solar flares and turned the sun into a neutron star; the earth had only a few years to live.

Step: A pile of nanotech goo.

Step: a strip-mined slag heap.

Step: Irithrué and Nir stood in the center of a giant hive in which genetically altered bees made a perfect honey that contained all nutrients that a human body needed to survive; these bees and those in a billion other hives provided all the food that was eaten on earth.

Nir opened his eyes to stare at this second unchanging thing in the chaos of alteration. The War Chief recognized the tall, red-tufted woman he had surrendered to before. He was surprised that she was alone, and had not even drawn her weapon.

Nir realized that he could concentrate solely on this single being and gain the same focus as he had by paying lone attention to his standing.

"Speak," Irithrué said in the language she had used to communicate before.

"Speak?" Nir said, unsure if he had heard correctly over the din of change. "Speak about what?"

"Speak," the Adjutant said again. She pointed up toward the sky.

Every Time Warrior knew what up meant.

"Speak about the Instant?" Nir asked.

The woman pointed up again. "Speak, there."

Nir reached for one of the grenades on his bandolier. "Not surrender."

"Not surrender," Irithrué said. "Speak to commander. Parlay."

Nir was stunned at the word. Parlay was a concept never used in the Instant. Every tribe knew that every other tribe was its enemy. There could be no trustworthy interchange, no bargains could be struck. No one talked to anyone outside of their own tribe except in the context of threat and interrogation. But this strange warrior was offering a parlay.

That was not the same as being a captive. Alone and far from home he was, but if this warrior's leader meant to speak on even terms then Nir could do so. But why should he believe her? For in truth he did believe the offer; yet he distrusted his belief.

And then Nir's thinking changed, removing the distrust. His mind sparked into awareness and he realized quite clearly why he believed: because there was only one warrior here instead of a whole troop, and because he had first been captured outside the broken island. The War Chief realized that Irithrué and those accompanying her had been scouts. They had not been sent to capture Nir but to find out about the breaking. And Nir knew something about it. The woman's commander, whoever that might be, must want to know and must want to be able to trust the knowledge gained. Information taken in torture was always risky to rely upon. For that commander to trust the knowledge, Nir had to trust the commander.

"Parlay," Nir said, pointing to the sky. The two of them vanished into the Instant. Irithrué began to swim futureward and Nir followed, crossing the millennia in easy strokes. None of Quillithé's soldiers came within a thousand years of the two swimmers, so it seemed to Nir as if he and Irithrué were quite alone.

"Twenty warriors, one century futureward," Third Voice said when they reached a point one hundred years pastward from Quillithé's camp. A few strokes more.

"Correction, twenty-five warriors."

Third Voice kept up a running total, continually augmenting the number as they swam closer. Nir was amazed. No tribe was this large. Nir knew how many warriors he could keep together in a battle before their waves interfered with each other. This camp, this army, was impossible.

"Camp appears to be organized in seven rings of clustered warriors, total radius two hundred years," Second Voice said.

"Confirmed," said Third Voice as Nir and Irithrué swam through the outermost ring. "Estimate two hundred fifty to three hundred fifty warriors total. Tail lengths average twelve years. Exceptions in the center of the camp."

"What exceptions?" Nir said.

"Seven warriors with average lengths of three months, and one a century long."

A century? Confirm that! Nir commanded.

"Confirmed. One warrior one hundred years in extent."

"A warrior that long should not be able to move in the Instant," Fourth Voice said.

That warrior must be the commander, Nir thought. But what use is a leader who cannot enter battle?

Irithrué led the War Chief through the six inner rings into the presence of Quillithé and her seven fathers.

Image from Irithrué: Irithrué coiling herself up before the strategist. Orders carried out.

Image from Quillithé: Quillithé and Nir floating alone. Leave us.

Irithrué swam out of the inner ring to resume her accustomed place among the scouts. Quillithé's seven fathers darted away from the presence of the lone enemy in the center of their camp. Fearful images passed back and forth between them as they tried to understand what their unfathomable but infallible daughter was doing.

Quillithé and Nir faced each other across a gap of six months and settled down to parlay on the waters of the deep, seeking to bridge the span of one hundred millennia that separated them.

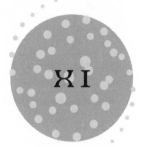

XI

Nir was overwhelmed by the grip of separation. So far from his home, Nir faced a being unlike any he had ever confronted, unlike any he had ever heard of. He had no conception of what this being perceived, how it thought, or what the nature of its language was. But he knew one thing. He knew that it wanted to have all he knew about the broken Island.

Quillithé took into account a minor vision of separation. Quillithé faced an ordinary ten-year-tailed Time Warrior, limited in its perceptions. She speculated that it possessed only a single sense, probably touch or taste. Its language, whatever it was, would be simplistic and almost impossible for the century-long being to use. There was only one thing that was strange about this otherwise common being. It had shown a gift for improvisation, a tactical awareness unmatched by any Quillithé had ever fought. It was that gift Quillithé wanted to explore, and once she had taken in that broad understanding of the being's mind, then and only then would she seek to learn the nature of the dark lands.

The feeling and the sight of silence filled their mutual separation. Nir waited for an inspiration to strike and transform his mind, giving him a means of opening speech. Quillithé floated, contemplating the multifarious different options available, seeking the best gate of entry into the Ghost's thoughts.

What did they share, what did they have in common, these two beings from opposite ends of time? The answer came to both of them; they shared the common experience of all the dwellers in the Instant from the shallows to the deeps, the common inheritance of the timeless: War.

Nir began the colloquy. He arched a few seconds of his tail and flipped out a very small wave-spike a few seconds wide, too tiny to injure anyone in the Instant. Then he tapped out the Ghost words, "Cutting wave."

Quillithé quickly grasped that the first emission had been a demonstration and the second was a word. But the tapping waves were not clear to her. Still, she tried to respond. She crafted an image, simple in her language, lacking nuance and color, of two groups of warriors facing each other across a calm sea. "Prelude to battle."

The image washed over Nir, tingling in various places along his length, but the picture was not comprehensible to his sense of touch.

Analyze that wave, Nir commanded Second Voice.

"Two clusters of touch impulses separated by an unfelt space."

Two clusters? A language not of touch or sound, then. He wondered if it could be visual. No tribe in the Instant that he knew of used vision for communication. That had been one of the facts Second Voice had taught the Ghosts. A fact without any given cause but with a hint of fear to it. Nir's mind changed and he realized that this immense creature was responsible for this fact. Something about the use of vision as speech would make a tribe more vulnerable to her and her army than the other tribes. Those that had used such a means of communication must have abandoned vision after she came along. Sight's language had been ceded to this creature.

Nir opened the eyes of his mind as he rarely did in the Instant and he saw as well as felt his own thoughts.

Assume the wave is a picture, he said. Show it me.

Second Voice reformed the sensory impressions, shifting them from tactile to visual. Nir saw two groups of vague objects separated from each other by empty space. It reminded him of the battle games he and his friends had played with stones when he was a child living time-bound in the Now, hoping one day to be a Ghost. Stones for soldiers, an open patch of grass for a board, lines laid down with sticks, games of war.

As a game, Nir saw it, but a game was not what Quillithé had intended it to be seen. To her the images were the reality, not an abstraction of the reality. In the vast caverns of her mind there was no need for the shortcut of abstraction. An image of a tribe showed the tribe itself in all its nuances with all the latent possibilities of its actions.

Nir tapped back the word "battle."

Quillithé studied the tiny motions of Nir's tail and the small ripples that emerged. Without touch or hearing she could not feel the rhythm of the words, could not sense the subtle variations using long or short strokes, quick or slow taps that made the language of the Ghosts so useful in combat, where complex variations in orders could be given with only a minute change in the pulse of the tapping tail.

The strategist tried to duplicate Nir's tap, but she could not manage the control. A slew of words echoed out, interfering with each other.

"Battle, war, stratagem, plan, schemes," rippled from one part of her.

"Battle, killing, slaughter, spree of vengeance," rippled from another.

"Battle, raid, enslavement, theft."

"Battle, melee, riot, confusion, chaos."

And on and on through a hundred chains of related concepts, a web of interflowing meanings, nuances shading one into another like the subtle variations of a spectrum.

Second Voice dutifully recorded all the versions that came out of Quillithé like the ripples of a pond after a stone has been dropped in. Nir reviewed the variations and determined that if he wanted to communicate with her he would have to use only the centers of words, the harsh core taps that gave basic meaning; he had to cut off all the grammar of the Ghosts when speaking to Quillithé. It would make his language sound harsh and brutal but he would be able to communicate at least a little. That satisfied him as a beginning point for their speech.

Tap by tap Nir gave Quillithé a basic vocabulary of the Ghost language, so that she could speak of war and death, defense and attack. Nir leaned back on his tail, expecting converse to begin in earnest.

Quillithé, however, was not satisfied with this crude tapping speech. She wanted to explore Nir's mind, and to do that she needed for him to be able to speak at least some form of her language. He had found a way to see that she had presented battle, now she had to show him how to make the images.

"Battle," she tapped again, and she waited.

Nir quickly realized what she wanted.

Make a map of two groups of stones on a grass field, Nir said to Second Voice. Program motivators to tap out moving waves to represent the stones in their arrangement.

Second Voice jerked a few hours of Nir's tail into an arrhythmic bumping, which it hypothesized would create the flowing image Nir had commanded.

Image: Two groups of unmoving, featureless objects floating on a flat space.

Quillithé was startled. How could such a lifeless picture represent battle to the Ghost?

Quillithé spoke again.

Image: One group of warriors spreads itself out into a crescent shape in order to focus assaulting waves on the other group.

"Deployment," Nir tapped, correctly interpreting the image.

"Deployment, arrangement, allotment, fortune, luck," Quillithé responded.

Nir believed that Quillithé was making the first move in the war game. He regarded the situation and chose his own deployment, then he ordered Second Voice to send his response to Quillithé in the form of a picture.

Image from Nir: The other group of stones lined themselves up into a phalanx, point toward the focus of the crescent; thus the assaulting waves would not be able to strike the vulnerable lengths of the defenders.

And in this manner of image and counterimage the battle/language lesson/game continued.

Words were exchanged across the interchange of battle, a simple even conflict, two equal tribes, equally armed, equally capable, Nir and Quillithé studied each other over the most basic test of military command. Quillithé deployed her forces according to a strategy that saw the whole web of interlocking possibilities; she conceived the orders she would give to her actual soldiers and had her image warriors behave accordingly, battling with their leader absent.

Nir designated one of his pieces in his own mind as representing himself. From that piece all orders flowed. Swift and sure, he changed the operations and orders of his stone water warriors a hundred times over the course of the game.

Each of them began with some appreciation for their opponent's capacities, but as the game progressed, that appreciation grew into fear. Nir quickly realized that Quillithé was following a devised plan. The War Chief had always been contemptuous of those who believed battles could be fought solely from the backward position of the strategist, but that contempt did not apply here. Quillithé did not give orders like a disinterested commander floating back in a disconnected headquarters. It was clear that she saw all, including the capacities of her warriors, and gave commands that allowed them enough use of their own minds so that a tactician was not needed.

Quillithé on her part had always regarded improvisation as the duty of minor commanders, not the work of true leaders, but in Nir she saw how it could hold the keys of life and death in battle. The War Chief of the Ghosts, who at first seemed to regard his pieces as interchangeable stones, showed in the course of play that he was aware of them as individuals. But he did not keep that always in mind. He would move half a dozen stones in a concerted attack, then have them split up and each take on characteristics of their own. One stone would demonstrate a capacity for defensive wave making, another would become a skilled ambusher, diving down into the Flux and shooting back into the Instant without warning.

He makes the invisible visible when he needs to, Quillithé thought.

She sees all, missing nothing, Nir thought.

And both began to dread the day they would be engaged in combat with each other, for all tribes were enemies in the Flux and before the war could end all battles would have to be fought.

Quillithé began to consider the possibility of killing Nir then and there. The War Chief was alone and friendless in her camp; surely he was at his most vulnerable. Methods of killing the War Chief appeared in the corridors of Quillithé's mind. But along with those ideas came a worry that grew until it occupied a full quarter of her thoughts, then half, then all. Nir had willingly entered the circles of her army. He must have some confidence that he would be able to leave. Quillithé could not predict what lay invisible in Nir's mind waiting to stir up. Also there was the matter of the blackness that Nir had been inside. Quillithé still needed to know about it. No, it was not worth the risk to her army and herself. The War Chief would live.

Nir, for his part, had considered the value of losing his life for the benefits of slaying the strategist. It was tempting, and if it had not been for the broken island and the dangers it posed for the Now, he would have done so. But she, who could clearly see so far, who had so great an army at her command, she must know about the broken island. Nir needed to get what information she had and bring it back to the Ghosts. The strategist would live.

The battle of stones and images ended in a draw, each side

retreating with half their forces decimated. The languages of battle had been passed back and forth between Nir and Quillithé. Both their minds now turned to the subject at hand.

Quillithé looked out on the half of time's ocean that was within her vision. Pastward she looked, through the deeps of time to the center where the tribes fought one upon the other, tens, twenties, and thirties of warriors, battling in a thousand battles, filling the world with change. She formed this image in her mind, then added to it what she had learned from captured prisoners of the regions beyond her vision. The shallower areas of the center, then the even shallower parts where tribes fought more for slaves than for weapons, shallower still to the Diaspora, and finally to the mythic region of the Now, so shallow that the waters stood nearly still and the bottom of the ocean lay just beneath the tails of the Ghosts.

She rippled out this complex map and let it wash over the War Chief. Second Voice chewed this map up and swallowed it easily. It had learned to comprehend Quillithé's mapmaking even if it still had great difficulty with her other images.

"She has sent a map of the Instant," Second Voice said.

"The Instant," Nir tapped.

Quillithé sent another image, the same map but with the dark region marked by blackness. This she limned in the blue of questioning. But Second Voice could not feel the colors, only the map. Nir did not know a question was being asked.

Nir waited. Quillithé tried again. This time she sent an image of a black area with Nir emerging from it. But Second Voice could only see blackness and someone emerging, for it had no concept of what Nir looked like in the Instant.

"Out of emptiness?" Nir tapped.

"Emptiness, void, nothing, lack, blindness, shadow, foolishness, ignorance," Quillithé replied with echoing taps.

"Who out of emptiness?" Nir tapped, braving the asking of a question, a grammatic construction he had not attempted before.

Quillithé took in the taps. She could see that there was some complexity to the ripples that she had not seen before. She let the words enter her mind and diffused them through the rooms, corridors, and caverns of her thoughts, seeking to know what this complexity was. Possibilities rose up and faded away until one stood out as most likely. The Ghost must be asking a question about that which had emerged from the darkness.

Quillithé washed a single wave over the whole of Nir's ten years and he understood that it was he who had come from emptiness. But which emptiness? The Now?

Send back the map of the Instant, make the Now larger, Nir ordered Second Voice.

Image: The Instant, but the shallows occupied a full third of the space. Quillithé drew in the impossible map and tried to interpret it. Surely the Ghost was not claiming that his warriors had conquered the pastmost thirty millennia of the Instant. No. Could it be a statement of ambition? No, that did not fit the context. It was a question. Blind, he had used size to indicate emphasis.

Image: The Instant, the dark region made larger to fill a third of the ocean.

"The Broken Island," Nir tapped, realizing what she was talking about.

"Broken, shattered, cracked, dispirited, saddened, crazed, bewildered. Island, isolate, lonely one, wanderer, fool, madman."

"Unchanging," Nir said, trying to elaborate the nature of the island.

Image from Quillithé: The Now, slow change, gentle waters, shallowness.

"No," Nir said. "Incapable of changed."

Image from Quillithé: Confused welter of waters crashing together, the image in Quillithé's language that expressed incomprehension.

Nir built an image and sent it: Water washing over stone, breaking waves, not affecting the stone.

"Unchangeable," he said.

"Unchangeable, fixed, immobile, rooted, buried, dead."

The echoing words sent a shudder through the War Chief's

body. He remembered the feeling of being buried alive in the cracking, and again recalled Nir the child's wondering at the Great
Mother's bones.

"Can you not see the cracking?" Nir said.

"No," Quillithé tapped, and the word carried no nuances, a
simple sharp denial.

Image from Quillithé: The map Second Voice had sent, the
inside of the cracking made large.

Nir understood that this was a command, not a question. Quillithé wanted him to tell her what was inside the dark veil over her
vision that kept that part of the Instant from the contemplations of
her mind.

Nir rocked back on his tail, and considered what he wanted to
say. He extended his touch to feel along the twists and turns of
Quillithé's century-long tail, and imagined her rolling into the broken lands, cracking the fragile bottom Instant as she plunged
through into the real world, sliced into trillions of one-second
pieces.

The War Chief of the Ghosts was momentarily tempted to lie
about the broken lands in hopes of luring this dangerous being to
her destruction.

Nir swam a few hours back from Quillithé's body and considered again. Quillithé and her army were obviously a potential threat
to the People. But she had not come to the Now and conquered
them. Indeed, from the way she had played the wargame, Nir had
concluded that she never left this spot, only sending her soldiers
to the nearby regions for battles.

She cannot move, correct? Nir queried Fourth Voice.

"Not without assistance," Fourth Voice answered. "A minimum
of forty ten-year-long warriors would have to roll her through the
waters."

Why does she stay here? Nir said.

"She moves too little to compensate for normal dangerous
waves," Fourth Voice said. "The shallower waters would slowly
erode her body."

That settled the matter. Quillithé was a potential but unlikely danger. The broken island was a real and present one. Nir decided to tell her the truth about his experiences inside the cracking.

Second Voice crafted an image, open space, cracked edges, coiled tail trapped inside, time-bound people staring.

Image: Waters crashing in confusion.

Nir tried again. Image: Nir sliding across ice, cracking, falling through.

"I fell into the Flux," Nir said.

Image: Waters crashing in confusion.

Nir tried again. Image: Open space, grasses, trees, plants animals.

Image: Waters crashing in confusion.

Then Nir realized that Quillithé could not understand what he was saying about the Flux. He tried the words in his own language.

"Tree."

"Tree, plant, shrub, fractal growth structure, overarching canopy, implication of shelter, tent, haven, refuge, house."

He tried again. "Cow."

"Cow, ox, animal, beast, carnivore, tiger, lion, pride, rage, hatred."

Nir was bewildered at the rambling changes in Quillithé's responses. It was as if Quillithé had no experience of time-bound life and so had no control over what she understood in his words. But that was impossible. Every Time Warrior came out of the Flux. How could she not know? Lay it aside. Explore that question later. What mattered now was to make her understand what had happened to him. Perhaps another source could be found from which she could draw knowledge.

Image from Nir: Tiny being, vibrating quickly, emerging from darkness.

"A Drum came from the emptiness," Nir tapped, clarifying the image he had sent.

An image washed out of Quillithé, but it did not flow toward

Nir. Instead it crossed two circles of her soldiers and reached those who had been given the duty of guarding Kookatchi.

Image from Quillithé: Four soldiers escorting the Drum into Quillithé's presence.

XII

Kookatchi had been learning the ways of the camp and refining his knowledge of their image speech. The beauty of the army's organization and the grace by which the soldiers followed Quillithé's commands had captured his attention to the extent that, rather than seeing himself as a prisoner, the Drum conceived that he was in the slow process of stealing all the beauty around him.

So when Quillithé sent for him, he came eagerly, and his guards had little to do save swim beside him, more an escort of honor than a solemn procession of imprisoners and prisoner.

Kookatchi swam into the center of the camp and stared again at the great, grand monster who had captured him. He rejoiced once more in the intricacies of her vastness, in the length of her life where he himself could be lost fifty million times over. So coiled, so complex, such grace. Then he noticed that there was another in her presence, one who was not of this army.

The Drum's consciousness recycled. He had been caught in a maze and this ten-year-long warrior had something to do with that labyrinth.

Recycled. A maze suddenly appearing in a shifting of the Instant. This man had made himself into a prison for the Drum.

Recycled. Interrogation about the broken island. Questions and response in the tapping language of the Ghosts.

Recycled. Memory gave way to questions. What was the War Chief of the Ghosts doing at the other end of inhabited time conversing with the doomsday bringer? And what did they want with him?

Kookatchi tapped a question to Nir in the language of the Ghosts. "Are you a prisoner of the Monster of the deep?"

"Monster of the deep?"

Kookatchi flicked a tiny wave toward Quillithé. "She is known and feared throughout the Instant," the Drum said to the War Chief. "Monster of the deep, Lady of the only army, Bringer of doomsday, Ender of all histories."

"I had never heard of her," Nir said.

"Only your tribe could possibly be ignorant of her," Kookatchi said. The Drum's consciousness recycled and all the legends of terror he had overheard from the other tribes washed into his mind. Each legend brought another of Quillithé's titles, Slayer of thousands, Hunter of tribes, the great Leviathan who floated in the depths of the ocean. The litany of those tribes she had destroyed flowed through his thoughts in a thousand different languages, sung across the ocean of time. Monster of the deep. Arbitrary Judge of tribes. Bringer of random destruction. Death to the eternal.

"She is wild and unknowable," Kookatchi said. "No one can comprehend her motives or her desires. She strikes without warning and without cause."

"Without warning, I believe," Nir said. "Without cause, no. I have faced her in mock battle. She is too good a strategist to act without cause."

"Believe what you like," the Drum said, "but we are both in terrible danger."

Quillithé had patiently waited through the interchange. She had only caught a few of the words that passed so swiftly between the War Chief and the Drum, just enough to know that Kookatchi was suddenly frightened of her in a way he had not been since she had first recaptured him.

Image sent to Nir: Small figure emerging from darkness.

"Yes," Nir said. "This is the Drum."

Quillithé realized that Nir had interpreted her statement as a question. He did not know that she had seen Kookatchi come from the invisible lands.

Image to Kookatchi: Nir and Quillithé exchanging words, waters breaking together in confusion.

"What did she say?" Nir asked.

"She says the two of you are trying to talk and having difficulty," Kookatchi said.

"That is true," Nir said.

"I do not understand," the Drum said. "Surely you are also her prisoner?"

"I do not think so," Nir said. "She invited me to parlay."

The Drum's consciousness recycled. He was floating in the center of Quillithé's camp. The rippling tides of the deep ocean flowed under him, washing his small form back and forth across a few minutes. The noise of the army came to him, three hundred soldiers, training, talking, laughing at the rough humor beloved of those whose life is war, and singing songs of their battles, songs sung in pictures loud with color, bright with triumph.

Two beings who did not belong together were speaking to him in two completely unlike languages, the War Chief of the Ghosts and the strategist of the deep-ocean army.

One word filled the Drum's mind, a word he had never before heard spoken in the Instant: parlay.

"What is this parlay about?" he tapped to Nir.

Image from Kookatchi to Quillithé: Nir and Quillithé speaking. Blue light limned the space between them.

"The broken island," Nir said.

Image from Quillithé to Kookatchi: Region of blackness, Kookatchi emerging from it then Nir emerging from it.

"Why do you care?" Kookatchi asked Nir.

Image from Kookatchi to Quillithé: Region of darkness limned in gold and blue, Quillithé limned in gold and blue. The image questioned why Quillithé concerned herself with this distant thing.

"It threatens the Now," Nir said.

Image from Quillithé to Kookatchi: Darkness sweeping across the Instant covering the deeps.

Kookatchi's consciousness recycled. He was in the middle of a discussion with two other beings who for their own reasons had an interest in the broken island, but were having trouble communicating. The Drum immediately concluded what his role in the situation was.

"You need a translator," he said to Nir.

Image from Kookatchi to Quillithé: Nir speaking to Kookatchi in taps, Kookatchi speaking to Quillithé in image, absence of waters of confusion.

A translator. Nir's mind shifted abruptly under the weight of the idea. The Drum clearly knew both languages and was having no trouble carrying on two conversations at once. But to give him such a role, to trust someone not of the People to speak truth. To convey honestly what was said. To trust this thief? How could Nir do that?

Mediation. Quillithé rolled the implications of that concept through the corridors of her mind. All her existence she had trusted her own sight, her own thoughts, and her appraisals of her soldiers' skills. Nothing else. Using the Drum like this she would have to accept his view of things, take into account that what she was seeing had been filtered through another mind. But was she not already doing that? Was she not using Nir's and Kookatchi's experiences of the darkness to help her sight penetrate where it could not directly go? Yes, she could use the Drum. That the words would be mediated was just another factor she had to take into account when considering the matter of the blackness.

Image from Quillithé to Kookatchi: Quillithé speaking to Kookatchi, Kookatchi speaking to Nir. Lessening of the waters of confusion, subtle yellow shadows around the confusion, threat implied if Kookatchi made the confusion greater.

"She has agreed to my translation," Kookatchi tapped.

"Is this so?" Nir asked directly.

"Yes," Quillithé tapped.

That gave Nir pause. Surely Quillithé could see the dangers in this interaction, the untrustworthiness of the Drum, the possibility of treachery. Yet she was willing to do so. Why? And then Nir knew. Because to Quillithé neither he nor Kookatchi could be trusted; both had to be restrained and kept in line. She had to be able to see them both. And then Nir realized that he could act the same way. He had interacted with Quillithé, he had watched her in battle. If the Drum lied, mistranslating words, then what would come out would not be like what Quillithé herself would say. The Drum would have to be able to think like the strategist to fabricate a likely lie. All Nir had to trust in was the uniqueness of Quillithé's mind, that a truth she told would not be maskable in a lie that came from the Drum's narrow consciousness.

"I agree to the translation," Nir said.

A moment. Both Nir and Quillithé acquiesce. The Instant changes with their acquiescence. Kookatchi changes with it. All three of these are the same event, the same moment, but only Kookatchi knows it.

Kookatchi is the mediator, that which is set up to bridge the distance from one end of the Instant to the other. Kookatchi the Bridge stands between the leader of the shallows and the leader of the deeps and lays himself open to their words.

Image from Quillithé to Kookatchi: Nir entering the darkness, Nir leaving the darkness. Blue limning around the darkness.

"She wants to know what happened to you in the broken lands," Kookatchi said.

"I know," Nir said. "I tried to explain it to her, but she had great difficulty in understanding what I experienced in the Flux. You may need to explain a great deal."

"I understand," Kookatchi said.

Nir related all that had happened to him in the broken lands: the increase in the cracking, the fall into the tiny fragment of time, the fact that only his Wavebreaker had saved his existence, the coiling and the madness of flickering about trapped in those few seconds, and his escape along the cracks themselves.

Kookatchi faithfully translated, sending his shorthand images to Quillithé. The events in the Flux were hard to render; images of solid time, of fixedness and rigidity were hard to wash over the changing surface of the deeps. But the Drum managed it, going piece by piece, event by event. Slow and steady, he gave the strategist the requisite awareness of the trap of time, a trap which most dwellers in the Instant remembered and held on to like a precious jewel, but which Quillithé had lost in the first moment of her freedom when the instant of death became the instant of her birth.

As the translation proceeded, Kookatchi grew into his role as interpreter and mediator. The circumstances under which he had come to be in this place talking to these people had faded from his mind. He ceased for that interval to be Kookatchi the Thief and became wholly Kookatchi the Bridge, Kookatchi the Messenger, Kookatchi who brings all things together in his perception.

So that when Nir finished his tale and Quillithé floated absorbing it, it was Kookatchi who posed the question to the War Chief. "Now that you have spoken, what is it you will do?"

And it was Kookatchi who sent these images to Quillithé: Quillithé seeing images. Quillithé contemplating. Quillithé ordering her army. Blue limning around the giving of orders.

"Do?" Nir said.

"To stop the cracking," Kookatchi said. "Is that not why we have come together?"

Image from Quillithé to Kookatchi: Quillithé giving orders. Blue limning around the giving of orders. Deep blue limning around the blue. Questioning the question.

Image from Kookatchi to Quillithé: Darkness retreating, vanishing. Instant returning to normal flow, Nir, Kookatchi, and Quillithé together speaking. Blue limning around the speech, tinge of violet to the blue, implication that the question is rhetorical.

Come together? Nir thought. Nothing comes together in the Instant. That was an article of faith among the Ghosts. Things are made to fall apart here outside of the proper course of time. But here we are speaking together. A temporary expedient, but nevertheless . . . The War Chief's mind changed. He became aware of a new commitment in himself; he refused to accept that commitment, but neither could he reject it. Nir rationalized with the following thoughts: If the strategist wants to end the cracking then I will use her vision and her thoughts to help me do so.

Quillithé looked at Nir. He looked so ordinary, a Time Warrior like any other, but he had fought her to a standstill. She who had never been bested in generalship had been countered, his improvisation matching her vision. None of her officers could match his mind, and he could go to the broken lands where she could not. Yes, he would be useful, he was at hand, and he was willing. The Drum in the swiftness of his changing mind had shown her the truth of the present situation. From this rare and very temporary agreement of purpose, she would contemplate the seeds of possibility and lay out the strategy to follow, then she would give that strategy to Nir and the War Chief would improvise his way through to the carrying out of her vision.

After that the moment of their agreement would end, and the Instant would return to normal. So the thinking went in most of her mind. But in a few dark rooms and hidden corridors of thought lay the possibility that things would never be the same in the ocean of time.

"Ask her what she thinks can be done," Nir told Kookatchi.

Image from Kookatchi to Quillithé: Quillithé coiled up, emitting a picture around the darkness. Blue limning around the picture.

The question washed into the strategist, flowing through the corridors of her mind, filling the chambers of possibility with its insistent inquiry. What were they to do? The question flowed around from here to there until it produced a child question, or rather an ancestral question. What could be the cause of the breaking? For only when the cause was known could they decide upon an action. This new question washed through the strategist's mind, watering the seeds of consideration until six possibilities blossomed forth. Quillithé coiled a few hours of her life around the moving seat of her consciousness and considered how best to show these six.

Throughout the army camp, rumors and questions were quietly exchanged in short pictures.

One image formed the core of these questions: Quillithé speaking with the two outsiders. Limning of blue and orange for stunned disbelief.

It amazed her soldiers that the strategist, who to them was greater than any other being that could possibly exist, was conversing on seemingly equal terms with two warriors from other tribes.

Her soldiers did not doubt the wisdom of Quillithé's actions. None of them could even conceive of setting their thoughts against her. But this action was so strange that even these soldiers who had so little curiosity were set to wondering.

The flow of rumors and questions gradually settled on the one officer who had some direct experience of what was happening. Irithrué found herself at the center of a vortex of inquiries for which she had no answers.

Image from a soldier to Irithrué: Nir limned in blue and emerald green. What is so special about this man?

Image from Irithrué: Same picture but limned in dark gray. No answer known.

Image from one of Kookatchi's guards to Irithrué: Nir and Kookatchi conspiring together in the middle regions of the Instant. Did they form some plot that they were now bringing against the only army?

Image from Irithrué: Nir keeping Kookatchi in the coils of his tail. No, the Drum was the other's prisoner.

And so it went, question by question, rumor by rumor, a growing confusion in the camp.

Quillithé watched all this from the seat of her contemplations and noted how the unprecedented was injuring the discipline of her army. That would have to be restored soon, but for now this matter took precedence. The six images of the possible causes of the cracking were ready; one by one she let them flow from her tail and wash over Kookatchi.

Image from Quillithé: A tribe floating in a circle; in unison they emit harsh waves into the center where they collide; the bottom of the ocean cracks and the waters wash away, forming an island.

Image from Kookatchi to Quillithé: Repetition of previous image, blue limning around the circular wave. Inquiry as to whether she means that exact action caused the breakage.

Image from Quillithé to Kookatchi: Same picture, gray-violet around the wave. Not literally.

"Her first possibility is that a tribe found the means to break the ocean floor and did so deliberately," Kookatchi said to Nir.

"I had already assumed that," Nir said.

"So had I," Kookatchi replied, "but she thinks there are other options."

Image from Quillithé to Kookatchi: Variation on a theme, tribe cracking the bottom of the Instant in the form of a barrier, creating a lake surrounded by an navigable reef.

"A defensive use rather than an offensive one," Nir said after Kookatchi had translated the image. "More likely, but both of these uses are dangerous. After all, the cracking can spread."

"Perhaps they did not know that when they broke the floor," Kookatchi said.

"Agreed," Nir replied. And he considered his own tribesmen, so many of whom would be willing to run that risk for the sake of protecting the People. Nir's thoughts drifted briefly back to the Now where others were probably speaking of him.

XIII

In the Now, the Elder called Col to a private meeting on an autumn midnight in the Year of Ghosts' Conferring.

Leaves crunched under the callused soles of the Elder's feet as she squatted on the Great Mother's mound. "What is being said among the warriors concerning the War Chief's absence?"

Col covered his ears for a moment, unsure of how to reply. The Elder had taken him into her confidence in Nir's absence, telling him of her concerns about the safety of the People and expressing interest in the protective powers of the broken island. At first Col had been flattered by the trust implied by the Elder, but lately she had begun to inquire about things spoken in private. He could not refuse to answer her, but still he was discomfited.

During Nir's absence, the Ghosts had begun to speak of him one to the other, and each had found how unlike one warrior's opinion was to another. It almost seemed to them that each Ghost had been led by a different War Chief: a commander of brilliance, a taker of intolerable risks, a cautious restrainer, a leader who survived purely by good fortune.

Col had been very confused by these quiet shared tappings and had come to believe that he had never known his own commander.

Fortunately there was the Elder to guide him. And yet she asked these questions.

"The Ghosts begin to wonder about Nir," Col said. "They are confused by his absence and perplexed that he did not bring back the gift of the breaking for the good of the People. Many of them trust that there is a good reason for this. A few wonder if Nir has gone mad, or if he always was so. One even wondered if the War Chief's mind is not truly focused on the vow and the People."

"And you, Col," the Elder said. "What is your opinion, you who traveled with him to the region of the breaking?"

"I do not know, Elder," Col said. "I hope he will return and explain, but I am no longer sure he will do so."

In the heart of Quillithé's camp, the colloquy continued.

Quillithé sent her third image to Kookatchi: It showed a small circle of tiny figures, a score of Drums, led by Kookatchi himself, tapping rhythmically against the floor of the ocean over and over until a tiny crack formed; then they spread the cracks, isolating a region of the Instant that could then be raided without any worry about longer-tailed tribes. In the center of this broken island lay a hoard of stolen treasure, the fabled loot of the Great Thief Kookatchi.

The Drum was horrified by the accusation. His immediate impulse was to deny it. But for the first time ever Kookatchi restrained himself, for he did not know if it could be true. He might have done so, might have been the cause of the breaking, and he might not remember. If he had been, then in the heart of that island lay his own treasury, sitting dry and forgotten.

The Drum's consciousness recycled, a little of Kookatchi the Thief poked up from under the awareness of Kookatchi the Bridge. The Thief considered the breaking, considered the changelessness of it, and found it not beautiful enough for his consideration.

"I do not think I did this," the Drum said. "But I cannot offer real assurance."

Both and Nir and Quillithé found this answer satisfactory; both knew that if the Drum had been deceiving them he would have denied the accusation vociferously. Perhaps they would later find out that he was responsible, and if so they would wring the necessary knowledge from his buried memories.

Fourth image from Quillithé to Kookatchi: Vague tall buildings, time-bound people standing around, moving jerkily. A large machine dominating the cityscape.

The machine shakes, lightning emerges shooting upward, striking the sky, cracking the heavens above the terrified people. Whole scene is limned in a dubious orange.

"She suggests the possibility that time-bound people may be responsible," Kookatchi said. "But she does not think it likely."

"Why not?" Nir said. "All things in the Instant are originally taken from the Flux."

Kookatchi transmitted the question.

Image in answer: One island in the Instant, then many islands appearing. Gold of emphasis around the repetitions.

"She points out that nothing ever happens only once in the Flux. Everything that enters the Instant recurs in many places and times. If something could be invented under one set of circumstance it could, and—given the changings of the Flux—would have, been invented under a myriad of circumstances. Like entry into the Instant itself, a cracking machine would have recurred over and over again in a multitude of times and places, yet there is only one cracked region. The uniqueness of the Island makes it unlikely that it was created by the time-bound."

"Agreed," Nir said after a little consideration, though he was not sure. This might be just the first such occurrence. There had been a first man in the Instant, after all.

Fifth image: A Time Warrior draws a new weapon out of the Flux; he uses it on an enemy; the waves that result thin the bottom layer of the ocean of time, altering the very nature of the relation between Flux and Instant. An island emerges; the cracking kills both the attacker and the defender.

"An accident?" Nir said after Kookatchi translated the image. The idea was startling to the War Chief. That the thing might have been created by mistake had never occurred to him, so used were the Ghosts to thinking of all things in the Instant as the direct and deliberate responsibility of one mad tribe or another.

The sixth and last image was even more surprising to the War Chief. It showed the bottom of time's ocean to be by nature thin and constantly at risk for cracking. The Instant itself had simply been waiting for a sufficiently savage event to occur in order to shatter.

"No one is at fault?" Nir said. That was impossible to believe. Everything in the Instant resulted from the actions of man; nothing could be given over to the vagaries of chance.

The War Chief consulted Fourth Voice, seeking confirmation in his disbelief. His atemporal advisor's answer was not what he expected. "Nature of the Instant not well enough understood to rule this out."

How can that be? Nir said. The Instant has been well studied.

"Fought over," Fourth Voice said. "Not studied."

Nir's thinking changed under the pressure of those words; he saw an assumption vanish. A descendant of slaves, he had assumed that the enslavers were evil but not ignorant. Now he realized the falsehood of that belief. The tribes had ranged over time seeking material and tactical advantage. They had guided and enslaved the time-bound, forcing them to work on weapons for the Instant. But what had they learned in all that battle? Precious little.

"Ask Quillithé what can be done to discern which of these possibilities is true," Nir said to Kookatchi.

Image from Kookatchi to Quillithé surrounded by six pictures. Army poised to receive commands. Blue limning around the pictures and the ungiven commands. Yellow line connecting images and orders.

Image from Quillithé to Kookatchi: Scouts from the army sent out, harvesting information, bringing it back to Quillithé.

"No," Nir said directly to the strategist, after Kookatchi had translated the picture.

"No?" she tapped, booming her tail on the interrogative.

The War Chief turned to the Drum. "Tell her that her scouts cannot see into the breaking. They would be useless. Tell her you and I will go and glean the information she needs to discern what is happening."

"We will?" Kookatchi said. Fear welled up in his mind, and Kookatchi the Bridge faded into Kookatchi the Thief; the Thief was too frightened to go back to that desolate prison of cracking. "Why should I go?"

"To establish your innocence or guilt," Nir said. "And to gain your freedom from her."

Kookatchi the Thief looked back and saw the monster of the deep. She could take him when she wanted, she could kill him if she felt like it. Better to curry favor, better to do as Nir wanted, at least for now. The Thief faded back into the depths of memory.

Kookatchi the Bridge relayed the War Chief's suggestion to the strategist.

To let them go? Quillithé considered. To rely on their information. But had she not been doing so already? She let the question echo through the caverns of her thoughts, and answer came back swiftly. Nir was right. Her own soldiers were blind. That blindness was no doubt responsible for the destruction of Adjutant Vanchen and his soldiers. She could not send more of her people to useless death.

But Nir's touch and Kookatchi's five senses might penetrate the darkness she could not. As to whether they would come back or not to relate what they found, Kookatchi knew that she could dispatch enough troops to capture him. And as for Nir, he would not relish the prospect of pitched battle between her army and his Ghosts. He might triumph but the cost would be disastrous.

Yes, they would be back.

Image from Quillithé to Kookatchi: The War Chief and the Drum swimming out of the camp toward the darkness. Quillithé watching them, her army prepared to render assistance should they need it.

Deed followed picture. Nir and Kookatchi swam out through the rings of soldiers, igniting confused rumors as they went.

Quillithé floated placidly, sending calming pictures to her seven fathers and her three hundred soldiers. She knew what she was doing. They need not concern themselves. And as she spoke those images, the strategist's mind returned to the six possibilities and began to elaborate them, seeking to identify the regions of thought and time where evidence might be found to identify the source of the great injury to the Instant.

XIV

Nir and Kookatchi swam side by side pastward, their atemporal bodies pushing against the prevailing currents of time's ocean, rippling in opposition to the flow of cause and effect. Nir swam with heavy strokes, coiling his years and thrusting out his own wake against the tides, pushing his ten years of life against the relentless course of history. Kookatchi, in contrast, skipped like a stone across the peaks of the waves, taking advantage of each little bit of countercurrent that washed backward against the larger tides; his Drum's perceptions saw the state of the Instant and led him toward each little bit of backflow, so that he could catch those little moments when future altered past instead of past creating future.

The two of them crossed two thousand years of the deeps in silence. Nir was turning over in his mind the six possibilities Quillithé had laid out, wondering how he would go about finding evidence for or against each one without having to venture onto the broken island and risk being trapped again or, more serious worry, risk destroying more of the Instant.

Kookatchi's consciousness was a welter of confusion. There were too many things he simply could not forget, but they would not settle down into a simple minute of thought. Quillithé herself was too many things simultaneously: Monster of the deep, grand strategist, Lady of the only army, the great beauty of the tides, the sum total of experience and conception. And Nir, who seemed at first so unimportant to the Drum—just another chief of a parochial tribe—yet he was held in surprising regard by Quillithé. What had he done to earn her respect? And Kookatchi himself, he had been so many things so swiftly that they lay in his mind like a jagged jumble: thief, interpreter, mediator, participant in this great search for truth. And the army, what was it that disturbed him about the army?

"They sing no songs of their past," the Drum tapped out, awareness dawning in the moment after recycling.

"What?" said Nir, surprised by the unprompted comment.

"Quillithé's army," Kookatchi said. "They have no songs of memory. Nothing to remind them of their purpose. Their only songs are in celebration of Quillithé herself."

"Quillithé gives them purpose," Nir said. "She decides, they obey. You are right, Drum. They have no songs, no litany, no vows. Nothing to hold them together except her vision and her strategy."

"So vulnerable," the Drum said. And neither of them thought it strange to see the Monster of the deep, the Lady of the only army as vulnerable.

Ghost and Drum swam for thousands of years, crossing from the deeps of time to the futuremost reaches of the middle Instant, the part of the ocean where the tribes contended one with the other.

The War Chief considered how best to proceed. It was strange to him to be traveling with one who was neither subordinate, captor, nor prisoner. How were the two of them to respond if danger threatened, and how could he take advantage of the Drum's senses if battle arose? Or could he even rely on Kookatchi? Would the Drum flee at the first sign of trouble, leaving Nir to fend for himself?

Discipline was needed. Kookatchi had to accept Nir's authority in the face of danger. But how was he to instill that discipline in the wildly changing consciousness of a Drum? That answer came swiftly to the War Chief; he would use the Drum's changes in the same way he used the changes of his own mind. He would lay upon the altering consciousness the goal he wished to achieve and then let it alter as needed.

"You will have to give warning if we near any tribes," Nir said, handing his need to Kookatchi.

"What will we do if I do see any?" Kookatchi said, resisting the other's will. "You are far too large to hide, and you lack the awareness of a Drum."

"True," Nir said. "But I have led many battles, and I have fought Quillithé to a standstill in game. And I have captured a Drum."

Kookatchi tapped his tail in grudging agreement. "So what are you saying?"

"That you should let me decide what to do if we near enemies."

"Let . . . you . . . decide . . . " The words perplexed the Drum. To rely upon another's judgment, such an alien thought. And yet was he not relying on Quillithé's judgment in undertaking this expedition? But his life depended on Drum's awareness and Drum's adaptability. This ten-year-long warrior could never understand what it meant to see the Instant as a whole; he was too chained by his illusion of perpetually relived life. Or was he? Kookatchi's consciousness recycled and he recalled his capture by Nir, that sudden transformation of the War Chief's life into a prison maze, a change of his body according to the change of the Instant. There had been no illusion of sequential passing there.

"I will obey you," Kookatchi said, "unless I can only survive by abandoning you."

"Accepted," Nir said.

The Drum had not made a vow of loyalty or even of true obedience, but he had chosen to accept Nir's direction in battle. That, at least, was a beginning. Nir turned his thoughts to the question of what they would do when they reached the broken

island, while Kookatchi turned his awareness outward and sharpened his senses for the approach of enemy tribes.

Fifteen thousand years futureward from the broken island,
Kookatchi heard a song:

> "In Mani's name we seek the light,
> In darkness beyond time.
> In Mani's name we search for light,
> Stolen and hidden beyond time."

The song continued in this vein, growing louder as they swam.
"The Manichean Seekers beyond the Dark," Kookatchi said to Nir.
"By the sound of them they must be only a few hundred years
pastward."

Second Voice retrieved from its storehouse all it knew about
the tribe and told it to Nir. "Fanatical tribe. They believe that destroying all the other tribes is a necessary prerequisite to finding
the true light hidden in the darkness of the Instant. They attacked
the Now once during the reign of the second War Chief. Captured
prisoners revealed that they believed that possession of the People
would give them access to the basic secrets of human life and allow
them to free the souls of all who lived in the solid world."

Third Voice filled the silence left when Second Voice completed its recital. "Favored tactic of this tribe is encirclement with
the goal of isolating and destroying enemy commanders."

Fourth Voice had nothing to say. The individual tribes were
not its concern; it looked only at the Instant itself.

"Have you ever stolen anything from them?" Nir asked Kookatchi.

"Of course," Kookatchi tapped in amused reply.

"What was it?"

"I do not remember," Kookatchi said, "though it must have been
beautiful."

"How wide-ranging are their senses?"

The Drum tapped a rough beat of scorn on the surface of the

waters. "No better than yours; they possess only a limited sense of hearing, by which they listen to the flow of the ocean and the speech of the tribes."

"Would they recognize Quillithé's picture speech?"

"In their own fashion," Kookatchi said; the details of the Manicheans were surfacing swiftly in his memory.

"And they know enough to be afraid of her?"

"Oh, yes."

"Then here are my instructions."

The War Chief and the Drum separated, Kookatchi swimming pastward and northward, Nir staying futureward of the Manicheans but swimming three hundred kilometers to the south.

The Manicheans, all fourteen of them, continued their cautious swim futureward. They knew that they were skirting the edge of the deeps where the monster dwelled, but they had suffered many reverses in battle recently and had swum here seeking new weapons from the far reaches of technological development.

Their leader, who had long since forgotten his time-bound name, was known to his soldiers by the title Light of the Elect. He had come during his long sojourn away from the world to hate the Instant and to fear all those who lived in it. But he could not show these feelings to his subordinates. A brave front was necessary if his dwindling tribe was ever to overcome the vast numbers of their enemies, particularly the creature who dwelled twenty-five thousand years futureward of them. A quarter of the long axis of the Instant away, and yet she still dominated these waters with her presence.

The Light of the Elect heard a strange buzzing noise, complex yet indistinguishable. It passed through the ten-year-long line the Manicheans made as they swam. The wave of noise was only a minute across, but there was something about the sound of it that was familiar. All the tribe listened to the wave as it passed southward and futureward. Then an answer came. This one was months in diameter, a loud booming noise, still inseparable, still complex;

but this sound was recognizable as the incomprehensible speech of the deeps.

"The Monster's minions are nearby," cried the Light of the Elect. "Swim pastward. Keep your hearing open. Beware of ambushes. Stay together."

An orderly retreat ensued and the Manicheans decided to search closer to the center of the Instant.

Nir swam to where Kookatchi waited for him.

"Well done," the War Chief tapped.

"What are you talking about?" Kookatchi said. He had already forgotten the incident, so simple had it been to carry through.

"You tricked them into believing that Quillithé's army was nearby. You sent a picture through their camp and I responded."

The Drum's consciousness recycled. "Oh, yes, now I remember. That was very amusing. But not a trick I would want to do again."

"Why not?"

"For two reasons: first, Quillithé would see me do it and become angered at my use of her reputation, and second I would need someone as large as you to make truly believable pictures. And even then—well, the Manicheans do not have sight; they could not see how crude your image was."

"That last is very important," Nir said. "As for your first objection, as long as we are acting on Quillithé's behalf, I think we are safe in using her reputation to our advantage."

"I suppose you are right," Kookatchi said. "And it was a good tactic."

"Yes, it was," Nir said, pleased that the Drum had followed his instructions and even more pleased that Kookatchi was gaining trust in his leadership.

The two resumed their swim pastward and by dint of such deceptions and careful avoidance of danger they reached the shallow waters forty years futureward of the broken island.

The bottom of the ocean scraped against Nir's body, giving him again that itchy feeling. He did not want to get too close to the Island, lest he increase the cracking with his ten-years' weight, but they could not stay too far away either.

"Follow me slowly," Nir said. "And watch the bottom, see if any more cracks form."

The Drum trailed the War Chief, a minute behind a decade. Slowly swimming, they neared the futuremost border, twenty years, ten, five, two. That was close enough for Nir. He wanted to be able to maneuver a bit in case of danger.

"No new cracking, yet," Kookatchi said.

"Good," Nir said.

The War Chief stretched out his sense of touch and felt the contours of the island, ragged, sharp, angry. He had been inside, had found himself by accident on that landmass. Before his only concern had been to escape that dry hell, but now he needed to know about it. What was it like to crawl up out of the ocean onto that land? Could any atemporal being survive long there? For that matter, what was it like for the time-bound in these artificial shallows? Did it in any way resemble the Now?

"We need to anchor," Nir said.

"What for?" asked the Drum.

"I need to know what their lives are like down there under the sky."

"Is this because of the possibility that they might be responsible for the breaking?"

"No," Nir said. "It is something else that concerns me, but we will endeavor to find that out as well."

The War Chief reached down and grasped the earthly side of time, vanishing from the Instant. The Drum followed. The waters two years futureward from the island became still and placid. The sea flowed only slightly, water rocking back and forth in second-sized waves, pushed and pulled by the little driblet ripples that flowed from the surrounding ocean into that shallow lagoon.

The Vault of the World Provision Center was the pride of Nepal, indeed of the whole Indian subcontinent. The Director of South Asian Sales Control for the Consumerist Mercantile Hegemony frequently boasted of it at meetings of the directorship. She spoke glowingly of how the Provision Center covered over half of the tallest mountain range on earth, and how its buildings had made them even taller. How the spectacular views seen from the three hundredth story of the Provision Center attracted sightseers and purchasers from all over the world.

The eight other sales control directors scowled at this boasting before the Grand Director of Designs and Control for the earth. The Grand Director was now three hundred years old and reaching the point where human life could no longer be extended by drugs, transplants, and artificial body parts. He had come to accept his death and was contemplating the choice of his successor. Who better than the woman who had shown such innovation in consuming those mountains?

But the other directors, jealous of the Grand Director's favor, had warned the South Asian Director that perhaps the place she had created and on which her future was pinned might attract the attention of rebels. The Director of South Asian Sales Control knew a threat when she heard one. For the protection of her ambitions, she assigned an army of security guards to hide in the surveillance halls behind the walls of her consumer-filled atria. She was not about to let any anticonsumerists, whether real or fabricated by her fellow directors, stop her from sitting on the tiger-headed chair of the Grand Director.

Nir and Kookatchi appeared in an apple-tree-lined atrium that filled the fortieth story of the seventeenth tower of The Vault of the World Provision Center. Sunlight streamed in through translucent green . . . blue . . . orange plastic walls.

"Strange," Nir said in the language the People spoke in the solid earth.

Kookatchi knew variations of the language, having heard many forms of it in the Diaspora, but this was his first exposure to the original speech of man.

"What is strange?" the Drum said, hoping that his synthesis of the language was correct.

Nir found Kookatchi's accent peculiar, but comprehensible. "These walls are changing slowly."

"What did you expect?" the Drum said. "The waters above are nearly still."

"So are the waters above the Now," Nir said. "But there, changes do not manifest in this inconsequential manner. In the Now, changes are few, but important. Here they seem to be many but slight."

"That is strange," Kookatchi said. His consciousness recycled and he realized that there was a thing he did not know, which had not mattered before, but now that they were anchored was of some concern. "Ghost?"

"Yes, Drum."

"How are you called in the earthly side of time? What is your birth name?"

"Nir," the War Chief said. "And yours?"

"Kookatchi."

A crowd of shoppers had filled the atrium after paying the fee to smell the apple trees and laze about on wooden benches while a blizzard howled outside the windows. These innocent buyers stood stunned in horror at the bizarre appearance of these two mysterious people; the fearful crowd huddled together, unsure of what was going to happen.

A few whispered to each other. "Have they come to destroy the building? Or to force us to give up our money? What are we to do?"

A particularly brave elderly man at the edge of the crowd, two hundred years old, proud of having fought for the Hegemony in his youth and even prouder for having been rewarded with great wealth, was not about to be cowed by one lone rebel and a strangely dressed man. This stubborn old veteran boldly walked out of the atrium and pushed a yellow . . . blue . . . orange and green hawk symbol on one of the smooth marble-and-slate walls. Security would take care of the rebel, and the old man would satisfy his ambition to once again be involved in some real military action, to strike a blow for the Hegemony as he had in his youth under the command of the man who became Grand Director.

A squad of four security patrolmen, clothed in garish orange . . . green . . . silver body armor, and carrying long silver staves that crackled with electricity and gave off a stink of ozone, appeared at the vaulted entryway of the atrium. The crowd of fearful onlookers breathed a sigh of collective relief. While two of the security men held their staves pointed at Nir and Kookatchi, the other two quickly ushered the fifty onlookers to the safety of a nearby atrium where food could be purchased to calm their nerves and a direct three-dimensional transmission of the incipient arrest would be shown to bolster their confidence in the Hegemony. The old veteran who had alerted security was rewarded with a glowing green . . . violet medallion stamped with a diving sea eagle that permitted him to enter the security dining room and eat one meal with the troops.

Nir and Kookatchi had paid little attention to the commotion. What concern had they with the actions of the time-bound? It was only when the four security men came up to them that they even turned to look.

"Four time-bound, three meters distant," Third Voice told Nir.

"Silver staves are electrical weapons, capable of stunning a human neurological system or if properly set, killing," Second Voice said. "Body armor is made of layered plastic, capable of stopping projectiles with momenta up to twelve hundred kilogram meters per second. Also provides electrical insulation."

"Threat level, nonexistent," Third Voice said.

"What do you want here, rebel?" one of the security guards said to Nir. He hoped his voice was steely and secure. After all, this would be seen all through the complex. Many guards had been fabulously rewarded for capturing rebels; he hoped to be one of them.

Nir had no idea what the man had said, but Kookatchi knew enough closely allied languages to be able to understand it.

"He believes you are a revolutionary," Kookatchi said to Nir.

"Ask him why he thinks that," Nir said.

Kookatchi turned to the guard, who held his staff in front of his own chest to ward off whatever violent activity this small gold-armored man might be intending. Strange about that armor. He was clearly in league with the rebel, but why was he clothed?

"Why do you believe my comrade is in revolt?" Kookatchi asked.

The security guard raised the staff as if to strike the Drum. Things were not working out properly. The rebel and his companion were not acting according to type. The transmission would make him look foolish. What to do? He was tempted to strike both of them down with the staff. But what if something strange was happening? What if this were some sort of test? Speak clearly in answer, that was what he would do. That would give him the best chance of doing the right thing. Thoughts of rewards still dangled themselves before his eyes, but now they were joined by fear of punishment, demotion, perhaps dismissal.

"You anticonsumerist, naked rebels are all alike. You flaunt yourselves before your betters, claiming to be without any belongings. We know you have stolen great amounts of produce and hidden them. We know that your protests are a pretense, a trick to delude the good people of the Hegemony." The guard hoped his voice carried well enough and that he had properly stated all the official objections to the rebels.

Kookatchi turned his back on the guard and faced Nir. "There appears to be a nudity taboo here. Apparently naked people are associated with a political faction that has no interest in buying things."

"Ask him how large his nation is," Nir said.

"What does it matter?" Kookatchi said. "It will change, before—ah, I see. History is quite fixed here only two years from the island."

"Exactly," said Nir. "If this nudity taboo is widespread it will make surveying this place difficult."

"How large is the Hegemony?" Kookatchi asked the guard.

The guard was now almost sure that this was some sort of staged event. Perhaps it was an educational device, meant to remind the children of the Hegemony of their great heritage. If the guard did well enough, perhaps he would be a symbol of the steadfast citizen; perhaps small figurines of him would be made and sold. They would be cast in quick-dissolving materials, of course, so that each household would have to buy replacements every few days. Yes, that would be a great triumph for him.

"The Consumerist Mercantile Hegemony covers the whole of the earth," the guard said, his chest swelling with pride. "Our Grand Director has brought prosperity to everyone. Only you vile rebels defy his bounty. Come with us. We will show you the error of your ways."

"He claims that his nation is worldwide, and he wishes us to accompany him," Kookatchi said, casting his gaze upward. "Shall we leave?"

"No," Nir said. "I want to see how static this place is. All we have seen change are colors and a few markers of style. No great changes of shape, nor of the people present. I want to see more of this."

"To learn what?" Kookatchi said.

"To learn how this slow change differs from the slow change of the Now."

"And what will that tell you?" Kookatchi said.

"The cause and nature of that difference."

"I see," said the Drum. There was a trace of greed in his voice as he caught a glimmer of the answer. It came to him in a moment of recycled consciousness. He saw the Now and the shallows of the island leap through his mind. Two slowly flowing regions like twin graceful dancers executing complementary parts of a dance, similar but not the same. There was beauty here, beauty in these two places. But to have that beauty Kookatchi the Thief would need to see not just the shallows futureward of the broken island but the shallows of the Now. No, bury that desire, do not let Nir feel it. The War Chief would never let him or any other outsider into the Now. Wait, hide the wanting. In the eternal changing of the Instant, opportunity would present itself.

"We will go with you," Kookatchi said to the guard.

The two Time Warriors let the four time-bound guards lead them out of the shopping center's public arcades, through a door carefully concealed behind a large fruit-bearing apple tree, and into a network of gray passageways behind the shops. The passages were lined with video screens displaying many views of the shopping areas.

Kookatchi watched in fascination as the colors of buildings, clothes, and the levitating boxes that accompanied each shopper changed minute by minute. Every so often a piece of decoration would change; the epaulets on the guard's shoulders cycled through eagles, hawks, falcons, vultures, and ravens, never leaving the confines of raptors and scavengers. The only emblem that never varied was a continual display of tigers on the ceilings. Tiger masks, tigers asleep, tigers leaping on deer, but always tigers. The Drum found the repetition had a soothing quality, like listening to the rhythm of rain.

Nir's attention was focused on the people. They never changed. Always these same guards, always the same shoppers, always the same technicians sitting at rows of monitor panels gauging crowd reaction, studying purchasing patterns, and so on. Such a fixity of persons. The War Chief envied them their solidity. If the Now could be protected from the changing of human lives, how safe it would be. But no, that was what the reactionaries would think if Nir brought this information back. And they would lose awareness of the danger the cracking presented, lose the true danger in this apparent safety. He needed to know even more before he could return home.

The guards took Nir and Kookatchi into a gray rectangular room, the west wall of which was lined with three-meter-high clear plastic-fronted cabinets. Inside the seeming closets were rows of merchandise: clothing, food, drinks in metal bottles, jewelry made of azurite and platinum, and many many green-and-gold plastic tigers.

The leader of the guards took a handful of violet chits out of a pouch that hung at his side and handed them to Nir. The War Chief took the dark brown pieces of painted onyx and studied them carefully as they changed colors.

"You will demonstrate your rejection of rebellion," the guard said, flourishing his arms for the watching monitors. Then he turned and led the three others through the irised door on the short north wall.

"May I have those?" Kookatchi asked.

Nir handed over the opalescent disks with disinterest.

"This is probably money," the Drum said.

He walked over to one of the cabinets, studied it briefly, then placed three of the chits into a hand-sized open box on the left side of the case. The box withdrew into the body of the cabinet, and six glowing panels appeared on the clear plastic front. Kookatchi touched one of them and watched as a bar of synthetic meat wrapped in a real lettuce leaf dropped down into the base of the machine, and was then pushed out an open slot near the floor. Kookatchi picked up the leaf-meat combination, took a bite, and with an experience of food that stretched for a hundred millennia and covered the entire globe, pronounced it passable but in need of pepper.

"Would you like some?" he asked Nir.

"Ghosts do not eat," said the War Chief.

"Why not?" asked Kookatchi, who enjoyed the pleasures of the earthly world whenever he anchored.

"So that we remember our separation from the living," Nir said.

"I understand," said the Drum, feeling momentarily the beauty of the Ghosts' commitment and their strong remembrance of the difference and unification of the two sides of time. The idea of that connection tugged at Kookatchi; such solidity, such earthiness in a watery being.

"I have felt enough here," Nir said. His mind had changed, his thinking and knowing were now rock solid, no guesses needed. He understood the time they were occupying.

"Felt what?" asked the Drum, jarred away from his contemplations. The beauty of the Ghosts' vow vanished into his memory to wait with all his other knowledge, lying in darkness until the right moment came and it would emerge into the light of beautiful contemplation.

"I have felt the pulse of the broken island; somewhere in it is an event or events that fix all important aspects of this place and time."

But Nir did not give all of his thoughts to Kookatchi, for he thought of the Great Mother's birth and how her existence fixed the basic course of occupied time. So strong an event, but even that did not have this strength of stasis. The Now changed much more than this place.

The Great Mother was also in Kookatchi's mind. He had never seen her, never come closer than two centuries to her life, yet he knew of her and had often wondered what kind of prize she was that so many tribes fought over her.

"I think you are right about an anchoring event," the Drum said, not betraying his thoughts of the Great Mother. "What should we do now?"

"Test the power of that event, see how far futureward its control stretches, and how that control manifests in later times."

"So we return to the Instant?"

"Yes," Nir said, releasing his grip on solid time. Kookatchi let go as well, and the two of them vanished, leaving the room to the vending machines.

In the hall outside, the guard watched his ambitions vanish into empty air. The future of rewards gave way to that of punishments.

How could he explain what had happened to the South Asian Director without destroying his career and possibly his life? Perhaps one of the special security watchers who kept vigil at the monitors would be of assistance, someone who had seen the impossible disappearance of the two rebels and would give him the recording instead of hiding it for sale to someone interested in sensational events. If he scraped enough money together, he might be able to salvage this. If he hurried. There was so little time in which to act.

Nir and Kookatchi unanchored into the artificial shallows two years futureward from the broken island. Minuscule waves of change washed over them with no more force than a sea mist.

"Futureward," Nir tapped.

"Lead on," Kookatchi replied.

The Ghost and the Drum swam slowly toward the deeper waters of change.

They traveled for over a century, watching the Instant around them go from a placidity unknown outside of the Now to shallows like the Diaspora, and so on until the tides almost, but not quite, achieved the accustomed choppiness of the midocean of time.

Nir asked his Second Voice to extrapolate a map of the lagoon from their observations. The Voice replied that it was roughly triangular. At its pastmost border it was as wide as the broken lands, but as one traveled futureward, waves encroached from the sides, narrowing the region of placidity to a single point two centuries from the island.

"An excellent place to go," Nir said.

"Where is that?" Kookatchi asked.

"The last calm point."

The two swam toward the apex of the triangle, but stopped eight decades before they reached it. A tribe was encamped on the exact spot they were seeking.

"It's the Persian Zurvanite Infantry," the Drum said to the War Chief after listening to the song coming from the encampment.

"What are they doing?"

Kookatchi watched as one of the Persians vanished into the

Flux, emerged carrying a few-seconds-long small dumbbell shape made of brass and agate, waited for a wave to pass over them, then entered the Flux again.

"Raiding the Flux," said the Drum.

Nir was annoyed that such a common activity was keeping him from the place he wanted to survey. He reached out his sense of touch to feel inside the encampment.

"Kookatchi," Nir said. "Does your sight confirm what I have just felt? Have they taken a dozen copies of the same object?"

The Drum looked at the small floating pile of treasure eighty years away from him. "Yes, twelve small double-bulbed things; they seem to be made of metal and crystal."

Nir's mind changed. Twelve of the same things taken one after the other despite the tides of time. Those objects must be part of the stasis in these shallows. Perhaps they were the last remaining thing to not change.

"Those objects are the essence of the fixed point," Nir said. "Whatever they are arose from the event that holds the time below us in the grip of history."

"That makes sense," Kookatchi said, and his sight sharpened in focus as the beauty of that stasis sharpened his greed.

"Steal them for us," Nir said, and he anchored down into the Flux to await the results of his orders.

The Drum darted futureward, spurred on by his desire to possess those delicious anomalies.

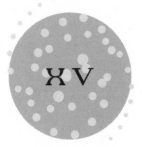

XV

The Persian Zurvanite Infantry was a force of twenty-five proud soldiers who had entered the Instant at the height of their earthly empire; they had come forth out of time to assist Darius the emperor in his conquest of the earth. Darius himself had sent them out of time to bring him weapons stolen from the future with which he might arm his warriors, giving them the might needed to subjugate all who stood in their way. It had been a great and noble dream shattered by the presence in the Instant of so many competing atemporal tribes.

The Zurvanites had been temporarily engulfed in despair when they emerged from the earth into the ocean of time and grasped the scale of the battles and the fragility of the putatively invincible empire that had sent them forth to gather the powers of time.

But despair had not lasted long; their impenetrable pride bolstered their martial spirits. Their commander, Prince Xerxes, declared that the struggle before them would bring greater glory to the name of their empire than the mere conquest of the earthly side of time.

Pride led them out to battle, and the craftiness of their Prince gave them many triumphs in the field of atemporal combat. They chose their fights well, attacking less well armed tribes or recently depleted enemies. Cautious in decision, they had never fought a foe greater than themselves. They kept to the middle of the Instant, avoiding both the army of the deep and the stubborn tribe of the Ghosts.

Prince Xerxes had learned to seek every advantage in atemporal combat: his enemies' weaknesses, the individual capacities of his warriors, the skills of time-bound slaves, and the properties of whatever technology came his way. He regarded the apex of the broken island's shallows as a source of useful material and he intended to exploit to the limit his good fortune in finding the strange unchanging objects that his diver pulled from that vertex of time.

While Xerxes contemplated the uses of the anomalies the diver herself continued to loot the Flux, drawing up one two-lobed bar after another. Xerxes rippled out the names of enemy tribes one by one, large tribes he had not dared attack; with these objects, he would defeat them one after another, until only the Persian Zurvanite Infantry remained in the Instant. Then he would reach his hand back to the beginning of humanity and recreate the empire of his ancestry. He would return to the Flux and sit forever on the throne of immortal Persia.

Kookatchi the Thief swam to within three months of the encamped Persians and prepared his mind for the joys of robbery. It was a thing he had done uncounted times before, the approach, the contemplation, the awareness, and then the act. This time he felt a faint discomfort. Kookatchi the Bridge was not happy at the return to thievery, but Nir had ordered that it be done and that settled the Bridge's doubts. Kookatchi the Bridge faded into memory and Kookatchi the Thief set about his work.

The Drum bobbed silently and unnoticeably like a tiny cork on the ocean of time while his unquiet mind recycled over and over again, washing away recent memory and filling his thoughts with present knowledge of his quarry.

At first his mind became filled with a torrent of details: the shimmering green of the Zurvanite troopers' armored tails, the repeated splash of the diver darting down, the inrush of water as she vanished from Flux to Instant, then the backwash as she reappeared. The whispers of two soldiers stationed on the western border of the camp, exchanged fears of pursuit, dreams of advancement, subtle hints of personal hatred toward their commander mixed with great respect for his abilities. The rippling words of Prince Xerxes, a litany of enemies, tribe after tribe, the entire known roster of combatants in the Instant.

After a few more cycles, the dross of irrelevance floated away and the gold of important information, the details of mind and arrangement that were useful to Kookatchi the Thief, remained in his thoughts. Several more iterations and the shape of the context around him became clear. The Drum could now perceive with all of his senses every single relevant factor for the planned theft.

Twelve of the soldiers were arranged in pairs along each border of the camp, north, south, east, west, future, and past, forming a perfect cube with their seven-year-long bodies, their tails coiled in interlocking spirals to form the faces of the cube, two warriors for each face. The pairs of soldiers left only month-long gaps between the prison bars they had made with their own bodies.

Inside the cage were Prince Xerxes, his personal guardsman, the diver, and the floating pile of treasure. The guardsman swam a tight circle around the Prince, protecting him from any possible assaulting wave. The diver floated a few days away from them, her tail coiled into a spring whenever she emerged with a new prize from the earthly side of time.

The remaining four soldiers patrolled in sharklike circles five years around the cubic camp. Kookatchi had easily slipped past them. Their concern was for approaching warriors; they could not notice the tiny shape of the Drum.

For armament, all the soldiers bore Ukrainian Wavesharpeners that damped all but one of the harmonics of their striking waves and added the force from the damped waves to the single crest remaining. The result was a clean knife-edge of water that severed the lifespans of their enemies without leaving ragged edges of flesh and time. The Prince and his personal guardsman had wrapped their tails in repeller coils that generated riptides around their bodies, making close approach dangerous. The scouts had Surfing Helices wrapped around their tails, which gave them greater buoyancy; the Helices permitted them to float and dart more easily on the crests of waves, as well as speed their passage through the Instant.

That was sufficient for Kookatchi's awareness. The Drum swam pastward to a few months beyond the perimeter that the scouts were circling. Then he waited until one of the scouts neared the closest approach to his position. The Drum skipped across the crests of waves and rippled out bits of deliberate change, subtle clues that any experienced Instant scout would recognize as the distant approach of a large force. Added to this, Kookatchi dropped in fragments of speech, little dollops of words from the language of Constantine's Conquering Sign, one of the enemy tribes Prince Xerxes had listed as too dangerous to battle now. (Though soon, if everything worked out, the Persians would face them in a conflict of killing waves and conquer them.)

Fragments of the memory song of the Conquering Sign came to the Persian scout from what seemed like a little more than two centuries pastward.

"For Constantine's City, for Rome built twice, then gone . . ."

That would suffice. The scout turned around and swam back to the cubic camp. Kookatchi followed, hiding in the scout's wake.

The pastward wall of the cube parted to let the scout inside the perimeter; Kookatchi surfed in as well.

Reporting, the scout coiled himself up humbly before Xerxes.

"My Prince, Constantine's soldiers approach from the past."

"Have you seen them?" Xerxes responded.

"No, my Prince, I heard fragments of their speech on the waters. They sounded about two hundred years pastward of us."

"Two centuries," Xerxes said. "No further than that. Two centuries pastward is the black realm of death. They must be approaching from the side and the realm has confuted the direction of their coming."

"As you say, O all-wise," the scout replied.

Kookatchi, coiled up into a ball five seconds in diameter, was intrigued to learn that the Persians knew something of the broken island. He wondered what the source of their knowledge was.

"Still, we cannot stay." The Prince flicked the tip of his tail toward the diver. "Pack up the fruits of your labors. We will return for the rest of the bounty when our enemies have gone."

The diver extended the end of her tail into the pool of floating treasures and swiftly knotted their ends together, turning the few-second chains into half a minute of intertwined objects.

Perfect, thought the Drum.

"Defense march formation," Prince Xerxes called.

The cube dissolved into long lines of march, six lines of three soldiers each. The soldiers perceived themselves as uncoiling their tails and straightening them out, but Kookatchi saw the truth with Drum's awareness. One moment the Instant contained a cube of soldiers. That moment changed into a moment of confused hesitation as the Persians reordered their minds. The moment changed again and the soldiers were in three lines. In the moment of hesitation, when the troops were translating in their own minds the change from one configuration to another, in that pause wherein they believed they moved in the Instant as if they were moving in the Flux, Kookatchi, who suffered no such delusions, acted.

The Drum suddenly was next to the knotted coil of stolen objects, suddenly had them placed against his body, suddenly was in the middle of the uncoiling tails of the pastward guards.

The Persians, wedded as most Time Warriors were to the belief that their movements in the Instant were like movements in the Flux, could not even perceive what had happened. All they knew was that just after the order was given, the bounty of their work was gone.

Prince Xerxes did not know what to do. All this effort for nothing. Which way to go, who to pursue? He could not let his men know of his indecision. Orders had to be given immediately.

"Futureward, quickly. Once Constantine is past we will return to discover how this prodigy happened."

The Persians set off futureward while Kookatchi swam pastward, hiding in their wake. A simple theft, but enjoyable. Now where to go to luxuriate in the beauty of this prize?

One cycle of mind. Oh, yes, he had someplace to go. Where was it?

Another cycle. Someone was waiting for him. Who?

Another. Nir. Why did he want to meet an enemy chieftain?

And another. Nir, Quillithé, the broken island. Kookatchi the Bridge reappeared and Kookatchi the Thief vanished. Now, where was Nir?

And another. Oh, yes, now he remembered. The peak of Mount Tai in China, ten years futureward from the broken island. The Drum made his way pastward to the correct spot and anchored into the Flux, carrying his braided prizes with him.

Nir waited patiently on the mountain peak, looking out over the expanse of China and watching the slow course of change. Spread out over the landscape lay the easy answer to his vow of protection. The lives of the people of the Consumerist Mercantile Hegemony passed before him, lives lived in serene ignorance of the battles of the Instant. Their clothes might change, their particular fashions and attachments, the things they might acquire would be altered by the gentle flow of change-waves muted by ten thousand years of cracking, but their lives stayed fixed in peaceful ignorance of the war waged above the sky.

Was it not his duty to bring this serenity back to the Now, to protect the People with the changeless shadow of another broken island, an island created before humanity came to be, an island that would encompass the Great Mother's life? Nir knew as surely as he knew the litany of the Ghosts that the answer to that question was no. But he could not yet justify that answer. It was for the sake of justification, for words to be spoken in the Year of Ghosts' Conferring, that he had come to this place, come to rely on the mind of Quillithé and the actions of Kookatchi. Come to wait for evidence that would give his watery surety an earthly solidity.

Kookatchi appeared next to him. The Drum looked down from the mountaintop at the mist-fogged lights of a city-sprawl in the valley below. The noise of three million humans engaged in a life of barter and acquisition merged together into a rising hum that filled his ears. So many people, so many things, so many lives. Such a short existence, constricted as it was by life and death.

"I retrieved the items," Kookatchi said. He held up one of the two-lobed metal rods, which abruptly flickered and changed into another one; the shape was the same, only the color had changed from deep brown to dark red. "They are knotted together."

"I see," Nir said. "Untie them."

The Drum vanished into the Instant and separated his braided prizes into twelve individual baubles that he then took back down into the Flux. Kookatchi reappeared next to Nir. At his feet lay a dozen of the bi-lobed devices, identical except for color. Even the sleeping silver tiger stamped on each of the lobes was the same from object to object.

"Identify these," Nir said to his Second Voice.

The memory voice reached out and touched the objects. "Universal Power Storage Units. Every device seen in this place/time uses these objects."

"Every device?" Nir said.

"Every device."

"These are power supplies," Nir said.

"Why would the Persians want those?" Kookatchi said. "What good would they be in the Instant?"

"They are used in all the devices of this culture," Nir said, realization dawning suddenly in his mind. "With possession of these power supplies this whole region of the Flux becomes an unchanging armory they can continually raid to resupply themselves for their battles."

"A power supply that does not change over the centuries," Kookatchi said. "How can that be?"

"These must arise from the anchoring event that lies pastward in the broken island."

"How can the consequences of an event be that solid?" Kookatchi said. "Events change. That is the nature of the Instant."

Nir's eyes gleamed with momentary awareness. "And is not the nature of the Instant one of the things Quillithé sent us to seek?"

The Drum smiled and bowed his head in agreement. "So what do we do? We cannot go into the broken lands to make sure of this idea."

"No, we cannot," Nir said. "But we can make sure that these power supplies are fixed throughout the triangle of slow change."

"Agreed."

The two Time Warriors unanchored into the Instant carrying their prizes with them. Only the mountain was left behind to look down alone on the city below.

"Where shall we start?" Kookatchi tapped in the language of the Ghosts.

"Close to the apex of the triangle, ten years pastward from where these were taken."

A short swim futureward and a dive down into the Flux.

They appeared in a small village near the southern tip of India in the middle of a battlefield. Five thousand naked insurgents armed with goo-grenades were trying to reduce a heavily armored shopping complex to its component atoms, while on the brightly colored walls of the merchandise market, soldiers played streams of highly accelerated neutrons over their attackers, felling them like wheat under a scythe.

"What do we want here?" Kookatchi asked.

Nir pointed up at the walls, unanchored, and reanchored next to one of the tiger-headed two-meter-long neutron cannon. Two soldiers manned the weapon; they were clad in crimson uniforms with hawk-head helmets and were glaring down at the rebels with expressions of mixed rage and fear. They had been fighting for three hours and their early confidence in a swift outcome to the battle had long since eroded. The rebels kept coming in angry waves. No matter how many were felled, more followed. Their grenades had already reduced half of the complex to a mass of useless polymers, and the neutron cannon were antivehicle weapons, not antipersonnel, devastating but hard to aim at small targets. But the Hegemony's armies could not afford to send better weapons here; the rebellion was winning all across the earth. If only the first Grand Director had lived longer, he would have crushed the rebels. But no, this was no time for helpless grasping of the past; they had to concentrate on this battle, right now.

The cannoneers looked up in horror as they realized that a naked man, a rebel, was standing right next to them. How had he gotten there? Did the rebellion have some secret technology that even the Hegemony government did not possess? Both men drew short truncheons and shoved them toward Nir. The War Chief ducked to the side, uninterested in the battle.

Nir reached out his hands, touched the ends of the florid cannon, and yanked seven hours of the neutron gun's existence out of the Flux into the Instant. Seven hours previously when the soldiers had first come on duty and the attack was nothing more than a rumor, a neutron cannon had vanished from the walls of the citadel. A replacement was brought up and mounted, just in time to repel the first wave of attackers.

But the waves kept on coming and the loss of one cannon was enough to tip the balance. The shopping complex fell, as did so many others. The rebellion eventually conquered the earth and set up a propertyless state that lasted all of ten years before a counterrebellion rose up using hoarded weapons from the old Hegemony. Eventually that rebellion conquered the world, then fell apart into squabbling factions, by which point it was so far from the broken island that the wars of the Instant became again the dominant factors in human affairs.

Kookatchi met Nir in the Instant. "What use is this?" the Drum asked, pointing to the bulk of the cannon. "It is too big for a tribe to carry through the Instant at a swift swimming rate."

"We will not be taking it far," Nir said. "Just help me move it a few hundred kilometers."

The two of them rolled the seven-hour-long cannon northeast, then dragging the gun with them, they anchored down onto a plain near the Yangtze River. Nir studied the cannon for a while, letting Second Voice familiarize itself with its operation. Then following the Voice's instructions, he opened a panel on the underside of the barrel. There, held in a zinc housing, was a two-lobed rod exactly like the ones Kookatchi had stolen. Nir removed the power supply and replaced it with one of theirs.

The War Chief aimed the cannon at a tall tree and pressed the clearly marked blue firing button. The tree wavered for a moment, then collapsed to the ground.

"Ten years without change," Nir said. "Let us try further pastward."

"Very well."

The two returned to the Instant and the cannon, no longer held down, bobbed up after them, floating uselessly in the waters of time. It made its way slowly futureward, carried by the common tide that washed events toward the deeps.

Nir and Kookatchi, carrying the remaining eleven power cells, swam twenty years pastward and dove back into the Flux. They appeared in an entertainment complex in Nepal; it had been built by the second Grand Director in an attempt to mollify the people of the Hegemony and stave off the spread of the rebellion. The plan was simple. The other directors called it crude and feared it would not work; many of them struck secret deals with rebel factions offering them weapons in return for their personal safety.

The multiacre building was a knotwork of corridors, so confusedly interwoven as to give fits to a topologist or a sailor. Rooms of various sizes jutted haphazardly off the walls, floors, and ceilings of the intricate hallways like buds and flowers on a twisted vine. Each room had a video screen on its outer door that showed pictures unsubtly hinting at the pleasures, pains, distractions, and amusements that lay in wait on the other side.

Visitors walked aimlessly through the halls, stopping at doors that interested them. After a few moments' deliberation, they would either move on or drop a few plastic coins into a slot next to the door. The door would open, and they would pass in to enjoy whatever awaited them.

Nir and Kookatchi watched this process for a little while before slipping back into the Instant. They moved over one of the nearby rooms and reanchored so that they appeared inside the entertainment area without having to bother with the pointless ritual of paying. This particular room was a dance studio. The walls were covered with mirrors, the ceiling glowed with a gentle violet light. The floor was made of some soothing springy material that gave a gently energetic boost to every step they took, and a slippery orange mist covered the lowest meter of the room, massaging their legs. Lined up on the far wall were thirty-five android dancing partners waiting with the infinite patience of all wallflowers to be asked out onto the floor.

The Ghost and the Drum strolled over to a short female android dressed in a patchwork sari made of little gauze squares and pentagons. She stepped forward and held out her hands, but Nir did not lead her in the dance. Rather, he turned her around and opened a panel in her artfully curved back. Held in an easily removed gold housing was one of the tiger-stamped power sources, which Nir replaced with one of his.

After a moment's deathly stillness, the android raised her arms and laid them squarely on Nir's shoulders. The War Chief ducked out of the way while the robot pirouetted across the floor, clutching the empty air to her like a lover.

"It works perfectly," Nir said to Kookatchi. The Drum nodded and the two vanished into the Instant, leaving the android to finish the dance alone and resume her place on the wall. There she would sit, coming to life when called upon, then receding back into death when the dance ended, until the goo-death handed out by the rebellion reclaimed her plastic body.

"Shall we continue checking?" Kookatchi asked.

"Yes," said Nir.

They moved to seventy years futureward from the broken island. In the Indian Ocean, they found a small one-man boat cast adrift with a delirious, half-starved man on board. The boat had used up the last of its stored energy before it reached port, but one of the power supplies revived it. The man struggled back to his feet and piloted the boat back to shore. There he told his fellow rebels about being saved by one of their number who had appeared on the ship. Confidence grew; surely there were rebel cells with secret resources, secret weapons. Once the cells came together the rebellion would blossom and conquer. It might take a hundred years, but now they were confident. The day would eventually come.

Sixty years futureward from the island, an orchestra-in-a-box accepted one of the universal power supplies and in gratitude gave Nir and Kookatchi a symphony of bell ringing and drum beating.

Fifty years, a home surgery machine.

Forty, an automated plow.

Thirty, a toy battle tank.

Twenty, a personal rejuvenator guaranteed to add a century to your life, sold with a five-year guarantee.

Ten years, a metal foundry.

Five years, a thirty-armed juggling robot.

"I think that confirms it," Nir said as he and Kookatchi floated in the shallow waters of the darkland. "These power supplies are anchored solidly in the broken island; whatever event created them maintains the unchangingness."

"As the Great Mother maintains the Now?" Kookatchi said. He had not meant to speak, but the impulse to respond came over him so swiftly that he spoke that which he had thought to keep silent.

Nir's stretched-out tail of ten years became again the prison maze that had held Kookatchi before. "Drum, what do you know of the Great Mother?"

Kookatchi the Thief surfaced and began to construct a lie that might mollify the War Chief, but Kookatchi the Bridge regained control of himself and in an effort to regain Nir's trust told the truth. "I know only that which I have heard from feeling the speech of your Ghosts, hearing the myths of your descendants in the Diaspora, and listening to the ambitions of the tribes that wish to conquer the Now."

"And have you entered the Now unawares?" Nir asked, pressing down upon the Drum with threatening months of his life.

"Not since your predecessor was War Chief of the Ghosts," Kookatchi said, surprised at the memory. He had forgotten that he had actually been in the Now, but the need to speak truth had drawn the memory up from the depths of his mind. "And then I traveled only a few years inward following an invasion force. I left when they retreated."

"Why did you come into the Now?" Nir's whole being covered the space and time around Kookatchi; the feel of death was very clear in the taps of the War Chief.

It would have to be the truth. "To see the beauty of the Great Mother," Kookatchi said.

"But you did not succeed," Nir said.

"No."

"And would you try again?" Nir asked.

"Only if I had forgotten all that had passed between us," Kookatchi said. "I know you could capture and kill me and that you would if I did come to her."

"So long as you know that, Drum," Nir said, and he returned to placid floating, "I will let you live."

"Thank you, Nir," Kookatchi said. "Is it permitted that I speak what I was thinking concerning the Great Mother?"

"It is," Nir said. "For your thoughts echo mine."

"Whatever else changes in the Now, you Ghosts maintain the life of the Great Mother."

"True," said Nir.

"Whatever else changes here futureward of the broken island, these power cells remain. They are fixed as you wish the Great Mother would be fixed."

"Also true."

"Then are you seeking a way to create a broken island, to keep her safe?"

"No," Nir tapped. "Though many of my Ghosts would want to do so."

"And why do you not want to?"

"I cannot answer that, Kookatchi," Nir said. "But I feel that the People and the Now would be in greater danger from the presence of a broken island than they are from the mad tribes who seek to enslave us."

"And will your Ghosts accept your feeling?"

"No," Nir said. "That is why we must continue our search. Somewhere we will find justification or refutation for my view."

"And if you find refutation?" Kookatchi asked.

"Then I will see to it that the Now breaks, and then the labor of the Ghosts will be done."

Nir's mind filled with the sad concept of the Now broken into an island, a fixture within the ocean of time. It would fulfill the vow of the Ghosts, but in a manner that would be the ending of the Ghosts themselves. They would no longer be able to dwell above the Now; they would exiled from their native time by the terrible cracking weight of their own long tails.

With that realization the War Chief's mind changed.

For what the Ghosts could do to the Now, every single one of the nomad tribes of time could do to some other part of time. They could shape a piece of the Flux into the future they wanted, then break the corresponding region of the Instant into a fractured island, preserving the history they desired in unchangeable shards of time. The endless battle over history would be resolved.

For a moment, the War Chief contemplated this version of peace in the Instant—but only for a moment. Two thoughts clamored for his attention, each objecting to the Instant he was contemplating. The first was a feeling of primal disgust at the idea of more broken ground. The second was a question: What will the tribes do if their ambitions are achieved, but they cannot live in the time and place of that fulfillment? Will the tribesmen be satisfied with fixed histories if they cannot be masters of those histories? Would they be satisfied to rest in timeless triumph if they could not enjoy the fruits of their eternal labors?

XVI

Quillithé watched Nir and Kookatchi's progress, tracking them through the millennia until they vanished into the invisible region. Once her vision was no longer occupied by concern for her agent-allies, she took up her own personal contemplations.

Asking: What is the nature of the Instant? She swirled the thought in the vast ocean of her mind, letting it ripple out like an eddy of change let loose in the Instant. She let it flow through the vast tides of her experience and watched it conjoin with other flows of thought, watching for the emergence of strong currents that might feed the deeps of her understanding.

There, a strong wave emerged as the question joined the tides of history. The wave carried a reminder that research into the Instant itself was the cause of man's presence in the waters of time. Dhiritirashta, who had first freed himself from what he later called the Flux, had been a seeker into time. But neither his research nor that of any other had ever lasted past the point of liberation. Greed for knowledge had always given way to greed for power when a time-bound person became free to swim through the waters, changing history to comply with vision. Over and over there had been a cycle of what was, to Quillithé's vision, a series of perfect recurrences. The newly free people of time would enter the Instant with the noblest of motives: to search for truth, to liberate their fellows from the yoke of atemporal oppressors, to sculpt the world into a utopia. All the new dwellers in the Instant conceived of this as easy to do.

But in that spiral of recurrence the hard realities of time's ocean took hold. Those noble desires actually took great effort to accomplish. There were foes to be conquered, plans to be laid, time to be altered. The newly freed became slaves to their own labor; they lost the awareness of the Instant in the awareness of work and war.

Quillithé realized to her great surprise—such a strange thing to see, surprise—that she too was caught up in this substitution of awarenesses. Her seven fathers had brought her forth for battle and she had battled, turning her vision and her mind to serve their purpose, their fear.

Quillithé looked at the seven men with their few-months'-long tails clustered and huddled around her century-body. Fearful pictures still flickered from one to the other, worries and questions, terrors never assuaged though they had been safe for so very long. What was she to make of them and their creation of her?

Was she not ruled by their fear as much as the other tribes were ruled by their desires?

Quillithé once more turned her vision to look at the tides of her own thoughts. Somewhere hidden below the surface of her thinking there would be countercurrents, deep-flowing fears that would dampen the change-wave of her question. Yes, in the wide-open seas of her mind where she contemplated battle, protecting her fathers had been her priority; and there in the deeps where she crafted orders for her soldiers fear ran strong beneath the surface, and in the choppy waters where she considered the other tribes and their attitudes, the tides of terror churned the ocean.

A tidal wave of pure self-awareness washed out from Quillithé's interior vision overwhelming the streams; all the flows of fear were calmed. All but two persistent undertows.

There and there, the two most stubborn regions of awareness, the two stern flows that would not be stilled so easily. The first unburnable terror lay in the pool where she considered her own body, her own vulnerable form, the Monster of the deep who cannot safely leave the deep. Her century of power and powerlessness. That all-pervasive, all-invasive current had to be stilled before she could look at the Instant free of her own biases. But how? She was what she was.

But what was she? Quillithé scattered that question through her mind, seeking a better answer, a reply that did not grow from her own vulnerability.

Possibilities echoed through her consciousness. Pride suggested itself: She was who she was, Monster of the deep, Lady of the only army, doomsday embodied. What had she to fear? But she rejected that pride, knowing that it would blind her vision, and blind she was nothing. Confidence in power offered itself: She was more dangerous to her enemies than they were to her; as long as she maintained the army and created wise strategy she had nothing to fear. But she rejected that as well. She had already met her match in Nir. If the War Chief became her enemy she might not survive the conflict. If Nir reached out to strike her, she might die.

The thought of that death echoed through her and she accepted it. It was true. Death was possible. In the changing of time's ocean she might be destroyed. And with that acceptance, death became possibility and her mind embraced rather than rejected it. The wash of death-fear vanished in the counterwash of acceptance.

One current remained, a stubborn wave ironically strengthened by the destruction of death. Quillithé feared her allies. She could not take into her thinking those two whose minds she did not know: Kookatchi with his Drum's thoughts and Nir with his swiftly turning tactician's mind. Fight them she could, defeat them she might, know them she could not. They were too unlike her and too unlike the normal minds that dwelled in Flux and Instant for her mind to truly encompass them.

But they lived, they survived, they thrived in the Instant as she thrived in the Instant and they showed her things and brought her truth from their own senses. Accept the truth, filter out their personal prejudices as Thief and War Chief, and she could see the truth they brought. To encompass that truth in her awareness she had only to abandon the need to encompass them in her predictions. Their present would give her all she needed if she gave up the need to know their futures.

The ocean of Quillithé's mind was purged of all change governed by fear. She returned to the question: What is the nature of the Instant?

Now the change-wave in her thoughts began to propagate freely. The Instant could be entered. Solid time was not a complete prison; by effort man could be freed from it. That told her much, a great deal about time and its two sides. New courses of awareness arose in the ocean. Nothing entered the Instant, save man brought it there. All motion in the Instant affected the solid world below; all movement of the waters created change. The current of thought broadened in extent, touching more and more of her mind.

What could exist in the Instant? Long-tailed warriors, Drums, objects taken from the Flux, and Quillithé herself. Consider those things one by one. Begin with the objects torn from the earthly side of time. Though she did not herself remember the Flux, she knew that those who passed back and forth between the two sides of time had to learn to live both ways, embrace an amphibious existence. They had both to walk and to swim. All in the Instant knew that. Ah, there was a strong flow to follow. All tribes knew this and took it for granted. It was a piece of the Instant's nature that one could pass back and forth and by so doing have two distinct existences; that was true for objects and people in the Instant.

The long-tailed warriors who comprised the vast majority of dwellers in the Instant, what could she discern from her knowledge of them?

She knew that they were the most comfortable of the dwellers in the Instant, that the ocean of time was easiest for those who were capable of swimming in the shallows of the Now or in her

own native deeps, that they passed most easily back and forth between Flux and Instant, and that this very ease permitted them their
blind unconcern for the world around them. They could care about
the war and about their dreams of settled histories and utopias because the earth and waters of time were comfortable for them. From
that rising tide waves of change blossomed. That the Instant should
be most comfortable for the long-tailed told her much about the
waters and the waves, about how safe man could be in the Instant
and how hard and sharp the waves of change had to be in order
to threaten them.

She turned to the current of the Drums. What did she know?
She knew that they did not perceive the Instant as others did. She
knew that their perception was more accurate than even hers. She
had learned from Kookatchi that the passage of events in the Instant
was an illusion. He saw constantly the truth of the Instant, but his
memory and his desire for beauty made it impossible for him to
seek further.

Only beauty could capture his attention and hold it cycle after
cycle, and the Instant itself was too familiar to him to be beautiful.

But begin with the truth he perceived. If the Instant had the
illusion of passage, what was the nature of the changing of the
Instant? An answer came cresting, a wave breaking in the golden
brightness of her vision. Man changed the Instant. His entry from
time's other side changed it, and all change of the Instant was his
action. A vision arose in Quillithé: a coiled loop of action twisting
strangely through Flux and Instant. She saw a deed done in the
Instant, creating change in the Flux, which brought forth more
change into the Instant. And in this loop of change the dwellers in
the Instant had imprisoned themselves. This loop that existed in
imitation of the true solid cause and effect of the Flux was not real,
and the Drums knew it. They were not bound by this prison of
change; they were free to move throughout the waters of time,
unfettered by the need to change the Flux in order to change the
Instant. But their awareness was based on the shortness of their
lives. Lives . . . that was it.

A thousand change-waves rose in her thoughts and conjoined into a world-changing tidal wave that overcame her entire awareness. It was the lives they had taken with them into the Flux that held the tribes in their delusions. Quillithé opened her vision and looked out across the expanse of half the Instant. The tribes warred, enslaved, stole, and killed to feed the memories of their lives. Only the Drums and she herself were free of that imprisonment.

But what of herself? True, her own life was no prison, but her fathers' lives were. She had been enslaved to their fearful lifespans. Now what did she see? What did she know of herself?

She knew that only the deeps were safe for her. She knew she could not swim herself through the waters. Did that not tell her much about the Instant and its limits?

The change-wave altered her understanding, making tides and flows and breakers that revealed all possibilities within their forewave and backwash, an infinite range of possible natures of the Instant.

Now she had to consider the broken island in relation to this new form of the ocean.

The broken island was a thing in the Instant. Somehow man in the Instant had created it, for all changes in the Instant came about by man. When she knew how it had been made, Quillithé would be able to choose what the new knowing of the Instant would be. Until then she would have to wait and stare at her ocean of possibilities, dropping in changes here and there, seeing which streams of possibility petered out, and which grew stronger as they moved toward the deeps of understanding. She would wait and watch, until Nir and Kookatchi returned with solid information with which she might break the tides of false flow and guide the currents of truth.

"The War Chief has not yet returned," the Elder said, addressing the Ghosts assembled gathered together in the dry season of the Year of Ghosts' Conferring.

"You have had to stave off one attack in his absence," the Elder went on.

The Ghosts silently remembered the battle they had just fought, a hard-won victory.

Henri Cinque's Royal Huntsmen of Time's Fields had assaulted the Now in search of what all came to the Now for, rulership of mankind's beginnings.

The Royal Huntsmen's attack had been long in the planning. They had scouted the defenses of the Now from a safe camp in the Diaspora, and had noted that the former activity of sending out Ghost scouts had ceased. Their commander, Prince Robert d'Orleans, had concluded that the Ghosts were fortifying themselves out of fear of something. Prince Robert had both in his time-bound life and his atemporal existence followed the battle maxim that a fearful enemy is a vulnerable enemy. By following this principle unquestioningly he had won as many battles as he had lost. Experience had taught him nothing; the maxim was all he regarded as important.

The attack itself was savage and noisy, a terrifying display of angry waves and cutting tides. Prince Robert had sought to increase the fear of the Ghosts so that they might flee or submit.

His initial attack cost two of the futuremost border guards two years of their lives each, but they had responded as Nir's standing orders commanded them: retreat and alert the other Ghosts. The Royal Huntsmen were gleeful as they swam pastward into the latter century of the Now, but their glee ended when the main body of Ghosts confronted them at the midpoint of the Now.

The battle was protracted as the Ghosts concentrated their efforts on destroying first one, then another of the Royal Huntsmen. Prince Robert's personal guards were slain first, their eight-year-long tails shattered into seconds by the concerted efforts of eight Ghosts. The rest of the Royal Huntsmen rallied around their Prince to form a defensive barrier with their own tails, but through this wall Col slipped by duplicating the trick by which Nir had captured Kookatchi. The scout reshaped his body in a momentary change, altering himself from a straight line facing past-to-future into a complex knot that crossed through the barrier of defending Huntsmen, then again into a straight battle line inside the living wall.

Col faced the Prince and in single combat slew him, carving his life up into mere moments. The Royal Huntsmen fled back into the Diaspora and from thence futureward to the safety of the middle Instant, there to choose a new leader.

In the Year of Ghosts' Conferring, the Elder sang Col's praises to his fellow warriors.

"Great service have you given to the People, Col," she said. "Your name and deed will be remembered and given to the People to sing at night over the fires, so that all later Ghosts will know you while they live."

Col covered his eyes with his hands and bowed to the old woman seated on the mound of bones.

The Elder's praise was great, for she thought she had found in Col a replacement for Nir; such battle brilliance was the quality she had been seeking.

"Tell me the source of your deed," she said, hoping to extract more evidence of the scout's worthiness to be War Chief.

"It was a variation of an action I had personally felt," Col said. "What action?"

"The War Chief used such a maneuver in his capture of a Drum," Col said. "I drew a new effect out of his method."

The Elder lowered her head in sadness. It was not enough. She did not want to replace Nir with one who simply discovered new variations on Nir's stratagems. She had seen the dangers of an un-imaginative War Chief, seen the risk to the Ghosts, the People, the Now, and the Great Mother herself if the battle leader of the Ghosts could not create new plans and schemes for war.

Before Nir's ascendancy she had been satisfied with the mettle and mind of previous War Chiefs. Now her standards were higher. Winning battles was not sufficient; whoever took on the mantle of War Chief had to continually think of the good of the People and continually guide the course of Ghostly existence according to the

Now and the ingenuity of his mind. No one of the Ghosts could do that. Still, she could do something.

"Col," the Elder said. "The War Chief is not here to decide what position you merit for your actions, so I am forced to make that decision for him. Until Nir returns I name you Voice of the War Chief. You will interpret the War Chief's standing orders and innovate as needed in battle."

"But Elder," Col said, "I am so recent a Ghost. All here have more experience than I."

"Many had more experience then Nir when he showed himself capable of being War Chief. No dispute, Col. My decision is made."

"Yes, Elder."

Col covered his eyes once more, as did the rest of the Ghosts. Then they vanished into the Instant, leaving the Elder in her place on the Great Mother's mound. A seed of ambition has been planted, she thought. Let us see if it sprouts into greatness in him. She hoped Nir would return swiftly and the matter would be unnecessary, but if not, perhaps she could make Col an adequate substitute for the absent War Chief.

The Elder vanished into the Instant, leaving the solid time of the Now. Its history had been changed again by the recent battle. The child who would have grown up to be the final priest of the People had died from the bite of a snake when only four years old. His uncle Col had never been conceived. Instead, Col's parents had brought forth twin daughters three months before Col would have been born. In the Instant, the scout reconciled himself to never having existed and by letting his attachment for his life become attachment to the People his mind became the mind of a veteran Ghost.

XVII

On a spray-swept beach on the island of Fiji, five years futureward from the broken island, Nir and Kookatchi squatted on the sands, passing back and forth from one hand to the
other the last of their stolen power supplies. That it was a clue to
the nature of the breaking was clear. But how to pursue it without
venturing into the broken island? That was the question that had
stymied them. Conversation had vanished into contemplation as
they considered the strangeness of this unchanging object, Nir waiting for inspiration to strike him, Kookatchi hoping that some appropriate memory would surface.

Two teenaged girls, wrapped from head to toe in the latest
figure-concealing beachwear, watched the two strange men tossing
the power cell back and forth like a toy. The girls had just that
morning flown from their home in Alaska to swim in the warm
Pacific waters before going to work at the direct-neural-stimulation
musical recordings factory in the evening. The two had been close
friends since birth but now were rivals for a promotion. They had
come to Fiji together in order to try and patch up their differences
so that whichever of them was promoted would not lose the friendship of the other.

"The tall one's a protester," one of the girls whispered, distracted from her purpose by the scandalous sight of Nir's naked form.

"He can't be," the other said. "Not out in plain sight. The police wouldn't let one of them run free in a public place."

"Why else would someone be naked on a beach?" the first one argued, wrapping her gauze blanket tighter around her body.

"I don't know," said the second. "What should we do?"

The first girl pulled a circular metal disk out of the fashionable lime green pouch tied to her thigh and slid a long fingernail, painted with the face of a cougar, around its outer edge. There was a momentary hum, then a voice came from the disk. "Fiji security police. How may we assist you?"

"There's a protester on the beach," the girl said in a hissing whisper.

"Turn on your transponder and an officer will be there within five minutes."

The girl tapped the center of the disk three times. A small spot of pink light began to blink on and off from the place she had touched. The two young women went to hide behind a large outcropping of rocks to watch the police apprehend these dangerous criminals. Both agreed this was the most exciting thing that had ever happened to them. Their future rooted-rivalry was quickly forgotten in the pleasure of the moment.

Neither Nir nor Kookatchi had paid any attention to their observers. Indeed, they were paying precious little attention to their surroundings at all. They had anchored onto the Fiji beach for lack of any idea of where to go or what to do. They had begun tossing around the power cell to fill the empty silence between them.

Kookatchi tossed the dumbbell through the air and watched it twirl in a graceful arc down toward Nir, an idle moment of beauty amidst the dullness. The War Chief reached up, grabbed the power cell, and tossed it in a straight line back to the Drum, a short practice of accuracy. Somewhere between the eightieth and the ninetieth toss, their silent game was interrupted.

From the northeast a gleaming red-gold police skimmer arced down through the air like a well-aimed arrow. The craft was three meters long and one meter across. Open to the sky, it resembled nothing so much as a flying war canoe. Its metal hull brightly painted with a shark's face was reflective enough to be seen from five kilometers away in the bright Pacific sunlight. The thing continued its curving descent until it was directly over Nir and Kookatchi, falling as if to impale them. Ten meters above the ground, the skimmer stopped in midair, turned sideways so its keel was parallel to the earth, and hovered ostentatiously on its antigravity repellers. The canoe's long shadow fell across the two Time Warriors, blotting out the sunlight.

"Protester, leave the beach or you will be arrested," a voice boomed from the canoe.

Nir caught the dumbbell and held it. His gaze drifted upward toward the police craft.

"This nudity taboo is becoming a distraction," Nir said. He flicked his gaze up to the sky. Kookatchi caught the significance of the glance and the two of them vanished into the Instant.

The two Time Warriors disappeared from the solid world, leaving two confused girls and six suspicious policemen. The latter eventually concluded that the two men on the beach had been holograms rigged up to distract the Fiji police from some diabolical act of subversion. A subsequent sweeping investigation of the Island's populace led to the extraction of more than one hundred confessions to acts of anticommercial terrorism. This brilliant piece of police work resulted in the promotion of the Fiji Police Chief to the post of Pan-Pacific Inquisitor. The two girls received a substantial monetary reward and their fame was such that both received promotions at their factory. A friendship that had been destined to fall apart within two years became lifelong, eventually leading to the uniting of both their families into one.

When the report of the investigation on Fiji reached the tiger throne of the Grand Director, he realized that the isolated acts of protest, which had been nothing but an annoyance to the Hegemony for the last fifty years, were not, as he had believed, the acts of isolated malcontents. It became abundantly clear to the Grand Director that there was a rebellion brewing, invisible to his eyes and his security forces. The only possible response was a worldwide crackdown on the protesters, the institution of severe penalties for nudity, and an increase in the number of officers in the Special Police sections in order to have more people available to infiltrate cells of the rebellion and extract confessions.

By such means did the cause and effect of the Flux carry the change-wave created by Nir and Kookatchi's presence and vanishing.

As he passed from Flux to Instant, Kookatchi could feel the propagation of the wave along the bottom of the ocean. The Drum was struck by a strange feeling, as if the bottom of time's ocean were corrugated, rough edged, almost contoured. And with this realization came another, seemingly unrelated.

"Nir," Kookatchi said, "let us see if we can change the nudity taboo."

"Change it?" the War Chief was scandalized. "You ask a Ghost to change the Flux?"

"Nir, we are sixty-five-thousand years from the Now. Nothing you do here can affect those you are vowed to protect."

"But to effect deliberate change, to follow the ways of the mad tribes of the enslavers! No, Kookatchi, no Ghost would do that."

Kookatchi's consciousness recycled. He remembered that they were arguing about change, he remembered the strange experience of unanchoring, the raggedness of the ocean bottom.

"War Chief of the Ghosts," Kookatchi tapped in the formal speech of time's beginning. "We know that not all things here can be changed. We know that though waves pass over the solid world certain things remain fixed. Is this not the only line of investigation we have? We must see what can be changed and what will come of it."

For a few seconds of his life Nir held on to stubbornness, to the strictures of the Ghosts. But then he remembered his predecessor, remembered the man's desperation, his struggle to find a way to save the People within the confines of the vow and his ultimate failure and madness. In fighting him, Nir had realized what no other Ghost had, that the vow was not a prison that held his actions but a ground from which his actions would arise. That awareness had been the foundation stone of all he had done since then. The War Chief had bent the customs of the Ghosts many times, but that bending had always been in true service of the vow and the People. That, as he saw it, was the War Chief's duty. Only he could make such decisions. He could not now retreat into obedience when obedience itself pointed him in the opposite direction.

"What do you propose?" Nir asked.

"That we see if the nudity taboo is as tightly anchored as these power cells. You will have to effect the changes; my body is too small. But I can instruct you in how to do it."

"There is no need," Nir said. "All Ghosts know the arts of change."

"You do?"

"We have forgotten none of the lessons we learned from our enslavers," Nir's words were tapped loudly against the shallow waters, drowning out Kookatchi's waves as a decade drowns out a minute. The War Chief hesitated one moment more, letting his mind settle into a new configuration. Yes, this experiment was in the service of the vow. Nir banged out his desire like a blacksmith hammering the form his will has conceived into recalcitrant iron.

"I will undertake this changing," he said, and it became so.

The War Chief and the Drum swam a short distance in space and a year futureward in time and anchored into the Flux, appearing near a small arcology that straddled the Yangtze River. The building was only two kilometers high and covered a mere sixteen square kilometers in area. It was constructed of alternating panels of semi-translucent plastic and light-emitting crystal. Clouds of flying vehicles landed and took off from the spiraled roof, like hordes of mosquitoes feasting on a drowsing man.

Nir and Kookatchi slipped back into the Instant, then reappeared inside the bustling building. Second Voice quickly mapped the place and informed Nir that the arcology consisted of three concentric cylinders. The outermost was a shell of shops that stretched from the skin of the building inward for a quarter of a kilometer. The next layer inward was a thick stratum of apartments, and within that lay the central cylinder of the building which housed a plethora of manufacturing areas. The arcology was an experiment created by the local Subdirector of Housing to combine manufacture, living, and shopping in one place. He hoped that if the arcology succeeded it would eventually replace the present system by which the people of the Hegemony traveled all over the world for the purposes of buying. The Subdirector had suggested that the arcologies would be self-contained areas of production and consumption, which would be much more efficient for the acquisition, use, and disposal of commercial creations.

"Kookatchi," Nir said as he looked out across the building from an artificial palisade halfway up the manufacturing sector. "Find me a maker of clothing."

"As you wish."

Kookatchi vanished into the Instant. The Drum began a random search of the building's center, appearing in one factory after another until he found one that made clothes, then he reported back to Nir.

The War Chief meanwhile had been consulting Fourth Voice on the standard tactics the tribes of time employed when they wanted to make careful changes in the Flux as opposed to the more haphazard changes caused by battle.

Few tribes had the opportunity to use such precise control, but they all knew how to do it, and they all dreamed of eventually using those skills to create the histories they wanted. The Ghosts, concerned only with the safety of the Now, did not practice this art, but as Nir had declared they knew how to perform the basic work. However, the deft subtlety Nir needed for this operation was unknown among the Ghosts—except to Fourth Voice, which guarded the knowledge until a War Chief needed it.

"The standard procedure," Fourth Voice said, "is to institute several small changes over the course of one or two decades. Each change acts as a guide marker toward the desired end."

I understand, Nir said. Continue

"A common strategy is to manipulate the life of one person and use him or her to carry out your ends."

Kookatchi reappeared. "Four hundred thirty-two stories down, fourth factory down the corridor."

War Chief and Drum flitted through the Instant into a small one-room manufacturing facility. One man sat in a chair, staring at changing abstract pictures on the wall. The pictures supposedly gave him inspirations for his clothing designs, but nothing had ever come from them. However, they were popular among designers and he could always use them as an excuse whenever he was asked about the source of his latest creation. When a notion occurred to him, he would sketch it on a computer screen, and then order the clothing construction machines to stamp out the actual apparel, creating as many copies of each design as the man ordered. Delivery robots then carried the clothes to several shops in the outer shell of the arcology.

Nir and Kookatchi hid in a corner of the room. The man, absorbed in his creation, did not notice them.

"Let me know as soon as he starts producing clothes that reveal much of the human form," Nir said.

Kookatchi nodded.

Nir vanished into the Instant. He began, slowly and gingerly, to flick out tiny change-waves, directing them toward the place in space and time where the man was designing the clothes. The process was somewhat haphazard, but since he was repeatedly affecting the same moment, any alteration that did not help his cause was instantly wiped out by the next one.

The designer sat in his comfortable chair, ignoring the random changing forms that danced on the far wall, focusing instead on the model of the human body that existed in his mind. Perhaps a mixture of materials that would change colors based on a combination of chemical sprays that could be applied each morning. Yes, that would do.

Change-wave.

Perhaps he could make an asymmetric poncho that revealed the top of the left shoulder. No, never. That flirted with nudity.

Change-wave.

Perhaps he could make an asymmetric poncho that revealed the top of the left shoulder. It flirted with nudity; that would never do, unless—suppose he made the effect comical, suppose it were a mockery of the nudist rebels. That would show them.

Change-wave.

Perhaps he could make a cover-blanket with several holes in places and with parodies of the nudist slogans on it. Yes, a mockery of the protesters, that would catch on; they would be shown up for the fools they were.

The designer punched the appropriate buttons on his computer and the new wraps were quickly pressed out of raw plastic, then dyed with inks, then words were carved into them with lasers.

Kookatchi appeared in the Instant. There was a strange echoing sound he could barely hear, but he could not trace its source. Concentrate on the matter at hand.

"Done," he said.

The two Time Warriors followed the new clothes into the six small boutiques that sold this designer's work. The daring new fashion had a brief flurry of popularity, then vanished. The designer quickly changed styles back to body-covering ponchos. Nir resumed his alterations, changing the choices of the shoppers in those stores until the innovative new line of outerwear became a best-selling style. The notion of clothes to mock the protesters caught the attention of the government, which gave a prize for patriotism to the designer. Soon everyone on earth was buying these new clothes, and other designers swiftly copied the notion, creating more and more daring fashions.

The protesters, finding their appearance mocked, switched their garb of choice. No longer naked, they began to appear in public wearing homespun clothing, plain gray in color with no adornment.

The waves of change Nir had created spread over the world, altering fashion sensibilities, but making no great change in the future. The government still came to believe that the isolated protests were the work of a well-organized conspiracy. The Grand Director still instituted repressive laws that angered more and more of the people until a true rebellion grew up where there had been none. That rebellion eventually overthrew the Hegemony one hundred years after the death of the first Grand Director. Those things seemed fixed, anchored by events that occurred in the broken time.

A swift exploration of the shallow centuries revealed these facts to Nir and Kookatchi, who had no trouble searching the region now that they were no longer hampered by the nudity taboo.

"A very fixed history," Nir said as they floated in the middle of the shallow lagoon. "Whatever we do only seems to contribute to its fixedness. Like the power supplies, the details can be changed but the core events remain."

"Yes, but how—" Kookatchi began to answer, but his consciousness recycled and he lost the thread of his speech. There was that sound again. Where was it coming from?

"How what?" Nir asked.

"Stop tapping," the Drum said. "I need to listen."

Nir floated without moving, keeping still since he did not know what Kookatchi's hearing would react to. The Ghost's deafness and blindness made him defer to the Drum's senses.

Kookatchi's consciousness recycled again. The sound was tinny, like water dripping on something. Another cycle. There, it was coming from the pastward direction.

"Follow me," the Drum said. "Swim slowly and keep still if I ask you to."

They slipped pastward, Kookatchi concentrating on the odd echo, Nir following a few months behind, trying not to interfere. For most of a century they swam until they neared the point where Nir had begun his changes.

When he came within a year of that place and time, Kookatchi swam back to Nir, and said, "You wait here. I must listen carefully."

Nir tapped out a quiet agreement. Kookatchi slipped pastward, leaving Nir to coil himself up and wait for the Drum's return.

Kookatchi returned after only a brief absence. "Follow me," the Drum said, leading Nir to a place just six months from the point where Nir had begun his alterations.

"Stretch out your touch," Kookatchi said.

Nir extended his only sense pastward over the shallow waters, over the rough ocean bottom, until he felt a jagged line, a cut in the ocean floor, an upthrust piece of dry ground a few seconds long by a few meters wide.

"A crack!" Nir tapped.

"Yes," said Kookatchi. "A crack made by your changes."

XVIII

"Confirmed," Fourth Voice said. "New breakage created. Source of breakage likely to be our change-waves."

"Strange," Nir said to Kookatchi. "How could a simple altera-tion, an action that has been done millions of times since the Instant was entered, have such a different effect?"

"There is no 'since the Instant was entered,'" the Drum replied. "The Instant is the instant. We change it, we change with it, and it is still the Instant."

Kookatchi's words itched in Nir's mind, but he could not make sense of them. His agile thoughts tried to adapt his thinking to accommodate these new notions, but could not do so. Nir, like all the other long-tailed dwellers in the Instant, habitually turned the sequence of perceived events into a history, a past-to-future like memory. This process kept minds anchored in the Flux while bodies floated free. The War Chief's experience in capturing Kookatchi had shown him that that perception was false, but he did not have yet enough experiences to let his mind transform into new aware-ness. So he let the Drum's words lie in his mind like a seed sown but not yet germinated.

The War Chief turned his thoughts away from pure atempor-

ality, back to the pseudotemporality that was the common manner
of thinking for the dwellers in the Instant. He retrieved his question
and reformulated it. What was different about this place that would
make his changes have such a catastrophic effect? For that question
there was an answer, and from that answer a need arose.

"Kookatchi, swim toward the broken island, cast your senses
about, tell me if the ocean bottom seems strange to you."

"To the broken island?" Kookatchi said. "How close? I do not
wish to fall in again."

"A month, a week, a day, an hour. Wherever you feel safe. I
need to know about the ocean bottom, and you can go much closer
than I can without risk to your life."

"Very well," the Drum said.

Kookatchi swam pastward. At first his mind was distracted from
the task Nir had given him by a sense of amazement that he had
felt often before. It was startling to realize that the long-tailed could
not see the Instant as it was, that they could not accept that from
one flicker of awareness of another the whole ocean of time would
be different. They clung hard to their time-bound conceptions, and
their years of life between recyclings helped them maintain that
clinging. Even Nir, whom Kookatchi knew to be dangerously facile
in the changing of his thoughts, could not easily grasp this. Even
Quillithé, whose mind so dwarfed his own that he was afraid of
being lost in her contemplations, even she who did not remember
the Flux at all could not easily abandon this way of thinking.

The Drum's consciousness recycled and he recalled his mission.
He was a single year futureward from the broken island and the
ocean floor was gritty, and something else. What was he feeling?
He cast his gaze down at the bottom. Were those striations in the
ocean floor, little channels that were guiding the water's course?

The Drum swam on, his mind focused on the bottom, trying
to see the beauty of the ocean floor. All other thoughts faded away.
Only the bottom with its tracks and channels remained in his perception, the details of the ocean floor growing larger as he swam

pastward. At first the channels were barely visible, only a fraction of a second wide. But as he neared the broken lands and the waters grew shallower, the channels widened until some were more than ten seconds in width, giving strange guidance to the lower currents of change.

So fascinated did the Drum become that he barely noticed the approach of the broken island, a month away, a week, a day, an hour, and then the currents began to gain an undertow and they started to pull him in, pull him toward the island itself.

Kookatchi's consciousness recycled. The broken island, he was falling again, sliding across the frozen ice—no, not ice, water was pulling him, the tides of time themselves were running backward near the bottom. An undertow. He remembered the word, remembered swimming in the waters off the coast of Australia during his time-bound life; he remembered the warnings of his family and his people who no longer existed, who never had existed. He remembered that the surface progress of the waves from sea to land carried an opposite current under it, a washing out to sea that might pull him away from the land.

Here in the Instant the opposite was happening. The surface waves were washing away from the island, but the undertow was pulling him back. Kookatchi swam up, away from the bottom to surf along the surface waves, away from the breakage, away from the shattering rocks of the island. Back to where Nir floated in patience.

"We are on broken ground," Kookatchi tapped as he reached the War Chief.

"As I suspected," Nir said. "The ocean bottom is broken, but there is enough water for us to float above it."

"Yes," Kookatchi said. "And there are channels guiding the tides, making only certain changes possible. The bottom of the sea has been sculpted and that sculpting is confining the course of the waters."

"And that is why only certain kinds of changes happen below

us," Nir said. "And when I made a change contrary to the sculpting, a new sculpting was made, and that created an upthrust, cracking the sea bottom."

"You seem pleased about this," Kookatchi.

"Not pleased," Nir replied. "Satisfied. We have enough to bring back to Quillithé. We know the confinement of change and something of the source and consequence of that confinement. And . . ." The War Chief's tapping trailed off.

"And what?"

"And we know that we are standing on broken ground. But we do not know if any actions of ours will cause the ocean floor to shatter completely, pulling us down into the prison of shattered earthly time."

"You are right. We must leave."

The two swam futureward with cautious strokes, their senses sharply focused on the ocean floor. For two centuries the channels in the sea bottom were sharp and visible to Kookatchi and clear to Nir's extended touch. After that they were perceivable for another two thousand years as tiny millisecond trails. Beyond that time neither War Chief nor Drum could sense them, but both wondered in silence if the minute striations were gone or had only become too small to be perceived.

Such were the thoughts that weighed upon them as they made the long, hard swim back to the depths of time's ocean to confer with the ruler of the deeps.

Quillithé saw Nir and Kookatchi emerge from the darkness and sent down four detachments of her soldiers to frighten off any tribes that lay along their return path. Adjutant Irithrué was given command of the first detachment, those who were to travel furthest into the past.

Irithrué's confidence in her commander was as pure and perfect as it had ever been, but that confidence was now accompanied by a certain nervous confusion. Irithrué was sure that whatever the purpose of Quillithé's alliance with two outsiders, it was for good reason and would no doubt give benefit to the army. But Irithrué was incapable of seeing how that would be.

Furthermore, there was the fact that Quillithé had sent these two outsiders to scout out the region of blackness. Irithrué could not fathom this. How could the strategist rely on those who would not obey her orders? And, though Irithrué would not admit this to herself, there was the subtle implication that the soldiers and officers of the army would not be capable of carrying out this command.

Still, Irithrué would never have conceived of questioning Quillithé's orders, for she knew as all in the army did that only Quillithé had the breadth of vision needed to comprehend the reasons for all things. So Irithrué led her detachment of twenty warriors down thirty millennia to meet Nir and Kookatchi and instruct them on the safest route to the future, the route that would lead them through the other three detachments and so on to the army camp.

The marching out of eighty warriors from the army of the deep did not go unnoticed by the tribes that frequented the futureward reaches of the ocean. Such a progress out of the camp usually meant a punitive expedition, and each tribe prepared its path of retreat should it turn out to be the target of the sally.

The Atemporal Corps of Technophages, a tribe spawned by a cyborg society that had existed eighty thousand years futureward from the Now, were particularly fearful that they might be the targets of this raid. The Technophages were fanatical in their acquisition of the latest technical equipment available in the Instant. To further this desire they frequented the waters just pastward of the deeps, and were themselves frequently subject to Quillithé's wrath as she sought to relieve them of one mechanistic advantage or another. The Technophages had often wondered why Quillithé had never destroyed them, though she had had several opportunities. They had come to believe that she was insane and that her actions defied all reason.

They did not know that Quillithé regarded them as an impetus for others to make changes in the Flux in pursuit of technology; their presence created more change and fed waves of alteration into the deeps. They were also useful as judas goats, stalking horses sent to find other tribes with new armaments that Quillithé could then take.

Worried about this latest foray from the deeps, the Technophages sent two scouts to watch the progress of the mustering of eighty soldiers. These scouts had been, when time-bound, human brains placed in six-meter robot bodies, composites of metal, plastic, restrained force, and isolated human intellect. In the Instant their bodies were no stronger than that of any other warrior; the waves of sharpened change could carve their hard matter into milliseconds as easily as atemporal forms made of soft flesh. The failure of this body-changing had taught the Technophages that what defends in the Flux may be useless in the Instant; later they learned the contrary lesson and so set out to take what was valueless in the Flux and turn it to vital purpose in the Instant.

Thus the eleven-year bodies of the scouts were wrapped with Wavebreaker shields and high-mobility undulators that permitted them to contort their atemporal forms more swiftly than their opponents. They could dart in and out of danger faster than any dweller in the Instant except for a Drum.

The scouts in confidence approached to within two centuries of Irithrué's detachment. At such a distance their atemporal sight and hearing became effective and they could watch the deployment of Quillithé's troops in safety.

Irithrué had spotted the scouts at a millennium's distance, but her orders were to ignore such things. As long as no armed force approached her troops, Irithrué was to do nothing.

The scouts paralleled the pastward progress of Irithrué's detachment. At seventy thousand years futureward from the Now, Irithrué met up with Nir and Kookatchi.

The Drum had seen them coming at a distance of two centuries.

"Some of Quillithé's soldiers are swimming toward us," he informed Nir.

The War Chief stretched out his sense of touch and felt their approach. "Twenty of them, led by the officer who captured me and brought me to the camp. Either they are an escort sent to assist us or Quillithé has changed her mind about our usefulness."

"Which do you think?" Kookatchi said.

"I think they are an escort. Let us go meet them."

At a year's distance, Irithrué sent a picture in greeting.

Image: Irithrué leading Nir and Kookatchi futureward to another detachment. Repeat three times until entry into the camp.

Image in reply from Kookatchi: Nir and Kookatchi accompanying Irithrué, gentle hue of rose to imply gratitude.

From their distance the Technophage scouts could not clearly see what was happening as Nir and Kookatchi swam without concern into the detachment of soldiers and then all of them swam futureward. The scouts did see that pictures were passed back and forth, and though they did not know the language of the deeps they recognized it when they saw it.

The scouts returned to their camp as swiftly as their undulators would carry them to report to their leader. The chief of the Technophages had no name. It was a hierarchical arrangement of thirty-one human brains connected by intermediary computers; it used its multiple minds to consider many sides of a thing, but in battle only the primary brain led. Now all thirty-one of its selves turned their intelligence to digesting the peculiar information brought back by the scouts.

Level five, brain number twelve: "An ordinary capture. The Drum and the other were taken by the Monster of the deep. Nothing peculiar."

Level five, brain number eleven: "An extraordinary event. The

Drum is the Great Thief; the other conforms to reports of the tribe at time's beginning. They went voluntarily."

Level four, brain number six: "Subsidiary brain number eleven is correct. Event is extraordinary. Voluntary action suggests some form of military cooperation."

Level four, brain number five: "Presence of the Great Thief implies that the action is not military but involves some treasure."

Level three, brain number three: "Subsidiary brain number five is correct. An alliance has been formed to gain some great prize."

Level two brain number two: "Subsidiary brain number three is correct."

Level one, primary brain: "Subsidiary brain number two is correct. Some great device is being sought. The leaders of the earliest tribe and the last tribe are combined to seek it with the aid of the Great Thief. We must discover its nature or risk the chance that the monster of the deep enhanced by its power will decide to bring down doomsday."

The leader of the Technophages gave orders to send out its scouts to find the prize before the alliance did. Along with its fears of death from the deep, the leader had hopes that whatever the treasure was, it would permit the Technophages to destroy Quillithé and, at last, conquer the Instant.

The actions of the Technophages attracted the attention of spies from other tribes, who swiftly learned the source of the cyborgs' activities. Wonder and speculation spread through the middle of the Instant: wonder at alliance, a thing never seen before, and speculation about the prize the alliance was seeking.

XIX

From the deeps Quillithé watched the flitting back and forth of scouts and spies and the rise of excitement in the middle Instant. She quickly concluded that her own actions and those of Nir and Kookatchi were the source of this frenzy of activity. It was possible that inconvenience might arise from this flurry, but most likely it would have no impact on their plans.

Then Quillithé set that line of thought aside, for her allies had returned to speak with her.

Image from Nir to Quillithé: Map of the two-centuries-long area futureward of the broken island, the ocean of bottom rendered large to indicate its importance.

Image from Quillithé to Nir: Her old map, showing that the region they had been in was dark to her.

Image from Quillithé to Kookatchi: Repeat of Nir's picture with inquiring blue limning the bottom.

Image from Kookatchi: The ocean bottom lined with channels guiding the waters above.

Image from Quillithé: Time turned upside down, the earthly side controlling the watery side instead of what they had all believed, that the ocean governed the land completely.

"Did you understand that?" Nir asked Kookatchi.

"Not completely. She seems to be implying that solid time is dominant. But we know that is false."

"Not   dominant . . . controlling . . . mastering . . . ruling," Quillithé tapped in her reverberating form of Ghost speech.

"If not dominant, what then?" Nir asked.

Image: Water changing earth, earth controlling the flow of water.

"Interacting . . . coming together . . . feeding back . . . cycling . . ."

All through the camp, the soldiers and officers of the army waited in silence, their sight focused on the pictures flashing back and forth at the conference in the center. No one dared offer a questioning image to another lest they be distracted from the interchange. Even the four squadrons of soldiers who had helped escort Nir and Kookatchi back were not queried about their journey by their fellows.

Adjutant Irithrué, standing just outside the center of camp, watched in fascination, wondering what would come of the converse and whether this report marked the end of the alliance. Truth to tell, she hoped it did. She feared both Nir and Kookatchi, feared them because Quillithé had had to rely upon their capabilities. Surely such people were too dangerous let live once they had performed the tasks the strategist had set them.

The only members of the camp who spoke were not part of the army. Quillithé's seven fathers, cowering some decades away from Nir and Kookatchi, exchanged fleeting images of hope and fear.

Image: Converse done, the army rushing the center and shattering the Ghost and the Drum. Bright gold of hope.

Image: Quillithé, their daughter, abandoning them for the sake of these two outsiders. Deep purple of despair.

Image: Quillithé torturing Nir and Kookatchi, gleaning all the secrets of the first fifty millennia of inhabited time and using it to control all the Instant. Blinding gold of hope.

Quillithé herself saw the silence of her camp and the discussion of her fathers, but declined to do anything about either. Her soldiers were attentive to her orders and that was good. Her fathers were always fearful; they had never taken solace in the safety she gave them, and they would continue to fret no matter what happened.

"My grasp of her language is not good enough for what I want to ask," Nir said to Kookatchi.

"I will resume my role as translator," said Kookatchi the Bridge, Kookatchi the Mediator, Kookatchi who had almost completely forgotten Kookatchi the Thief.

"Thank you," the War Chief said. "Ask Quillithé if she thinks that the broken island arose because of some anomalous form of interaction between the two sides of time if the cause lies in both the Flux and the Instant."

Image from Kookatchi: Earth and Water, water flows, earth guides, an empty place limned in blue, the island appears.

"Yes," Quillithé tapped.

"Then we must find that event," Nir said. "It will tell us what we need to know to unmake the island."

"Unmake it?" Kookatchi said, surprised at the notion. "You think that is possible?"

"Yes," said Nir, "The broken island is only a change of things. And here, in the Instant, is where all change is made."

The War Chief tapped out the words and then realized what he had said, how he had just spoken against the fundamental attitude of the Ghosts. Here in converse with Quillithé and Kookatchi, his mind had made a great turning without him noticing. He was not just experimenting with change, as he had done in the shallows futureward of the broken island. He was embracing change as the source of good for the Instant.

Kookatchi, whose experience of the changeability of the Instant was more visceral, more immediate than either of his allies, was not convinced. He knew that the Instant was not changed; the Instant was change itself. While all things could be effected from it, it might itself be immune to certain alterations. He did not know, never truly knew how to judge. He only witnessed. Awareness was not sufficient for judgment. Vision and decision were needed.

Kookatchi looked at his allies. Vision and decision lay before him. Together they could form judgment. If they could be made to see the Instant as it was, then he could rely on their capacities to understand it.

Quillithé had returned to the consideration of the tides of possible natures of the Instant. This concept of a thing arising in interaction between time's two sides had brought forth many new branches of possibilities she had not conceived of. That she regarded as a defect in herself. She lacked sufficient knowledge of the Flux to fully comprehend the notion of interaction. Once again she would have to rely upon her allies.

Image from Quillithé: Nir and Kookatchi entering the darkness. Nir and Kookatchi leaving the darkness. Hundreds of spots of inquiring blue in the darkness.

"What does she want?" Nir asked.

"She wants to know everything that happened to us, in detail."

"Tell her," Nir said.

"I do not remember it," Kookatchi said.

"Then I will tell and you will translate."

"Agreed," said Kookatchi the Bridge.

Tap by tap and image by image the sequence of events, the whole tale of their journey was related to the Lady of the only army, who absorbed it all without comment. Kookatchi took great care to relate the events that happened to them in the Flux with sufficient detail to overcome Quillithé's ignorance of time-bound life. When the last words had been spoken and the last images sent, Quillithé withdrew into contemplation while her allies floated silently on the waters of the deep waiting for her to give forth her vision.

All she had been told confirmed her initial opinion; something that happened between Flux and Instant had created this channeled ocean bottom. Somewhere in the broken island itself lay the source event. A means of direct exploration would have to be created. But while Quillithé sought to direct her mind toward the needed work, a seemingly unrelated question crept out from one of the unattended corridors of her vast consciousness, crept out, then made its presence known, showing itself to be of much more importance than it at first appeared.

Image from Quillithé: Quillithé speaking to Kookatchi, her words in blue, Kookatchi speaking to Nir.

"She has a question for you," the Drum said to the War Chief.

Image: Nir in the Flux, naked, surrounded by clothed time-bound people, staring at him. Officers coming to arrest Nir.

"It concerns the nudity taboo."

Image: Nir working to change the taboo. Blue limning around Nir and the works of change.

Further image from Quillithé: Ghosts working against change, Nir making a change.

"She wants to know why changing that was important enough for you to make deliberate changes against the taboos of your tribe."

"It offended my dignity as a Ghost," the War Chief replied, unbending his kinks and coils into a straight line ten years long. Then in a martial rhythm he tapped out one of the litanies of his tribe.

"Shorn from the People, we need no markings to display our status.
Shorn from life, we need no modesty among the living.
Shorn from the world, we need no protection against the world's dangers."

Kookatchi had difficulty translating this into pictures, but he managed it with a series of images showing the dignity of warriors from a thousand different cultures and tribes.

Image from Quillithé: Nir surrounded by the time-bound, they regarding him, he regarding them.

"She wants to know why the opinions of the time-bound matter to you," Kookatchi said.

Nir fell silent for a while, trying to formulate an answer that

would clarify things for this strange being who had so little connection to the solid world, the place of human origin. He stumbled
for a time, searching for words Kookatchi would be able to translate
into images.

"The Ghosts are for the People," Nir said at last. Kookatchi
represented this as a picture of Time Warriors bowing to the time-
bound.

"It is our honor to serve the good of the People," Nir continued.
Kookatchi flicked out a picture of soldiers battling to defend civil-
ians.

"The time-bound are all descended from the People," Nir said.
Kookatchi showed a sketchy map of the Flux emphasizing the connection between the Now, the Diaspora, and all subsequent human
existence.

"Therefore an offense against the honor of the Ghosts by the
time-bound dishonors the People." Kookatchi struggled mightily
with this concept, finally showing a triptych of connected pictures.
The first showed Nir injured, the second showed that injury being
carried back to the Now, and the third, the injury being transferred
to the People, injuring them in turn.

Image from Quillithé: Another Ghost in the same situation as
Nir. Blue limning around the Ghost.

"She asks if another of your tribe would have felt the same."

"No," Nir said after thinking through all his tribesmen. "They
give regard only to the People themselves, caring nothing about
anyone who lives past the final hour of the Now."

"Thank you," Quillithé said, tapping the words in Nir's language
as best she could. The interchange had told her what she wanted
to know. Though blind and confined by the shortness of his senses,
Nir was as aware of the whole Instant as she was. He did not see
it directly as she did; instead he knew that from his People came
all of inhabited time. Action following action, he conceived of the
Instant. Quillithé, at last, understood her own decision to accept
the help of these two, and understood their decisions to do so as
well. Though neither War Chief nor Drum knew it, they had made

common cause because each of them, in their own way, thought of the whole Instant rather than just their part of it.

A strange vision of relief came to Quillithé. She could keep the alliance going since she could rely upon Nir and Kookatchi to be free of the parochialism that made the tribes untrustworthy. With that vision, Quillithé knew it was safe to return to the question of the broken island.

Image from Quillithé. Some unspecified being entering the darkness and then emerging.

"More exploration of the shallows?" Nir asked when the image was translated.

Image from Quillithé: Map of the shallows, unspecified being entering the darkness pastward of it.

"Into the island itself?" Nir asked. "The ground would crack under anyone's weight."

Image from Quillithé: Kookatchi, his small size and lightness emphasized by gold limning, entering the darkness.

Kookatchi the Bridge vanished from the Drum's mind, and Kookatchi the Thief reappeared.

Image from Kookatchi: Same picture, gray of denial over the whole image.

"What was that?" Nir asked.

"I refused," Kookatchi said to Nir.

The War Chief was about to give his agreement to Kookatchi's stand, when his mind changed and he saw his own experience in the broken island in a new light, one that made Quillithé's plan feasible.

"There is a way," Nir said, "for you to pass safely through the cracking."

"I will not do it."

"I escaped from the broken island by shifting my weight onto the cracks themselves."

"I will not go."

"Those cracks must be the channels through which the water flows. Rivers and rivulets that you can swim the surface of."

The Drum's consciousness recycled. He remembered being on the broken island. Remembered the cracks. Could that have been water flowing through them, streams of safe water between the solid chunks of time? Perhaps. But it was still not safe.

"I will not risk my existence for this," Kookatchi the Thief said, and floated in stubborn silence, defying a decade and a century with his single minute of life.

The War Chief and the strategist waited, but the Drum would not change his mind, though he went through a thousand iterations of life. Either could have killed him with one tail swipe, but they would not do so. Nor would threats be of any use. Both tactician and strategist knew that if Kookatchi was to go, he would have to go of his own accord.

"I will protect you," Nir said at last.

"How?" said Kookatchi. "You could not go with me."

"I did not say I would go. I said I would protect you."

The War Chief shook his ten-year-long body and the protective helix of his Wavebreaker shield came away from him like the shed skin of a snake. The numbing of his extended touch vanished and he floated uncovered in the waters of the deep. All the tides of time, all the events of a hundred thousand years washed over and under his unsheathed form. Naked he swam in the center of the army camp. Any warrior could have slain him with a sharpened wave. No dweller in the Instant since the first battles fought in the ocean had been so unprotected. But the War Chief of the Ghosts knew that he had to do this for the good of his People. If death came, it came, but this had to be done and only Kookatchi could do it.

"This is the most recent generation of Wavebreaker," Nir said. "I have not sensed its like anywhere else. Not even Quillithé has these yet. It kept me with my ten years of weight alive on the broken island. It will keep you safe."

Quillithé was amazed at the calm embrace of whatever would come to Nir. She flashed a picture of the War Chief's gamble to her seven fathers, hoping that the sight of bravery might inspire them, but they only cowered more. Whispered pictures passed back and forth between them. Surely the War Chief had some scheme up his sleeve; no one would actually put themselves at such risk. It must be a deception of some sort, and their daughter whom they had thought so wise was being hoodwinked by this trickster from the far end of time.

Kookatchi was awed by the beauty of the gamble. Nir's glorious boldness and willingness to risk his existence were too perfect a pair of treasures; he had to gather them up and take bravery into himself. Kookatchi the Thief reached for the shield and Kookatchi the Bridge wrapped it in a tight, tight spiral around his minute body.

The Drum's senses dulled momentarily but he quickly adjusted his perceptions to accommodate the soft blanket of armor that swathed him in safety.

Image from Kookatchi: The Drum swimming pastward down the millennia into the shallows, then into the broken island itself. The Drum returning to the camp laden with the treasure of knowledge.

"I will go," Kookatchi said to Nir, "And I will return your shield to you."

"I know," tapped Nir, and the War Chief's confidence filled the Drum's mind with the beauty of trust.

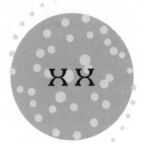

XX

Kookatchi swam alone out of the camp; no escort aided him
in his journey, nor did he need any aid. He was Kookatchi
who knew the whole of the Instant, Kookatchi who had seen it
from every vantage point, Kookatchi who had stolen from every
tribe. No part of the ocean of time was safe from him, no being
was a danger to him. A surprising thought, that last one. Two beings were dangerous to him. But he had just left them behind in
the camp of the only army, and they were not going to hurt him.
It was a strange feeling that flowed through Kookatchi's mind, comforting and warming like a gentle wave on an evening beach in
summer, a feeling of reliance, a realization that even if he forgot
what had passed between the three of them, Nir and Quillithé
would not. Even if he reverted to Kookatchi the Thief, they would
remind him and he would become Kookatchi the Bridge again.

But he did not think he would forget easily. The cocoon of the
Wavebreaker shield that covered his form would be a constant reminder. Nir's sacrifice and self-endangerment would not be easily
lost even in the layers of Kookatchi's memory.

Traveling alone through the ocean of time, Kookatchi unbur-
dened his mind of the need to think continuously. The concepts

of before and after, of sequence and of motion, left him, until his consciousness returned to the rare state of pure Drum's awareness. First to disappear from his perception was language. With no one to speak to, Kookatchi forgot how to speak. He no longer needed to put his thoughts in sequence; the whole of his mind was before him.

Next to go was the sense of his own length. No more a minute of life going through cycles, there was only Kookatchi moving through the ocean of time, changing with the changes of the Instant. Then the motion disappeared and Kookatchi was here; wherever he was was here, though here changed as the Instant changed.

Last to go was the sense of change itself. There was only Kookatchi and the Instant—Kookatchi, whose place in the ocean was only a point of perspective.

Kookatchi saw, heard, smelled, touched, and tasted the Instant, the trueness of the ocean of time. He experienced the nearness of the near waters, the farness of the far waters, and the beyondness of the waters he could not sense. But which waters were near, which far, and which beyond mattered little, save that there was still a purpose in Kookatchi. The shallows of the broken island should be near. So Kookatchi and the Instant accepted that those shallows were the near waters and the central waters of the Instant were the far waters and those waters that were futureward and pastward of the center were the waters beyond.

From her vantage point in the deep ocean, Quillithé watched Kookatchi swim. At first it looked to her as if he swam as all others beings in the Instant swam, moment of life succeeding moment of life. But from the corner of her mind that held some understanding of Drums came a reminder. And Quillithé looked again, seeing Kookatchi experience no time between the apparent moment when he left the camp, abandoning the mindset needed to speak with non-Drums, and the apparent moment when he reached the shallows futureward of the broken island. And Quillithé saw that though for her days of her life passed as Kookatchi swam, for him there was no swimming, only a vanishing and an appearing.

Image from Quillithé to Nir: Two pictures, Kookatchi swimming across time, and Kookatchi being, then not being, then being again.

The War Chief took in the images and his mind turned them over and over, seeking to make them one unified feeling of the Instant, but could not yet succeed. Nir and Quillithé would both have to wait for more sources of understanding before they could embrace the nonduality of these views.

Kookatchi the Drum knew that only events mattered in the Instant. All progression was illusion, so he felt no progression, recalled no passage since no events had happened. He had chosen to realign his position in the Instant, and his position had changed. All others perceived some passage of their own lives as Kookatchi swam, but he did not. He chose and he was there in the waters just futureward of the broken island.

But there in the shallows was an event that roused Kookatchi from the purity of his state and called back to his consciousness all the trappings of interaction in the Instant. A battle was going on seventy years futureward from the island. Sequency returned to his thinking and Kookatchi realized that if he did not stop the fighting, the cutting waves of war would carve out more space for the island, raising more of the ocean floor above the tides of change.

Battle brought Kookatchi back, restored the useful illusion of time, the deceptive voice of language, the awareness of his minute-long being, so fragile compared to the pure Drum unseparateness that made his being and the ocean of time one. But that purity offered his short stretch of humanity no protection against the cutting waves of the long-tailed. To survive Kookatchi had to be Kookatchi the Drum, who could see the Instant as separate from himself and interact with the tribes as they saw themselves. Had

Kookatchi ever paused to consider the matter he would have realized how difficult this bridging of two awarenesses could be. But he had never so paused; he did the bridging so easily that there was no impetus for him to think about it.

Senses open to the Instant and to the dwellers in the Instant, Kookatchi looked pastward at the battle and at the ocean floor below the battle. Two tribes contended. Kookatchi knew both of them. The Persian Zurvanite Infantry he had only recently had to dislodge from this region; they had obviously returned to resume their plundering of the Flux and recoup their loses. They had run into opposition in the form of the Lapland Crusaders.

This latter tribe was of medium size, fifteen warriors with seven-year tails, but they were all skillful fighters. While still time-bound the Lapland Crusaders had been an elite fighting force that had fought to liberate their homeland from the Swedish Democratic Oligarchy, a government that had ruled the northern half of the earth, sharing dominance with the Antarctic Combine.

The Laplanders had spent thirty years stockpiling weapons, training subsidiary cells of revolutionaries, and performing unsuccessful acts of terrorism against the Oligarchy. Their continual failures on this point had led them to discover the great secret of the Swedish Democratic Oligarchy, an atemporal warrior caste that protected the earthly government. The Laplanders had stolen the technology to enter the Instant and battle their enemies. They succeeded and the Timeless Shadows of the Swedish Democratic Oligarchy ceased to be a force to be reckoned with in the Instant. The Laplanders swiftly discovered the extent of battle in the ocean of time and joined the conflict with the hope of making the world into a safe place for their people.

Many battles had been fought since then. The solid world had changed greatly. The people who inhabited Lapland had no similarity in ancestry, language, or culture to those that had spawned the Crusaders. The Crusaders' goals had changed. They had made many enemies in battles unrelated to their initial purpose and had come to regard the defeat of those enemies as their true reason for

being. As had most of the other tribes of time, the Lapland Crusaders had long since lost the connection between their original
desired ends and the actions they were now pursuing.

This battle with the Persians was a case in point. Both tribes
had heard the rumors of some strange alliance between the Monster
of the deep and the Great Thief. The Persians had realized that it
was Kookatchi who had tricked them and stolen their prizes. Prince
Xerxes had concluded that they must have been close to the Great
Thief's treasure hoard, so he had returned to the site whence he
had encountered Kookatchi to search more closely. A spy for the
Laplanders had overheard the converse inside the Persian camp and
had reported back to his chief. The chief of the Crusaders led his
men in attack on the Persians in order to drive them off and so
give the Crusaders a chance at uncovering Kookatchi's mythic treasure hoard.

So it was that Kookatchi returned to witness a battle fostered
by rumors of his own activities; two tribes that had been renowned
for their awareness of when to fight and when to flee were locked
in a death struggle over a hoard of technology that did not exist.

The Persians seemed to have gained the upper hand in the fight.
The field of battle was littered with fragments of Laplander tails,
some as small as a few seconds, but most about a week in length.
There was one unmoving chunk of a Crusader's life that Kookatchi
guessed to be at least six years long. The smell of blood wafted
futureward on the currents of time, stinging the Drum's senses. But
that was not where Kookatchi's attention was focused. On the
ocean bottom, lines of new cracks and channels were growing under
the carving waves, spreading east, west, north, and south. If the
battle continued, then the broken island would cover not just southern Asia but northern Asia up to the Arctic Circle, the Indian
Ocean, the eastern half of Europe and on out.

Kookatchi was surprised that he saw this possible spread. Before
he would simply have seen the battle and decided whether or not
to steal something from the middle of it. But his awareness had
been bolstered by his interactions with Quillithé; momentarily the

Drum grasped the breadth of her vision and realized as she would have realized what the implications of this spreading would be. Kookatchi saw that the island might grow so far in space as to cover the whole of the earth. If that were to happen the cracked region would form a girdle of ice, a glacier around the center of time's ocean that would block the flow of change from past to future, sundering the tides of time into two parts. The ocean of time that had been one would become two, and the passage of events, the great unity that only his Drum's awareness could truly perceive, would end.

From that impersonal breadth of vision came a knowledge that was wholly personal to Kookatchi: only he could understand what was happening, only he was present to care about it, and only he could stop the battle that was precipitating this danger. He, Kookatchi, the least of all the warriors in the Instant, had to end this conflict even if doing so would end his life.

The Drum hesitated, startled at the thought. Nir's self-sacrifice, his willingness to risk his safety for the success of their agreed-upon task, had infected Kookatchi's thinking, and he found he did not mind. There was a beauty in this giving up of his own safety, a beauty he embraced with abandon.

As the Drum approached, the eight surviving Lapland Crusaders were making a tactical retreat pastward, seeking to regroup and lure their attackers into an ambush. The Persians, apparently not satisfied with routing their enemies, were giving chase, exactly as the Crusaders wanted. The fleeing Crusaders covered their retreat with a relentless barrage of change-waves. Kookatchi was horrified by the damage this regressing patch of chaos was causing to the ocean floor.

The conflict continued without a thought for the world around it. Kookatchi quailed at the noise of change and the savagery of the cutting waves carving up soldiers and terrain alike. The clash of tails and waves was far too loud for him to create the kinds of distractions he favored. All his Drum's instincts shouted at him to stay away when larger warriors unleashed their anger upon the In-

stant. But the golden beauty of self-sacrifice was greater than his
experience of danger and he swam pastward, surfing between the
angry peaks of the battle tides.

The Crusaders turned at bay thirty years futureward from the
broken island. In unison they sent a single wave front into their
attackers, spikes laid on top of spikes in fractal devastation that
carved up four of the Persians before Prince Xerxes could order the
retreat. The ocean bottom cracked, digging channels, shallowing
the shallows even more. Kookatchi could see that one more such
attack would be all that was necessary to turn these decades from
water to dry land.

He had no choice. The Drum had to lure these warriors away
with the only prize they would value more than killing each other.

In plain view of all, Kookatchi darted through the middle of
the conflagration, his Drum's awareness giving him the choice of
the small valleys between the killing peaks. Persians and Laplanders
alike saw the Drum as he skittered across the surface of time's ocean,
surfing eastward and futureward.

"The thief!" Prince Xerxes shouted. "Follow the thief."

The Persians abandoned their attack on the Crusaders to follow
Kookatchi. The Laplanders, who normally would have been wise
enough to retreat and fortify themselves against future battles, were
too enamored of the legendary hoard. They swam after the Persians, not to attack them but in hopes of catching the Drum.

Spurred on by the golden vision of death and life in his mind,
Kookatchi surfed on the waters of time, catching the height of
every wave to gain such advantage as he could over the long-
stroked swimming of his pursuers. His consciousness recycled again
and again until all of his thoughts were turned toward the luring
away of these tribes and the nobility of his actions.

Kookatchi swam for seven centuries and six thousand kilometers, maintaining a distance of thirty years between himself and his
pursuers, but the tides were slowing, growing deeper, with fewer
peaks. Soon he would lose his advantage of speed and they would

catch him. Unless—ah, there, another battle only seventy years away; that would do.

The Drum turned and swam toward the clash of riptides and the smell of blood in the waters above Alaska. Battle called to him and he answered eagerly.

Above northern Alaska the Aleut Time Raiders and the Antetemporal Order of St. Denis were fighting over a supply of Wavereflectors that the Aleuts had pulled out of the Flux. The Aleut Time Raiders were staunch isolationists; they stayed in one place and time and fought off all other attackers. They had patterned themselves after the Ghosts, regarding them as the model for any tribe committed to protecting a culture.

Sadly for them, the Aleut Time Raiders could not protect their lands and people as the Ghosts did, since change-waves from the past had long since destroyed the culture the Aleuts were sworn to protect. But they clung stubbornly to their model and served as guardians of whatever people lived below them in the Flux. In return for this protection they took much technology from the cultures below them. Some of those cultures regarded themselves as thralls of the Aleut Time Raiders, but the Aleuts paid no attention to that; they knew that they were protectors, not slavers.

The Antetemporal Order of St. Denis had no illusions about themselves. They had entered the Instant with the highest of motives, seeking to liberate all mankind, but the realities of battle in the Instant had long since stripped them of their pretentions. They were now no more or less than professional soldiers, fighting for survival and gain, reconciled to the unchanging war of the Instant. They no longer cared about anything except their survival and progress. They kept the name of their tribe unchanged, savoring the irony of battling under a saint's banner for their personal profit.

Kookatchi saw the battle and visibly hesitated, turning one way and then another, giving all the appearance of helplessness and despair as if his only hope had been dashed. Then with a dramatic ripple of fatalism, he anchored down into the Flux and waited.

A score of savage waves washed over the Alaskan tundra—artistically grown redwood forest—thousand-acre temple complex—stench-filled caribou theme park—bomb crater—spaceport.

Four people anchored down, only half a kilometer south of Kookatchi. The Drum peeked out from behind the cover of the grounded starship—hedgerow—megalith.

Two Lapps armored in green sheaths of micromolecular machines that crawled all over their bodies faced two Persians wearing full steel-and-brass chain mail. Some temporary truce had clearly been forged as they did not attack each other, but rather were searching in concert for Kookatchi.

He had only to wait; they would spot him in the changing of the world. In a flicker of alteration his cover vanished and they saw him. The four searchers vanished into the Instant and reappeared around Kookatchi. The Drum sat upon the ground, tears welling from his eyes.

"Lost, all lost," he said in the language of his long-vanished people.

"Give us your hoard, thief," one of the Lapps said.

"Tell us where you and the Monster of the deep have hidden it," said one of the Persians.

Kookatchi the Bridge concealed his surprise at the mention of Quillithé and hid himself under the gloomy face of Kookatchi the Thief, finally captured at the end of his great career.

"It does not matter anymore," said Kookatchi. "The hoard is lost."

"Lost to who?" said the Lapp.

"To the Order of St. Denis. They are attacking my guards even now. Lost, all lost."

"Your guards? The Aleuts?"

"Yes," said Kookatchi the Thief, confessing before his inevitable destruction. "That is why they stay in one place, so they can protect and use my hoard. But it is useless. I have come too late to save them. And the Monster's army will not arrive swiftly enough to take custody."

Those last words tipped the balance in the minds of the Persians and the Lapps. If Kookatchi were telling the truth their only hope for the hoard was to enter the battle now and win swiftly before Quillithé's army came to claim the spoils of war. Kookatchi himself did not matter as much as the hoard, which offered final victory to whichever tribe possessed it.

The Persians and the Lapps vanished into the Instant and their cessation of hostilities vanished with them. The battle of two tribes became a conflagration of four.

Though spectacular and savage, the course and outcome of this fight are unimportant, for the four tribes involved fought over temporary advantage and illusion as all the tribes of time did. Only the fact that the cracking did not spread, and that Kookatchi fled safely away back to his exploration of the broken island really mattered for the fate of the Instant and the fate of those who dwelt in it.

Kookatchi returned to the shallows futureward from the broken island, and the incident of the four tribes faded from his consciousness. All that remained was the gold of self-sacrifice and the elevating awareness that he had done some good for the whole of the Instant. Buoyed up by this feeling the Drum faced the cracked and broken body of time, and in words derived from the pure simplicity of the song of the Ghosts, Kookatchi vowed to restore the land to its proper watery form.

> "This is the Instant.
> The Instant shall be change."

Kookatchi's consciousness recycled and the vow rang in his mind, sharpening his senses to focus on anything that would serve the promise he had made. Kookatchi turned his fivefold perception upon the broken island, widening his awareness to better understand the upthrust land. Sight clarified first, giving detail to the solid mass that loomed only five years pastward from where Kookatchi floated. A rocky beach against which the waters of time lapped in their backward undertow. Scarred fragments of time thrust up like a mass of stones at the water's edge.

In between the stones the Drum saw rivulets of water flowing out of the broken island. Nir had been correct; there were passages through which the water flowed from past to future. Those waves of change were too muted to greatly alter solid time, but they were wide enough to bear Kookatchi's weight.

Hearing followed sight, bringing the sound of crashing surf flowing backward against the island. As his hearing grew more acute, Kookatchi heard a subtle undertone, a gentle washing sound audible between the crashes of the waves, the sound of the streams emptying from the island into the ocean.

Smell brought an acrid scent, like something long decayed that had been locked away from man's senses. The Drum could not identify the odor, but he knew he did not like it.

And touch, the ragged feel of the ocean floor in the shallows became differentiated. No more did the Drum feel an itch from the time below him; now he could feel the contours of the sea bottom and tell which way the waters were flowing. With that sense Kookatchi knew he would be able to navigate the streams and rivulets that flowed through the cracks.

Prepared, Kookatchi swam pastward to enter the broken island. He crossed the five years of shallowing until he reached the rock-strewn beach. Waves broke backward, mingling with water flowing forward from the streams. One leap from wave to stream and he would enter the island itself. The leap had to be perfect, lest he land on one of the rocks and fall through into the prison of solid time. But perfect motion had never been a problem for Kookatchi; all he needed to do was take up the perfect Drum's awareness and embrace the Instant. Then there would be no movement and no danger.

Kookatchi opened his mind, abandoning the common conceptions of the Instant to touch its reality. The waters of time became one water, and Kookatchi was of that water. But—the island, the solid parts, did not join the waters; they were not of the Instant.

Harsh intrusion of solidity; the stones of the beach refused his awareness, refused to cease their individuality. Their sharp edges and ragged forms were not water and would not be water.

The Drum, caught between two forms of perception, teetered on the crest of a wave, almost falling over into the rocks. Perception froze poised on the knife-edge of the wave, and the knife-edge of dichotomy. It should have been easy to take up one and abandon the other, but Kookatchi could not do so. Passage vanished, no apparent time passed. Almost Drum's awareness, but not truly, this was a courselessness born of fear, not understanding. Perfect movement was not open to him who had always relied upon it; beauty had vanished. Only pain and death lay before him. Unless . . . the Drum let go of perfection, abandoned the desire to be one with the Instant, and fell over into the waters, passing through the wave crest to appear in the stream. Not pure and perfect his arrival, rather Kookatchi entered the island in an undignified fall into a river.

The confusion of the two awarenesses battered at him: unified water and isolated land, two irreconcilables. He tried to cling to the unity, but the beach around him refused to change and the waters carried along by the cracks between the stones refused to accommodate themselves to perfect unity.

Kookatchi had no choice. Aching and fearful, he abandoned Drum's awareness, letting go of what he knew to be true. But he would return to awareness of the truth, he vowed in the silence of his mind. Once the Instant is restored, truth will again be known. Then out loud, tapping in the language of Ghosts against the thin sheen of flowing water.

> *"This is the Instant.*
> *The Instant shall be change."*

Fortified, the Drum swam pastward against the current of change. Or rather, since he was on a stream three meters wide and only ten seconds deep flowing at a pace less than that of the shallows of the Now, a trickle of change. As he swam, his body often grazed the bottom. He felt the knife-sharp cracks that lined the stream bed, but the Wavebreaker shield protected him from the cuts of jagged time, and his small size prevented him from falling through into the fragmented earth below.

Pastward he swam, into the body of the island, slowly, so that his senses might have a chance to further adapt to this place that was truly neither Flux nor Instant but partook of the character of both. Hearing, smell, and touch grew more acute, but no great change came to them.

The Drum's sight had been dulled since leaving the beach. All he could see were the edges of the stream, the waters flowing toward and away from him, and a faint tracery of colors off in the distance, which he suspected was other streams. The broken island itself had faded into darkness, because Kookatchi's sight had become aligned with Quillithé's manner of vision.

Then between one cycle of consciousness and another, the Drum's sight realigned itself. No longer seeing only change, it looked at the stasis of the broken island and transformed the darkness of unchange into the light of awareness.

In a flash, as if the sun had appeared in a midnight sky, Kookatchi saw the island around him. A vast plain stretched off in all directions, a plain of beautiful colored stones, an expanse of gems, glinting in the sheen of water that washed over them from the streams of change. Polished jewels of time, some round, some raw, some faceted. Enough beauty to excite the lust of any thief.

Kookatchi the Bridge vanished under the assault of this temptation and Kookatchi the Thief stared out at the plain of jewels and wanted to possess them, to keep their beauty forever with him. He surveyed the gems with hungry senses, taking in the vision of rubies several minutes long and dozens of kilometers wide, juxtaposed against little chips of diamond, less than a second in length, and brilliant pieces of jade intricately carved and covered with traceries of cracks, beautiful in their flaws.

All thought of unmaking the broken island vanished from the Drum's mind. Here was the hoard of beauty he had longed to possess, here was a never-ending variety of treasure from which his senses would never tire. Here he would settle down to contemplation of beauty as so many of his tribesmen had before him. Here was the resting place of Kookatchi the Thief.

Resting place. The words mingled in the Drum's mind, mingled with the acrid smell that had impinged on his senses since he first neared the island. He had never smelled it before, but now he knew what it was: stale blood, grated meat, the scent of shattered tails, long since fragmented by the sharp edges of the gemstones he coveted.

Billions of millisecond fragments torn from shattered tails were strewn throughout the cracks. The plain of jewels was a sieve that had grated the tails of tribesmen into pieces too small to hold any consciousness. The smell was the never-rotting flesh of the timeless bodies of time warriors.

Kookatchi's consciousness recycled and again his mind was assailed by two incompatible ways of seeing. The plain of gems was all about him as was the charnel ground of the broken island. He was in a treasury and a slaughterhouse. How to reconcile them? Then he knew. He would not reconcile them. He would keep his vow. The plain of gems would remain in his mind, but only as a warning. He would be Kookatchi the Bridge and he would free the broken corpses from the broken island.

"This is the Instant.
The Instant shall be change."

Kookatchi, who had been inspired by self-sacrifice and commanded to go search the broken island, took up his mission again and swam pastward through the fields of temptation, seeking for some anomaly, some greater clue to the nature of this place.

For a century he swam through the stream, till he heard the sound of running water, not a trickle like the rivulet, but faster, wider. Somewhere nearby was a river, wide and long, much safer for him to travel on. The Drum looked out across the plain of gems and saw the river, one hundred kilometers westward and fifty years pastward; the stream he was swimming on had diverged from it, a backflowing tributary stealing from the wider passage of change.

Kookatchi swam the distance, reaching the point where his stream came out of the broad path of change, twenty kilometers by four hours wide and deep enough that he did not immediately touch bottom, though he could sense it not far down. Room for him to swim between the banks of the great river, room to maneuver and plan. Room to be safe in.

The Drum took a cautious whiff, and was surprised that he smelled nothing. This water-carrying crack, unlike its smaller dry relations, was not a charnel pit for the nomads of time. Kookatchi slid his tail along the ragged banks of the riverbed. At first all he felt were the sharp edges of broken milliseconds that he had come to regard as the normal state of things in this region of the Instant, but then the tip of his tail struck a smooth patch along the eastern bank—smoothness, a thing he had not felt since entering the broken island. Whence came this anomaly? No answer came, but Kookatchi vowed to remember the smoothness and search out its source.

The Drum left the bank for the cool familiarity of the water. He splashed in the river for a little bit, remembering the wonderful feel of change against his tail. Then he turned pastward and swam salmon like against the river's flow. He focused his sense of touch on the river's edge, feeling for smoothness along the sharp stones that lined the stream.

He swam against the river's current for a distance of a hundred years, during which he found only a dozen smooth patches along the banks, each no more than ten seconds long. Those twelve little spots inspired an unaccountable hope in Kookatchi's mind. A theory began to take root, becoming more and more solidly planted each time his consciousness recycled.

The Drum began to believe that the river of change, instead of causing more breakage, was weathering down the jaggedness of the cracked lands. Somehow the currents of change were smoothing the edges of the gems. He became firmly convinced that a constant flow of water was polishing the stones of time.

Upstream he went, so intent on feeling the riverbank that he lost track of how far he traveled. Smoothness so occupied his thoughts that, had it not been directly in his path, Kookatchi might have missed the great treasure that lay in the great river.

But there it was in the middle of the watercourse, three kilometers wide at the center, an hour in length: a long thin gem, a perfect unflawed emerald ten times as large as any other stone he had seen.

Kookatchi the Thief surfaced again in his mind, staring in lust at this center stone of a royal pendant, the kind of gem that would be the focus of a work of lapidary art, a perfect emerald around which a cohort if not a legion of small rubies and diamonds would be set as minor consorts befitting a jewel of such stature.

So beautiful and so smooth. Smooth, that was the interest of Kookatchi the Bridge. This stone was larger and smoother than any of the others. Whatever lay inside it was a treasure indeed. No, not a treasure—down, thief, down—a great source of understanding. There had to be some reason for the anomalous size and smoothness of the stone. Kookatchi the Bridge needed to know what it was/Kookatchi the Thief desired to possess it.

The Drum leaped out of the water like a salmon and landed on the surface of the stone. It bore his weight and he did not fall through. Relieved, the Drum grasped the gem and anchored down into the hour of time bound within its lustrous form in order to find the knowledge/take the treasure hidden within that perfect jewel.

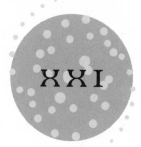

XXI

Noon approached on a sweltering day during the dry season in central India. The sky was cloudless, and the sun's extravagant warmth beat down in parching streams. Waves of heat rose from the dusty jungle clearing, making the tigers slow and listless. A half-dozen tourists enclosed in an air-conditioned sky-skimmer floated overhead oohing and ahhing at the lethargic cats and occasionally waving to the adolescent boy who was minding the fierce carnivores.

The boy's name was Saryu and he was a rarity even amidst the multitudes of people that could exist within the earth of time. He combined an inborn genius for working with energy with an ambition for material achievement. The vagaries of time had seen fit to have him born at a moment and in a place where his genius and his ambition could both be realized. Two parts of proper mind and two parts of proper fate created a man who could curve the course of the world, so long as nothing from above the world changed that course.

At the age of fourteen Saryu nurtured dreams great enough to swallow the world. But they were not idle dreams. He knew where his talents lay; since childhood he had been fascinated with the controlling and taming of energy to power everyday devices, frequently taking apart and putting back together the few machines in his mother's kitchen, tracking wires, trailing through computer controls, studying the flow and transformation of energy. Too poor to afford schooling, Saryu had been indentured to the government of his homeland for ten years' service in return for five years of teaching that would be given him at the end of his labors.

The government of the Midcontinental Utilitarian Republic had assigned Saryu the job of herding tigers in the North Indian Display Park. They had done so without any regard for his interests and ambitions, concerning themselves only with their employment needs. Every morning of the four years he had spent in this service, Saryu had vociferously expressed his anger at the Republic's indifference to his capabilities before setting forth to carry out their commands. And every day, Saryu had searched for some means of increasing his knowledge of energy, whether it was studying the movements of his tigers or covertly taking apart the static-electric stun mechanism in his tiger herd's staff, or endeavoring to boost the efficiency in the small force field he wore to protect him from his charges.

Saryu had vowed to himself that he would not waste these ten years before his formal education began. Every day, he would find something to further his quest for a new way to manage and store energy, a way that would bring him untold wealth.

Saryu knew what stood between him and the fulfillment of his desires: time and only time. Time embodied in the tiger-head posts of the park's main gate. Those golden tiger poles contained the computer that monitored his indenture, the computer that kept track of where he was and whether or not he was fulfilling his duty, the computer that would add to the length of his service twice the amount of any time he was absent from duty. Many indentured servants never earned their way to freedom and reward because of their shirking, but not Saryu. For four years of work, he had never so much as added a minute to the time he owed.

So the temporal jailer marked a continual reduction in the

marked period of indenture: one day spent, one day less to spend. Saryu longed for the day when he would pass through that gate, that prison of the present that held him from his future.

On this day, in this hour, Saryu was diligently carrying out his duties, making the tigers do tricks for the entertainment of the prospective buyers in the flying skimmer that hovered overhead. The monitor computer was particularly watchful during such moments and Saryu was not about to be docked for not amusing the customers.

An electric tickle from his staff and the tigers would jump over each other, roll on the ground, or leap high in the air offering mock threat to the skimmer, a metal craft floating thirty meters in the air, far too high for the animals to reach. This was the common labor of a tigerherd, which Saryu was more than capable of performing; doing this duty posed no threat to his ambition.

Then the shimmering, transparent man appeared in the midst of the herd of tigers. Saryu was amazed; such a thing he had never seen before. No man he had ever encountered, no technological device he had ever heard of could make someone seem to flicker in and out of existence like that. Although . . . he had a vague memory of his mother once threatening him with water-borne demons that could pass through walls and would come and punish him if he did not eat all his food. But such demons were myths; they could have nothing to do with this flickering man who had come from nowhere.

Kookatchi half appeared amidst the jungle cats. The Drum was surprised to find that he was not properly fitting into the block of solid time. Normally, when a Time Warrior anchored back into the earth, he would come into full existence and be indistinguishable from the time-bound around him. But not in this case. The Drum could feel the gem pushing against the change his presence imposed.

The Drum moved his arm slightly. It flickered and a tiny

change-wave passed over the gem, changing it slightly, but not as much as the motion should have. The air tried not to move aside for his movements, making Kookatchi feel as if he were passing through some gelatinous substance. And only half of the light that fell on him reflected off; the rest passed through him as if he were not there. Under the afternoon sun he cast a stained-glass shadow that revealed much of his inner body.

Kookatchi reached the end of his one-minute tail and his consciousness recycled. To his surprise he found his tail forced out of the gem, instead of automatically reanchoring in the next minute. Kookatchi pulled himself back down, now consciously holding on to solid time, forcing his watery being upon it, lest he be forced back onto the surface of the stone.

The tigers roared at this terrifying apparition and leaped upon it.

From Saryu's staff a ball of lightning emerged, which stunned the tigers and passed harmlessly through Kookatchi. The Drum turned around and faced the stony figure of the boy.

"Are those your cats?" Kookatchi asked in the language of the Consumerist Mercantile Hegemony, the Drum assuming that the language would not have greatly changed in the two hundred years that would elapse between his present position and the futureward border of the island.

The air languidly transmitted his words as if he had spoken at half the normal pace of speech. But the question carried and reached Saryu, imposing a change upon the fixture of his mind.

"I am in charge of these tigers, noble sir," Saryu said.

The boy's words also changed the gem slightly, since they were a response to this agent of external change. Kookatchi could feel the gem's solidity rebelling against the alterations and wondered if it could be cracked from the inside; but there was no sign of such incipient breakage.

In the air above them, the prospective customers, terrified at the apparition below, had turned their skimmer around and fled eastward, eventually vanishing from the gem altogether. More change-water sweated from the gem, flowed over the side of the stone, to feed the Great River.

Kookatchi and Saryu were left alone with the dazed tigers. Time-bound and free studied each other, each perplexed by the other's appearance, each wondering how the other could be used to further his plans.

Kookatchi the Thief took in all the details of the jungle, the boy, and the tigers. Somewhere here was a treasure to be taken. This boy was the only visible native; he would serve as a source of information.

Kookatchi the Bridge had seen how his speech had carried waves of change to the boy and noticed the sluggish alteration in his time-bound life. He suspected that Quillithé would be able to make much of this information, provided he brought her a thorough study of the phenomenon.

Saryu's mind was divided by two feelings. First, there was fear, fear of this demonic creature: half transparent, half solid, half here, half somewhere else. Second, there was desire; surely the man was using some technological device to produce this strange effect. If Saryu could find out what it was, determine how he was letting the light and air pass through him, it would aid his energy-transmission researches tremendously.

Divided, Saryu could not act. Divided in purpose but united in conception, Kookatchi could. "Tell me where I am," Kookatchi said.

Fear and desire united in Saryu; both knew they should answer the question, hard though it had been to make out the words. "The North Indian Display Park, noble sir."

Saryu gestured with his staff, taking in the jungle around him. The harsh sunlight splashed into flecks of rainbow on the boy's protective force field, surrounding him with a multitude of tiny spotlights.

"Tell me about this park," Kookatchi the Thief said, hoping to find some hint of the treasure.

"It's for display, noble sir."

"Display?"

The boy sidled closer to Kookatchi, angling around to watch the light pass through him. One moment all of him was solid, the next he was transparent except for his head, then the golden armor he wore would be clear, but his skin would be solid.

"For people who want to buy animals and trees," Saryu said walking all the way around Kookatchi. "I watch over the tigers and show them to people."

Kookatchi the Bridge felt the changes in the stone as the boy circled him; the fascination that the Drum's presence had engendered in the tigerherd was altering the gem. But Kookatchi could feel no cracking in the stone around him, only a smoothing down. This gem was unlike the prison that held him on his first entry into the broken island; where that stone drew in, this one repelled, where that one cracked this one became more solid.

In Saryu desire briefly won over fear, and he mustered a question. "Where did you come from, noble sir?"

"From the Instant," Kookatchi the Bridge answered.

"From the what?"

"The Instant," Kookatchi said. "From the waters of time; from the place outside; from Dreamtime; from the eternal; from the all and never changing. From the ocean above the sky. From the place of the eternal war; from the battle to settle history; from the sea of true freedom."

Saryu stared at him blankly, amazing the Drum. How could there be a time-bound being who did not know of the Instant? All cultures that had existed since the time war came to the Now knew of the Instant and the battle waged outside of history.

Saryu had vaguely heard of a place outside of time; it had been told to him by his mother in the dark of his room on nights when he had done something particularly unforgivable, like taking apart the central control system for her kitchen. She had warned him of the Asuras, the demons outside of time who could come and take your life away, stealing your breath and making you one of them. So she had heard from her father and he from his, down through many millennia. After hearing this tale for the tenth time Saryu the pragmatist had posed a question to his long-suffering parent: "Mother, has anyone ever seen such a demon?"

And she, more honest than angry, replied, "Not for thousands of years, but before that, they ruled the whole world."

And Saryu had turned over and opaqued the canopy of his bed to sleep in peaceful darkness, sure that a thing unseen for that long would never be seen again.

"What is your name, boy?" Kookatchi asked.

"Saryu, noble sir," the tigerherd replied.

"You keep these tigers."

"For the length of my indenture, then I will be able to go and study."

"What would you learn?"

"About energy storage and transmission. I have ideas to improve them."

"Have you?" Something niggled at the memory of Kookatchi the Thief, a hint of where the treasure might lie. But Kookatchi the Bridge snatched away the recollection and held it away from the other Kookatchi, tantalizing him with a reminder that they were seeking an anchoring event.

"Noble sir, how comes it that you are not solid?" Saryu asked.

"I would tell you," Kookatchi said, "but you would forget it within an hour."

The boy stood up straight. "My memory is excellent, sir. I never forget a matter of science."

"The quality of your memory does not matter," said Kookatchi, feeling his location in the gem. "For you, time ends in forty-seven minutes and fifteen seconds."

The boy shuddered and clutched his staff closer to his chest. "Do you mean I'll die then?"

"No, you will continue to live in disconnected bits and pieces. Of course, your whole life has been fragmented, but you would not be aware of that."

"Please, noble sir, you're confusing me."

"Do not worry," Kookatchi said. "You will forget all about it soon enough."

Or would he? Kookatchi realized that he was assuming something about the nature of the broken island, something he should test out first before he carried out the plan forming in his mind.

What plan? Kookatchi the Thief wondered. But Kookatchi the Bridge held the thoughts away, keeping them from his other point of view, locking up the idea in a conundrum about freedom and slavery.

"I will return," Kookatchi the Bridge said to Saryu.

The Drum vanished, leaving behind him a confused tigerherd and a lethargic band of tigers, slowly recovering from their recent stunning.

Leaving the stone was not like the usual unanchoring, not the same as letting go and permitting atemporal buoyancy to carry him from the earth of time to the waters above it. No, when Kookatchi released his grip on the gem, it was as if he were being forced out by a great pressure like a seed ejected from a squeezed fruit.

The Drum appeared atop the gem, followed by a small ripple of change-water that came into being with him. The wavelet flowed futureward across the gem from the place he had just left.

Kookatchi slithered behind the wavelet, feeling its effect on the surface of the stone. His awareness inside the gem had been correct; there were no traces of fissuring in the wake of the alteration, only a greater smoothness. The changes his presence had created had ever so slightly polished the gem.

The wave reached the futuremost edge of the fragment and flowed over the side, forming a microwaterfall that added just a little impetus to the Great River.

The Drum studied the array of gems across the river, searching for one that was likely to contain a future piece of Saryu. There, that small spinel four minutes long and a quarter kilometer wide should hold the piece of jungle where the Drum left the tigerherd forty-seven minutes ago. Kookatchi swam across the river and fell down into the stone—fell, he did not have to push himself. This stone had none of the polished resistance of the large gem he had just inhabited.

Saryu sprawled listlessly on a mossy stone, protected by over-hanging leaves from the sun's rays. The park had been placid since that tourist flyover, about fifty minutes previous. The tigers had grown sluggish in the midday heat and had decided to take a mass nap. The boy had fallen into a reverie composed equally of tinkering with the most common form of energy storage and daydreaming of the wealth that would be his once his ambitions were fulfilled. The lapse into thought was only broken when an unfamiliar man wearing strange gold-and-purple metallic clothes appeared next to him and shook his shoulder.

"Who are you?" the tigerherd asked.

Kookatchi flashed a broad smile. "Thank you, Saryu. You have told me what I needed to know. Do not worry; you will forget me in four minutes."

There was a cracking in the sky as Kookatchi's actions irrevocably altered Saryu's awareness; that alteration was a crucial attack against the solidity of this piece of time.

"Ah, I see," said Kookatchi the Bridge, as he watched the fracturing of the sky, and then vanished before his tail was sliced in two by a new flaw in the gem.

The Drum pulled himself out of the stone and fell back into the river as the four-minute-long gem splintered into a dozen pieces.

The huge gem is unique in its resistance to change, Kookatchi the Thief thought. How can I possess it?

By possessing the only valuable thing in it, Kookatchi the Bridge answered, tempting his other viewpoint to follow where his thoughts led.

Back into the large stone, this time sure of the prize he sought. This time Kookatchi the Thief would steal it/Kookatchi the Bridge would take the thing he needed to complete his mission. Kookatchi anchored down one minute after his disappearance.

"Show me around the park," Kookatchi said. "Quickly. We only have thirty-five minutes to find the things we need."

Saryu gasped in surprise at the reappearance of the half-present man or demon. He had begun to feel relief that the incomprehensible being had vanished and had hoped that he had seen the last of the there/gone man. But now he had returned and was giving orders.

Orders, those Saryu understood; he could forget the impossible presence and consider the demand that he lead the demon through his domain. Saryu's first reaction was to say no. If he left his charges the tiger-head gate would dock him, adding time to the period of his indenture, a span of the future he had tried to keep as small as possible. But then fear and desire won out. If this thing was a demon, then what choice had Saryu but to obey him? And if a man, then he was a man possessed of secrets that would well serve Saryu's ambition. Let the gate add to his time. If the creature spoke true it would only be thirty-five minutes away, a mere hour and ten minutes added to his indenture.

"What do you want to see first, noble sir?"

"Show me where you live," the Drum said.

"This way, noble sir," Saryu said.

The boy led the Drum down a winding path through the jungle. The air was filled with the heady scent of cinnamon trees, and reverberated with the twittering of birds amplified by sonic resonance panels cleverly concealed amidst the branches. Kookatchi noticed that the carefully manicured pebble pathway was supported by a rubbery substance that soothed his feet as he crossed over the stones.

Kookatchi was mildly amused and wondered if any of the visitors to this park were fooled by this attempt to simulate the rustic; he himself was far too familiar with all the artifices of fakery to be taken in.

Then a voice called into the pathway, a voice with a mechanical snarl and a quality like the low growl of a wildcat. "Saryu, you have left your tigers. Return immediately or face docking of your indenture time."

"Who spoke?" Kookatchi asked.

"The gate," Saryu said. "It tracks where I am. If I am derelict it increases the time I owe the state."

"No matter," said the Drum. "Soon you will not have to worry about your time of service."

"You will help me buy my freedom?" Saryu asked, his eyes wide with hope.

"I will help you to freedom," Kookatchi the Bridge said.

"Thank you, noble sir," the boy said, and his smile radiated gratitude.

Kookatchi the Thief smiled at the boy's miscomprehension. The Drum was quite used to people hearing what they wanted to hear rather than what was said. Even Nir and Quillithé were not immune to that affliction. Only a Drum could see reality.

"There is my dwelling, noble sir."

Saryu pointed to a square hut, three meters on a side. From the outside its walls looked to be crudely carved logs and its sloped roof appeared to be thatched with grass, but Kookatchi could see the concrete peeking out through the cracks in the facade.

The boy and the man walked through the curtain of plastic vines that served as a door into a concrete cubicle. Inside were Saryu's government-issued furnishings: a blandly utilitarian green plastic bed along the north wall, next to a two-meter-high bare chest of drawers, and in the center of the room a purple table with a single straight-backed, uncomfortable-looking chair.

Taking in the dullness of the place, Kookatchi understood why the yet-unformed Consumerist Mercantile Hegemony would be so overburdened with ornamentation.

The Drum noticed a red square incised into the floor in the northeast corner. "What's this?" Kookatchi asked.

"It is a trapdoor that leads down to the park's transport tunnels, noble sir. A tram is down there; it takes park servants around quickly."

Kookatchi's consciousness recycled and he realized that he needed something for his plan to be practicable. The Drum flicked his finger at Saryu's force field, feeling the resistance build as he moved his digit toward the shimmering, just as he had hoped. "Do you have another of these?"

"Yes, noble sir, a spare in case this one breaks down. Are you in need of its protection?"

"No," said Kookatchi. "You are. Bring both of them."

"Yes, noble sir."

Saryu pulled a gray plastic box out from under the bed, opened it, and looked over his meager possessions: a plain blue shirt his mother had hand stitched, two cheap mass-produced books on electronic engineering he had paid for with his tiny stipend, and, of course, his experiment.

The latter consisted of two clear glass globes containing two molecular batteries joined by force-field links. Saryu had been seeking a way to maximize energy storage in molecular bonds using force fields to contain the excess power. He needed education to know how to orient the molecules and the force fields and how to reduce the power cost of the fields themselves, but even without the needed teaching he had made great progress since he had conceived of the idea years ago.

Kookatchi the Thief stared at the experiment and his mind filled with pure delight at its beauty. Thief-thought was paralyzed by rapture, Bridge-thought spoke out loud.

"Shall I tell you your future, Saryu?" Kookatchi the Bridge said.

The words inflamed the boy's ambition. His throat became dry as if he needed to slake a thirst for foreknowledge. But fear accompanied ambition, fear that this prophet was truly a demon from out of time.

Hands shaking in a attempt at self-restraint, Saryu moved the experiment to the back of the box and retrieved the cobalt blue belt that controlled the spare force field. Then the boy looked up at the flickering man.

"What future, noble sir?" Saryu said.

"You will create an energy storage medium that will be so successful that it will replace all others. Because of this you will gain control of so much wealth you will be able to dominate the whole earth and create a mercantile empire that will survive even after your death."

The boy stood up slowly; his heart was beating wildly. The strange man/demon's words fueled his ambitions more than he had ever conceived. Wealth he had wanted, comfort, success, pride, all these things, but that his invention would so revolutionize the way things were done as to lay the world at his feet, not even his ambition had dared to conceive such a thing.

"Noble sir, will this truly happen?"

"So long as time remains fixed," Kookatchi said. "Now we must go. We have only twenty minutes to reach the futureward apex of this gem."

None of those words meant anything to Saryu, but he did not care; the Drum's prophesy had engulfed him in a flame of future thinking and he had lost all concern for the present.

"Saryu," Kookatchi said. "We need to go two kilometers west of here within four minutes; that will allow us to walk to the apex. Will the underground tram take us there?"

Saryu blinked and acted to answer Kookatchi's question. The boy tapped an almost invisible metal triangle on the north wall and a map of the tunnel network appeared in glowing lines of blue. "Yes, noble sir, there is an exit two hundred meters from the spot you wish to go to."

"That will do nicely if we hurry."

Saryu slid his hand around the edge of the red square on the floor and it vanished, revealing a narrow stone staircase, wide enough for a thin, small man such as Kookatchi or a boy like Saryu. The man followed the boy down into a spacious tunnel where an open tram car waited for them, floating a few inches above a single ceramic track. The tigerherd entered the front of the conveyance and punched three triangular buttons while Kookatchi settled himself onto the back bench.

The tram accelerated noiselessly, pressing Kookatchi onto the plastic cushions that lined the bench. After thirty seconds hurtling through a crudely carved tunnel lit only by dim purple rods, the car stopped beside a stairway identical to the one under Saryu's hut.

Man and boy emerged from the empty heart of a false tree into another part of the jungle.

"Southwest," Kookatchi said as he strode off. Saryu followed him, more bewildered than ever.

Fifteen minutes later they reached what seemed to Saryu to be a nondescript part of the park, but which Kookatchi could feel was the western border of the time fragment. The Drum had been so focused on his single idea to bridge/steal the treasure of this gem that he had almost forgotten the exploratory nature of his mission. But here was an opportunity to learn more if he acted quickly.

"What now?" Saryu asked.

"Walk one hundred meters west," the Drum said, "then come back."

Saryu obeyed, or he thought he did. He remembered the first few steps outward, and he remembered returning a few minutes later, but he could not exactly remember the trip to and from.

Kookatchi stared in fascination as the boy seemed to recede into the distance beyond the border and seemed to come back again. The Drum's atemporal hearing, however, told him that Saryu had traveled no more than the ten meters that separated Kookatchi from the western edge of the gemstone. The boy believed he had gone much farther than he had; that told Kookatchi a great deal about the confinement that these fragments created. Normally the Drum would have worried about forgetting this information, but the treasure would help him remember.

"Follow me," said the Drum.

"Yes, noble sir." At that moment Saryu would have done anything for the prophet of his greatness.

Kookatchi led Saryu north and east, following the contours of the gem. He wanted to remain in the fragment until the last possible second, but to do that they had to reach the few meters of space that coexisted in the gem with that final moment. Water splashed over the stone as they walked, changing the course of Saryu's life, giving him a longer existence in the stone than he had previously possessed. Wavelets washed above them adding polish to the emerald's tip, smoothing the stone.

Saryu grew confused at the inexplicable actions of his companion. He had seen Kookatchi avoid perfectly good trails because "they curved beyond the facet edge," and had been bewildered when he was told to duck down and scramble along the ground because "everything above it belonged to another piece."

"Crawl on the ground, Saryu," Kookatchi said, scrambling across the jungle floor on hands and knees. Above the sky, the water washed over the stone into the Great River. Half a minute more and they would touch the apex.

"Yes, noble sir," the boy said, scraping his body across the grassy park floor.

"Come here," Kookatchi said, pulling the boy to the base of a heat-seared tree.

There. The last second. Kookatchi gripped Saryu by the shoulder while letting go of his hold on solid time. The fragment spit out the Drum and the Drum tore the boy out with him, pulling Saryu screaming out of the life of his ambition into the realm where no changeless desire could be satisfied.

XXII

Time ends in a thunderclap.

Saryu's memory of the past and his dreams of the future shattered as the solid line of his life vanished into a single moment. His heart, caught in midbeat filled his frozen mind with a resounding echo that would not die. His consciousness was paralyzed, his mind holding to a single thought and image: the tiger-head gate counting off an eternity of absence, endlessly doubling and redoubling his guilt until a thousand lifetimes would not be enough to win him freedom from indenture.

Kookatchi's atemporal body strained at the exertion of pulling sixty times his duration out of solid time. If the stone itself in its resistance to change had not been trying to push him back into the Instant, he would never have been able to dislodge Saryu's entire hour-lifetime.

Kookatchi was amazed at the joy he felt in freeing Saryu. The Drum had never before taken a person from Flux to Instant, never brought a new life from the chains of solid time into the freedom of watery atemporality. He had witnessed the event often before; he had been witness to the creation of whole new tribes as one by one pieces of life were cut from the earth to become living Time

Warriors. He had never before found any beauty in the activity, but now that he had done it himself, he felt the rapture of giving liberation.

The freedom in Saryu's mind was too vast; the earth-taught manner of his thinking could not contain the openness of the moment, could not accept the infinity of possible action around him. His consciousness retreated into a need for succession, a demand that one thing follow another thing, but there was no place for such succession at the end of his hour's life. Saryu's mind sought a way to regain the sequence of one event coming after another, forming a chain, one second by the second that came after it. It retreated along his hour-long tail to the beginning of his atemporal life, and in the course of that retreat shattered Saryu's precious memories.

Kookatchi the Bridge looked at the hour-long child he had just torn from the womb of the earth, momentarily helpless, incapable of surviving without assistance; compassion filled Kookatchi the Bridge. Kookatchi the Thief was annoyed. Was this the treasure he had sought? A being too short in length to be a warrior and too long to cultivate Drum's awareness—worthless, useless dross, not the great prize he had sought.

The joy and compassion of Kookatchi the Bridge heard the disgust of Kookatchi the Thief and pushed against the older way of thinking. Rapture drove out loathing, forcing the rival mind-set down into the forgetful layers of Kookatchi's stratified memory. Kookatchi the Bridge became the sole attitude that would color the Drum's awareness.

Saryu's well-ordered memories with proper places for past, present, and future fell into a whirlpool of disarray as his consciousness battered through them to reach the place of longest duration, the seat at the beginning of his life.

Demons out of time were coming, or had his mother told him of them? No, she had warned him to stay away from the tiger gate because it would eat him. No, the tiger gate would allow him to channel the energy between the two nodules. No, that was what he wanted when he ruled the world. No, he had been ruling the world all along, but he dreamed of serving and herding tigers. No, he hated the smell of tigers, the way their leaves rotted on the ground in the wet season. No, that was trees, tall trees bound together with force fields, tall transparent trees that flashed in and out of existence. No, that was the demon; no, it was him—or the demon. Which was which?

There, a beginning, the first moment of his life; now things would progress in orderly fashion again. But there was nothing coming, no sound, no light, no smell, no taste. No sensation, no action. Saryu was lost, tumbling senselessly through a void in all things.

Saryu was deaf, dumb, blind, unfeeling, and terrified. From mercy Kookatchi the Bridge set about to rectify some of those conditions, to take away the helplessness that was the lot of all newcomers to the other side of time.

Kookatchi turned his awareness inward, seeking to remember that moment when he himself had been taken and his new atemporal body impregnated with the devices and capacities needed for survival in the Instant. He felt the length of his own tail, seeking the spot where the seeds of future Time Warriors had been planted in his existence in case the need should arise for him to sow them in the grounds of other lives. There at the tip of his tail they lay, dormant since his own ceremony of freedom had been enacted by those who had enslaved the first Drums.

A few remembered thoughts and instructions wafted up from the buried layers of his narrow but deep memory. Yes, that was how it was done. Kookatchi slithered across the diamond-solid gem and touched his one-minute length to the base of Saryu's hour-life.

The Drum began to vibrate, sending a wave shivering up and down the length of his own existence. The reverberation built upon itself, rippling faster and faster through the Drum's tail. Amidst this wavering a glow arose, a web of energy formed from the implicit power of change that lay in Kookatchi's movements. The light turned Kookatchi's tail into a luminescent shimmering blur flickering like a single firefly against an empty sky. Rising out of his body, carried along the energy web, were the molecular machines that would adapt Saryu's body to his new existence.

From the incandescence a thin tracery of coiled light resolved itself and shook away from the Drum's body. The glowing spiral slithered across the infinitesimal gap between Kookatchi and Saryu and wrapped itself around the tigerherd's tail. The coil stretched itself into a wide helix spanning the single hour of life that sustained the boy in the unwelcoming environment of the Instant.

The coil of light continued to spin out from Kookatchi's tail, weaving back and forth, wrapping Saryu tightly in a gleaming chrysalis. When the boy's entire length was completely shrouded in light, Kookatchi gave a single sharp flick of his tail. The sheath of light imploded, burying itself in Saryu's body.

The cocoon invaded Saryu's life, fusing itself into every second of the boy's existence. Once inside the tigerherd's tail, the machine of molecules and light built a network of atemporal sensors under his skin. Then it burrowed deeper until it reached his nervous system. Microthin coils of synthetic nerves coupled with the boy's naturally grown brain and spine, connecting his newly created senses to his formerly time-bound sense receptors, conjoining complex ripple emitters to his old language faculties, and adapting bipedal motor controls to his new ocean-adapted form.

While the boy underwent his transformation, the Drum saw to his protection. Kookatchi took the two strands of Saryu's force fields and laid them across the tigerherd's tail. He wrapped one of them many times in a coiled loop around the midpoint of Saryu's life, then he laid the other one along the hour of the boy's length. Two force fields flickered into atemporal existence; one of them lay parallel to the natural progression of Saryu's life, but the other was forced to coil in and out of itself throughout the same moment. The two fields twisted against themselves and each other, forming a flashing net of lines and sparks. A primitive Wavebreaker, but it would suffice as long as the boy did not leave the Great River or venture forth into battle with a long-tailed warrior.

Kookatchi surveyed his handiwork and found it acceptable. The

Drum snapped the cord connecting his tail to Saryu's, and the newly grown web of atemporal powers activated in Saryu's mind, giving him motion, voice, and all five senses that Kookatchi possessed, a generous bounty of power and awareness.

Sensation detonates in Saryu's mind; the world returns in unity with awareness.

Sight: a long piscine tail stretching back from his head, and a small fish flopping next to him on a stone.

Sound: something flailing around, water splashing, a banging of flesh on rock. Somebody talking, the words not yet making sense, as if he did not understand the language or as if the speaker were a long way off.

Smell and taste: wet air, the stink of fearful sweat, a tinge of blood.

Feeling: hard smooth stone, slick with water, garbled memory of a childhood beach, lying on the rocks while the ocean washed over him. His leg were flailing—no, not legs, he was legless, armless, a cripple, he would have to beg for his bread, his ambitions unfulfilled. No, there was something; it felt like a supple limb at his command. What was it? That tail, it was part of him.

The boy screamed out an inarticulate change-wave, lashing out ripples of alteration from his terrified tail. Water splashed over the hour-long stone, polishing it further.

In his mad thrashings Saryu pushed himself off the gem of his birth into the rushing waters of the Great River. Kookatchi dove in after him.

"Calm yourself, boy," the Drum rippled out in the language he had programmed into Saryu's receptors. "Calm yourself," he repeated now that he had enough water to speak in.

"Help!" Saryu cried. "Whoever you are, help me."

"You know me, boy," said the tiny thing floating next to him. "I took you from your former life. You saw me as a flickering transparent man; here you see me in my true form."

"What did you do to me?" Saryu shouted, adding a sputtering of waves to the river.

"I've freed you," Kookatchi said.

"Freed me?" Saryu said. "From what?"

"From the trap of broken time," the Drum said. "And the larger trap of unbroken time. From the earth, from being changed into being change."

"I don't understand," Saryu said, watching in amazement as his words formed plaintive ripples in the flowing water.

"Stop thrashing about," Kookatchi said. "Just float on the river and listen. I will tell you all you need to know and can yet understand. Just float and give me a chance to remember."

"Remember?" Saryu said. "You don't even remember where we are."

"That I remember," Kookatchi said. "I need to recall the song of the Instant. We are so far from the ocean that I have momentarily forgotten it. My size limits my memory."

Few of Kookatchi's words made sense to Saryu, but the boy ceased struggling against the river, floating instead between the banks. Was this the man/demon who had so bewildered him before or was it some new trick? A simple question occurred to the boy. "Why are you having trouble remembering? You had no problems before."

"In solid time there are many reminders, many strata that can call up the needed associations. Here there are few. Ah, now I recall. Float and listen, Saryu."

"Yes, noble sir," the tigerherd said, hoping to hear some words that would make sense of where he was and what had happened to him.

"Time is earth and water. . . ." Kookatchi began.

His extended touch rippling through a hundred millennia of intermingling change, Nir floated. He was in the center of the camp of the only army exchanging halting pictures and taps with Quillithé as, bereft of a translator, each sought to master the other's language.

The War Chief and the strategist had returned to games of

battle in order to extend their vocabularies and their understanding of each other's minds. From simple interchanges of one tribe against another they had moved to multitribe interactions, with all the subtleties of lust for power, long-term planning, and the seizing of momentary advantage that marked the broader battles of the Instant.

It was always Quillithé who began the mock battles since only she could ripple out the complex maps that defined the terms of the game. She had been forced to improvise her language to make up for Nir's inability to see color; it had been difficult at first to define objectives for the battles since the War Chief could not see the questioning shades of blue and the golds of desire.

Nir, for his part, had found Quillithé's lack of touch a difficulty. Many times in the course of a game he would have one of his pieces subtly alter the flow of change around him; Quillithé would see the alteration, but could not always appreciate its consequences. Indeed, they had had a full-blown argument about the outcome of one battle owing to just such an alteration. No settlement came of that dispute, only the conclusion that their sensory limitations precluded certain interchanges between them.

This most recent game ended in a draw as most of them had, and Quillithé laid out a new scenario.

Image: Shallow waters, thirty Time Warriors designated as Nir's side, a place that needed defense at the far end of the shallows, one of the pieces designated as leader. Invading force of twenty-five warriors.

"A battle in the Now?" Nir tapped out.

"The Now, the present, the unchanging, the source, the stillness," Quillithé responded. She had gained some control over the echoes of her taps, but still gave several answers to all questions.

"Why?" Nir said.

Image: Repeat of the previous picture but the leader piece made larger and the other pieces encircling it.

"You want to know more about how I lead my warriors?"

"Yes," Quillithé tapped.

Image from Nir: Same as Quillithé's but a second large piece was added to the side of the Ghosts.

"I do not lead alone," Nir tapped hoping to clarify the image. "The Elder governs above me."

In the Now, the Elder had instituted a series of tests seeking to find a new War Chief. Nir had been gone so long that she had concluded that he must be dead. At least, that was what she told herself and the Ghosts when she instituted the testing.

Her pronouncement, given on the last day of the Year of Ghosts' Conferring, had been simple and clear. "The War Chief has died. A new one must be chosen from among the Ghosts."

None of the warriors, guards, or scouts had verbally questioned her declaration, but in their minds was a uniform disbelief. For the first time, all the Ghosts thought the same thing about Nir: that he still lived somewhere in the Instant. But the Elder was not to be questioned and her decisions were not to be disputed save by the War Chief himself, and he was not there to oppose the declaration of his death.

Col privately wondered why the Elder had made such a radical decision. No new attacks had come to the Now. Indeed, the Diaspora was strangely empty of tribes.

The absence of the tribes that usually haunted the Diaspora had been a subject of much dispute among the scouts. But restricted as they were by Nir's command they could not venture forth from the Now to find the cause. Thus the Ghosts did not know that the tribes were gradually migrating into the center of the Instant, seeking the treasure of the Great Thief who had struck up an alliance with the Monster of the deep. Many battles were breaking out; old enmities were revived and new ones formed. Fruitless searches were undertaken. Many of the seekers found the broken island and many died trying to penetrate its secrets. None of the hunting tribes considered the Now a likely hiding spot for Kookatchi's treasure, so they left it alone, much to the confusion of the Ghosts, who had

long regarded the People and the Great Mother as the only prize
worth taking in the Instant.

This absence of enemies had comforted Col, giving him hope
that Nir would return before there was any new trouble in the Now,
but the Elder had dashed his hopes and he could not bring himself
to ask why.

Even if he had been able to do so, the Elder would not have
been able to answer the question without breaking a silence that
spanned the whole of the Instant. Certain things were not discussed,
not spoken of in any tribe, for fear that the speaker would be considered insane. The Elder's fear had arisen from one such unspoken
source.

The Elder's tail was only a year in length, long enough for
survival and defense if necessary, but not enough for true battle.
During Nir's absence, her consciousness had progressed to the end
of her tail and come crashing back to the beginning, momentarily
disrupting her awareness of the progression of things.

It was an uncomfortable phenomenon, common to all dwellers
in the Instant and the source of the great silence. The Elder, like
all of the long-tailed, had tried to ignore the moment of asequen-
tiallity, the flash of simultaneity, the thunderclap of timelessness.
They ignored it, even though every such event brought odd scraps
of awareness, hints of the Instant beyond their ability to sense,
implications of pure atemporality unadulterated by the remnants of
time-bound thought. The long-tailed had no use for such thinking;
they regarded those fragments of perception as the hallucinations
of the crashing of mind. The Drums could have told them otherwise, but they knew the long-tailed would not listen or understand.

When the Elder's mind collapsed in the ending and beginning
of her life-line, she had such an awareness, sudden and undeniable,
a sense that the War Chief was conferring with another, that someone else was giving Nir the understanding he needed in order that
he might best decide how the Ghosts should be commanded.

And in that moment, which was the whole of the Instant, that
moment of Drum's awareness, the Elder knew that this other being

was giving Nir broad understanding, not the narrow guidance of repeated orders, but a wash of comprehension as deep and open as the ocean of time itself.

In its presence the Elder came to feel as if she herself were earthly time and this other being was watery time, which changed the earthly as it saw fit.

The Elder had emerged from this moment back to sequential existence. The first memory she had was the vow of the Ghosts and she swore it.

"We are the People,
The People will not be changed.
This is the Now,
The Now will not be Flux."

If Nir was taking guidance from a creature of change, he could no longer be relied upon to command by the vow. So the Elder had pronounced him dead and called the Ghosts together to choose a new War Chief.

"The Elder gives the guidance of the vow," Nir tapped to Quillithé. "And the remembrance of the Ghosts' purpose."

"And if the purpose . . . intention . . . design . . . plan . . . scheme . . . necessity should change . . . alter . . . be washed over with waves . . . lose its confinement . . . slip the bounds of time?" Quillithé asked.

Nir was about to say that such could never happen, but he stopped himself. He knew that the purpose had already changed; at least, it had changed for him. Either the Ghosts would change with him or he would cease to be War Chief. But if he was no longer War Chief, how would he fulfill the vow?

A feeling of desperate nostalgia washed over Nir, a longing for the shallows of the Now, where he could feel the bottom of the ocean, safe and secure. Not like the currents of Quillithé's deeps in which flows of change interleaved and intermingled, creating an abyss of change that stretched far beyond the range of his extended touch. He would have to return to the Now, have to reclaim his place or accept its loss. But he could not leave until Kookatchi returned and the three of them had made a decision regarding the broken island.

"But what am I to do here?" Saryu asked Kookatchi when the latter had finished the story of the Instant. "How can I ever complete my plans?"

"What are your plans?" Kookatchi said.

"I told you, I wanted to complete my indenture, perfect my invention, and live well."

"Your plans are already achieved. As the Flux now stands you do indeed complete your work and you achieve what passes for wealth and power in the Flux."

"But how can I enjoy it, floating here in this river?"

"Future fragments of your life are enjoying it," Kookatchi said.

"But they're not me," Saryu said.

"Then what is you?" Kookatchi asked in a gentle ripple.

Saryu tried to respond to the question but realized he could not. If this strange being, this Kookatchi, this Drum, as he styled himself, was telling the truth then his future was set, fixed in stone in an unchangeable part of time. Was that not what he wanted? No, for he would not be there to enjoy it. Some future self would be there, but a future self he, Saryu, would never become. He could not work or even just wait to be that Saryu who would rule the world. But that Saryu was still Saryu, was he not?

"Help me, noble sir," the boy said. "I do not understand."

"I know," Kookatchi replied. "Time catches us all in confusion. But eventually we learn."

"Learn what?"

"To live in the Instant and to alter our desires to our new life, to see time as it is—changing, not fixed."

But even as he said those words, Kookatchi the Bridge wondered at their truth. This boy wanted his life of ignorance back, a fixed history to enjoy without any concern for the changes of time. Were the tribes any different? Kookatchi the Bridge let that question suffuse his consciousness until it became an atmosphere that colored his perceptions, a sharpening of his senses in search of answers.

Saryu found the Drum's words unhelpful and confusing, but at least they pulled him away from the mind-bending question of which Saryu he truly was. The boy chose a different line of inquiry hoping it would lead somewhere he could comprehend. "Why did you bring me here?"

"Why?" Kookatchi said. "For several reasons, some of which no longer matter since I am not now what I was when I formed them."

"I do not understand, noble sir."

"I will tell you the reasons that are true for the moment."

"Thank you, noble sir," Saryu said.

"First I took you to see if it would shatter the stone of time in which you lived. It did not. If anything, the gem is more solid, more secure than before."

"So?"

"Every stone in the broken island is injured by change, except this one," Kookatchi said. "The event you lived in is made stronger by alteration. That makes it unique. Uniqueness is beautiful and important. Quillithé will need to know about this."

"Who is Quillithé?" Saryu asked.

Quillithé filled the Drum's mind, all the coils and twists of her life, the expanse of her vision, the power of her mind to see and grasp possibility, the beauty and the terror of her. But no words came from the Drum. He did not dare try to speak of her, knowing that even he could not encompass her in words. "You will see her for yourself eventually when our work here is done."

"Our work, noble sir?"

"Yes. There is one other reason I brought you here. There are too many strange things in this island, too much for me to remem-

ber at once. I need assistance remembering. I wish you to serve as
my aide in recollection."

"Noble sir, I do not understand what you are asking. I do not
understand what this place is. I just want to go home."

Kookatchi flicked a ripple toward the gem. "There is your
home, Saryu."

"That? It is no longer than I am. I would feel trapped in that."

"I know," Kookatchi said. "Come with me, do what I ask and I
will give you a new home, the ocean of time, which is larger by
far than anything that lives, and yet if you will see it properly it is
as comfortable as your home and hearth."

"Where is this ocean?" Saryu said. "All I see is this river and the
land."

"The land should not be here," Kookatchi said. "Come with me
and we will learn what must be done to sink it again beneath the
seas of time."

"No, I want to go home."

Saryu leaped out of the water onto the gem of his birth. The
gem, hardened by Kookatchi's changes, resisted the boy's attempt
to return, pushing against the hour weight that lay upon it. Saryu
scrabbled, pushing down, wanting to be home, until grabbing the
solid time below him he pulled himself down into the fragment of
Flux that had been his home . . . his egg . . . his prison.

There was a moment in which Saryu felt nothing, saw nothing,
heard nothing. He screamed in fear, remembering the senselessness
he had experienced before Kookatchi gave him awareness. He
could not even feel his body, could not tell if he had a tail or arms
and legs, did not know if he was on land or water.

The moment passed. He was back in his forest, near his herd
of tigers. He had limbs, not a tail. He had lungs and could breathe
again; Saryu realized to his horror that he had not been breathing
in the Instant, had not even worried about drawing air into his
body.

Saryu raised his arms and cried aloud to the skies, "I am human
again."

But his arms were half transparent, and the world was moving in jerks and fits, not flowing smoothly. Saryu remembered what Kookatchi had looked like when he first appeared, and the boy knew that he was not back, was not human, at least not what he thought humans were.

He looked up at the sky and screamed his rage, but the shout died in his throat. "The sky," he whispered. "There was no sky up there in the Instant. Nothing above me."

Kookatchi watched the boy vanish from the Instant, noting that Saryu's point of consciousness had anchored down about halfway in the gem. The Drum left the water and anchored down just behind Saryu.

"There was no sky up there in the Instant. Nothing above me," Saryu said.

"No," said Kookatchi. "Only water, water and this island that should not exist."

"Should not exist?"

"The Instant is one," Kookatchi said. "If you were a Drum you would be able to know that. The Flux is many, the Instant is one. But this Island makes it not-one."

"And what happens to my life if you take away the Island?"

"You are of the Instant. You will remain of the Instant."

"But my plans . . ."

"Will be washed away in the waters of time," Kookatchi said. Kookatchi the Thief would have lied, but Kookatchi the Bridge wanted Saryu's help.

"Why should I help you undo all my future work?"

"Because once the ocean of time is made whole then you will be able to do so much more than your simple earthly ambitions could ever conceive."

A voice called out from the trees around the compound, the voice of the tiger-head gate. "Saryu, report your position. Explain your absence. You have already been docked one hour and seven minutes for deserting your post."

That cold mechanical voice sounded to Saryu like shackles being locked around his arms and legs, shackles of added time. But he was free of time, free to leave and reappear, free of the tiger-head gate, free of the gate of the future. And that was thanks to Kookatchi.

A chain of thoughts formed in Saryu's mind: Kookatchi had freed him; Saryu was grateful for the freedom; Saryu would help Kookatchi and so gain access to the power he wanted.

A second chain of thought formed parallel to that one: Kook-atchi had torn him away from his home and his plans; Saryu hated Kookatchi for doing that; Saryu would follow Kookatchi and learn all there was to learn about the Instant and then . . .

"I will do what you want, noble sir," Saryu said.

"Good," Kookatchi replied. "Let us return to the Instant."

"How?"

"You have only to let go of solid time," the Drum said, and vanished.

Saryu vanished from the clearing and the voice of the tiger-head gate continued to call his name for the remainder of that hour and continued to total up the time that Saryu owed on his inden-ture, time that would never be served.

Saryu appeared on the gem of his birth and rolled off to join Kookatchi in the Great River.

"What are we to do, noble sir?" Saryu asked.

"We will follow this river and hope that it will take us to the heart of the island," said Kookatchi the Bridge, and, leading his protégé, minute before hour, they swam upstream toward the past.

XXIII

Saryu did not believe that the ocean really existed. He had followed Kookatchi through the Great River swimming pastward, looking for any sign of the Instant the Drum had told him about, but there was none. The newly freed boy had come to suspect that he had been tricked, that all the Drum's words had been lies. The future-grasping boy had begun to believe that Kookatchi's only purpose in taking him into this other realm was to keep him from fulfilling his ambitions.

Aiding this belief of Saryu's was the recurrent damage to his memory. It seemed to Saryu as if at the end of every hour his mind tore itself to pieces in a rage of confusion and then, like a sulking child under a watchful parent's eyes put itself back together with little regard for a few fragments left out here and there.

Once this moment of disassembly and reassembly was over, Saryu would find gaps in his memory, bits of the journey missing, parts of his past vanished. The boy resolved to fill his consciousness with reminders of what he wanted so that he would never again lose the future.

Thus it was that Saryu crafted the song of his ambitions.

"Tiger gate/Future gate held me in bonds.
Ten years before I passed through.
Tiger gate/Future gate leads to the school.
Five years to learn what I must know.
Tiger gate/Future gate, I will make bonds.
Holding the power between two cells.
Tiger gate/Future gate, you will be mine.
Tiger throne/Future throne I will rule on."

Each hour after his consciousness recycled Saryu would sing this song privately in his mind and look at the small swimming form of Kookatchi, and Saryu would wonder how he would be able to free himself from the timeless bonds of the Drum.

Kookatchi paid little attention to his charge; he had become absorbed in the beauty of the Great River, his senses sharpened into an awareness of these new waters so like and unlike those of time's true ocean.

Where the ocean flowed uniformly, carrying the waves of change through the strata of cause and effect that lay below it in the solid world of time, the river followed its own course, uncaring what happened beneath it. The guidance of the change had a perverse beauty to it, solid time charting the course for the fluid. The notion that the solid could control the liquid was so against all that was known in the Instant that Kookatchi could not resist reveling in it, though even in the reveling he feared it, this upthrust of solidity that threatened to cut the oneness of the ocean into two.

He swam with joy and despair through the twists and turns of the river, surfing over change that flowed now from past to future, now east to west, now north to southwest and pastward. He wondered what this odd progress of alteration must be like in the world below him, but he could not venture down. The stones of the river-bed were too small even for his atemporal body.

As he swam he waited for recycling of consciousness to bring this strange place into harmony with the Instant that Drum's awareness knew. Moment by moment, he tried to reconcile solidity in the watery realm; but the world refused to change around him to the satisfaction of his Drum's awareness. The fixity of the watercourse and the broken island glared at him defiantly, mocking his capability to be one with all change. Kookatchi's awareness struggled to change and accommodate, to encompass this stasis in its comprehension of change. More than once in the course of the journey the Drum wished that Quillithé could have been there to take in all this and turn it over and over in the corridors of her mind, seeking a way to reconcile the presence of the beautiful watercourse with the ugliness of unchange.

The lingering mind-set of Kookatchi the Thief said that no such reconciling could be possible and that a means of stealing the watercourse should be found and the broken island itself ignored; the Thief wished to leave and find more fertile places to pilfer from. Kookatchi the Bridge, however, had a growing conviction that searching this place that seemed inhospitable to oneness would bring about some true coming together of ocean and river, a commingling that would unmake the broken island.

But to do that, he had to find the source of the river and the secret of its existence. Why did the water flow through the river instead of draining away into the cracks as it did in the rest of the island? What was special about the riverbed and the islet of stone from which Saryu had been pulled?

Saryu? Oh, yes, Kookatchi had to remember him. The boy was very important. He was the first person Kookatchi had ever liberated from the Flux—no, he was important as a source of longer term memory—no, because his life anchored the events that flowed out of the broken island—no, because he had been pulled from the fragment that refused to break, that became stronger when changed—no, because he was as ignorant of the Instant and its ways as the first man who left the bounds of earth to enter the ocean of time.

All these things were so, but Kookatchi could not hold them together as one; he could not place all the important aspects of Saryu into a single whole that could be held in his one-minute mind.

And in his inability Kookatchi found the answer to his inability.

"Saryu," Kookatchi rippled as they passed a wide turning in the Great River, "I want you to remember some things for me."

"Yes, noble sir," the boy rippled back.

"Remember your importances."

"Noble sir?" Saryu said.

"The reasons I took you. You have to remember them for me."

Reasons? Saryu thought. Since when do demons have reasons for their malevolence? But all the boy said was, "I will remember, noble sir."

Kookatchi focused his mind on the boy's form floating next to him, sixty times his size. In the greatness of the ocean, such a multiplication would have meant little. The Drum frequently out-witted warriors many millions of times his length and he had struck an alliance with the longest creature in the Instant. But here in the confines of the Great River, which was itself only a few hours across, that mere sixtyfold scale had a vastness lent it by perspective. It was, to be sure, a limited greatness, only a hint of the true size of things beyond, but it was vastness nevertheless.

That sense of size troubled the Drum. The broken island limited his awareness, prevented him from encompassing all things in a single knowing. The fractioning of space and time impinged even on his perfect acceptance of time as it truly is and took away his immunity to the assaults of most dwellers in the Instant.

Fortunately there were no enemies present. Only the boy could present a danger, and he knew nothing of warfare in the Instant. And besides, what cause had he to be angry at Kookatchi, who had freed him from the bonds of time?

"Here are your importances," Kookatchi said. "Remember them."

"Yes, noble sir."

"You are the first. You have an hour to remember. You anchor

278 · Richard Garfinkle

the future. Your egg accepts change but remains solid. And you are like the first."

"I will remember, noble sir." But what Saryu committed to memory was only a repetition of his song. Tiger gate/Future gate, he thought.

"Good," Kookatchi said. "Now I can concentrate on the river."

The Drum returned his attention to the flow of change, and cycle after cycle, permitted more and more his awareness of Saryu to dribble away from his consciousness.

The Great River flowed around and over the two, carrying a selection of change from before the island to after. As it carried it carved and smoothed, making banks and islets out of the shattered stones of minutes and seconds. It flowed on with a stately inexorableness that caught Kookatchi's attention and gave him cause to speculate.

At a turn in the river where the course of change altered from north-to-east to past-to-future, Kookatchi decided to turn speculation into action. The Drum focused his attention on the river bend, looking for a stone of appropriate proportions. Not too smooth, a jagged stone, one he would not wish to swim over. But not too rough either. The stone had to be in the process of smoothing out. Yes, there was one, a small thing, two seconds by three meters by four centimeters by half a meter, curved like the inner edge of sickle.

Waters of change washed over it, splashing onto the dry parts of the island where the momentum of alteration was damped into nothingness. A good stone for the Drum's purposes.

"I am going to attempt something," Kookatchi said. "You must remember what happens and remind me when I ask you."

"Yes, noble sir," Saryu said.

"Watch and listen," Kookatchi said. He snapped his tail hard against the center of the arcing stone. A thin tracery of cracks spread across the crescent shard. Tiny flakes of time fell off into the river to join the sand at the bed. A tinkling sound washed over the stone, then echoed back, adding a tiny ripple to the river of change.

Saryu skittered back in surprise at the shattering of the stone. "I did not know a tail could do that."

"All too easily," Kookatchi said. "Our lives are the instruments of war in the Instant. But that is not important now."

"What is important, noble sir?" Saryu said, not wanting to be caught in an error by the demon.

"We wait," Kookatchi said. "But you have to remember something for me."

"What?"

"Remember that I cracked this fragment. Repeat it to yourself over and over again, because I am going to forget it."

"Yes, noble sir," the boy said. "I will remember that you cracked the stone."

Saryu sang the song of the gate a thousand times. At the end of each singing he reminded himself that Kookatchi had cracked the stone and in that reminder a notion of his own power in the Instant began to grow.

Having swiftly grown bored with watching a stone, Kookatchi's mind wandered aimlessly, flitting from one memory to another, but holding on to the notion that he was supposed to wait in this place. He soon forgot why he was waiting. Had Nir told him to? No, the War Chief was nowhere about. Perhaps Quillithé had given the instruction. No, she was not there either. Perhaps he was planning a theft. No, there was no one to steal from. And nothing beautiful around to look at.

Eventually even the memory of having to wait left Kookatchi. One cycle after that last shred left his consciousness the Drum looked around and found Saryu floating next to him.

"What are we here for?" Kookatchi said.

"You cracked the stone, noble sir; you told me to remember that."

"Which stone?"

Saryu sent a gentle ripple of words flowing toward the smooth crescent-shaped stone, unmarked by any damage. "This one, noble sir."

The Drum studied the stone with sight and touch and he neither saw nor felt any flaw in the stone; the lines of cracking had been healed. The water streaming over it in a constant flow had taken away the damage.

Constant flow, that was the beauty of the river. It took the intermingling tides of disparate changes, melded them into a single smooth flow and with that smoothness healed the cracks. But constant flow was rare in the Instant. The shallows had few waves but those were sharp with battle and deliberate change. The middle region was full of all possible tides and waves. Some were smooth, but those did not last; war would replace them with cutting wave fronts. Only the deeps had any constancy, and there only the surface waters flowed smoothly. Between the solid time below and the gentle rocking currents on which Quillithé floated lay twists and turns and vortices that had torn apart many a warrior.

But here in this river where change was guided by the shape of the bed below was a unique smoothness that healed the injury of shattering waves.

Kookatchi twitched his tail in joy, almost dancing on the waters. "Half done," he called out to no one in particular. "Answer have I, now only cause is needed."

Saryu slid backward down the stream, afraid of what this mad demon might do in its exaltation.

Kookatchi danced his ecstasy through ten cycles of consciousness, then coiled himself into a contented ball for two more cycles.

"Saryu," he called after releasing himself from his own hug.

The boy slithered cautiously toward the Drum. "Ye-yes, noble sir."

"I want you to remember all of this. Remember that I cracked that stone. Remember that the river healed it. And above all remember the constancy of the change."

"Yes, noble sir." Saryu remembered what Kookatchi told him,

but stronger than that memory was the recollection of the power of an angry tail.

Past the bend the river widened into a stretch three days across. The constant wash of change developed eddies and undercurrents and the banks no longer held the smooth stones that had given Kookatchi the hint he needed to discern the healing. The Drum was somewhat perplexed; the nuances of change he felt lying below the surface should not have existed in waters this shallow. The Drum felt down to the riverbed and there he touched intricately carved channels, large trenches half an hour wide and in them smaller trenches a few minutes or seconds in width, channels within channels that preserved currents and undercurrents that should have been homogenized into a single flow.

The Drum grew so fascinated with this microcosm of the deeps that he almost did not hear Saryu's cry for help.

The boy's tail had dipped down below the surface and been caught by two countervailing currents; one tried to pull him eastward, the other futureward. Deep channels gave strength to the flows that threatened to tear Saryu into two half hours.

Kookatchi dove down below the surface and swam under Saryu's thrashing form. Drum's awareness was greatly impeded by the improper solidity around him, but it still enabled Kookatchi to dart between the random cutting waves that the fearful boy emitted in his splashing.

At the river bottom lay the point where the two channels crossed. A whirlpool five minutes across had formed above this point, pulling and tearing at Saryu. Kookatchi flashed through the vortex to the calm center, then lashed his tail at the river bottom, seeking to shatter the solid place where the channels converged and disputed.

New cracks formed in the riverbed and the two broad currents broke into a hundred narrow ones. An eddy of confused change welled up, spurting out a geyser that pushed Saryu's tail to the surface away from the danger of the lower currents.

"Be more careful," Kookatchi said as he surfaced. "Keep your tail on top of the waters unless you need to anchor."

"Yes, noble sir." Saryu's mind tried to wrap itself around gratitude for the Drum's saving of his life, but he could not manage it. Anger and the sense of having been robbed of his future kept the boy in a state of ambivalence. Still, he felt a need to acknowledge what had been done. "My thanks."

"Just be careful," Kookatchi said, returning to his pastward swimming.

"Yes, noble sir." Saryu followed, keeping his tail on the surface.

As they swam, cycles passed in Saryu's mind. In those cycles he drowned the memory of being rescued in repetitions of his song, until he had drowned all gratitude.

The two swam upstream in silence, following the course of the Great River for a thousand turning and twisting years. In the fractured time below their passage, Saryu's ancestors slaved under a score of different governments, each striving to make its mark upon the world and each ultimately vanishing into obscurity. And in the myths of the peoples who lived in that broken time, the tales of the Instant faded from hope and fear into threats whispered to children at bedtime. Memories of atemporal power in action became the idle speculations of pure theoreticians. A hundred attempts to harness the well-documented capacities of the Instant met with failure and the knowledge of time beyond time faded away so that the ancient texts on the ocean above the sky were seen as mere metaphors of other teachings instead of direct descriptions of the truth.

In the waters of truth, Kookatchi and Saryu swam up a narrow passage with a deeply grooved riverbed, and in those waters Kookatchi heard something flowing toward them from the past, a crashing, rushing sound like the simultaneous breaking of a hundred waves.

Past a turning the Drum saw the source of this noise. Three waters from three tributary rivers were feeding a triune torrent of change into the Great River. The land from which these cascades flowed had been pushed far up into the absent sky, creating a great descent ten years in height, a terrible fall of time. Waters of change poured down, swirling and sparkling with intersecting tides. And in this mingling torrent Kookatchi smelled again the scent of blood and broken flesh.

"Is this the source your were looking for, noble sir?" Saryu asked, rippling out wide questioning waves that would be audible over the inarticulate thunder of the falls.

Kookatchi felt down toward the river bottom. The cascades of change had carved deep trenches in the solid time below, but there was no feeling there of an initial event. These falls brought three streams together to form the Great River, but the beginning, the cause of the broken island, was not here.

"No," Kookatchi said. "But whichever stream is carrying the smell of blood will lead to it."

"Blood?" Saryu said.

"Blood comes from battle," Kookatchi replied. "And battle is the cause of change in the Instant."

The Drum looked over the falls at the three streams. One came directly from the past, another from the north, the third from the east.

"Wait here," Kookatchi said.

"Yes, noble sir," Saryu said.

The Drum swam toward the vortex where the waters mingled in angry conflict before resolving themselves into the inexorable course of the Great River. His one-minute form skated with ease and practice over the savage intermix of disputing change. Like a salmon Kookatchi leaped up the northern falls, darting from one breaking wave to another until he reached the top ten years past-ward from the bottom. A small stream barely half an hour wide fed a single course of change down into the Great River below, but there was no smell of blood up there.

The Drum sailed back over the falls, descending easily as if floating over calm waters. Saryu could not believe the sight of Kookatchi apparently falling, carried along by the savage tide, and then emerging unscathed from the whirlpool below.

Kookatchi climbed the eastern and then the pastward falls. The former also lacked the scent of blood, but the hour-wide stream that carried a dozen different currents from the past, that one stank of war and death.

"That is the way we must go," Kookatchi said.

Saryu looked up at the angry crashing deluge that fell from stream to river, and wondered if it was for this that Kookatchi had taken him from his home, wondered if he had been harvested from solid time to be torn apart in this current.

"How can I go up there?" Saryu asked.

"I will show you," Kookatchi said. "Though I doubt you will remember it. How long does it seem to you since your memory last cycled?"

"Noble sir?"

"Since your mind shattered and reformed? How long does it seem to you?"

"It has been perhaps two-thirds of an hour, noble sir."

"Then we will wait," Kookatchi said. "You must tell me when you feel the end approaching."

"Yes, noble sir." Saryu acquiesced in trembling.

They floated near the edge of the whirlpool. Kookatchi focused his attention on the water, shutting out the land, concentrating on the oneness of all change. Forgetting that there was change outside the island, he let the waters of the four rivers be the whole of alteration. Full Drum's awareness rose within him as far as it could. Events ceased to follow one another, the illusion of time progressing went away; he was floating in the ocean, was the ocean, but the ocean was so small, so confined that he could have been anywhere with the merest thought.

Saryu's mind began to fragment, memory fell apart; he tried to hold on to the silence, but his decision went away, replaced by Kookatchi's command.

"Noble sir, it's happening."

Kookatchi created an event, but what that event was depends on how one chooses to see it. To the Drum all that occurred was a reordering of the Instant so that he and Saryu were at the top of the falls rather than at the bottom. Saryu's fractured and confused memory recalled it as a terrifying trip darting up through the waterfall, around each cutting wave, but he also recalled it as a vanishing from one place and an appearing at another. Had there been a long-tailed warrior to observe the event, they would have seen Kookatchi touch Saryu and wrap him in a cocoon of light as if he had just torn him from the Flux, then it would have seemed as if the Drum rode the boy up the waters and onto the relative placidity of the ten-year-high stream.

But none of these views would have been completely true. Only Quillithé, after hearing of the event and contemplating it in the right context, truly comprehended what happened; but in the apparent progress of things, Quillithé had not yet been informed, so let the manifold errant descriptions suffice until that moment seems to come.

Saryu and Kookatchi floated in the stream, an hour pastward from the waterfall. The intermingling currents of the hour-wide watercourse washed over them, carrying the scent of blood and shattered lives.

The riverbed beneath them was not the smooth carpeting of centisecond sand that had lined the Great River. This stream's bottom was a rocky causeway lined with half-second and quarter-second stones, jaggedly thrusting upward.

"Keep your tail on the surface," Kookatchi said.

The words sounded familiar to Saryu's reforming consciousness. He had heard them before, but he could not remember when or where. And how had he gotten to this place? He remembered a waterfall he had climbed; no, he had somehow bypassed it, or—no. What had happened?

"Come along," Kookatchi said, and swam off against the current of change. "And do not touch the banks. They are very sharp."

"Yes, noble sir," Saryu said. He shook away the confused memories of the falls and returned to what mattered to him. Tiger gate/Future gate . . .

Kookatchi turned his attention from his protégé and focused on the smell of blood flowing down the tributary. The Drum set off swimming at a leisurely pace, so that his sense of smell could grow more keen. Yes, the scent of death was strong; somewhere farther upstream many Time Warriors had died. A large battle, perhaps forty slain.

Saryu and Kookatchi skated into a four-decade-long series of curves and bends, sharper and narrower than they had encountered before. The water was choppy and the scent of blood grew stronger with each year they traversed. After a final turn that curved three-quarters of the way around a beach of jagged rocks, the two of them emerged into a broad lapping lake of change.

It was the first standing body of water Kookatchi had seen since he entered the broken island. It extended ninety hours from past to future and fifty kilometers in every spatial direction. The lake waves squalled angrily as if in the nonexistent sky above them a storm was laying gale winds upon the water. Ripples of change bounced off the banks and interfered with each other in riptides and whirlpools. So savage was the interplay of change that it could not be seen through; Kookatchi could not discern with vision the farther shore of the lake, though his hearing told him how far away it was.

On this wild, contained cataract, ragged-edged pieces of flotsam bobbed up and down, cast this way and that by the currents and tides.

"Noble sir?" Saryu asked.

"What?" said the Drum as he studied the swirling waters dark with blood and anger.

"How can the water be flowing out of this lake into the river?"

"These are the waters of change," said Kookatchi the Bridge. "They flow according to the paths of alteration. Do not let the form of this place deceive you. This only appears to be a lake surrounded by a rocky beach. That is how your sight has been taught to see it. If it were possible to give up that convenience you would see time as it truly is, an emptiness filled up by its own actions."

Saryu looked out at the hellish pool that violated all of nature's laws, roiling without cause, spilling out from lake to river instead of following the proper course of waters. And there were things floating in the lake, torn pieces of something.

"What are those, noble sir?" he asked.

"Corpses," Kookatchi said. "There was a battle here."

"A battle?" said the boy and asked the question always asked by those who hear of wars. "Who won?"

"The sand and the water," said the Drum, sourly. Kookatchi was surprised at his own anger. He had seen more battles in the Instant than anyone could possibly remember, but this was the first that had made him angry, though he could not say why he felt that way.

Saryu fell silent, afraid to further stir the Drum's wrath.

Kookatchi skated out into the lake to study each broken piece of Time Warrior in turn. The carnage was astonishing, even to a looter of battlefields. Each corpse had been torn apart from all directions. The Drum had seen many Time Warriors sliced into pieces less than a second long, but the torn pieces of these soldiers had also been cut spatially into ragged parcels of human form. Centisecond torsos were pushed by the waves forced up against jigsawed millisecond arms and half-second skull and spine remnants.

The Drum's mind conjured up an image of the savage spiking of wave fronts that these warriors had unleashed on each other. His consciousness recycled while his mind was fixed on that image, and he suddenly realized that the rippling tides of the lake were the muted remnants of those battle waves. In time's ocean the waves would have joined to others and gradually become new tides as they progressed futureward, but trapped here in the lake of battle they could only reverberate back and forth. All the crests of battle remained save for those few progressing waves that escaped into the stream to join the Great River.

But how was it possible that most of the change-waves remained? Why didn't the waters of change seep out into the broken island? How could the waves be contained by the banks of the lake?

Kookatchi returned to Saryu. "We have to follow the shoreline," the Drum said.

"Yes, noble sir," Saryu replied.

"Swim carefully. Some of these waves could still be dangerous to you."

They swam half an hour from the eastern shore following the contour pastward. The beach at first looked solid, as if it were a vast expanse of unbroken earthly time. But Kookatchi noticed that as the waves hit the beach, they were tempered slightly as if they had fallen into minute cracks. The Drum focused his sight on the place where water touched land. There, little grains of time washing into the lake. Kookatchi realized that the apparently intact earth was in reality solid-packed sand, microsecond-micron granules of space-time that been carved up and then jammed together by the force of the waters and now served to echo back the very waves that had shattered them in the first place.

Around the eastern extremity of the lake, the Drum saw the promontory, a single pinnacle of true solid stone rising up from the beach of apparent hardness. The promontory lay near the pastward edge of the lake, a rocky outcropping, standing defiantly against the waves, a truly solid piece of time against which the waves lashed to no avail.

Half an hour by four kilometers across, it rose up an hour into the emptiness above. The rock was covered with a tracery of scarring, not a smooth stone like the gem of Saryu's birth. This one defied the waters by its echoing curve, a shape battered into it, not polished like the perfection of the gem in the Great River.

To Kookatchi's adapted sight, the stone seemed perfectly carved to deflect the angry changes and modulate them into temperate ripples.

"There," Kookatchi said. He swam swiftly over to the prominence, followed tentatively by Saryu.

"Wait here until I return," Kookatchi said. The Drum leaped out of the lake and dove into the stone, vanishing into the Flux.

"No," Saryu said.

But Kookatchi had left the waters and appeared in the earth, too late to hear the words of his student . . . protégé . . . servant . . . colleague . . . slave.

The Drum appeared in a dark plain in southwestern China amid the cold, twisted wreckage of a nuclear battlefield that had been turned into a preserved historical site and opened for tourists every day from sunup to sundown.

It was near midnight so no tourists were present. And yet, amidst the carefully groomed devastation designed to preserve the look and feel of postapocalyptic lifelessness, someone stirred. A living figure walked among the blast scarring and the angry sculptures of formerly molten steel, now cooled by time.

A man walked and sang to himself in a language Kookatchi knew but did not remember the name of:

"We rode our horses across the steppe, from the ocean to the mountains.
We carried the Czar's banner across the steppe and showed it to his foes.
We left the steppe, we left the horses, we left the Czar behind.
But his banner we carried into the ocean and carved his name in time."

The song clearly had more verses to come but the singer stopped when he noticed Kookatchi.

"There is nothing here to steal, O Great Thief," the figure said as it moved toward Kookatchi and resolved into a man, tall and white skinned, heavily bearded and wearing a thick woolen jacket. A ceremonial iron sword hung at his side and a short-barreled copper gun of some kind was in his hand.

"I did not come to steal," Kookatchi said.

"Then I will take revenge for the thefts you perpetrated on my tribe." The man's voice was stilted but there was a hint of fire in it, and a sense of relief at being able to vent anger.

"Which tribe is that?" Kookatchi asked. "I have stolen from so many of them."

"Czar Ivan's Grand Army of Time," the man said with obvious pride.

"I thought I recognized your song," Kookatchi said.

The warrior raised the gun and took aim. "In the name of His Majesty Czar Ivan the First, I execute you for looting in wartime."

Kookatchi vanished into the Instant and reappeared behind the Czarist as a vengeful spray of red bolts of light flew through the space he had vacated.

The Czarist whirled around. "You are not trapped here! Thief, have you come to mock me in my prison?"

"No," Kookatchi said. "To learn the cause of your entrapment."

The hands that had confidently grasped the gun opened wide in sudden despair; the weapon clattered to the ground. The empty hands then clutched the weeping face of the Czarist who had been forced to glimpsed the freedom he had been denied.

"Tell me about the battle," Kookatchi said.

The Czarist howled inarticulately, his voice carrying upward to the image of the midnight stars, though in truth the stars themselves were elsewhere, free floating in time's ocean, untouched by the actions of man.

"Tell me," Kookatchi said. "I am trying to help."

"Help?"

"We want to repair the damage, restore the broken island to the Instant."

"Broken island?"

"Above us, the land has thrust up through the waters and shattered. No long-tailed warrior can survive up there."

"That I know," the man said, his voice a snarl. "I watched my comrades in arms die up there."

"Tell me," Kookatchi said.

"What can you do, Drum?"

"By myself not a great deal, but I have allies."

"Allies? In the Instant?" The tears of pain gave way to hysterical laughter.

"Tell me!" Kookatchi said, imitating as best he could the tones of command he had heard Nir use.

The military perfection of Kookatchi's voice snapped the soldier out of his agony. His report jumped out at a quick-march cadence. "We were engaged with the Babylonian Timeless Infantry. Both sides had recently obtained Heavy Wavebreakers, which made inflicting damage with normal attacks nearly impossible."

"Continue," Kookatchi snapped, to keep the man from faltering in his recitation.

"Our commander, Czarevitch Alexei conceived the idea of forming a phalanx, a line of tails athwart the marching line of our enemies. They came toward us, and we lashed our tails in unison to make a single great cutting wave, a great blade of water. I was the farthest back in the line. It was my duty to give the signal and begin the wave. The Czarevitch's plan worked perfectly. The hugest, sharpest wave ever made by the tails of man flooded out from our line and smashed into the enemy.

"It tore the Babylonians to pieces, and we gave a great cry of victory. But then something happened. There was a noise like thunder, and the waters parted. I could see the ocean bottom, and then the bottom disappeared and there was a void, an emptiness where our sword of water had cleaved the ocean. Our single wave split apart, reflecting off in all directions. The wavelets fed on each other, forming even sharper cutting lines. A line of vicious spikes came hurtling back toward our phalanx.

"Some of my people tried to scatter, but they were cut apart by the other waves. The main shock front struck the phalanx and ripped us to shreds. My comrades gave their lives to blunt the force of the attack. This piece of time, this prison, is intact because we lay between it and the oncoming wave. I was the last in line. Just as the wave hit me, I tried to dive into the Flux. Only a few minutes of my life survived.

"I lost nine years to that wave. Nine years of life and memory! All I have left is half an hour, which I live over and over in this cell. I have lost most of the songs of my tribe. I lost the names of my comrades, the names of our enemies. All I have left is the first song, the battle, my Prince, and myself. And those I have vowed never to lose. I will never forget the song of the horses, I will never forget Czarevitch Alexei, I will never forget the battle where he died, and I will never forget myself, Mikhail Dimitri Alexandrovitch."

Kookatchi concentrated on the information he had been given. He tried to form it into a single clear thought so he would be able to remember it until he could transfer the knowledge to Saryu's longer memory.

In the Instant, Saryu finished scouting out the prominence into which Kookatchi had vanished. The boy had watched the places where waves flowed in and out without damaging the block of time; he had seen how the sculpted stone blunted the knife-sharp tides, and he had seen a way past that line of defense.

Saryu stood to the north of the rock and lashed his tail transverse to the waves, then he darted to the south end and did the same. Both of his waves struck the promontory. A keening rose up from the isolated prominence, a wail of long-delayed destiny. The memorial stone of the battle that created the broken island screamed out the final war cry of two armies and shattered into sand.

Saryu swam out into the lake and fled singing through the tides to the stream, hoping to make his way back to the Great River and his home.

> "Tiger gate/Future gate, the demon is dead.
> Tiger gate/Future gate, freedom is mine."

XXIV

The lash of Saryu's vengeance wave struck the memorial stone. Drum's awareness knew it as it struck, knew that water cut earth; Kookatchi knew the promontory was breaking up around him. It was not like the normal knowing of the state of the Instant while anchored in the Flux. This had a greater immediacy, a feeling of the stone changing essentially, as if instead of merely the contents of solid time being changed by the waters, the solid time itself was altered.

Water was coming down, water of time invading the earth, not changing it, not washing above it, falling down into it, carving the stone into pieces, carving the weeping Czarist's sad remnant of life into unknowing fragments of flotsam.

Mikhail's fragments floated up out of the cracked ground to join the shattered remains of his fellows in the lake of the phalanx.

Earth and sky splintered as waters of change poured down through that which should have been changed. The land fractured into pieces, and the water pushed the segments of earth away from each other, breaking the contact of cause and effect, shattering the long chain of time into a million short chains. A cascade of water pushed each millisecond of time away from the next, each cubic micron of space apart from all those nearby places.

Kookatchi found himself trapped by the inevitable destruction around him. He had one moment to act. One moment was enough for a Drum to escape almost anything, but this prison forged of time's two sides filled that moment with death undeniable.

But in the moment of death, Kookatchi remembered Nir, remembered a mind that changed faster than moments. Drum gave up being Drum and became the memory of War Chief; mind changed according to the changing of mind. Kookatchi became Kookatchi again, but he saw things differently and the moment of death became a moment of action.

Water flowing down as earth had risen up; both sides of time were coming together against their proper ways. Water's way was to flow above earth, changing it. Earth's way was to guide the flow of water. It was not just the ground that had been broken by the phalanx, it was the water as well.

But he was a Drum. All the waters of time were one to him. Even these cascades that shattered the world around him, even they were one to Drum's awareness. Water and earth were not to be one but two, and between the two there was to be a bridge. Kookatchi the Bridge let go of the shattering stone, let go of the single view of awareness and rose up on the many streams of water. On a thousand cutting waves, Kookatchi welled up in unity to the ocean of time, leaving the solid world behind.

And yet he did not reach the ocean, only the lake where men had died to create the broken island. The Drum rose up on the waters as the deluge of change shattered the promontory into sand, rose up in anger at the breaking of the world and the foolish intermingling of time's two sides; one was to change, one was to guide, not two to helplessly intermix.

Kookatchi the Bridge leaped away from the crumbling stone and as he saw the earth and water come together in helpless confusion renewed his vow and added to it.

"This is the Instant.
The Instant shall be change.
That is the Flux.
The Flux shall be guide."

The pastward wall that kept the waters of the lake in check crumbled and the roiling battle crests that formed the pool of death were now free of their prison of sand and stone. Out the past gate of the lake the waters fled, draining the blood-perfumed pool of all reminders of the battle of the phalanx.

Backward ran the waters, carving a new river into the broken island, a river that ran from future to past, breaking and changing the course of time. The pull of the lake took hold of the stream that washed out of it, reversing its course. Now in apparent accord, but truly in violation of nature, the stream flowed into the lake and backward through time.

In the earth below the streambed, cause and effect reversed themselves. An old woman visiting the nuclear war-park dies suddenly of a heart attack; that is cause leading to effect. The waters flow backward. Her death occurs, death causes her heart to seize up, the seizing causes beating, the beating causes breathing, the breathing causes eyes to open and see the world, but she is still dead, for the death happened and reversal is not unmaking.

Kookatchi darted and danced across the lake, avoiding the damaging flood with Drum's awareness. No effort was needed on his part. His mind swiftly focused on the question of what had caused the destruction of the promontory. The answer was immediate. Someone had come, someone small enough to survive in the broken island, but large enough to let out a destructive wave. A warrior about an hour in length, the same extent as Saryu.

Kookatchi suddenly remembered his protégé. Where was the boy? Had the strange attacker killed him? No, no fragments of Saryu were present amid the flotsam of the battle. The boy must have fled, following the stream, traveling through the only part of the Instant he knew. Kookatchi swiftly set out against the onrushing current to catch up to Saryu. The Drum had to make sure the boy was safe before seeking the mysterious attacker.

The lake drained down to dregs of change, revealing a ragged dry bed. Dagger-sharp points of broken ground dug into Kookatchi's tail; only the Wavebreaker kept his fragile minute of life intact. The Drum fled toward the river, hoping to outrace the coming drought.

Saryu swam in terror against the reversed current of the stream. He lashed his tail fiercely, trying to put countervailing waves against the prevalent pastward flow. Panic gripped him. He pushed against the sharp-stoned bottom of the river and felt the knives of solid time bite through his improvised Wavebreaker. Fingers and toes were carved away from several seconds of his life; he lost a hand five minutes before the end of his tail, and an ear near the beginning.

"Stay on the surface," he said to himself, and whimpered at the pain.

It had all seemed so easy; break the stone as he had seen Kookatchi break a stone. The demon Drum would be destroyed and Saryu would be free.

"Tiger gate/Future gate . . ." But he could not remember the whole of the song; his mind was too focused on the need to swim and stay alive.

Swim he did, pushing his tail against the waters for seeming hour after seeming hour. He kept swimming through the repeated pain of losing parts of his body. Every hour-cycle of relived life he experienced the vanishing of his hand, then Saryu would scream and weep tears of change into the backward stream.

Six times he lost and regained his hand, until at last he reached the waterfall. The backward-flowing falls now drew change out of the Great River, halving its depth, drying up its banks, taking away the life of the waters from which the boy had been born.

Saryu stopped swimming as he looked over the reversed cataract and wondered helplessly how he would survive going over the rising falls of change.

No hope, no way down. If only he could remember what Kookatchi had done. It had seemed so easy then, just a moment, a moment in which they swam up the falls. No, a moment when they were below, then above. No swimming, no moving, just a change of being. But the boy could not do it alone, did not understand what had happened. He was trapped, swimming against the falls, against the current.

Kookatchi swam swiftly through the reversed stream, his mind jumping from thing to thing. Too many to hold on to, but he had to recall them all: the phalanx and the battle, the cracking of the ocean floor, the healing of injured stone, the Great River, Saryu's egg, Saryu, the destruction of the promontory, the unknown enemy.

Too many things. He had to winnow them down or he would not be able to focus enough to move through the angry currents and the drying-up tributary. Drying up, yes. The water was being exhausted. Too much was being pulled back. The sharper stones of the river bottom were starting to peak up through the waters, spikes of solid time that glistened momentarily with droplets of change before turning arid like desert rocks.

Saryu, enemy, phalanx, remember those three and swim, swim swiftly, find the foe, rescue the boy, tell him about the phalanx.

Kookatchi saw Saryu, struggling against the waters. The Drum could tell that the boy was completely focused on survival. That would do. Kookatchi swam over to the boy, touched him and laid the golden corona of Drum's awareness over Saryu, pulling him safely down the waterfall in the same event/nonevent that had brought them up before.

"Do not hurt me, noble sir!" Saryu thrashed out in panicked waves as they emerged in the now-shallowed Great River.

"Hurt you?" Kookatchi said.

"For destroying the stone." The boy was too frightened to lie or conceal anything. He was certain that Kookatchi would momentarily reveal his terrible demonic powers and condemn him to an eternity of suffering.

"You should not have done that, Saryu," the Drum said. "Someone was trapped there and you killed him."

"Killed?"

"Yes," said Kookatchi. "The last of the warriors responsible for this island was held captive by that stone and now he has been shattered like his comrades."

"But it was you I meant to kill." Saryu's mind had lost all coherence, all he could do was babble his plans and his idea of what Kookatchi was like. It came flooding out in a cascade of confused words that washed over the Drum.

Kookatchi took in the boy's viewpoint and saw through Saryu's awareness. It had a beauty born of fear, a dark gloomy view of things filled with regions of blackness and nuanced shades of gray. The Drum admired it momentarily as if he were looking at a carved piece of onyx, then tossed it aside.

"Your view of events is not right," Kookatchi said.

"But you took me from my life," Saryu said.

"I gave you life," Kookatchi replied.

"You made me a slave."

"I made you free."

"You stole my power to act."

"I gave you the power to act."

"You made it impossible for me to fulfill my ambitions."

"Oh, Saryu," Kookatchi said, completing the song they had made together. "Come with me to the ocean and I will show you more possibility and more ambition than you could ever hope to achieve."

"To the ocean?"

"Yes," said Kookatchi. "My work here is finished. You must

remember two things for me and then we can return to my allies."

"What two things?" Saryu rippled his tail nervously. Was there hope, was he going to survive?

"Remember the phalanx and the battle."

"The phalanx and the battle," Saryu repeated, relieved beyond measure that no revenge was being carried out upon him. "I will remember, noble sir."

Then the boy screamed out an incoherent wave, for he had just passed over the moment of his first injury. Kookatchi looked at the hour-long tail and noticed the damage.

"Float quietly," Kookatchi said. "I will heal you."

The Drum spun another cocoon of light over Saryu, again connecting his tail to the boy's. Using the state of Saryu's temporal body before and after the injury, Kookatchi interpolated the missing pieces of Saryu and the web of light and molecules rebuilt them, restoring hand and ear and tips of toes, a thousand tiny slices healed. The golden chrysalis vanished and Saryu possessed the wholeness he had lacked.

"How do you feel?" Kookatchi asked after breaking the link between them.

"Well, noble sir, I feel well."

"You are lucky," Kookatchi said. "You were not severed temporally and you did not lose any vital parts, so I did not have to truncate you."

"Thank you, noble sir," Saryu said.

"You are welcome. Now come with me," Kookatchi said, and swam off through the shallower Great River, darting through the futureward current and pastward countercurrent. Saryu followed meekly. In his mind, Kookatchi had changed from the demon who was keeping him from his desires to the divinity that would grant them all.

They swam past the stone of Saryu's birth and the boy looked at it, remembered his ambitions, and changed the verses of his song.

"Tiger gate/Future gate, freed now from time.
Tiger gate/Future gate, time will be mine.
Tiger gate/Future gate, the ocean to see.
Tiger gate/Future gate, all come to me."

They swam on past the stone and down the Great River, following its course until it emptied change into the ocean. Saryu stared in wonder at the expanse of waters beyond the island of his birth. He was enraptured by the myriad waves of alteration cascading into each other, rippling together, interfering with each other, swirling and dancing one into another. The changing waters of the Instant filled his senses with a chorus of rapturous song and a swirling show of intermingling lights like fireflies dancing in front of clouds and rainbows.

"Noble sir, it is so beautiful."

"Yes, Saryu, all beauty lies here, if only you could see it."

"I can see it, noble sir," Saryu said.

"No, you cannot," the Drum replied. "You cannot see the Instant whole and entire. That is where the beauty lies, not just in the interaction of flowing water, but in the whole of change."

But Saryu did not really hear Kookatchi, for in the interacting waters he came to understand the purpose and the power of his tail and came to embrace the ability of change. He realized what Kookatchi had meant about giving him the power to act. Saryu swam out of the broken island and knew that he could alter the solid world by the swish of his tail. The fires of ambition rekindled in him and he grasped the chance to change the world according to his vision.

Kookatchi did not know that his protégé had come to the same conclusion as all the tribesmen before him had, nor that he had implicitly decided to enter the war as a tribe of one. The Drum's attention was focused was on the forty thousand years that separated him from his allies and separated his knowledge from Quillithé's ability to plan, and Nir's capacity to act.

"Tell me when your mind begins to fall apart," Kookatchi said to Saryu, "and we will cross the millennia in that moment."

Nir and Quillithé had evolved their war games and their compre-
hensions of each other's languages to the limit of their senses. Battles were now fought in series of engagements stretching all across
the hypothetical Instant. Multiple tribes sought many disparate
goals and began battles when the work to achieve those goals was
thwarted by the presence of another tribe. Grand schemes of real
and invented tribal leaders were carried out or dashed to hopeless
defeat. Strategy and tactics contended and each learned the ways
of the other.

But, as said, there was a limit to that learning. Nir could not
see; he relied on Second Voice to translate Quillithé's pictures into
feelings, and feeling could not capture the nuance or subtlety of
color, shade, light and darkness. Quillithé, for her part, could not
feel, so the texture of Nir's maps, the configurations and interactions
of small wave changes were beyond her ability to translate into
vision.

Eventually these gaps in comprehension came to dominate the
interaction of the two as a battle would stop so that the two combatants could try and overcome a missed nuance with an elaborate
description.

"The Turkic Upland Atemporal Cavalry was shielding itself behind the crosscurrents of the middle Diaspora," Nir tapped, trying
to explain why he thought one of Quillithé's maneuvers would not
work.

Image from Quillithé: A Drum in the tribe of the Tortuga Cor-
sairs of the Wind beyond the Sky, shading the color of the cross-
current so the Turks would not know to rely upon them.

Impasse. For the twelfth time in as many battles, an impasse of
the senses.

Taps and images ceased to pass back and forth as a visual and
tactile silence grew in the center of the camp. The Lady of the only
army and the War Chief of the Ghosts, two minds clear and sure,

each capable of innovation unknown to the rest of the Instant's leaders, floated in stymied voicelessness.

Near the forward tip of Quillithé's tail, twenty years of life from her present point of consciousness, the strategists' seven fathers exchanged images of fear, fear that their daughter had met her match.

Image from the first father: The army fighting the Ghosts, long protracted battle, Nir and Quillithé locked in combat, their daughter's century of life carved into decades by the War Chief, decades then cleaved into years, years into days, days into minutes, minutes into a spray of dead milliseconds.

Image from the second father: Red of denial, a different fear than the one just given. Quillithé and Nir joining in perpetual alliance, abandoning the seven fathers for their own schemes of Instant conquest.

Image from the third father: Red of denial, yet another fear. Nir convincing Quillithé that the seven fathers were no more to her than the rest of her soldiers, the strategist using them in battle instead of protecting them.

And so it went, fear feeding on fear while at the center of camp silence fed on silence.

In the outer rings of the encamped army, the soldiers waited, prepared for whatever orders would eventually emerge from the strategist. Rumor had ceased to fly, and the army had settled down to await the next event in the strange alliance. Quillithé's warriors floated, waiting with a patience unrivaled in the Instant, a patience born of pure confidence in their leader.

Quillithé had always encouraged and endorsed that confidence. After all, she had never made a mistake, never erred in strategy, never lost an opportunity to expand the possibilities of her command. But now she had a problem she could not seem to solve. She looked across the gap of silence at the only equal she had ever found, and did not know how to cross that gap.

Nir floated on the tides of the deep and felt down through the interleaving currents of time. One hundred thousand years of deliberate and random change-waves had come together to create this complex wash of motion and countermotion. His extended touch could feel it all and his mind could move him safely through it, so that if he wished he could have swum down, touched the bottom and entered the wildly changing Flux below. With practice he could even have adapted to that flashing world, transforming completely moment by moment; but he could not find a way to understand the subtleties Quillithé gave to her images, could not reach to the heart of her strategies.

The War Chief's mind, the perfect model of adaptability, could not find a way to take in that missing sense of visual nuance. There was something missing, something that could not be supplied by the adaptations open to him. Nir, who had become War Chief for his swiftness in thought, who had changed the Ghosts from a struggling huddled tribe into the invincible defenders of the Now, who had himself crossed a hundred millennia through the whole of the inhabited Instant, needed something that lay outside of himself.

A thought began to form simultaneously in both of their minds. Quillithé approached it by considering the possibilities of their present situation and pruning away the untenable answers. Nir came toward it by letting his mind transform freely, letting each stray notion carry him along until it exhausted itself and another would take its place; an undisciplined way of thinking, but Nir knew it was the best way to let a new notion come into being.

Quillithé had pared down the branches of possibility to reach a growth premised on the concept of seeking a source of new senses. Nir had come near to the thought by allowing his mind to wander along the limitations of Ghostly existence, and consider how, if the opportunity presented itself, he might go about improving the capabilities of his warriors. They had almost simultaneously reached the self-same idea when Adjutant Irithrué swam into the center of camp bearing news.

Image from Irithrué: A Drum and an hour-long Time Warrior, swimming in tandem toward the camp. Subtle shading of black, gold, and blue on the two figures, implying that they had emerged from darkness.

Nir missed the color subtleties, but the overall import of the picture he understood. "Kookatchi has returned?" he asked.

"Yes," Quillithé tapped.

War Chief and strategist regarded each other with touch and sight. The thought that had been growing in both their minds remained unsaid but unforgotten. They would wait to speak it until they had heard the words of the Drum and decided what to do about the broken island.

Kookatchi and Saryu had traveled forty millennia in a moment of thought. They had swum by many tribes caught in the confusion of battle, and evaded a hundred life-threatening enemies and twice that many sea-borne storms that, had they lacked the moment of Drum's awareness, would have shattered them into milliseconds.

The moment had ended and they floated ten years pastward from the camp of the only army. Kookatchi's mind adjusted swiftly to the need for pretended sequency. But Saryu, who had only been gripped by the power of Drum's understanding once before, had difficulty resuming the apparent passage of events.

"Come," Kookatchi said. "That is the camp of our allies."

Words. Saryu had heard words. Words had followed one after another. One after another. Things happened one after another. Past led to present led to future. Future. Tiger gate/Future gate . . .

The song of his ambition yanked Saryu completely out of Drum's awareness. The moment, that long, vast moment that stretched so far across the ocean and consumed so many people, so many battles and dangers, that moment vanished utterly from his mind. He was Saryu, he had come to the waters of time to fulfill his ambitions. Ahead lay those who his mentor had allied himself with. He had come to help his mentor report, and then, then . . . Somehow he would gain aid in his plan to shape the future.

"Noble sir," Saryu said as they swam futureward, covering the last few years. "Those people ahead, they seem very long to me."

"Most of the army soldiers have fifteen-year tails," Kookatchi said.

"Fifteen years?"

Saryu looked across the distance at these warriors and the wakes they left behind them. One hundred thousand times his own length, fifteen years of life to have all at once. To use that much time to make changes—oh, how he envied them. One hour, how could that be adequate to do what he wanted? Yet Kookatchi had only a minute and he could do what he wanted. Perhaps the length of the being was not enough.

As Saryu mused, the soldiers of the army passed them through the rings of the camp, carrying hour and minute through the centuries to the center. There Saryu saw Quillithé for the first time. Coils wrapped within coils, twists and turns of a hundred years wrapped around themselves. Her body was like an unsolvable labyrinth that drew the boy's senses in and snared his mind with the puzzle of her life. In the vastness of her complexity, Saryu did not even notice Nir, so innocuous did the War Chief seem in the presence of the Monster of the deep.

Kookatchi swam away from the boy over to his two allies. As he swam, Kookatchi the Bridge, Kookatchi the Mediator floated up to become his whole consciousness.

"Nir," he tapped, "I have learned the ways of the broken island."

Image from Kookatchi to Quillithé: Darkness receding, the broken island revealed.

"And what have you learned?" Nir said.

Image from Quillithé: The broken island, limned in questioning blue.

"Saryu." Kookatchi washed a wave over the boy, breaking his trance. "Come here."

"My memory will tell you," Kookatchi said to his allies, and he flicked his tail in a marking gesture toward the boy. Obedient and nervous, Saryu swam slowly forward and submitted his memory for examination by the three minds there gathered.

XXV

"And what treasure is this you have brought back from the broken island?" Nir asked Kookatchi.

"The treasure of memory," the Drum replied.

Image from Quillithé: Long-tailed warrior fallen into cracked ground, losing all but an hour of his life. Kookatchi pulling the hour-long warrior out. Blue of inquiry over all.

Image from Kookatchi: Repeat of Quillithé's image. Red of denial. New image: Egg floating in the waters, Kookatchi pulling Saryu out of the egg.

"I did not understand that," Nir said.

"I pulled the boy from an hour-long fragment," Kookatchi said. "I freed him from the Flux."

Nir and Quillithé rocked back on their tails in disbelief. A new silence rose up in the center of the camp, and the wash of the deep tides flowed in to fill the space between the four who floated there. The War Chief could not imagine deliberately taking one who was not of the People out of the Flux. The strategist, for her part, could not comprehend deliberately liberating a warrior who would not be committed to her service. Both Nir and Quillithé believed that the last thing the Instant needed was a source of more contention.

But neither War Chief nor strategist could ignore the truth in front of them. Kookatchi had liberated a person he could neither rely upon nor enslave, one who was not of his people nor subservient to his cause.

Nir's mind changed and the truth before him became part of the idea he had been nurturing.

Quillithé looked at the unprecedented act and took the awareness into the vastness of her mind. Kookatchi freeing Saryu darted from corridor to corridor, room to room until it settled down next to the notion she had been cultivating.

Both Nir and Quillithé placed the notion near the idea that had been churning their thoughts before Kookatchi returned. Both concluded the same thing: If for the sake of his mission the Drum could free one who was not of his people, then perhaps they could do this previously unthinkable thing.

Saryu, who did not know either the language of the Ghosts or of the deeps, had floated nervously while the other three had spoken. He ventured to break the silence with a question to Kookatchi.

"Noble sir, what am I to say to these great beings?"

"Nothing yet," Kookatchi said. "I will ask for reminders and you will tell me what I have forgotten."

"Yes, noble sir."

The Drum flicked a questioning image into the silence that remained between Nir and Quillithé.

Image from the Drum: Kookatchi regaling the War Chief and the strategist with the tale of his journey. Blue of inquiry.

Kookatchi then repeated the question in the tapping speech of the Ghosts, "Shall I tell you what I found in the broken island?"

Image from Quillithé: Kookatchi speaking, Nir and Quillithé attentive to his words.

"Speak on," Nir said.

The Drum began his recitation. Having forgotten the battle he engendered before entering the broken island, Kookatchi omitted that tale from the report. He began instead with the first unforgettable thing.

"There is a Great River," Kookatchi said. "It carries a corridor of change through the island."

Image from Kookatchi: Broken ground, a single swath of change-waters flowing through it.

"So change does pass through," Nir said.

"Yes, but very confined, and the passage of change is distorted," Kookatchi said. "In the middle of the Great River I found an island inside the broken island, a solid egg amidst the shattering."

Image from Kookatchi: Oval gem, bright emerald in the Great River. Gold of gloriousness about the gem.

Image from Quillithé: Repetition of previous image, blue of inquiry around the gold of glory.

"What is she saying?" Nir asked, incapable of telling the colors of nuance.

"Quillithé wants to know what the beauty of the egg was."

"And what was it?"

Kookatchi poised to answer, but found himself unable to move. Kookatchi the Thief had been overcome with the desire for the gem, but Kookatchi the Bridge was the one who found the beauty of it. How to speak this?

The Drum's consciousness recycled and he became again both Thief and Bridge.

Image from Kookatchi: The broken island a vast tracery of cracks, little stones, sand, and this one big stone. Superimposed over this image was an image of Kookatchi pulling Saryu up out of the Flux, the act of freeing limned in the gold of glory.

Words tapped out from the forward thirty seconds of Kookatchi's life. "That emerald was so large, so great, how could I resist it?"

Words tapped out from the rearward thirty seconds of Kookatchi's life. "In that stone was the event that anchored the future. I pulled that event away and the future did not lose its anchor."

The Drum's consciousness recycled and he was once again Kookatchi.

Nir and Quillithé exchanged taps and images of confusion, but they did not want to distract the Drum.

"Say on," Nir said.

Quillithé echoed his words in pictures.

Image from Kookatchi: Kookatchi and Saryu swimming pastward up the river.

"We swam on," the Drum tapped.

"I understood your picture," the War Chief replied. "What happened then?"

"I do not remember," Kookatchi said. He switched to the language he shared with Saryu.

"What did I ask you to remember after we left your egg behind?"

Tiger gate/Future gate. The boy thought, returning himself to the base of his memory. What was it? Oh, yes. "That you cracked a stone with sharp waves and healed it with slow rhythm."

"I healed a stone?" Kookatchi said in surprise; then his consciousness recycled and the whole event came back to him. He recited it carefully in taps and images, showing the crescent stone and the wash of the Great River, a smoothing power that healed the damage.

In the corridors of Quillithé's mind the tree that held her models of the Instant's nature changed; branches fell off and the trunk grew up swift and sure as if a hundred years passed in a moment. Possibilities came to her, strategies began to form. The broken island would be healed.

Nir felt only a great sense of relief at the news that cracking could be undone, a realization that he might be able to go home to the Now and see if he was still War Chief or if the Elder had exiled him.

"What then?" Kookatchi asked Saryu.

"The waterfalls," the boy replied.

Waterfalls? Kookatchi thought. What was important about the waterfalls? Recollections bubbled up in the Drum's memory like the

breaking waves at the bottom of a cataract. The three streams coming together, yes, that was relevant, but not terribly important. Why
would the boy remember? Oh, of course, carrying him up. No
doubt that would confuse Saryu, who lacked Drum's awareness.

Image from the Drum: Kookatchi and Saryu at the bottom of
the falls. No passage of time, Kookatchi and Saryu at the top of
the falls.

To Nir, the Drum said, "We floated at the bottom of the falls,
then when Saryu was not fixed in the delusion of passage, the configuration of the Instant changed and we were at the top."

Nir, who had once used this change-without-passage to capture
the Drum, thought he understood what Kookatchi was saying, but
in truth he missed crucial elements. What the War Chief heard the
Drum describing was a means of travel open to the short-tailed that
the long-tailed could not employ; thus it fell away from Nir's mind
without having great impact upon him.

But Quillithé put the image Kookatchi had sent her together
with the tapped words he had spoken to Nir and saw something
else. Not yet did she gain a complete understanding; that would
have to wait for another event. But she learned a great deal, which
she embodied in a montage of pictures, three streams of images
sent back to the Drum.

First sequence of images: Saryu floating, Saryu's consciousness
a bright silver light traveling up his tail. Saryu's consciousness vanishing in the crash that all who dwelled in the Instant experienced.
Saryu himself disappearing as the silver light vanished.

Second sequence of images sent along with the first: Kookatchi,
a silver light of consciousness suffusing his minute-long body, his
body half-present, half-gone in the light, then vanishing completely
along with the light.

Third sequence of images: Waterfall alone. Waterfall with
Kookatchi and Saryu floating in the pool at its base. Waterfall
alone. Waterfall with Kookatchi and Saryu floating on top, in the
waters above the cataract.

Then one single image: One point, nothing else.

"Yes," the Drum tapped out in the language of the Ghosts, awed that Quillithé, the longest being in existence, could see this truth that only the short-tailed knew.

But Quillithé herself was not satisfied. She had gleaned the nonsequency of the Instant, but she did not know how to use it. Her immobility chafed at her and the lapping waters of the deeps ceased to comfort her. There had to be a way to put this understanding into application, but she could not see it.

"Continue the telling," Nir tapped.

Quillithé considered interrupting and demanding more knowledge of this transport up the waterfall, but she stopped herself. The War Chief was right; the safety of the Instant came first.

"What next?" Kookatchi asked Saryu.

"The lake of blood, noble sir," the boy said and a tingle of fear ran through his mind. What if Kookatchi told the Monster about his betrayal, and what if the Monster was not as forgiving as his master?

"The lake of blood," Kookatchi said. "And there was something else, was there not?"

"The phalanx and the battle, noble sir," Saryu said, hoping that was what Kookatchi was asking about.

"The phalanx and the battle," Kookatchi repeated, and the memory of his converse with the Czarist came to him pure and perfect in every detail. "Yes, but first the lake of blood."

Image from Kookatchi: The roiling pool of water is filled with the shattered bodies of the dead. The waters lap at the sands and are repelled. The wash of change flows out of the lake into the stream and therefrom feeds the Great River.

"The microsecond fragments kept the lake intact?" Nir asked.

"Yes," Kookatchi replied.

"So the gaps in time were too small to let changes through."

"Yes," Kookatchi said, and then he remembered a crucial element he had forgotten. "And they were too small to have channels to guide the waters."

"Guide the waters?" Nir said.

"The carving of the sea bottom guides the waters of change," Kookatchi said.

The War Chief stretched out his sense of touch, feeling downward through the interleaving layers of the deep tides until he felt the ocean floor. There in the everchanging passage of time his touch felt grooves, hard, carved, tiny channels barely a thousandth of a second in width, reinforcing the course of change, guiding the flows in the deeps.

Nir's mind changed of a sudden and he felt the Instant in a new way; no longer did he feel only the savage change-waves lying over a hapless solid time. The War Chief touched two things two together, the water and the earth. But they were not separate, one dominating the other, they were two things that were one. Not water over earth, not earth below water, but water and earth, time as one thing with two ways to feel it. A longing filled the War Chief's mind, the need to return to the Now and give this understanding to his Ghosts that they might at last understand their oaths and so at last fulfill them.

"I must leave soon," the War Chief tapped. "I have the thing I must bring back to the People."

"Not yet," Quillithé tapped. "There is more for you to return to your People."

Image from Quillithé to Kookatchi: The Drum continuing his tale.

Image from Kookatchi: The promontory, Kookatchi entering it and vanishing into the Flux. Confrontation with the Czarist.

"I met the last survivor of the battle that created the broken island," Kookatchi tapped to Nir.

"Tell us about that battle," Nir said.

Images from Kookatchi: The strong Wavebreakers of the Babylonian Timeless Infantry. The phalanx of Czar Ivan's Grand Army of Time. The escalated wave, the cracking, the earth thrusting up through the waters, the waters falling down through the earth. The knife blades of solid time, carving both armies to pieces. The promontory as the memorial stone of the conflict and the fifteen-minute piece of Mikhail Dimitri Alexandrovitch clutching his last few memories like prizes from Kookatchi's nonexistent hoard.

Quillithé took in the images. Some she placed in her considerations of the Instant's nature. The stress that the floor of time could take before cracking she now knew; that was the last piece of information she needed for her tree to bloom fully. The Instant could be healed, earth could be returned to earth and water to water. But one of the images did not go to that part of her mind. The battle itself stayed with her.

Image from Quillithé to Nir: Game beginning, the phalanx of the Grand Army against the heavily armored Timeless Infantry. Quillithé could control the Czarists, Nir the Babylonians.

The strategist and the War Chief began to play out the battle, first as it actually happened, plan by plan and wave by wave. At the end both agreed that the leaders of the two tribes had fought well and as sensibly as could be expected from limited commanders.

Then Nir and Quillithé tried again, seeking different ways to carry through the battle between one greatly weaponed and one greatly armored side. Images and taps flashed back and forth between the two while Kookatchi and Saryu looked on.

The boy was confused by this interchange, but did not dare to ask what the Monster and the warrior were doing.

The Drum was caught up in the beauty of their means of communication. Imperfect as it was, it crossed the gap of the senses unmediated. Sight saw feeling and feeling felt sight, a distance unbridgeable without the mediation of one who possessed both senses, and yet Nir and Quillithé had bridged that distance.

Almost, they had bridged it. It became clear to the Drum that this beauty of interchange was a flawed beauty. Errors in comprehension cropped up continually. Nir's blindness kept the subtleties of Quillithé's actions hidden, and Quillithé's unfeelingness hid Nir's motivations from her awareness, and yet, they were still communicating.

A hundred battles were played out, fifty with Nir commanding the phalanx, fifty with Quillithé, a hundred battles and only one way to avoid a rout by one side or the other.

"Only the crescent defense, the phalanx wave, and the cracking leads to an even battle to mutual destruction," Nir tapped to Kookatchi. "Every other possibility leads to annihilation for only one side."

"But the phalanx wave leads to destruction for both and for the Instant itself."

"Yes, Kookatchi," the War Chief said, "but the leaders of the tribes would always choose mutual annihilation over the death of only their people."

Image from Quillithé: The Instant. At a thousand different places in the ocean, a thousand phalanxes fight a thousand shielded tribes and a thousand broken islands bloom. The ocean of time is gone. Only a desolate landscape remains.

"She says that this will happen again," Kookatchi said to Nir.

"I know," said the War Chief. "Even if we heal the Instant, the escalation of armaments will lead to another phalanx and another island and then another. The madmen who lead the tribes will not stop for the sake of the Instant. Their sole concern is the establishment of their tribe's history."

Image from Quillithé: The broken island sinking back under the waters at Quillithé's direction.

"You will heal the island?" Nir said.

"Yes."

"Then I will find a way to stop it from coming again," the War Chief said. "This I vow."

"This is the Instant," Kookatchi tapped.

> *"The Instant shall be change.*
> *That is the Flux.*
> *The Flux shall be guide."*

The War Chief of the Ghosts, half leader of the first People, swirled in a sudden ring, coiling himself around the Drum. Anger took hold of Nir's whole mind, a blinding rage at this perversion of the Ghosts' vow.

Kookatchi the Bridge floated unconcerned in the War Chief's coils. Rippling death waited around him in all eight directions. His minute of life, his moment of existence could have been shattered with a single thought. But the Drum did nothing.

And that doing of nothing, that single act of no battle drained away Nir's rage like a torrent of change striking the broken island. The wave of wrath passed out of the War Chief's mind and in its place was acceptance. Kookatchi had spoken rightly. Nir's new vow was like his ancient vow.

"We are the People," Nir tapped.

> *"The People will not be changed.*
> *That is the Now.*
> *The Now will not be Flux.*
> *This is the Instant.*
> *The Instant shall be change.*
> *That is the Flux.*
> *The Flux shall be guide."*

Quillithé saw the words and interpreted them. In the corridors of her mind she saw a great possibility that Nir would be cast out from his people for changing their vow.

Image from Quillithé to Nir: Nir traveling the Instant alone, peril swimming everywhere around him.

"I have assistance . . . aid . . . tool . . . beneficence . . . useful gift . . . benediction for you in your plan . . . goal . . . strategy . . . effort . . . action . . . need . . . necessity," Quillithé tapped.

Image from Nir to Quillithé: Quillithé floating aided by her army, attempting to heal the island, safe from any danger.

"And I have aid for you," he tapped.

The War Chief swam close to the strategist. A day separated them, then an hour, then mere seconds.

Image from Quillithé's seven fathers to Quillithé: Nir attacking, seeking to carve her up, then killing them. Deep yellow of fear washed with ruby red of denial.

What he was about to do Nir had done half a dozen times before, but always to a fledgling Ghost, newly taken from the Now after the newcomer had succeeded at the tests and completed the ritual of passing on.

What she was about to do, Quillithé had done three hundred times, each time to a new soldier taken from the Flux of the deeps to fill a place in the army; each new soldier had been taken from a state of the Flux in which all the time-bound were loyal to Quillithé and would follow her commands without question.

But this time Nir touched one who was not of the People, voluntarily leaving the earthly world to become a Ghost.

But this time Quillithé spread her gaze on one who was not bound to her by intrained fealty, taken from the earthly world to become a soldier in the only army.

Quillithé saw a coil of golden light spin out from the base of Nir's tail and wrap itself around her century of existence.

Nir felt a line of matter and energy, thinner than a hair, thinner than a heartbeat's duration spin out from Quillithé's body and coil itself around him.

From his nearby vantage Kookatchi stared in wonder as the coils of gold and black light, the spider threads of Instant survival passed between his two allies. The Drum reveled in the beauty of the moment. Events like this event happened over and over in the Instant, the passing on of ability from the old to the new, but the beauty here lay not in the act but in the actors. Two minds that had long experience of the Instant were about to be changed, augmented by each other.

The threads from Nir completed their coverage of Quillithé, then detonated inward, filling every moment of her century with new feeling.

Quillithé's web enmeshed the War Chief, then embedded itself in every second of his atemporal brain, filling his decade with new vision.

The waters of the deeps, every current, had a flow and a feel to them. Their intermingling was soothing, comforting, waters of home; so many different strains, each with its own pace. Choppy waves and smooth waves, swift passage and broad deep flow. And every current carried nuances of change, nuances of feeling to add to the breadth of sight. This current came from a battle thirty thousand years pastward, high peaks and narrow troughs. That tide was from before Quillithé could see, a long, old passage of events perhaps as far back as the Now, gentle and washing over her, bubbles breaking against her tail.

The only army was arrayed around Nir in a circle three hundred years across, further than he could feel, but not further than he could see. He had a thousand years of vision, and with it he saw each soldier individually, clear and obvious. That long ebon and violet being was Quillithé. The seven green creatures floating in her coils must be her fathers. That flickering, darting rainbow-colored tiny thing was Kookatchi, and the dour brown nervous creature next to him must be Saryu.

All the years of touch came into Quillithé's mind and she correlated them with sight, letting the new understanding that came with this new sense enter the corridors of her mind, adding texture to her vision. Every possibility she held in her labyrinthine consciousness gained a feeling: the prickliness of the unsolved, the smoothness of the known and comprehended, the satin of understanding, and the rough granite of the unknown.

Nir's ancillary Voices screamed their confusion into his mind.

"New data, visual information in the Instant, violates programming. Orders needed," Second Voice said.

"Hallucinations," Third Voice concluded, taking the swiftest possible explanation. "Injury to brain likely."

"We have been changed," Fourth Voice said simply. "Specify nature of change."

We have been given the sense of sight, Nir said to Fourth Voice.

The War Chief's special advisor fell silent, accepting the new source of understanding.

There has been no injury, Nir said to Third Voice. We have a new tactical advantage, greater detection range and more capacity to gauge the actions of enemies.

The tactical advisor fell silent, accepting a new assistance in battle.

The new data is visual, Nir said to Second Voice. We can now see the Instant.

The keeper of memory fell silent and reprogrammed itself for ease of translation.

"We must go," Quillithé tapped, and the words were exact without vibrating in meaning.

Image from Nir: Picture of the Instant from the Now to the deeps. Blue of inquiry.

"Where?" he asked, watching the ripples that emerged from the taps of his tail.

Image from Quillithé: The broken island, bright gold of emphasis around a region of the waters a single millennium futureward of it.

"There, the whole army must go," she tapped.

Image from Kookatchi: Quillithé leaving the deeps, blue of inquiry tinged with silvery gray of disbelief.

Image from Quillithé: Quillithé leaving the deeps, suffering injury in the midwaters, steel gray-gold of absolute necessity. The broken island healed.

Quillithé's seven fathers saw the image and clustered close to her, whimpering pictures of fear and abandonment.

Image from Quillithé: Thirty of her soldiers remaining behind to guard the seven fathers.

Still they whined and begged, but their century daughter would not heed their fears.

Nir tapped a gentle message to Kookatchi. "I need my Wave-breaker before I undertake such a journey."

"Yes, of course," the Drum replied, and shivered the protective helix off his body, flipping it back to the War Chief, who wrapped it again around his ten-year form.

Quillithé rippled her entire body. All one hundred years of life shivered out a picture, a single image propagating in a sphere through the camp. A burst of variegated light covered the whole three centuries of the army. In that impulse of color and shape was a new ordering for the soldiers, a place for each to take up. A marching order was shown comprising three columns: ninety soldiers in a front line fifty years pastward of Quillithé, ninety directly next to Quillithé, and ninety soldiers fifty years futureward of her as a rear guard. The remaining thirty were formed in a protective ring around the seven fathers.

The image passed through the camp, and as the order implicit in the image touched each soldier that soldier took up the place assigned. In that single burst of light the many-ringed camp was transformed into three echelons geared for marching.

Nir had watched this use of image-speech with fascination. Such a power of ordering, and now it was his to command as well. With such a capability the Ghosts would be able to respond more swiftly than mere touch had permitted them. Quillithé had given him a great gift; soon he would bring it to his People, if only they would take it.

Kookatchi had been dazzled by the brightness of the image and the flash of change, a perfect transformation of the Instant. No delusion of passage had marred the motions of the army. To most there it seemed as if Quillithé had commanded and her commands had been followed, but Kookatchi had seen the truth. Quillithé's command and the carrying out of that command had been one thing, one transformation of the Instant; desire and action had happened in a single event with no intervening delusions of movement.

"Perfection," the Drum tapped in the language of the Ghosts.

The word rippled over to Quillithé, tickling her newborn touch with its implications.

Adjutant Irithrué had obeyed the command instantly along with the rest of her comrades. The issuing of the command had stopped all other picture speech among the army. Quillithé, she whose image-name was center of all plans, had made a decision and the only army would carry it out with no questions asked, no confusion permitted.

Irithrué herself had been placed in charge of the ninety soldiers whose task it was to move Quillithé herself. It was a singular honor and one Irithrué took up with zeal. The first task of the ninety warriors was to straighten the strategist out, uncoiling the maze of her tail so she could lie flat across the deeps, one end of her facing east, the other west, a single line perpendicular to the future-past axis.

Once Quillithé was uncoiled, Irithrué's soldiers formed a line one hour futureward of the strategist and created a slow surface wave front; no sharp peaks were formed, just a rolling surf moving pastward, carrying Quillithé away from her native deep tides.

The three lines of the army set out, the vanguard followed by Quillithé, then Irithrué's rolling troops and then the rear guard. They left behind the honor guard of the seven fathers and their terrified charges.

Nir, Kookatchi, and Saryu swam a year in front of Quillithé, bobbing up and down on the great waves her century-body formed. Deep tides of change flowed from her as she was carried along the ocean's surface.

The War Chief found the sight of Quillithé being pushed and rolled by her soldiers a source of great sadness. He had known that the strategist could not move herself through the freedom of time's great ocean, but to actually see this forced movement as one of the first sights his Instant vision took in, that was hard to bear.

Kookatchi's senses were fixed on the overall rhythm of the army's movement, the cadence of the deeps being carried down into the shallower waters of the central Instant. The Drum vibrated in tune to the heavy bass percussion of that great swimming.

Saryu's attention was as fixed on Quillithé as Nir's was, but where the War Chief saw helplessness, the boy saw a fearful creature moving with menacing inevitability toward the time that had given him birth. The great waves of change that flowed out of Quillithé's hundred-year body spelled doom for Saryu's ambitions. How could any human design and scheme of man's mind hold up against that relentless barrage of alteration?

Tiger Gate/Future gate, what can I do?

The boy could find no answer to that question.

The army's passage down the millennia did not go unnoticed by the assembled tribes. Scouts who had been sent to spy on the army swam back to their encampments and brought the word.

"The Monster of the deep is coming!"

That message was carried to the leaders of each tribe in turn and each took it in and spoke its meaning to the warriors of time.

"The end of the kalpa has come upon us," said the commander of the Kala's Kshatriyas.

"The apocalypse is here," said the chief Keeper of the Chalice of Time's Waters.

"The great flood is about to inundate our people," said the Lord High Guardian of the Eternal Spring.

In language after language and myth after myth the sentence reverberated. Doomsday had come.

A thousand tribes echoed this fear; the battles of the Instant ceased as the great unconquerable enemy made her way through the ocean. Each tribe was sure that the Monster of the deep had come for them in particular, for each regarded its own ambitions as the great threat to Quillithé's dominance. Each abandoned its petty rivalries in order to do battle with the true and great enemy of all.

One thousand years futureward from the broken island, Quillithé flashed out a new configuration and the army reformed again. The camp now consisted of Quillithé floating in the center and one hundred and twenty of her soldiers arrayed around her in two concentric circles, an inner guard of forty stationed at a radius of thirty years and an outer ring of eighty at a radius of one hundred years. The remaining one hundred and fifty soldiers were parceled out into five squads of thirty each. To each of these groups Quillithé rippled out an image-order, and, obeying the commands, the five groups departed from the camp, swimming pastward.

"What task have you set them?" Nir inquired.

Quillithé rippled out an image of the broken island. Along its pastward edge the five squadrons were deployed and set to rippling rhythmic waves into the island.

Saryu, who had slowly come to grasp the basics of the visual language, understood the meaning of the picture and spoke immediately. "She is digging new rivers."

"What did your memory say?" Nir asked Kookatchi, and the Drum translated from his verbal language to the tapping speech of the Ghosts.

"Correct," Quillithé said.

While Quillithé spoke with her allies, the inner guard of forty soldiers coiled up her body in order to give her some degree of comfort in the shallow waters which bit and scratched at her neophyte sense of touch. Once she was well wrapped up in an area twenty years by ten kilometers, the guards withdrew to form their defensive ring, leaving Quillithé with Nir, Kookatchi, and Saryu.

Image from Quillithé to the other three: Rivers flowing all through the island, polishing the stones, healing the stones until the river bottoms become like the true ocean floor. Then more rivers, until the broken island is drowned and healed by the timeless waters of the Instant.

"A good plan," Nir tapped. "You have your task well under way. I must undertake mine."

"What must you do?" Quillithé tapped.

Image from Nir: The War Chief returns to the Now and gathers up the Ghosts.

"I would like to come with you," Kookatchi tapped. The words came out of his body before he realized what he was saying.

"Why?" Nir asked.

"I do not know," the Drum replied, and then his consciousness recycled and he remembered a little of something that had passed through his mind in very different circumstances. "I need to go to the Now and see how your People anchor events. Only when we know how things do not change can we make the Instant safe to be change."

The War Chief's first instinct was to refuse. It seemed obvious that to let an outsider into the Now was to betray his oath, but that same obvious seeming made all his actions since joining with Kookatchi and Quillithé look traitorous. And he had his new oath to consider as well.

"The Instant shall be change," he said. "You may come unless Quillithé needs you."

Image from Quillithé: Nir and Kookatchi leaving the camp, swimming downtime, Saryu remaining behind with her.

Image from Kookatchi: Saryu with Quillithé, blue of inquiry.

"I have need of your memory," Quillithé tapped. "Saryu knows the inside of the island. He will be of use in charting the passage of the rivers."

Saryu had no idea what was being said about him, so he was shocked when Kookatchi swam to him, and said, "Nir and I must leave. You will remain with Quillithé and assist her in the reclamation."

"Noble sir?" Saryu said. "Did you say remain with that . . . that . . ." He could not find a word to complete the question.

"Yes," Kookatchi said. "You will help the Lady of the only army. Do whatever she tells you to."

A wash of helplessness came over the boy's mind and he felt again that powerless sensation that had come over him when first Kookatchi had torn him from his home. And then he remembered what had come of that feeling. He had tried to kill his mentor and had in fact killed someone else, someone he had never met.

"I will do as you say, noble sir," Saryu said. But in his mind the fear of Quillithé lurked and darted around, whispering to his ambition.

Tiger gate/Future gate, a way will be found.

The War Chief and the Drum took their leave of the strategist and the boy and swam out through the thirty-year ring and the century ring of the camp. They turned eastward and pastward and began the long journey toward the beginning of things.

Quillithé watched them go until they disappeared around the eastern edge of the blackness that lay a thousand years pastward from her; unseeable, it mocked her, but though she herself could not penetrate it directly, she had been given knowledge of it, and already her soldiers had begun the work of remaking the deathly solid darkness into time's ocean of varicolored life.

XXVI

A thousand years from the darkness, Quillithé and Saryu waited for the return of light. The hour-long boy floated amidst the complex coils of the century strategist, swimming through channels and passages all of which were Quillithé. Every-where Saryu looked there was a bit of Quillithé, floating in itchy discomfort amidst the uneven waters.

The boy's thoughts were evenly distributed between fear of this great being and a desire to know what was happening in the solid world below him. He knew that this point in space and time lay a single millennium after his ambition had conquered the world. And he wondered if he anchored down now and asked someone who Saryu was, whether they would tell him the story of his life and give him the coda to the song of ambition's gate.

Quillithé's thoughts were also divided. A sizable segment of her mind was working on the reclamation plan by which the broken island would be healed. Some of the vast labyrinth of her thoughts was given over to the endless practice of planning battles with the tribes camped around the island, so that should one or more of them make a desperate attack against the camp she would be able to respond immediately. A little of her attention was given to Saryu;

a few rooms and corridors of thoughts rearranged themselves over and over again, seeking the right manner and moment in which to use his knowledge of the broken island's geography. In a few corridors there would be repeated flashes of concern for her seven fathers left with only an honor guard to protect them. Fully a third of her cavernous being was expending the considerable effort needed to integrate her new, more intimate sense of touch with the vastness of her vision. And, of course, her mind constantly worried about what Nir and Kookatchi were doing in the past beyond the realm of darkness.

Swimming pastward from the change-abating of the broken island, the War Chief and the Drum took up the journey away from the heart of the matter and toward its beginning.

But there was a barrier across their path. The tribes assembled lay between the two travelers and the shallows of time. Nir's new millennial vision saw the panorama of encamped warriors strewn tribe by tribe across the way to the pastward half of time's ocean. Just-given sight made out clots of vivid red and orange camps floating on the blue-green waters of change, a thousand bands of warriors like flickering flames on the tides. Each tribe had laid claim to a half-century-by-hundred-kilometer patch of water, and there each one floated glaring its defiance and acceptance of doomsday.

There they waited, helplessly biding their time in order to see how the Monster of the deep would come upon them. But even while awaiting the killing waves of Quillithé's army, they could not keep from old arguments and old battles. Those tribes camped near to the island kept watch on each other and on Quillithé's work crews as they began to dig the rivers, but those further away, five hundred or more years pastward from the center of all activity, remembered their ancient grudges, and if one tribe found itself near an enemy old memory and old ambition would rouse them to new battle.

Image from Nir to Kookatchi: The thousand years before them, that band of time's ocean covered with enemies and battles.

"I do not see a way through to the shallower regions," Nir tapped.

Had the Drum been alone he would simply have passed invisibly through in a moment of awareness. The thought of that easy passageless passage flitted through his mind and almost vanished into idle whimsy; after all, no long-tail could follow that way of travel. But the Drum snatched at the thought. Perhaps he might be able to show Nir this way of travel; after all, the War Chief had shown himself capable of exploiting the suddenness of the Instant. It was worth the attempt.

"We could go through as I took Saryu up the waterfall," the Drum said.

"Do you think that is possible?" Nir asked, surprised at the suggestion that he take a Drum's way.

"It might be."

"What must I do?" Nir asked.

"See the Instant as it is," Kookatchi replied. "Open your new and old senses. Look at it and forget the movement of the tribes, just see the water."

Nir stared out at fire and water and waited for his mind to change, and change it did. Fire vanished and there was only water, a vast expanse of blue like a great unanswered question.

"There is water," Nir said.

"Now, let the water go," Kookatchi said.

And Nir's mind reached out and grasped the water and let it go and there was nothing, only Nir and the Instant. There was no passage. Time was gone. Only the present was with him, the present was the Instant and the Instant was Nir. Even Kookatchi was gone; no advice could be given. There was only Nir and the Instant, but the War Chief was aware of what the Drum was saying though the Drum was not there.

"Now let go of the past and future, of what you have done and what you wish to do."

"No!" Nir said, and the Instant was back, the tribes were back,

Kookatchi was back, and time again seemed to pass.

"Why did you stop?" Kookatchi said. "You were almost right."

"I cannot be War Chief without past and future," Nir said.

"Yes, you can."

"How? The past gives me cause and the future holds my actions. How can I give them up and retain my position?"

The Drum had no answer, but he knew one was coming. The Instant would change and there would be the answer, but the change had not yet been brought about.

"You must wait," Kookatchi said.

"I cannot," Nir said. "We must pass through the tribes."

"Then we will have to make a way," Kookatchi tapped. The change would come and Nir would know and the Drum would not be alone in the Instant.

Nir's mind had shifted away from the singleness of view and he saw again the flames of the tribes scattered before him, a thousand burning obstacles.

Image from the War Chief to the Drum: Kookatchi swimming two centuries pastward of Nir, the Drum entering camps and sowing discord with nearby tribes. The tribes abandoning their places to battle each other. A path of empty water plowed amidst the conflict and Nir swimming down the path through the region of the encampments.

The Drum swam off to carry out the War Chief's design, and carry it out he did. There is no need to detail the battles Kookatchi caused, the rivalries he reignited, the temptations of wealth and power he laid before the chieftains of the assembled tribes. Their minds fell eagerly into delusion and desire and their senses, drunk with want, did not see the War Chief of the Ghosts swim past them toward his home.

Five thousand years of conflict were created, battles that flared into red-and-gold destruction and then fell silent again as the surviving warriors, battered and bruised, returned to their encampments unaware of the trail of water Nir had left behind him.

Nir and Kookatchi swam through the waters thirty thousand

years futureward from the Now. No tribes occupied that region of the ocean; it was as uninhabited as the waters pastward of the Now. And yet the tides of time still flowed, change still progressed from past to future, alteration continued without the tails of man driving it.

The millions of deliberate alterations of solid time and the millions of battles that had been fought had carved channels in the ocean floor, channels that now gave impetus to and carried forward the waters, so that where there would have been stillness there was movement. These channels created tides and flows and waves that washed futureward, bringing ingrained ways of change into the middle Instant and endlessly altering the Flux below. But these alterations were not like the haphazard changes of battle; they were predictable courses of change, like regulated water passing through irrigation ditches.

In the solid time below these trenches mankind spread across and dominated the earth, for this was what the tribes of time had created by their efforts. But where man settled and where he built his cities and what he chose to regard as important and value and worship, that was not fixed. Those things were changed by the waters that flowed through the channels laid down by the dominance of the tribes.

Had the slaver tribes been present at those points in time and anchored themselves into the Flux they would have found a thousand cultures springing up and vanishing. Every one of those cultures would have been suited for slavery, for the channels of dominance and submissiveness had been carved deep in the course of time.

Had the liberator tribes been present then and there and sought to teach the ways of Instant freedom to the societies that flickered in and out of existence they too would have been pleased by the results, for the channels of rebellion and atemporal ambition had also been deeply carved.

But the only two dwellers in the Instant who swam through those waters and anchored down into that earth to see what was happening were the War Chief of the Ghosts and he who had once been the greatest thief in time, he who had since become the mediator and protector of change.

"This is what you meant about the channels in the riverbeds," Nir said to Kookatchi.

"Yes," the Drum replied.

The two of them were standing on the eastern bank of the Nile River twenty-four thousand years futureward from the Now. They stood passively watching civilizations appear and vanish around them. The pace of transformation was relatively gentle and Nir would often have five apparent minutes pass before one culture would vanish and another appear.

Fifty cities came and went astride the Nile's waters, the peoples of those places variously builders in stone or mud, workers in bronze or iron. A hundred bands of nomads settled for a season, then passed upriver or downriver or across the desert sands depending on where they were going and whether they traveled by horse or camel, on foot or on boats.

The Drum found a certain grace and beauty in this recurrent change where details would appear and vanish like smoke but commonalities would remain amidst the myriad peoples that lived on the Nile shore.

The War Chief did not know what to make of this strange dance of uncaused alteration, but he had a glimmering of a notion that here in this course of being he might find the seed of solution to the danger the tribes posed to the Instant itself. Thus the War Chief waited through the transformations of the world, hoping that his mind would change with it and the seed of thought blossom into a course of action.

But the seed remained a seed; there was not enough here to germinate it. This eventually became clear to Nir as the fiftieth city came to be and his mind stayed stubbornly the same.

"Enough," Nir said, and flicked his gaze skyward.

He and Kookatchi released their grip on solid time, returned to the ocean, and continued their pastward swim to the Now.

A wave of change left by Nir's passage washed over a city of gold and brick that had been built on the Nile. On a bridge of woven reeds one of the city's scholars saw the two men vanish and he remembered whispered stories of Ghostly guardians that had been carefully preserved from the ancient times. The stories claimed that the Ghosts ruled over the earth and that they had merely to will a thing and it would happen. Lusting after that imagined power, this scholar hunted through the city's archives for the means the great ancestors had used to preserve themselves outside of time. In a reliquary he found a device long ignored and used it to enter the Instant, taking a few stalwart comrades with him.

The scholar's people had no names, only titles. His had been Keeper of the Nearly Forgotten, but, freed from time, he named himself Ghost Lord of All and his companions he called the Honors of the Ghostly World.

In that empty region of the waters of time this new tribe emerged. And sensing no others, they concluded that they alone dominated time, so they ventured to explore their new domain, traveling futureward through the ocean until they came to encampments of the tribes and learned to their cost that the Ghost Lord of All was neither the first nor the strongest person who liberated himself in order to use the other side of life for the furtherance of ambitions.

Saryu's consciousness recycled and he sang again to himself the reminder of his ambitions.

"Tiger gate/Future gate . . ."

Quillithé had turned her attention to the boy and waited for his mind to settle down so that she might begin questioning him. Her converse with Kookatchi had told her all she needed to know about the rivers and the pace of change needed to heal the broken island. But there was one place in the island that, if the Drum's narrative had been accurate, would not be returned to the waters by change. The gem of Saryu's birth would only be polished to greater beauty by the healing waters, and that gem needed to be reclaimed if the ocean of time was to be made whole.

Image from Quillithé to Saryu: Gem in the Great River, Kook-atchi pulling the boy out of the Flux. Blue of inquiry around the emerald stone.

Saryu had learned enough of the image speech to know the question being asked by the coiled creature that surrounded him. Fear led him to swift truth and he told Quillithé in pictures about his life in the stone.

One hundred years pastward of the past border of the broken island, the river-digging gangs commenced their work. Adjutant Ir-ithrué had been put in charge of the central gang, the crew that coordinated what all five bands of workers were doing.

Irithrué stared futureward at the vast expanse of blackness that she had been dispatched to bring to light and gave the order for the crews to begin. Command images washed out of Irithrué, flow-ing east and west to the other work gangs. Orders received, the members of each crew linked their tails together so that each band of twenty formed a semicircle facing the darkness. Then in unison, the living half-circles began to vibrate with a firm but gentle pace, each crew creating a slow current three kilometers wide flowing into the broken island.

The waves struck the pastward border, seeping into the cracks, flowing water gently smoothing the sharp edges of broken time, submerging corridors of upthrust earth, digging new channels into the land. Five streams came into being; five channels of water dug their way into the island.

Irithrué stared in wonder as five spots of light that came to be in the darkness. The Adjutant had never doubted it would happen, for Quillithé had said it would. But still, Irithrué could not contain the strange sense of joy that grew in her mind, for what had been invisible to her only sense was now growing bright and clear.

Other dwellers in the Instant also witnessed the beginning of the miracle. Those tribes that were bolder or more fatalistic than the others had camped themselves near to the island, between fifty and three hundred years away from the cracking. When the squads of warriors had swum in around the pastward side of the island, these tribes had been sure that the predicted doom had arrived. The brave among them had prepared to fight and lose their lives in brave defense of their visions of history. The doomsaying had been prepared to fight helplessly and lose their lives as a futile gesture for their visions of history. Both sorts of tribes had been disappointed; no attacks had come. The five groups of warriors from the only army had focused their attention on the dangerous land just futureward of the camps and showed no interest in dispatching the brave and fearful.

Thus the tribes turned their attention to the island, for what concerned the Monster of the deep regarding doomsday concerned them all. Each tribe saw the island differently depending on their senses and beliefs. Those who perceived only the movements of time's waters felt the space as blank and empty; those whose awareness centered on the presence of things felt a vast solidity in the island.

The Great Wave of the Khan Eternal, a tribe of twenty warriors, believed the ocean of time to be a gift to them directly from their gods, and the other tribes to be trials placed in their way to test their worthiness to make history over in their image. The island seemed to their sharply tuned hearing and smell to be a huge cavern into which the waters of time spilled to be trapped. They conceived that at the center of this cavern was a lake of change and blood, and if they could find their way to this center they could lure their enemies in and slay them all, thus gaining their rightful place as lords of the great waters. To this end, when they smelled Irithrué's crew digging channels into the cavern, they camped themselves only seventy years pastward from the Adjutant in order to seize the right moment to enter the cavern.

In contrast, the Eternal Martyrs of Mount Athos believed, and their touch and hearing told them so, that the island was a huge egg that the Monster of the deep had laid, and now that it was mature Quillithé had come pastward to aid in the hatching of her child. The Eternal Martyrs believed this child would span ten thousand years and in its coils all the warriors of time would be crushed. Even Quillithé herself would die, and the only living being in the Instant would be the doomsday child.

But whether they saw doomsday as opportunity or danger, none of the tribes could do anything to affect it. All that was within their power was to wait until Quillithé's work was done. Though together the tribes numbered nearly a quarter of a million, they could not lay aside their fear and hatred of each other or give up their ambitions for the conquest of time in order to band together against the Monster of the deep.

All this Quillithé had known when she dispatched her warriors in apparently vulnerable squads; the fear the tribes had of her was a fundamental element of the strategy she had devised. So, placid and safe against attack, she continued to question Saryu.

Image from Saryu: The place where he lived; the expanse of the stone; marked are his tiger herd, the little box he called home, and the tiger-head gate.

Image from Quillithé: Saryu next to the gate. Gold of glory, blue of questioning.

It took Saryu a little while to understand the question but he eventually realized that Quillithé wanted to know what was important about the gate. Without knowing why, the boy sang his song to the Monster.

"Tiger gate/Future gate . . ."

He sang it all and transformed his words into images so that Quillithé could understand him. Eventually she did.

Saryu's genius, ambition, and invention, the dedication of his life was the anchoring event that bound the region of time futu-reward of the broken island. Genius and ambition anchored Saryu, and the gate that held him prisoner was the anchor of his ambition. Anchor in anchor in anchor, a solidity of purpose that defied all change waves. Solidity nested in solidity nested in solidity, reinforcement of the solid side of time against all change was the force that preserved the stone.

In the caverns of Quillithé's mind one thing became clear: the emerald stone would have to be broken by Saryu, and to do that the boy's attachment to ambition would have to be destroyed. The strategist loosened her coils, giving Saryu a few months in which to swim, a reminder of the freedom of the Instant. That reminder would serve as a beginning of Quillithé's effort to free Saryu's mind as Kookatchi had already freed his life.

Nir and Kookatchi passed through the gently rippling waters of the Diaspora and came within a thousand years of the Now. From that vantage the War Chief turned his open sight upon the waters of his birth; what he saw pleased him not.

"My warriors are not at their assigned posts," Nir tapped.

"What does that mean?" Kookatchi tapped in response.

"It means the Ghosts have a new War Chief," Nir replied. "It means I cannot offer you safe conduct into the Now. You will have to wait for me here or return to Quillithé, for it is very likely that I will not be able to return to the deeps."

"And what of your vow?" the Drum tapped after a suitable silence. "You swore to the Lady of the only army that you would prevent the Instant from being broken again by the tribes."

Nir did not speak, for he had as yet no answer.

Nir floated in the shallows of the Diaspora watching the Ghosts move about their duties in the confines of the two-century pool that was the Now. Their guard arrangements were adequate but flawed; he could already see a dozen ways that an attacking force could penetrate the perimeter. Whoever was now War Chief would need his assistance, would need the aid of his new sight and his tactician's mind. The proper thing for Nir to do was enter the Now and accept the judgment of the Elder and the new War Chief. If they exiled him he would go back to Quillithé and serve her. If they took him in, he would remain in the Now and serve the War Chief.

But if he was sent from the Now, how could he fulfill his vow to the People?

And if he stayed in the Now, how could he fulfill his vow to the Instant?

Nir's mind changed and an answer came to him, a grim one. He could not give up being War Chief. The Ghosts would have to accept him. Only if he could bring that about would he able to fulfill his vows.

"I must go to the Now, Kookatchi," the War Chief said. "You must wait here. If I succeed I will send for you; if not, return to Quillithé."

"I understand," said the Drum.

Nir swam off pastward leaving Kookatchi in the gentle waters of the Diaspora.

But the Drum did not remain where he was left. He waited until Nir was two centuries from him, then he swam after the War Chief, hiding in his wake as only a Drum could. Kookatchi knew that if Nir did not deliberately look for him, then he would not be found. And if the War Chief was busy in the Now, Kookatchi would be able to accomplish his purpose, for none of the other Ghosts had the slightest hope of finding him.

Nir swam up to the futuremost border of his home time. The feel of those gentle waters lapping tiny changes was a comfort to his deeply wracked body, but the new sight of the Now troubled his mind. The relentless flow of change that persisted in the Instant even without the actions of man existed even here. The actions of the Ghosts in the Instant, careful though they were, had dug shallow channels in the ocean floor. All the way back to the life of the Great Mother, the Now was Flux, and there was nothing that could be done about it. The vow of the Ghosts was a sham.

Two of his warriors met Nir at the border of humanity's beginning. Wyr, a veteran Ghost who had been one of Nir's great supporters since his appointment, and Aul, a newly made guard who Nir had judged unfit to be a scout and had set to this task of guarding.

"Nir," Wyr tapped. Ripples of hope and worry flowed out of the banging words. "You have returned."

"Yes, Wyr," the War Chief said. "I bring much back to the Now."

"The War Chief and the Elder have given instructions concerning you," Aul tapped, emphasizing the title "War Chief" with hammer blows of his tail against the border waters.

"And what are those instructions?" Nir said.

"That you be taken to the Year of Ghosts' Conferring. That you make an account of your absence. And that you surrender your Fourth Voice and take your place among the warriors."

"I will come to the Year of Ghosts' Conferring and make an account of my absence," Nir said.

The Chief tapped a brief message along a narrow ripple that only Wyr could feel.

"All will be explained, loyal Wyr," were Nir's words. "I see that you still trust me."

Pleased, Aul led Nir pastward. Wyr followed the War Chief in puzzlement, wondering what had given him cause to express such trust—and with such a time-bound concept as sight.

Word spread through the Now. Nir had returned. The Ghosts would meet again in the Year of Ghosts' Conferring. The primal tribe of time, long unified in purpose, came together and two waves of thoughts flowed among them. One group was relieved and hoped that Nir would be reinstated as War Chief, for they knew his skill and wisdom. The other group was angry at him for defying tradition and was pleased that he would be demoted to their ranks or perhaps even exiled for his willfulness.

In the Year of Ghosts' Conferring, on Midsummer Day at noon under harsh sunlight the Ghosts appeared around the mound of the Great Mother's bones. The soldiers and the scouts anchored first into the solid half of time, then the two War Chiefs appeared on opposite sides of the grave. Then at last, the Elder came into being, seated on her throne of the Great Mother's bones.

All the Ghosts save one covered their eyes at her appearance.

Nir would never blind his sight again. The Elder glared at him, but he stared back at her, flaunting his open eyes. He had spent too much of his recent life with one far wiser than she and could no longer defer to her judgment.

The other Ghosts one by one uncovered their eyes and saw the battle of wills between Elder and War Chief. They stood paralyzed, unable to act, all except for him who had been chosen Nir's successor.

"Even the War Chief must defer to the Elder's wisdom," Col said. "That is the way of the Ghosts."

He found his own words stronger than he had imagined. Col, newly chosen leader of the Ghosts, who had been selected because of what Nir had taught him, spoke imperiously to his former leader, reminding Nir of his duty.

The new War Chief's voice bit deep into Nir's mind. It was not Col's words that affected him but the tone of them. In exactly that way had Nir spoken to the War Chief before him when Nir had captured him; he had used the pure voice that arose from the vow of the Ghosts, that First Voice that none of those who had sworn to the People could ignore.

But Nir's mind turned and he realized that the two situations were not the same. His predecessor had acted from an idea that had given birth to fear and hopelessness, but he was acting from senses and understanding that had given birth to awareness. He had come back to the Ghosts with a new seeing that they needed and he would give it to them.

"The way of the Ghosts is the vow," Nir replied, matching First Voice with First Voice.

In the moment of those words the Ghosts split asunder. Those who had been relieved at Nir's return vowed silently in their minds that he would be their War Chief, and those who had been angered at his absence vowed that Col would lead them. The oneness of the first tribe was ended.

In that same moment, in the waters above the first region of time, Kookatchi, sailing on Drum's awareness through the two centuries of the Now, reached the life of the Great Mother. Passing easily through the guards and pickets laid to defend it, Kookatchi the Bridge prepared to anchor down into the village of the People. His crossing of the whole inhabited ocean of time from the deeps to the shallows was complete. He had reached the greatest prize ever sought in either side of time, the great treasure of man's beginning.

XXVII

The new rivers carved their way into the broken island, healing the breaches between moment and moment. Five new channels gave passage to the waters of change, letting passages of the ocean flow over and sink the upthrust earth that had before defied alteration.

In the Flux below the new river, events came together again. A herd of horses frozen in midgallop proceeded forward across the steppes of Mongolia; the thunder of their hooves came forth again in air no longer frozen.

In southwestern China the moment of lighting a funeral pyre joined again to the moment of wood burning, which in turn connected to the moment of the frail body of a starved man being consumed and turned into ash and smoke.

In one of the poorer quarters of an overcrowded city on the Ganges River, a marriage broker brought two families together to contract the joining of a nineteen-year-old boy and a fifteen-year-old girl. The point where the families agreed to the wedding was once again connected to the point where the wedding took place so that the two came together to live out their meager lives and produce one son who would have one idea by which he would seek to better himself and gain dominion over the whole world.

The rivers spread, branching and branching as they followed the circuitous course of the island's lowest contours. Then more rivers were made, adding to the tracery of water that flowed through the shattered times. In the lowlands rivers pooled into ponds and ponds grew into lakes. The once-monolithic broken island became several smaller islands surrounded by the waters of change. The ocean was reclaiming its own.

Quillithé could see regions of light forming where before there had been only darkness. The broken island became a patchwork quilt of presence and absence, sight and blindness. As the waters of change returned the island to the Instant, Quillithé restored the regions she could see to her mind's contemplations.

Saryu did not see the island as regions of light and dark. He saw the land itself sinking under the waves, and he knew that as the waters washed over the island, the fixed time that fulfilled his ambitions was being washed away in a tide of alteration. Helplessly, he saw the world of his creation vanishing into nothingness.

"Tiger gate/Future gate, time ends for all."

Image from Quillithé to Saryu: Saryu journeying into the patchwork, back to the gem of his birth.

Image from Saryu: Repeat of Quillithé's image, blue of questioning.

Image from Quillithé: Saryu shattering his stone.

"Never!" the boy shouted in the language Kookatchi had taught him.

Image from Quillithé: Repetition of her command, gold of glory and steel gray of inevitability. Saryu would return to the stone and destroy it.

The boy floated in coiled defiance, holding up his hour's life against the force of a century. He thought the Monster would kill him for his refusal. But Quillithé had no plan to harm him. Instead she wrapped him in a cocoon of images to teach him the error of his ambition.

The tribes watched the sinking of the island and in its disappearance saw their own destructions. Each chieftain, whether wise in battle or foolish with overconfidence, could see that by this intervention the Monster of the deep had made clear that the middle waters of the Instant were part of her dominion. No longer would she only exert her power in the futuremost reaches of the Instant. All time was hers to act upon. None of the tribes numbering in their tens and twenties could stand up against her power.

As if to confirm that she was truly ruler of the entire inhabited Instant, the Lady of the only army was staging this display of might, this showing that the substance of the Instant itself bowed to her designs. The chieftains looked upon her works and saw that Quillithé alone had command of history and they had no hope against her.

Despair became the common lot of the dwellers in the Instant. Battles ceased as even the most long-memoried of enemies gave up their dreams of eventual triumph. The tribes assembled floated on the waters of the middle Instant and waited for their doom, for what else could they do?

In all their experience of the Instant the tribes had only learned one way to govern and guide the course of events: water controls earth. That had been the way since Dhiritirashta had entered the Instant. The Instant dominated the Flux and whoever was skilled in controlling the waters of time ruled.

But in the art of controlling the ocean for change or for destruction they were no match for the only army and they knew it. A few of the tribes, the madder ones, tried to move forward to attack the enemy, preferring death to the horrors of waiting for death. But the rest of the tribes moved to stop them, pushing them back with concerted waves of attack. Their fear was a simple one;

if only the army was roused to battle, it might destroy them all, not just those who had assaulted it.

Silence came over their camps and soured ambitions filled their minds. They did not seek new ways to act for they were as sure of the futility of such an undertaking as they had previously been sure of their power to create and control the substance and course of history from end to beginning.

At the beginning of history two War Chiefs faced each other across the grave of history's mother. They had spoken, First Voice to First Voice, laying out their assertions about the purpose of the Ghosts. No more words needed to be said, as one by one the Ghosts assembled divided themselves into two camps, half lining up behind Nir in a phalanx and half standing in a loose array behind Col.

The Elder looked down in horror from the mound of bones as she saw the division of her tribe and knew that she had brought it about. In that moment the Elder realized that it was only because she had feared Nir's return that she had made Col the War Chief.

The two War Chiefs would have to settle the matter between themselves.

Nir and Col stared at each other, but neither could act to break the deadlock of separation. They were in the Now. To bring about battle in the Now would violate the vow of the Ghosts; to leave the Now and fight elsewhere in the Instant would be to abandon the People and violate the vow of the Ghosts. No options lay open. The two War Chiefs were frozen in the Year of Ghosts' Conferring.

Kookatchi flitted past the four Ghosts whose eternal duty it was to guard the lifespan of the Great Mother. Those four had been given their task by Nir so that never again would a being from the Instant come near to the source of humanity and risk taking her out of the Flux. Those four never anchored, never brought about disturbance in the solid world below. They remained vigilant and nonpartisan; they took no sides in the dispute between the War Chiefs, regarding their duty as greater than any other Ghosts.

But, though stern and careful, their sense of touch greatly extended to feel the slightest change in time's waters, they could not sense the Drum's approach in pure simultaneity, nor could they notice him anchoring down into the jungle around the village that held the first of the People.

Village indeed. Kookatchi could only laugh at the beauty of the sight that confronted him: a compound half a kilometer across, surrounded by steel walls fifty meters high. Around those walls were four flickering concentric curtains of force through which the sunlight made waves of rainbows jump and dance across the steel barriers. Atop the walls were a variety of emplaced weapons: solid slug cannons with barrels half a meter in width, clusters of lasers lashed together into omnidirectional bristlecones, antiproton guns at each of the corners, capable of killing anything that came within two kilometers of the village. And as a final defensive touch antigravity mines, fist-sized bombs, floated in the air between each of the layers of force. A hundred different means of death were assembled around that box.

"Oh, Nir," Kookatchi said to the absent War Chief, "you are a greater thief than I have ever been. Such a wealth of stolen violence. If the tribes knew of this they would cease looking for my hoard and come for yours. What a grand and beautiful chest you have built to keep your treasure in."

And under the direction of the Kookatchi the Bridge, Kookatchi the Thief strode forward to pass through the best defenses ever created in the solid side of time.

Under Irithrué's guidance, the digging crews had made a hundred rivers, set them flowing into the broken island, and with them carved ten thousand smaller isles out of the former megalith that had dominated the center of inhabited time. The rivers came together, forming an isle-filled sea—shallower than the waters of the middle Instant should have been, but a sea nevertheless.

In the Flux below this, time had largely come together. Change flowed into change, altering the course of lives, but the lives had whole course. No longer were there fractured existences in which a man's birth, youth, maturity, old age, and death could be completely disparate. Life became unified for all the dwellers in the Flux.

All save one. Saryu's mortal existence was still anchored into the event of the great gem, a gem Saryu no longer occupied. The boy was born, grew up, took his indenture under the tiger gate, emerged from that onerous decade with ambition intact, learned the skills he needed to give manifestation to his genius, and then saw his ambition flower. Inevitably, Saryu, the Grand Director, conquered the world with his invention and created the Consumerist Mercantile Hegemony, which eventually fell to rebels.

But there was a hole in this history. For one hour Saryu did not exist. That hour was separate from the rest of solid time, that hour refused to rejoin the ocean, and no waters of healing could bring it back. All the water did was polish that place and time into a brighter luster, making the emerald glow in the heart of the Instant, a defiant beacon of solidity amidst the waters of change.

Quillithé laid out before Saryu a thousand possible lives he might have lived. Each decision he made in the ladder of action that led to his rulership of the earth, each event that helped him achieve his ambition, each person whose desires happened to accord with his own, all were shown him in a century-long spectacle. And Saryu joyed and gloried in this display of his success.

But then Quillithé began to change the panorama of multiple lives. First a few events were different, a few things did not go his way. In one of those lives, instead of being blessed with a teacher who helped transform his idea into reality he was placed under the tutelage of a self-centered, self-important incompetent who fought against his new ideas. That cost this alternate Saryu five years of success.

Saryu watching Saryu was displeased by what he saw; up until then he had thought his ambition was his destiny.

Now Quillithé made life harder for the image Saryu. She changed the incompetent teacher into a thief who stole the idea and became the founder of the Consumerist Mercantile Hegemony. Saryu was relegated to serving the thief; the Grand Director kept the tiger-head slave around and picked his brains for ideas.

Saryu was very displeased with that. Now he saw that his destiny was not even his to fulfill.

Quillithé returned to the main line, in which Saryu succeeded. She changed the people who came to serve him. Instead of a council of ambitious but loyal Directors, Saryu was given a crew of backstabbers whose concern was only their own ambitions; they cared nothing for the Hegemony and worked to unseat Saryu from the tiger throne. Because of this court intrigue Saryu lived long enough to see the Hegemony fall and to see himself tried for crimes by the rebellion.

Saryu offered protests, suggesting ways in which he could act differently and still fulfill his ambitions. But by so doing he was pitting his ability to plan against the mind of the strategist. It was no effort at all for Quillithé to show that any time-bound plan could be countered by fortune.

Forced under this pressure, Saryu's ambition changed. No more would he concern himself with his former life. Now he would use his position in the Instant to bring about the changes he wanted.

But Quillithé had anticipated that response and changed the image barrage to a showing of the wars of time, each tribe's ambition pitted against the others, battle, endless battle. And what would Saryu do alone against the might of the tribes?

Image from Saryu: The boy floating like a supplicant before Quillithé, asking for her aid.

Image from Quillith. Saryu carrying out her orders first.

Image from Saryu: Repetition of the previous picture but the orders limned in blue.

Saryu waited patiently while Quillithé instructed him. He would do whatever she wanted, for only Quillithé had the power to help him realize his ambitions in the Instant.

Kookatchi passed through the force fields, the mine fields, and the steel box with an ease born of long practice. After a little effort, he found himself inside the village of the People. Fifteen years from the beginning of the Now, only one Homo sapiens lived in that settlement of two hundred prehumans. The Great Mother lived in a box inside the box, a solid steel house with sealed doors. She lived alone but protected, guarded from above the sky. The fifteen-year-old virgin had never seen her guardians, the Ghosts, never seen any of the five men who in this formulation of time would father her children not yet conceived. She had never seen the sun, the moon, or the stars, never walked out under the sky. She was locked up in a treasure chest within the treasure chest.

Kookatchi flitted through the Instant to pass through that inner box as well. He appeared and found the sad-eyed young woman seated on a cushioned wooden bench, alone as she always was.

The Drum appeared next to her and the dark-faced girl leaped up, disarraying the long zebra-hide toga that had appeared in her box one day, a gift from her invisible guardians.

"Ghost!" she cried. Then she saw the golden armor Kookatchi wore. "You are not a Ghost. You've come to hurt me, to catch me. They told me this would happen."

"No, Great Mother," Kookatchi said. "I have not come to harm you or enslave you, only to look at you and see how you live."

Kookatchi the Bridge reached out his hand and touched the Great Mother on the shoulder. She shrank back in fear, sure that her life was about to be torn apart as she had been taught would happen if an enemy tribesman ever came to the Now. But nothing happened. There was only the touch of Kookatchi's hand, rough from a billion thefts, but deft from thievery as well.

"How do I live?" she said, and a wave of sadness flowed over her. The Great Mother gestured expansively, showing off the five-meter-by-five-meter steel room that was her home. "This is how I live. How else could it be?"

Kookatchi the Mediator, Kookatchi the Bridge did not know how to answer that question. All he knew was sadness and the beauty of sadness.

Saryu set forth from Quillithé's camp with an honor guard of ten warriors. He had been told to meet up with Adjutant Irithrué's digging squad ten years pastward from the gem of his birth.

Saryu swam through the reclaimed waters over the changing world below. Changing, except that one thing alone was fixed: Saryu completed his invention and did found the Consumerist Mercantile Hegemony, ruling it from the tiger throne. That the Hegemony came into existence was not changeable so long as that single hour remained separate from the rest of time.

Saryu's pastward progress was noted by the scouts of assembled tribes. So rare was an hour-long dweller in the Instant that the scouts reported back to their chieftains. None knew what this strange being was doing and how he was associated with Quillithé, but all the leaders took it as a further sign of doom. A few considered attacking him, but the presence of the only army kept them in check as it had since Quillithé's fearsome migration to the middle Instant.

Adjutant Irithrué and her squad of twenty met Saryu and his escorts at the appointed place and time.

Image from Irithrué to Saryu: Saryu in front of Quillithé, orders given by the strategist to the boy. Blue of inquiry limning the orders.

Image from Saryu: Saryu anchoring into the stone, the stone being absorbed back into the ocean.

At noon on Midsummer Day in the Year of Ghosts' Conferring, the twin squadrons of Ghosts waited in silence behind their silent War Chiefs. Col stared across the clearing at Nir. The young War Chief held himself defiantly against his former leader, but in his heart Col quailed under Nir's iron-eyed glance. He knew himself no match in battle against Nir and he feared that he would never equal the other's ability to see what the Ghosts needed.

The Elder, caught between the two War Chiefs, wanted to lend support to Col, but one gaze at the troop behind Nir told her that if she opened her mouth to speak she would lose authority over that half of the Ghosts. Silence was her only recourse, a silence that galled her, for she felt that if only she were wiser she would be able to find a way out of this prison-decision she had made.

Nir, eyes open, waited for his mind to change itself so that he might see the way out of this impasse. He knew the change was coming; he could feel his thoughts changing, his mind turning in new paths, new ways of formulating notions, new mind arising. He had only to hold on to the moment until vision came.

Saryu appeared in the jungle near his tigers. The stone of time tried to force him out; so solid and secure had it become that it accepted no intrusion from the Instant. Saryu the dweller in the ocean could barely force himself inside—but the gem had to accept Saryu the tigerherd, Saryu whose ambition was the basis of its survival.

The tigers leaped away from the flickering, barely-there being who sometimes resembled their master but mostly seemed to be a cloud of sparks. Saryu walked slowly through the heavy space that weighed upon him, trying to deny him the power to change it. Walk he did across the clearing and through the jungle to the tiger-headed gate.

Four meters high, cobalt blue and arched like the sky at night, the two-headed gate stared down at Saryu and spoke to him.

"Saryu, you have left your herd. You will be docked two minutes for every minute you are away from them."

Saryu looked up at the red machine eyes of the two tiger heads, glaring down at him with their tracking sensors. For a moment he quailed at the growling voice threatening to condemn him to further time. That twinge of fear showed two sights to his mind: the gate itself and the tiger-headed throne he would have sat upon in order to remember these years of servitude.

"Tiger gate/Future gate, now you are mine."

From his back Saryu took the weapons Quillithé had armed him with, two heavy black cylinders joined by a single silver wire. The strategist's soldiers had taken them from a defeated tribe and kept them in the only army's store of destruction, waiting until Quillithé had a use for them.

Saryu put one cylinder at the base of each pillar.

The tiger gate emitted a roar in voice and radio to call for help. "Explosives present, terrorist threat. Saryu, you are fined fifty years for attempted sabotage."

But the call for help could not pass the barrier of broken time, could not pass outside of the gem to reach a security post that no longer existed in a place and time changed by the currents of alteration.

Saryu pulled a plain onyx box out of his belt and pressed the single button on it.

The gate of the future vanished in light and thunder. If there was no gate, Saryu could have left. If there was no gate, Saryu could not have been taught. If there was no gate, Saryu's life and Saryu's destiny parted from each other. The inevitable ceased to be inevitable. The waters of possibility flooded into the stone of destiny.

Changed beyond its ability to be itself, the gem of time, the last fragment of the broken island, lost its grip on solidity. The ocean of time washed in to that last remaining outpost and sank it in a whirlpool of change.

A moment: The whirlpool was small, a waterspout of change circling the hour of Saryu's freedom in the channels of what had been the Great River.

A moment: The whirlpool was ten thousand years across, swirling through the channels dug by all the rivers that had drowned the broken island.

A moment: The whirlpool covered the hundred millennia of inhabited time. It rose in power and swiftness through every channel ever dug by man's alteration of history until all of the Instant was a spiraling maelstrom of change.

XXVIII

I n the Instant is a whirlpool, one thousand centuries wide.
The whirlpool is the Inhabited Instant.

The Flux, eternally controlled by the whirlpool that is the Instant, loses the coherence of normal time. In the spiraling of the waters the direction of passage changes. Past events need not lead to future ones, as change moves sideways in the wild eddying of alteration. A baby is born, but his next breath is not dictated by his last one; rather the contiguous changes his life as if it preceded him. The rocking of his cradle by his mother becomes the last event, so he does not breathe again; rather he rocks again, rocks to death, but comes back in the moment after, as the crying of his mother becomes his living crying. And so it is through a hundred thousand years of the Flux.

Quillithé's digging crews, at the heart of the alteration, see the oncoming danger. Between first moment and second moment they seek to anchor into the solid world, but the third moment catches them by surprise. They are pulled away from the center of the Instant, hurled to its borders before they can anchor.

Scattered to the eight directions by the change of moment, the diggers gain control of their actions and anchor; the digging crews leave the Instant.

Adjutant Irithrué, alone and confused, grasps earthly time and appears in the Russian steppes one thousand years into the Diaspora.

From second moment to third moment, the tribes assembled in the central Instant are struck by the waves. In the circling tidal pull the tribesmen are pulled apart one from the other. Each warrior is carried away in space and time from his fellows. Each warrior, helpless to guide his own path, anchors down somewhere, somewhen in the hundred millennia of the inhabited Instant.

The tribes leave the ocean of time.

First moment, Quillithé sees the oncoming change. She emits a single image covering the army encamped her, ordering them to anchor. Without question, without thought the one hundred and forty soldiers of her army vanish into the Flux, leaving Quillithé alone and unprotected.

The main body of the only army leaves the waters.

Saryu sits anchored at the calm center of the whirlpool. The tiger gate is gone, the stone of his birth is shattered. The Flux accepts him again and the boy, completely visible, completely present in the earthly world once more, settles down to rest out the moment in solid time while the world around him distorts into acausal confusion.

Saryu remains outside of the Instant.

In the Year of Ghosts' Conferring, the timeless deadlock is broken. Nir sees all the changes around him and feels the spinning waters above the sky. Col only feels and fears. Vision changes Nir's mind. He knows what has happened in the Instant; only he who knows and can act can be War Chief.

"You must do as I say," he says to Col. "Fourth Voice alone cannot help you with the new tasks of the Ghosts."

And Fourth Voice says to Col, "The War Chief is correct."

Col accepts Nir's command.

The Ghosts wait in the Flux before returning to the Instant.

In the deeps thirty soldiers surround the seven fathers, guarding their fragile lives. The whirlpool comes; thirty soldiers throw their lives into defending the seven, casting change after change to blunt the anger of the coming storm. Their lives are enough. The seven fathers survive alone and afraid in the Instant.

Kookatchi is aware that the Instant is changing. Drum's awareness understands that all the settled facts in the Flux will be consumed by the change. His eyes look upon the fifteen-year-old form of the Great Mother, starved for human company, starved for human speech, starved for human life, and Kookatchi the Bridge decides to save her from the change that is coming.

In the Flux itself the Drum does what he has only done in the Instant. Embracing Drum's awareness fully, he abandons the illusion of sequence even in the solid sequenced earth. He obliterates the normal ordering of events in his own mind and by so doing compels the world to lose that ordering. Kookatchi appears in a hundred places at once and with sharp tail spikes attacks the anchoring points where the hoard of weapons and steel, force fields and antigravity mines, all the stolen pieces of the first box/first treasury/first prison are held down against their atemporal buoyancy. The box explodes, creating a wave of shattering debris in the Instant. The wave of incoming matter forms a breakwater against the tide of change.

The devastation of the whirlpool is stopped fifteen years into the Now, and the Great Mother is vouchsafed fifteen years of life.

Fifteen barren years, childless years.

Humanity, never born, vanishes from the Flux. The People are gone; only one human being is ever born, ever lives. But she does not die, for the proper ordering of causality vanishes on a day when she is fifteen years, three months, and eighteen days old. The Great Mother has one glimpse of sunlight, one breath of unfiltered air, and one scent of jungle aroma before her life disappears into confusion.

Kookatchi does not reenter the ocean.

From the Now to the edge of the deeps only Quillithé remains in the Instant. Quillithé who cannot move, Quillithé who cannot anchor, Quillithé who has only her vast mind to protect her from the onslaught of braided change that is the whirlpool that is the Instant.

The corridors of Quillithé's mind fill up with possibilities, ways she can react to the imminent all-consuming transformation. But every possibility fails, every option leads to her death in the maelstrom. Death shatters her to pieces in the storm. Death imprisons her by anchoring down. Death ties her into a knot when she seeks to defend herself by throwing parts of her body in the way of the waves. Death does all to her.

Only one glimmer of hope resides in a deep recess of her all-encompassing consciousness. Kookatchi's words reside there, Kookatchi's description of Drum's awareness, Kookatchi's firm conviction that there is no sequence of events in the Instant, there is only the Instant. Lodging there are the images showing Kookatchi and Saryu traveling up the waterfall. In all of Quillithé's mind only this place holds life.

And she knows that to reach that life all she has to do is give up her consciousness and the sequence of her life. In this cycle of thought and memory she has reached her eightieth year. Twenty years remain before her consciousness recycles. Twenty years in which to fill her mind with the means to remember all that has happened to her. Twenty years to create a treasury of memory to guard against the thief of shattered consciousness. But she cannot build the treasury nor store away remembrance. She must give up all, sacrifice the twenty years to come and with them the past eighty of accumulated experience. She must take up death to reach life.

The strategist acts without hesitation. The sacrifice is done with the surgeon's knife of her own thoughts. All possibilities are thrown away, all knowledge is cast out, all surety of what she is and has done vanishes.

And the greatest, the longest of the dwellers in the Instant takes up the awareness that only the shortest and least had ever known.

But Quillithé has something that no Drum has, a vision that extends for fifty thousand years around her. She lets go of sequency and embraces death and life; Quillithé rises up in the center of the Instant and sees for all one hundred millennia of inhabited time.

Seeing, Quillithé knows what the Drums know and more. She knows that the moment of her abandoning consciousness is the same moment as the moment of the whirlpool, she knows that the Instant is the whirlpool and the Instant is her, for she sees it all and vanishes from existence in the moment that she gives up life to gain life.

The Inhabited Instant is not the whirlpool. There is no whirlpool. There is only the Instant, the flowing waters of time, swirling haphazardly from the shallows to the deeps. In the deeps of that great ocean is Quillithé. She floats resting in the waters, surrounded by her seven fathers. Quillithé has consciousness again, has awareness again, has Quillithé again, but she remembers nothing of the last century of her life. Most of her mind knows that she should remember, should have left markers and clues to help her reconstruct things after the crash of consciousness.

There is only marker, only one important memory. One corner of her mind contains the knowledge that there was no past century, that there is no past in the Instant, only an ever present.

And in that corner of Quillithé's mind sits an understanding, the same understanding that Nir's mind has turned to, and the same understanding that has surfaced from the depths of Kookatchi's flashing remembrance/awareness/forgetfulness.

There is no whirlpool, is no past to hold the whirlpool; but the Flux and the Instant are now guided by the whirlpool's tracks, the tides of time are guided by the circular channels of unnatural causality.

XXIX

Image to the seven fathers from Quillithé newly come again into being: The army in its seven rings around her and the seven of them. The army gone, blue of inquiry surmounted by stark silvery gray of disbelief. Where have the three hundred soldiers of the only army gone, why do we float alone in the deeps of time?

Huddled together, terrified at the deaths of their guards and bewildered at Quillithé's sudden reappearance after the whirlpool, the seven fathers conferred in swift short pictures and then the first of them gave answer.

Image from the first father: A mustering of all the tribes under two leaders, a Drum and a Ghost who brought the entire armed might of the Instant down on the deeps, attacking Quillithé's army.

Image from the second father: Quillithé brilliantly deploying her three hundred against the half million, carving down their numbers, but all the while losing her soldiers.

Image from the third father: In desperation, Quillithé employs her soldiers somehow to create a whirlpool that scatters the assembled warriors pastward through the Instant.

Image from the fourth father: Quillithé battered by the effects of the whirlpool, confused and lying helpless for a while, then recovering into her present state of incomprehension.

Image from the fifth father: The two evil leaders of the attack reassembling the tribes, deep yellow of fear. Might this not happen?

Image from the sixth father: A renewed assault on Quillithé and her fathers alone and helpless, deep yellow of fear.

Image from the seventh father: Quillithé recreating the army and sending them forth to kill these two malevolent warriors who had destroyed the first army, bright gold of hope.

Quillithé took in the story they told, both the past parts of it and the hoped-for future parts.

In the center of the Instant, Saryu arose from the Flux and found himself among the main body of Quillithé's army, which had abandoned its grip on solid time as soon as the whirlpool was gone. Around them the waters of time flowed in circles and spirals; the tracks carved by the whirlpool made a mockery of past and future. From the heart of the Instant where they floated there was no way to tell which direction was which. Space and time were one, past and future confused and conflated, cause and effect were undone and helpless.

Images passed back and forth in the one hundred and forty members of the army, images of confusion and helplessness.

Image: Marching to Quillithé, mustering around the strategist and again acquiring purpose from her.

Image: Quillithé bearing the brunt of the shock wave, shattered into pieces. Helpless immobile strategist slain by the waters of time.

Image: Denial of last image. Quillithé, immortal, unkillable, center of all plans. Find her.

Image from Saryu: The Instant, directions marked down. Blue of inquiry which way to go.

As they talked and debated, tribesmen floated up from the Flux, confused and saddened. No whole tribes, just warriors in their ones and twos, soldiers from all the disparate factions of the Instant, in a thousand different languages, in converse of sound and sight of touch and scent, all reported the same information.

"There are no humans left."

"Mankind is gone."

"History is gone."

And all asked the same question, "What purpose can we have here and now, in the day after doomsday?"

The Year of Ghosts' Conferring no longer existed. The village of the People was not there, the Great Mother, who vanished at the age of fifteen had had no children, had left no bones behind. The Ghosts, assembled in an empty clearing, were vowless and purposeless, all save their War Chief, who was sure that there was something to salvage from the sundering of man from history.

"The Now is destroyed," the Elder said, covering her eyes with her hands. "We have failed the vow."

"We are only in one year of the Now," Nir said. "Let us return to the Instant and see what survives."

One by one the Ghosts vanished in obedience until only Nir, Col, and the Elder remained.

"How did this happen, War Chief?" Col asked. "What brought about this destruction?"

Nir did not answer, for he knew that only the healing of the center could have brought about so great a change. If he spoke, the Ghosts would think Quillithé at fault and attack her in folly. With silence he was sure he could find a way to heal the healing.

Nir gestured upward in mute command. Go and look, he said without words.

But Col turned to the Elder, unwilling to enter the Instant just yet. "Relieve me of Fourth Voice. I am not War Chief."

"No," Nir said. "I have need of you to serve as War Chief if I am absent."

"Only one bears Fourth Voice," the Elder said, taking her hands from her face and looking at Nir with a trembling attempt at defiance.

"That is no longer so," Nir replied. His voice had the soothing quality of a grandchild reassuring a grandparent, but in his words his undeniable will came through.

The Elder tried to muster the old force of her domination, but failed. The way of the Ghosts had changed and she knew it. The devastation around her, the destruction of the People, were beyond her ability to devise answers. She yielded to Nir and gave over the deciding of Ghostly actions.

"To the Instant," Nir said, and they vanished.

The Ghosts, blind and saddened, floated helplessly, feeling the rough contours of the ocean floor. But Nir, looking pastward, saw things floating near the border of the Now; flotsam, shattered steel hundreds of meters long by mere seconds in length floated on the barely moving waters. And the waters pastward of that wreckage did not move at all. The whirl of change had not consumed everything. Fifteen years remained to the Now.

"The Great Mother still exists," Nir tapped. "The pastward reaches of the vow can still be fulfilled."

The Ghosts hoped the War Chief's words were true, though they could not bring themselves to believe the bald statement. They followed him pastward to feel the truth for themselves, swimming down most of a century to just after the beginning of things.

Floating amidst the wreckage were the shattered tails of the Great Mother's four guards. They had thrown themselves defiantly against the whirlpool, but without sight they had no idea of what was attacking them. They had died in hopeless confusion.

In the village that would have been the village of the People, in the minute before the orderly progress of time vanished into the chaos of the whirlpool's aftermath, Kookatchi and the Great Mother stood staring at the noonday sun.

The fifteen-year-old mother-not-to-be laughed and wept at the sight of the gleaming golden ball shedding light she had never seen.

"Thank you," she said, and was no more.

Kookatchi vanished into the Instant as the Great Mother vanished into the Flux.

The Drum appeared amidst the assembled Ghosts. Tails were coiled to strike the interloper, waves of wrath ready to be unleashed.

"Stop!" The War Chief slammed the command against the shallows of time.

Image from Nir to Kookatchi: Kookatchi in the Now. Blue of inquiry.

Image from Kookatchi: The Drum anchored down in the village, speaking to the Great Mother. The whirlpool comes, Kookatchi shatters the village, the whirlpool abates, the Great Mother lives.

"I freed her from her box of deprivation as I freed Saryu from his," Kookatchi tapped.

"The Ghosts owe you thanks, Kookatchi," Nir tapped, making his words reverberate through the thirty years of floating Ghosts. "You have saved the mother of the People, the mother of humanity."

In the deeps Quillithé had finished considering the tale her fathers had told her and found it to be a vast ridiculous fabrication. The attack they described could never have happened; no one could unite the tribes against her. The battles they showed her were fictitious romances, bearing no resemblance to the conflicts of pure strategy she employed. That alone would have been enough to convince her that she had been told great falsehoods by her fathers. But there were two things more, two newnesses that clearly implied that strange events had been happening and that she had done things unlike any she had contemplated.

First, she possessed a sense she had never had before. She could feel the waters flowing over her, soothing her body; she could feel the ocean bottom, its carvings and its carryings of water, and she could feel all the thoughts in her mind and know whether they were right or wrong.

And second, there was the enclave in her mind, pure and undefiled by confusion, a place that declared the Instant to be timeless, that showed her that event did not follow event; rather in the ocean of time event became event and that event/becoming was the ocean of time. She saw that her memory was a construct, a facade created to retain the illusion of sequence in the atemporal.

As she explored it Quillithé saw that this enclave of awareness contained images, images of her moving through the Instant—no, that was not it. It was an image of her and the Instant as two and then as one and then as two again, but her place in the Instant had changed from the first duality through the unity to the second duality.

And these two things, feeling and unity, were marked in her mind by images of two people, a Ghost and a Drum, those who her fathers claimed had led the attack.

Image from Quillithé to the seven: The Ghost and the Drum. Blue of inquiry. Who are they?

The seven fathers prepared to muster their fear-born lies in order to tether Quillithé down again.

Before the first false picture was emitted Quillithé repeated her demand. The Ghost and the Drum. Blue of Inquiry. Gold of greatness. Iron gray of threat. Who are they? The truth, or you are no longer my fathers.

Fear clutched at the seven and they acceded. Image by image they told the tale of the island and the alliance and the whirlpool.

Quillithé took in the truth and turned her gaze toward the middle Instant.

Saryu and the body of the army waited as the mass of tribesmen grew around them, one thousand, two, ten, fifty thousand. They came to the center, no two of the same tribe in the same place, all confused, injured, and disheartened. All separate, but united by their despair, they formed a living barrier against the only army.

"You will not pass," they said in all the languages of the Instant, "until you tell us what must be done on the day after doomsday."

Fifteen years into the Now, Nir and Kookatchi felt the contours of
the ocean bottom. Deep spiral cuts were directing the waters in
their improper courses, cutting off the inhabited Instant from the
source of humanity.

"We must dig new channels," Nir said. "From past to future.
Then time will flow properly again. The Instant will be change."

"And the Now will not be Flux," Kookatchi replied.

"The Now will not be Flux," the Ghosts assembled echoed the
Drum's words.

"But we do not know how to guide such a digging," Kookatchi
said. "We need Quillithé to tell us."

"She could not survive in these shallows," Nir said.

The War Chief cast his gaze around, seeking anything that
might help, and saw a figure swimming through the Diaspora, floundering in confusion.

"Adjutant Irithrué is eight hundred years futureward from us,"
Nir said. "She will know how to dig."

Kookatchi vanished into Drum's awareness, leaving the Now. He
reappeared next to the startled Adjutant.

Image from the Drum: Digging, new channels to remake the
Flux and the Instant.

Image from Irithrué: Her crew scattered across the waters, she
knew not where. Quillithé somewhere unknown. Who would dig?

Image from Kookatchi: The Ghosts assembled under Nir.

Kookatchi swam pastward, surfing over the circular tides of
time. Irithrué followed into the uncomfortable shallows of the Now.

Image from Nir to Irithrué: The Instant covered with incorrect
channels. New ones must be dug, starting here. The channels must
guide life so that humanity continue to exist.

Irithrué thought for a while. To dig without Quillithé's direction seemed impossible, but the thought came to her from the small

set of rooms in her mind that Quillithé had given her the orders to dig and in carrying out the digging she, Irithrué, had learned how it was done. Irithrué could continue to obey the strategist's orders by making new channels here. But there was a problem.

Image from Irithrué: The Ghosts stumbling through darkness, incapable of seeing her instructions, misdigging false channels, adding to the chaos of the Instant.

"Col," Nir tapped. "Come here."

The second War Chief came to the first. A web of gold flowed out of Nir to embrace Col and give him the gift that Quillithé had bestowed on Nir.

Col looked out across the Instant in wonder.

One by one, Nir gave sight to the Ghosts. Each in turn opened his gaze and saw the Instant, saw the shallows of the Now and the turning of the tides, and each Ghost saw the others.

Last to be so gifted was the Elder, who saw that she had been right to cede control to Nir. The War Chief had brought a greater gift than any ever conceived by the Ghosts. The Ghosts had changed and she could no longer guide them. It was time for her to rest and let the vow of the Ghosts change.

The tribe united looked out across the Instant and at last saw the ocean of time and they took up the greater vow that Nir and Kookatchi had taken.

> *"The People must not be changed.*
> *The Now must not be Flux.*
> *For from the People and the Now comes all possibility.*
> *And the Instant must be all possibility.*
> *The Instant shall be change.*
> *The Flux shall be guide of change and source of humanity."*

"And now we will recarve the Now and return humanity to the Flux," Nir commanded in taps and pictures.

Irithrué laid out the course of cutting channels and the Ghosts began their work.

In slow unison, they made waves above the moment of the Great Mother's vanishing. The circular channels the whirlpool had dug wore down and down and new straight channels grew, carrying forward from past to future, returning time to its normal flow.

When the Great Mother was fifteen the steel box of the village shattered. The Great Mother looked up at the sun and laughed and cried. The moment ended and she continued to live. She grew a year older and bore her first child, the first begotten of the People born in sunlight and breathing open air. Or it took another year for the first one to be born as the slow waters of change lapped across the new-made village. Small changes came to be. The People were born, they lived and gave birth to more of the People. But who exactly they were and when they came to be, that changed as the waters flowed through the newly dug channels.

The Great Mother lived in light and air and eventually died of old age having seen three generations of her descendants. She was buried in a mound at a specific place. The Ghosts made sure that the waters of change flowed narrowly over that point in space and time; they would have the sacred place of her birth and the Year of Ghosts' Conferring back again.

Two centuries of carving and the shallow waters of the Now flowed once again in straight paths. The People lived again, and the Ghosts renewed their vows again.

> "We are the Ghosts of the People,
> The People will not be changed.
> This is the Now, the Now will be humanity's birth.
> The Instant shall be change.
> The Flux shall be guide."

Col swam over to Nir. "War Chief, your orders have been accomplished. The People are safe; our work is over."

"No," Nir tapped. "Humanity must be returned to the rest of the Flux. Only then will the Instant be as it should be."

"We are to leave the Now?"

"Only a few of us," Nir said. "Col, you will remain and be War Chief in my place until I return. Kookatchi, Irithrué, and I will take five warriors and carve straight tracks through the ocean floor until we reach the deeps."

"But War Chief, will that not just start the wars again? Will the tribes not take up the battle to recapture history if you return man to the Flux?"

"If I do not then all the tribes will descend on the Now and try and take the only humans from us."

And in his thoughts Nir renewed the vow he took to Quillithé. He would stop the fighting so that the Instant would never be broken again. The War Chief did not know yet how he would do this, but he could feel that his mind was poised to change itself and give him the answer. All he needed to do was set out into the middle Instant, carving the way of man as he went.

Image from Nir to Irithrué: The eight of them entering the Diaspora and setting humanity free from the box of the Now.

Image from Irithrué: The size of the earth, the width in space; too many rivers would have to be dug to permit mankind to spread out from the Now.

Image from Nir: Beginning of that work, a few rivers dug immediately. Gold of greatness, iron of command.

Irithrué saw the order from Nir. At first she could not believe that any except Quillithé could command her. But the strategist regarded the War Chief as her equal; could a subordinate of the only army do less?

Carving began. Routes out of the People's village were laid down in the chaos of the Flux, ways for humanity to flow out in multifarious changes. Through the confusion of spiraled alteration rivers were carved, proper courses for change. Mankind could pass northward or eastward along narrow corridors only a few hundred kilometers across. In those several hundred-year passages change flowed from past to future, the People became separate peoples, they set up their villages along the rivers and became many.

Above the Nile River, 1,853 years futureward from the Now,

Nir and his followers found a Time Warrior floating in the ocean of time. His name was Sen-hotep, a loyal member of the tribe called Ptah's Might beyond the Sun. He lay helpless and desperate, alone above the land where he was never born, where no humans had ever lived or ever would live if the course of change remained as it was. Doomsday had come. Sen-hotep had been sundered from his tribe, and he had found himself alone in the Diaspora, wishing that dwellers in the Instant could weep change so that he might feed a few tears into the ocean of time.

"Kill me if you wish," he said. "The Son of the Sun will never again be born and sit upon the throne of the two Egypts."

Of the eight who were present with him, only Kookatchi understood his words. "Perhaps he will," the Drum said in the formal language of Sen-hotep's tribe. "We are carving the ways for mankind to return."

"Mankind is gone," Sen-hotep said. "You cannot trick me, Drum. I have nothing worth stealing."

"Enter the Flux in the past that lies in the straight tide behind us and see if mankind is no more."

A trickle of hope dripped into Sen-hotep's mind. If the Drum spoke truth—but no, it had to be some trick. The Great Thief never spoke truly. But what gain could there be to the Drum? Sen-hotep had nothing to steal and nothing could be gained from tricking him. Could it be true? He had to find out.

Sen-hotep swam fifty years pastward, his tail striving against the current that flooded through the deep trench Nir and his followers had dug. The Egyptian anchored down into the Flux. He appeared in North Africa and to his delight saw a group of nomads traveling eastward . . . southward . . . establishing a temporary camp . . . grazing sheep . . . raising barley . . . building a village into a city.

A hundred and fifty kilometers west of the orderly human change, chaos still dominated. Change flowed from north to south and the Mediterranean tried to turn the coast of Africa into ocean. But this strip of change was too deeply cut, the tide too strong for the cross flow. Those alterations vanished when they touched the carved region. Only past to future, cause to effect could happen in the trench the Ghosts had dug.

Sen-hotep returned to the Instant. Delight filled his mind. The day after doomsday had brought life back to the Flux. The true history might yet be created, the Son of the Sun might sit again in his proper place. If . . . if his tribe lived, if he could find them again and return from his whirlpool-made exile, and if the eight who were working to heal the Instant did not stand against them, and if the only army did not return to bring back doomsday. Despair took Sen-hotep again.

"Ask him to help us," Nir said to Kookatchi. "We cannot dig through the whole of time alone."

So far had Kookatchi's thinking been changed that he found it not at all strange to ask assistance from a tribesman.

"Help us dig," Kookatchi said to Sen-hotep. "There is much work to do in restoring the Instant."

"Help you?" Sen-hotep said. "Help you lay down your own history opposed to ours?"

"We lay no history," Kookatchi said. "We have taken a vow. 'The Instant shall be change.' So have we sworn."

"How can I join you? My tribe is vowed to a fixed history."

"There will be no fixed history," Kookatchi said. "The eternal war has carved paths in the ocean floor. The ocean of time can never be still again as it was when the blind man came into the Instant. Change is inevitable. Only a new breaking of time would make a single history possible again. And to break time, violent uncontrollable change is needed. The tribes cannot have what they want. Utopia cannot be made. History cannot be fixed."

"Then I will not act," Sen-hotep said, and returned to floating in despair.

Kookatchi swam back to Nir and reported what the Egyptian had said.

"He will not join us," the Drum said as a coda to Sen-hotep's words.

The War Chief listened and considered giving up on Sen-hotep, but then he remembered his interactions with Quillithé and remembered the way she would play out many variations on one theme. Nir's mind changed in realization. There was a way to use the digging of channels to keep the tribes from ever again shattering the floor of time. The War Chief found that he was already doing the deed that would fulfill his promise to the strategist.

"Go to him again," Nir said to Kookatchi. "Tell him that we will carve a deep channel above this region of the Nile, tell him that cultures like the one his tribe arose from will exist in such a channel. They will not be fixed, but they will come and go and many will be like the history he desired, in a thousand flowing variations. Tell him that we will let him plant the seeds of his history along the shores of this river and he will come as close to his desire as any tribesmen can in the Instant."

Kookatchi carried the message back to Sen-hotep bearing Nir's words. Three thoughts passed one after another through the warrior's mind. First he thought, never would he do such a thing, never betray his tribe. Then he thought that he would go along until he had an opportunity to change this work of digging into a work of fixing time. But last, he remembered the broken island, remembered the gathering of the tribes and remembered doomsday, and he knew that if the tribes returned to battling as they had before, Quillithé would come again and destroy all inhabited time.

"I will help you," Sen-hotep said. "Show me what I must do."

"First take the vow," Kookatchi said.

> *"This is the Instant*
> *The Instant shall be change.*
> *That is the Flux.*
> *The Flux shall be guide."*

Sen-hotep repeated the words and felt a great weight pass from him. The struggle to retain and regain a single fragile strand of history had lain heavily on his mind since first he entered the Instant; now he was free of it.

The digging resumed now with a crew of nine. The carvers cut a wider swath through the passage of time. As they dug futureward they found more and more tribesmen and offered them the same chance that Sen-hotep had been given. Many refused, preferring to keep their attempts at history intact, but others accepted and the diggers grew from the original eight to eighty to eight hundred to eight thousand and more as they carved straight, deep channels through the floor of time, making their way from the Diaspora toward the center of the Instant, restoring the flow of past to future, letting change occur, under the guidance of man.

In the deeps, Quillithé contemplated the true tale her seven fathers had told her. She found it surprising that she did not foresee the eventuality of the whirlpool. Surely she should have done so unless something in her thoughts, some overly practiced way of thinking, had prevented her from seeing all the possibilities. She turned the corridors of her mind inside out searching for that lack, that hole in her capabilities.

And she found it, a hole in the center of her awareness, a dark place in her open mind. She had not seen the threat of the whirlpool for it had been hidden behind the threat of the Island and the threat of herself. She had seen only two dangers in the whole of the ocean; the broken island had been a danger to her and she had been a danger to all other things. The last shred of pride and fear vanished from her mind, and Quillithé took in the sight and feel of the Instant and made her mind the same as that sight and feel. She turned her gaze outward/inward and looked at the center of the ocean swirling with the waters of the whirlpool's passage.

In the center of the Instant, Saryu floated at the center of the main body of the army. Surrounded by a quarter of the Instant's population, the one hundred forty soldiers remaining from the only army had arrayed themselves in a defensive posture and there they floated, waiting. But the tribesmen did not attack. Though many tens of thousands strong, they still feared Quillithé and wondered

where she was. She had brought about doomsday, and the tribesmen feared that if they attacked her people she would bring the
maelstrom back and this time they would not survive.

Saryu floated in the still point of swirling time, his hour's length
coiled around a few seconds of the shattered tiger gate that had
been torn from the Flux in the whirlpool's first moment. The bones
of his ambition were caught in his coils, the dead reminders of his
lifelong desire. He no longer wanted the future he had conceived,
but he felt the lack of it, the absence of a plan for his existence.

"I am not yet free," Saryu said. "Noble sir or great lady,
wherever you are, please come and finish freeing me."

The still point ceased to be still. Currents were flowing under
it; straight paths of change arising from the past came up to Saryu,
digging away at the circular tracks of the whirlpool.

The furthest pastward of the tribesmen saw something coming
futureward from the shallower waters. Rolling change in rhythmic
waves, slow but inexorable, consuming the circularity of the maelstrom's tracks, replacing them with a gentle tide that flowed according to the way of time. Guided by human mind and realized
by concerted human action, the world was being restored.

Doomsday was over. Renewal had come to the middle Instant.

XXX

The digging tribesmen, united in will by Nir's command, in colloquy by Kookatchi's memory, and in guidance by Quil-lithé's wisdom embodied in the person of Irithrué, reached the center of the Instant. The channels they had dug had grown in force and definition, so that even though the carving of solid time ceased when the assembled diggers reached the midpoint of time, the waters flowed on their own. The straight tides of time passed through the center of the Instant, removing the circularity of the whirlpool. Change and the guiding of change passed futureward to the deeps themselves. Passage in the Flux was restored, past and future existed again under the dominion of the ever present.

The laborers looked out upon the middle Instant and saw the vast floating camp of their tribesmen who waited in their many concentric doom-thinking circles around Saryu and the body of the army. Vows newly taken were tested by the reminders of past lives, past battles, past glories, past hatreds, and desired futures.

The surviving members of the Persian Zurvanite Infantry were reunited five centuries pastward from Saryu's encampment. Prince Xerxes beheld ten of his soldiers, five of whom had been digging new tracks through time, learning the art of building the earthly guides of water to complement the long-known art of using water to alter earth.

The other five tribesmen had found their way back to the center of the Instant, mourning the loss of mankind, the ending of history, and had gathered themselves under their chieftain. Xerxes had considered forcing his way to the center of the hundred rings of encampment around the middle Instant to find out what was to be done now that doomsday was over. He could not bring himself to sacrifice the last of his soldiers in battle against half of the only army. But now his numbers had swelled from five to ten, or so he thought.

The Prince, coiled in his glory, swelled in importance in his mind. "Soldiers, the time has come to confront the source of doomsday. Attend me."

Two of the five he had gathered from the despairing multitudes swam close to him to form a guard of honor. One of the five who had come futureward with Nir, bringing humanity back to the Flux, swam out as well, but the rest remained, three who had floated in despair and four who had swum futureward with hope. Xerxes' words did not affect them; the despairers still despaired and those who had come with hope still had hope.

"Prince Xerxes," said Ahasarus, one of the newly vowed diggers, "we cannot attend you. Half of time is still without proper guidance. We must finish our labors."

Xerxes, who had been brother of Persia's emperor (but there had never been a Persia nor an emperor save in Xerxes' memory), who had always been obeyed (except by all the tribes of the Instant save his own), who had planned carefully how to restore the Flux to proper history (except that his plans could not possibly have been implemented given all the opposition in the Instant), lashed his tail in anger at the defiance of his former soldier, seeking to strike him with killing waves.

But fifty warriors of disparate tribes who had accompanied Ahasarus futureward in the renewal of time lashed out defensive waves to blunt the assault. Xerxes could not believe what his senses were telling him; the members of enemy tribes had banded together to defy his will.

Across the pastward border of the hundred rings this scene was played out over and over as chieftain after chieftain realized powerlessness. Their warriors would not muster to their words; even the songs of the past would not sway them to come again to battle.

Of all the tribal rulers, only the War Chief of the Ghosts commanded at the center of all things, and his command had grown far greater than governance of the People's guardians. With a tapped command his line of diggers advanced and the circles of despair dissolved before the living wave. Ahead of his subordinates, Nir swam into the center of the Instant where the remaining half of the only army lay encamped.

Kookatchi swam behind Nir, and at the sight of his master, Saryu left the protection of the two innermost rings and swam out to meet the Drum.

"Noble sir," Saryu said to Kookatchi, "why are all these tribesmen here? What do they want?"

Kookatchi had been listening to the voices of despair and confusion that had flitted through the middle Instant, the grumbling of chieftains, the whispers of hatred and desire.

"They want the ease of war back," the Drum said. "They want things to be simple for them again."

And with those words from his master Saryu came to understand.

The tribes had entered the Instant where all things became possible, and just as Saryu had done they had taken with them the narrow ambitions of life in the Flux. They wanted to rule the world as he had, to have their decisions fix time as his had. And since that chance had been taken from them, they despaired.

"Tiger gate/Future gate," Saryu sang. "You held them all."

But the tiger gate was gone and a new song was rising in Saryu's mind, a song to put before the other songs of the Instant. It was not yet complete, but it was coming to be.

From the deeps Quillithé watched the meeting at the center of all things and knew that she should be there. She could feel, though not yet see, that an event was growing there. The Instant was poised to change greatly once more; like a seed about to burst forth, something new was coming. In the corridors of her mind, Quillithé saw the two possible events that could come from that seed. In one grand room lay the possible healing of the whole Instant, joining ocean and dwellers in the ocean. In another open chamber lay a living whirlpool that would shatter the whole of inhabited time.

Which event would arise, which would the Instant be? That depended, as always, on those who could control the course of change.

Nir could direct the proper action through the accumulated influence of his diggers.

Kookatchi could sense the unrest coming and the fatal decision as it was happening.

But only Quillithé could see far enough to know which way action and awareness would lead.

She needed to be there to give them her vision and make the right change in the ever present.

Quillithé remade her mind, filling the rooms and corridors with solid reminders of what had happened. The tale of the breaking, the alliance, and the whirlpool she reviewed and placed in its proper context. Redundantly remembered, it filled half the rooms of her mind. The other half of the infinite number of rooms and corridors were dedicated to reminders of the event that was being formed, the transformation of the Instant that would lead to life or death.

Quillithé's seven fathers, their minds filled with fear, wallowed in misery at their daughter's disregard for their terror. How could she prepare to abandon them again? Had they not created her? Was she not theirs to command?

And for the first time they looked at Quillithé. Not as their possession, not as their triumph against the Instant, they looked at her, grand and terrible floating in the waters of time; and then they knew that they had not created her and that she was not theirs to command. Quillithé was inevitable. She had arisen from the Flux with their aid, but if not them, others would have brought her about. They were not her creators, not truly her fathers. They had helped her come to be, and she had more than given back to them for that single act. They had tried to guide the Instant with their fear, and she had permitted that guidance until something too important came along. She would never go back to their rulership.

Four of the fathers coiled themselves in terrified knots, afraid to face this new existence; the other three swam away from Quillithé's body a distance of a few months. Then the three approached again, swimming slowly like subordinates reporting to their leader.

Image from the first father: The three of them submitting themselves before Quillithé, deep orange of regret for their previous actions.

Image from Quillithé: Repeat of that image. Bright silver of acceptance.

Image from Quillithé: Quillithé leaving the deeps.

And in the tapping speech of the Ghosts, the first father rapped out a single question unsuited to the language of images. "When?"

"There is no when in the Instant," Quillithé responded. "Only Now."

And Quillithé let go, sacrificing all one hundred years of her life to leave the deeps and appear in the middle of things. In that sacrifice she knew that all changes of the Instant lead to death and life. Entry into the Instant required the death of the time-bound and the new life of the free. Movement in the Instant required the death of the present configuration of things, for movement made waves and waves were change. Even death in the Instant had life in it; death was shattering, sundering to pieces too small to act, but each piece was a fragment of life in death. All things in the present are death and life. Only the form of death and life changes.

Where Saryu had been, floating at the center of the living rings of warriors, she whose name meant Center of all plans . . . Heart of all creations . . . Base of events . . . appeared, a solid century of weight floating on the spot where the heart of breaking and the calm center of the whirlpool had been.

At her arrival, the possibility of destruction vanished. She had only to send Nir the image he needed to understand the upcoming transformation of the Instant. She knew that Nir's mind would comprehend, and from that awareness he would decide how to direct the change of event. And Nir would give that direction to Kookatchi, who would transmit the direction, and the Instant would be.

Quillithé rippled her century body, drawing the knowledge from the whole of her mind, changing what she knew with the sight of the whole inhabited Instant, all one hundred millennia laid out in swirling tides of color and shadow. The image flowed from her, passing through the two inner rings of her army, growing in complexity as it traveled.

Nir saw the image. All the dwellers in the Instant there in the center. One source of guidance, he and she as one. A thousand different disruptions to that guidance were present, embodied in the chieftains of the tribes, each one a despairing pit of blackness, each chieftain represented by a broken island. But the image held more; it showed the Instant itself and the work Nir had done to reclaim it, it showed the tidal pools of history where the memories of the workers had carved pathways to make times like their times of origin, and the tidal pools were colored gold of glory, each pool dissolving a single mote of darkness.

Nir's mind changed.

"Kookatchi," the War Chief tapped. "Find the tribal leaders. I have a bargain for them. Death or life."

Kookatchi listened as Nir elaborated. The Drum reached out and touched Saryu with his tail and the two of them vanished to speak to each leader in turn.

"Persia-like, but not Persia," Kookatchi said to Xerxes. "Appearing and vanishing in the tides, ever changing but guided by your memory."

"No," the Prince said, slapping the waters of time with his tail.

"This is the Instant/ The Instant shall be change," Saryu sang to Xerxes.

> *"In the Instant*
> *Memory is the only past*
> *Hope and work the only future."*

Xerxes said nothing, coiling his tail in defiance.

"If you die," Kookatchi said, "the memory of Persia and the hope of Persia will be gone. If you will live, the tidal pool of almost-Persia and remembering-Persia and aspiring-to-grow-from-Persia is yours to work upon."

The soldiers of the Persian Zurvanite Infantry swam up around their leader and he knew that if he again said no to Kookatchi that they would act without him, and he who knew the whole song of Persia, he who held the whole memory of that land would not be there to guide them in bringing forth the bounty of Persia-arising-from-memory-of-Persia.

"Yes," he said.

> "This is the Instant.
> The Instant shall be change.
> In the Instant
> Memory is the only past
> Hope and work the only future."

And from those opening words, Prince Xerxes began to sing the songs of his tribe, reminding the soldiers of their duties, old and new intertwined in one. In Xerxes' mind the vow of bringing back his land and the vow to preserve the Instant became one vow. The pool-of-Persia and the tidal guides below it would be his and his tribe's to labor in. They would see a billion different Persias, none perfect but all together greater than the stagnant history he had lusted for. The guttering flame of ambition burned out and a light replaced it; in the light Xerxes would see all the variations of time as his treasure, instead of a single carved stone. Water and earth were one in precious time and he was owner of it all.

Kookatchi and Saryu vanished and offered Nir's bargain again and again to each tribal leader in turn.

Some chieftains chose life and became lords of all time; other chieftains chose death, seeking to make a helpless battle against the unity of the Instant. All the tribes survived—some with different leaders—but all took up the treasure of earth and water, the treasure of the present. And all added Saryu's preamble to their songs.

The center of the Instant grew many waves of singing as each tribe came back together to sing its songs and remember and hope.

In the center of the singing, Nir, Kookatchi, and Quillithé came together.

> The Instant is.
> Change comes.
> From the Now to the deeps,
> Unchained by past and future,
> Not bound by past and future,
> Remembering past and hoping future.
> They act in the present.
> Together in the Instant
> That is.

Glossary

anchor: The act of entering the Flux from the Instant. So called because to anchor requires grasping the bottom of the ocean and pulling oneself down into the earth below.

change-wave: A disturbance in the waters of time that causes alterations in the Flux below.

consciousness: The moment of awareness that permits perception and action. A Time Warrior's consciousness moves up his tail until it reaches the end and then recycles to the beginning of his tail.

currents of time: The accumulation of change-waves into a coherent stream.

the deeps: The far futureward regions of the ocean where the currents of time have become layered and complicated and the ocean floor is far down.

Diaspora: The region of time that spans the few thousand years futureward from the Now. During the Diaspora, Homo sapiens travel to and settle in all parts of the world.

Drum: A Time Warrior with a tail one minute long or less.

Drum's Awareness: Perception of the Instant as a unified whole, rather than as a progression of moments.

Flux: The earthly side of time, the side that suffers change.

futureward: The direction in which most change naturally flows. The direction that the currents of time follow.

Ghosts: The Time Warriors of the People of the Now.

Great Mother: The first Homo sapiens.

Inhabited Instant: The region of approximately one hundred thousand years stretching from the Now to the deeps. All Time Warriors dwell in the Inhabited Instant.

Instant: The watery side of time. The side from which change originates.

long tail: Any Time Warrior with a tail at least one year long. A long tail can easily effect change and can cause injury to other long tails.

middle Instant: The region futureward of the Diaspora and pastward of the deeps. Most of the tribes dwell in the middle Instant.

the Now: The region approximately two hundred years in length in which the People live. The most pastward part of the Inhabited Instant.

pastward: The direction opposite to the normal flow of change.

the People: The first generations of Homo sapiens. They live in the Now under the protection of the Ghosts.

recycling: When a Time Warrior's consciousness reaches the end of his tail, the consciousness returns to the beginning; this is called recycling. Recycling is mentally disruptive to everyone except Drums.

short tail: A Time Warrior with a tail less than a year in length. Short tails are not considered dangerous (except for Drums).

tail: To enter the Instant in the first place, a Time Warrior takes a segment of his life with him; this is called his tail. The beginning of the tail is the earliest part of life taken into the Instant, the end is the last part. Consciousness moves up the tail from beginning to end and then recycles. When a Time Warrior anchors into the Flux the part of his tail that contains his consciousness appears in earthly time. Each moment that passes for his consciousness brings the next moment of his tail into the Flux and releases the previous moment back into the Instant. The length of a Time Warrior's tail determines how much force he can exert on the waters of time and therefore how great a change he can effect.

Time Warrior: Any inhabitant of the Instant.

the tribes of time: A group of Time Warriors from the same culture who desire to create the same history is called a tribe of time.